I0771972

SECOND ACT

SECOND ACT

Joe Navratil

Old Vine Press

Old Vine Press

This book is a work of fiction. Except where noted, the characters, names, places, and any real people and places are fictitious, or are used fictitiously. Any resemblance to people, living or dead, or to places or activities, is purely coincidental and the sole product of the author's imagination.

Hardcover ISBN: 979-8-9914711-2-1
Trade paperback ISBN: 979-8-9914711-1-4
Ebook ISBN: 979-8-9914711-0-7

Manufactured in the United States of America. 

 jnavratilauthor   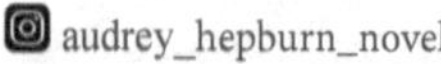 audrey_hepburn_novel    joenavratil.com

For Edda van Heemstra

PART ONE

I couldn't quite fathom that she was real. There were so many paradoxes in that face. Darkness and purity; depth and youth; stillness and animation. She had a fresh look, a beauty that was ethereal.

—Antony Beauchamp, photographer

In some circles (Palo Alto) has acquired the mythical reputation of a postmodern El Dorado, where money flows by the billions from the investors on Sand Hill Road to hundreds of garages where scrappy coders are changing the way we do everything, from driving around to eating food ... A few people seem convinced that Palo Alto is in fact the center of the world.

—Malcolm Harris, Palo Alto

Chapter 1

HOW IT BEGAN

I first fell in love with Audrey Hepburn after being lured into watching the film *Roman Holiday*. The far graver one struck as a despondent Audrey sobbed on the couch in my Silicon Valley home—more than thirty years after she left this world.

Tears streamed down Audrey's famous face as she broke the gaze between her big brown eyes and my bloodshot gray ones. I'd learned her hairstyle was named *coupe infante '66*, from *How to Steal a Million*—cropped short in the back and swept forward on the sides. Audrey's side-parted bangs hid her tears until she looked up again, reaching for me. She couldn't mask her trembling as her warm hands grasped mine.

"Bradley, I have a question. It's very difficult for me to ask this of you, and I have no right."

I responded instinctively. "Anything. You can ask me anything." Then she asked it and her shuddering transferred to me.

But perhaps I should start with how I came to watch *Roman Holiday* with its star. I'd been taking baby steps toward social acclimatization by swiping through the dating app my company AImmersion invented called *Cupid or Stupid?* As my right hand held the cell phone, my left decided whether each woman could put up with me. Swipe, swipe, swipe. No, no, no. None interested me, and I'm sure the feeling was mutual. I did my breathing exercises to stave off my constant companions, enochlophobia and haphephobia: *in, two, three, four, out, two, three, four.* My fears of being in a crowd and touching someone—even shaking hands—made me swelter with hives and sweat. Deep breathing sometimes stemmed more extreme symptoms like ringing ears, tunnel vision, and panic heaving.

Satisfied I'd tamped down my anxiety for now, my finger returned to the phone, and I projected a few eligibles onto the eight-by-six-foot OLED screen on the wall. I air-swiped at a few like a batonless symphony conductor, before stopping on a Japanese woman named Nicole.

I spoke aloud, "Bring up all information on Nicole Bone-*nay*, spelled B-o-n-n-e-t, Tokyo, journalist." Playing cards of information splayed across the monitor. She's also twenty-four, a freelance reporter for tech magazines, graduated from the University of San Francisco's Media Studies program a few years ago. Her social media profiles are decent, many with photos. I'm particularly drawn to her angular dark eyes. No, her high cheekbones … her long neck … lush eyebrows. She's maybe five-seven—a few inches shorter than me—and slender. Her videos at Tokyo Tower showcase lithe movements and a broad smile. I air-swiped right—a keeper.

A shrill whistle indicated she was simultaneously checking out my profile. I tinted red and drew an X in the air, closing the app. *In, two, three, four, out, two, three, four.*

A double bell broke my deep breaths, alerting me to an incoming message. Of course, it's from Nicole. Breathing escaped me and sweat rushed my palms.

Why did you run away so fast? flashed on the screen. An oily sheen lubricated my casual wear.

I don't like this app even though my teammate Advik créated it. He calls it speed searching but it doesn't allow for anonymity. If you pause five seconds on someone, they get an alert that you're lurking. I used voice-to-text to send Nicole my reply: *Sorry, have to get to work.*

Immediately, a counter came in: *I see you live in Palo Alto. Are you in tech?*

I began to draw the X in the air again but saw her profile pic and couldn't. Since she lives in Tokyo, I deemed it pretty low-risk to have a quick chat. My work wife, Ara—there is no home wife—would be proud of this baby step.

Your profile says you are.

Oh yeah, that. So, I replied, *Yes.*

I write about tech.

It should take only about ten seconds for Nicole to figure out who I am. I didn't use my full name—just Bradley W—to throw off the scent, like many who don't want to be readily known on dating apps.

I'm not worth writing about.

Ha, I doubt that. Anyway, is Tacolicious still open in Palo Alto?

Indeed! I didn't tell her I had ten tacos delivered by drone just last night. *What brought you to Palo Alto?*

Oh, I used to go to the Stanford Theater! The exclamation points took our relationship to the next level. *I used to love when they'd show classic movies. Do you like old Hollywood films?*

Sorry, no. I don't think I've ever seen one to be honest.

Not even The Sound of Music?

No. I'm more of a Star Wars *fan.*

Well, we need to expand your horizons then. Are you up for it?

I shook my head like a wet poodle and slapped my face awake. She had to know who I was by now and might be phishing for work info. If not now, then eventually. That would be quite the Silicon Valley scandal: Tokyo tech journalist honeypots AI savant through his company's own dating app.

No, sorry. I really need to go. I was still scanning her socials on the huge monitor above my computer suite and noted a photo of her at Disneyland Tokyo. Mickey Mouse ears and all. My heart fluttered.

Okay, Bradley. I know a brush-off when I see one. Thanks for chatting.

She was gone before I could reconsider.

NICOLE

The big screen wasn't even the centerpiece of my home studio; anyone could buy one of those. The three-dimensional cameras for *Cardinal*'s hologram technology, the world's fastest graphics processing unit, and in-home server room provided me the architecture to invent the kinds of things AImmersion was introducing this week up the road in San Francisco at AICon. I should have been tweaking things for the launch, but I was on *Cupid* again: swipe left, left, left, left again—discarding all suggestions. Then Nicole Bonnet's profile again froze my finger in place and that sent me looking anew at her socials. A new pic since yesterday appeared—Nicole in a sleeveless dress with an impressive tattoo running from her left shoulder to her elbow. I enlarged the photo: it was an Art Deco rendering of a woman smoking a cigarette.

You're back popped up on the big screen. I jumped at the incursion, reminding myself to set up extra controls for that. *Does that mean you're not working? Isn't it only early afternoon there?*

I didn't know what to do. So, I did nothing.

Helloooo?

Finally, I found my voice. *Hi, Nicole. I am working, yes.*

Working by swiping on a dating app? I'm in the wrong line of work! That forced me to remember her profession: tech journalist. I decided to look for an early exit again. I said, *Well, I'm taking a quick break.*

Oh, I'm just having morning coffee. Tomorrow morning to you, with the international date line and all.

I couldn't resist. *You woke up and started looking at dating apps?*

Guilty! At least I'm off the clock. What's your excuse?

The program buzzed and chimed—Nicole sent a video chat request. Red, itchy hives instantly blotched my skin and I froze, not answering. After ten rings, Nicole finally gave up. *Whew. Okay, back to work.*

Buzz, chime, buzz, chime—she called again. I went to push the red air-button but inadvertently hit the green one to accept the call. I flushed and moistened further when Nicole appeared on the screen and said, "Hello, Bradley. You aren't very good at this, are you? It works better if you look up at me. That camera must be connected to a big monitor I'm looking down from." At least the background was my open-walled bedroom and not the very sensitive computer suite. She made a show of craning her neck as if to look past me. "It looks like you aren't much better at making your bed."

She was a vision on the big screen in a black tank top and Yomiuri Giants ballcap. There was also that massive tattoo.

Nicole noticed me looking, smiled, and said, "Audrey Hepburn."

"Sorry?"

"My tattoo, it's Audrey Hepburn. That's who I try to look like as much as I can, Japanese American genes permitting—and that's who I'm named after."

"I'm not following, sorry."

"I'm named after one of her movie characters."

"Really? What movie?"

"You said last time that you don't watch classic movies. Have you seen any Audrey Hepburn films?"

"No."

"So, does it matter which character of hers I'm named after if you've never seen one?"

"I guess not." My intrigue wouldn't let me disengage and hang up. Here was an enchanting woman speaking with me, with interest. I asked, "But if I ever check out one of her movies, which one do you recommend?"

Nicole smiled again, and I noticed that she had a slightly crooked front tooth. That was a Japanese stereotype, but I saw it in this otherwise flawless woman. Nicole said, "Always start at the beginning. As a matter of fact, I was going to watch *Roman Holiday* tonight. Would you like to join me? Through your *Cardinal* program, perhaps?"

I looked up to see her still smiling at me. "Yes, I figured out who you are. Impressive. I imagine you researched me as well?"

I raised my hands in surrender.

"Bradley, let's just watch a movie together. Everything will be off the record. Sometimes a girl just needs a night off curled up with an old movie and a glass of pinot noir. I miss the wineries near you in Napa and Sonoma, but I have a great wine store close by here in Tokyo."

I had let my guard down long enough; it was time to force it back up. "That sounds tempting, but I really must get back to work."

"Do you realize that you have a similar name to a character in an Audrey Hepburn movie also?"

"Really?" I chuckled. "Who would that be?"

"Yes, from *Roman Holiday*, the movie I'm going to watch. The name is Joe Bradley. He's a do-good journalist in the film. Kind of how I can be with you, so I think that you are really meant to watch it with me tonight. If that's not being too forward."

Forward? Who talks like that anymore?

Then she added, "Your faith will not be unjustified. That's my favorite line from the movie, by the way."

Chapter 3

ROMAN HOLIDAY

I couldn't get Nicole out of my head. The invitation to watch *Roman Holiday* was certainly a ruse for her to gain information about AImmersion's technology, but I would only be able to find out her angle—and head it off—if I asked her some questions during the old movie. Since we would be watching virtually—me from home and she from Japan—I derived the risk was low.

I found several articles Nicole had published in the past two years. Her stories about the future of artificial intelligence and extended reality from a reporter's viewpoint were solid but lacked an insider's knowledge. That was good news, as long as I didn't become her insider.

Cardinal chirped; it was Nicole, right on time for our virtual … date, was it? I air-touched the green ACCEPT button.

"Hello, Joe Bradley. I'm sorry—Bradley Joseph. It takes a girl a minute to reverse those names, since I've seen this movie so many times."

She made me smile. I couldn't help it—she somehow put me at ease. My heartbeat was steady, no flushing, and no sweat. I began with a disclaimer.

"Just as a reminder, everything we talk about, even during this movie, is strictly off the record. Thanks for returning the signed nondisclosure agreement. We can deviate from that only when I say we're on the record. And that won't be tonight."

"Agreed, Bradley. See, I can learn and adapt, Bradley Joseph."

I told myself to stop staring at her. Her dark eyes were mesmerizing. Her bright sundress showed long, sinewy legs. I stopped gawking enough to ask, "What time is it there?"

She paused to check something—her phone probably—and replied, "Just after two in the afternoon. And there it's, what, ten at night?"

I nodded and saw that tattoo again on her arm when she removed a shawl. "Let's not keep Audrey waiting any longer, all right? I'm very excited to introduce you to her."

The black-and-white world transmitted on my advanced setup initially seemed antiquated, but as soon as I saw Audrey Hepburn as Princess Ann, my heart pounded, and the film swallowed me up. I looked from the movie to Nicole and was surprised at how she favored the actress. There were differences, but she could certainly get away with styling herself as a Japanese version of Audrey Hepburn.

She caught me looking back and forth at the dual display and said, "I've been dressing and trying to look a bit like Audrey for a while. I've always been a fan of hers, hence the tattoo of Holly Golightly. She was quite popular in Japan, by the way. Still is."

Princess Ann loses and regains her shoe at the gala, making us chuckle. I was smitten by the time she escapes her room while on sleep medication, wakes up in Joe Bradley's apartment, gets a short haircut, and rides around the Roman Colosseum on a Vespa. The princess falls for Joe but leaves him in the final scene. Even worse, Joe doesn't turn back to fight for her.

"Why!? Does it really end like this? Is there a part two where they get back together?"

"Don't you see? It's a Cinderella story in reverse. She flees her royal restrictions and has a brief love affair that flirts at changing who she is, but she must return to her duty. It may have been the first romantic comedy that didn't have a happily ever after. People weren't used to different endings in the 1950s. After World War II, they only wanted idealistic conclusions to movies, but this was the first to say that isn't always the case. It was a dose of realism that people needed to see."

"But they both seem okay with it. He smiles at the end. He doesn't have anyone else to go to. Why didn't he try?"

Nicole re-cued the movie to the start of the penultimate scene and rolled it without sound.

"Not exactly. Do you see how confident Joe is? He thinks that she will inevitably say or do something like kiss him in front of all of those people, and she gives him one final gift with her words, 'So happy, Mr. Bradley.' That was all she could give. As she returns from the press line, he looks up at her and kind of gestures with his eyes. 'How about us?' She does the slightest shake of her head, no, with tears welling in her eyes. She decides she can't disappoint her nation. Then the truth dawns on him and all hope fades. Look at that hard swallow. He didn't expect it but now realizes he will never see her again. Like most people who see the movie for the first time, you still don't fully believe it and are along with Joe as he walks out, hands in his pockets. Then one more glance back to see that she doesn't come running down the aisle for him, and the scene closes. It's absolutely perfect."

"No! We were along with them for their whole day together. There was no indication she was going to rebuff him. The ending should have followed the rest of the script! We were deceived. That long walk out by Joe—the audience is practically willing a return by her, or at least the promise of a future reunion."

Nicole laughed, and I felt stabbed.

"Think of it this way," she said. "They shared a day, a moment really, something they both will remember forever. That means more than an impossible relationship. No one can take that day away from them. Their love will linger forever. Besides, your imagination as a viewer can still carry out whatever you want to happen all these years later. Maybe you can dream about it tonight. But like Joe Bradley's memory, we always have the magic of *Roman Holiday* to return to and feel that sentiment."

I didn't have anything else to add until Nicole said, "There's a bigger reason this movie is so important, other than being Audrey Hepburn's first Hollywood movie."

"That's impossible."

"Think about this. *Roman Holiday* was made in the era of buxom, sultry movie vixens like Marilyn Monroe, Ava Gardner, and other actresses you apparently haven't watched. Then along comes Audrey as Princess Ann—she doesn't want a man, she wants adventure. Women in the audience in 1953 could see themselves as Ann. Not as a princess, but as someone who needs an escape from the everyday demands of family duties."

"Yeah, but she returns to that in the end."

"Yes, but as a changed person and on her terms. This was unheard of in movies—and in real life—back then. Ann defined her own rules and rejected those of her royal family."

"For a day—*just one day.*"

"Yes, and look what she found by seeking adventure: a liberating new haircut, gelato on the Spanish Steps, romping on a Vespa, and breaking free from security at the dance. She found love! It came to her, and now she knew love could find her through adventure instead of arranged marriage. This broke the mold in movies worldwide! And that's just the script! Now, about Audrey herself ..."

I snapped my head. "Yes, what about her?"

"She said herself that she wasn't the prettiest actress of the era. Check out, say, Hedy Lamarr and Loretta Young, not to mention Marilyn Monroe. She didn't have the best body; in fact, 'waif' is the word most people used to describe her. She did win the Oscar for this movie but never won another, so she didn't have the acting chops of Katharine Hepburn—no relation, by the way—or Bette Davis. And did you notice her teeth transform during the movie? They go from rather crooked to perfectly straight?"

"No. Well, yeah, now that you mention it."

"She resisted wearing caps when filming started, but they convinced her as filming progressed. There are funny stories that they had to reshoot scenes when they fell out as she was speaking. Anyway, put all of that together, and what do we have?"

I sighed and my head started to spin. "I don't know."

"Bradley, we have a new mold for women in movies and real life too. And it seems she is still breaking hearts today—and all because of this charming movie with an ending that many find incomplete."

I could only reply, "How did I not watch that movie until today?"

"Life changing, isn't it?"

I couldn't find the right words and settled for one. "Maybe."

Nicole laughed. "So, let me ask. Did you fall for Audrey Hepburn or Princess Ann?"

I hadn't thought of it that way. "Is there much difference between them?"

"You mean is there a difference in a reverse-Cinderella story between a movie princess who runs away from the crown to fall in love with a commoner versus a real woman who barely survived World War II by mashing tulip bulbs into flour? Yes, I'd say there is quite a difference."

"Well, I am taken by Audrey Hepburn as Princess Ann. We'll start there. Does she play that type of character in any other movies?"

"Well, not a princess, but does she play a desirable, new type of woman who enchants you with her mind, her eyes, her face, and her character instead of her bosomy sex appeal? Yes, she definitely has a few of those."

"Can we watch them? Or one more?"

"Not today. I have an assignment, and it's past midnight for you there." Nicole thought a second and said, "I understand AImmersion is launching something new at AICon. I look forward to learning about it."

That jolted me back to remembering Nicole was a reporter and, despite the fun education I just had, I needed to stop these meetings. Before I could tell her, she said, "Sorry, I have to run, Bradley. Talk soon!" And she disconnected.

I stared at the big screen, upset at myself for allowing things to go as far as they had. Then I realized my phobia symptoms had stayed dormant during our talk. Of course, we weren't in a crowd and we didn't touch, but I'd been completely at ease with her through the computer.

Chapter 4

THE LAUNCH

A single bead of sweat branched from my scalp and rivered down my spine as I watched the headlines scroll across my big screen: *Big Tech Insiders Warn Artificial Intelligence Poses Extinction Risk*. My skin turned as red as my Stanford hoodie as the next ones came: *Doomsday AI Addressed by International Tribunal,* and *Hollywood Pushes Back Against AI.*

Then, grouped caustically with the others, the one about me: *AICon: Silicon Valley Mogul to Introduce AI "Advancement" Today.*

Ouch. Did they really have to use quotes around *advancement*? It *is* a huge advancement, as people are about to learn. Movies, and maybe life itself, will never be the same.

Technically, it wasn't me introducing my—*our*——latest technology. I'm not the mogul; that's Charlie Hemming. Yes, that Charlie Hemming, the Ken-Doll-looking owner and CEO of AImmersion. You'll recall we brought you *ConVRsate* (mine), the virtual reality experience that pairs you with celebrities and influencers for pretend relationships. We also did the aforementioned 3D holoportation meeting room *Cardinal* (also mine), and *Cupid or Stupid?* Not bad for what was a three-person startup only two years ago.

Charlie Hemming, clap-clap-clap-clap-clap originated in the Chase Center and echoed through my home speakers. Charlie had asked me to launch this one at AICon in San Francisco—in front of twenty thousand adherents. The room began spinning just envisioning that, and I went down on one knee and closed my eyes.

I stripped off my hoodie and looked down at my now-damp leisure wear, upgraded to Lululemon at the behest of my teammates Ara Day and Advik Patel.

They are the only ones allowed in my house besides Charlie, and Ara had been disgusted last week to see my attire and the mess surrounding the world's most advanced computer suite.

"You can't live like this, Bradley. It stifles your creativity, living like a hoarder and dressed in your middle school sweatpants."

"Well, it got me this far. And they still fit."

Ara rolled her eyes. "Bradley, you aren't the teen-aged prodigy anymore. You're twenty-four now, like it or not. You've probably forgotten a dozen new inventions around the dirty espresso cups and half-eaten—what are these? Cheese sandwiches?"

"Swiss on rye. Delivered by drone straight to my door. Don't knock it."

"We've got to get you out in the world dating. Or at least going to Trader Joe's."

I had instantly hurled at the suggestions.

"Bradley, I'm so sorry!" She held my too-long hair as I retched, fortunately away from the electronics. "Your skin is so hot. I'll get a wet towel for you and a mop for the rest."

I gave a thumbs-up from the downward-facing dog position and took note to keep the trashcan closer whenever she came over and pushed being social again.

Raucous cheering snapped me back to the screen as the AICon hostess walked to center stage. "Well, it's time to introduce the person you all came here to see. Charlie Hemming from AImmersion is with us! What he is launching today is sure to revolutionize the entertainment industry, bringing the right kind of AI into films to make them even better! Please welcome back Charlie Hemming!"

Charlie walked out to an ovation better suited for music royalty, nodding and waving a few times, then genuflecting to the Big Tech CEOs in the front VIP section who'd offered upward of one hundred million dollars last week to buy our company. They had also offered to pay off the remaining litigation costs from *ConVRsate* after helping our lawyers create the blueprint for revenue-sharing with celebrities in exchange for their consent for parasocial dating. We declined their offers.

Charlie cleared his throat and said, "Here's a quick video."

He was a man of many words, but our public relations team had been working with him on brevity when launching new technology since we didn't want to give away any secrets. Charlie pressed a button on a remote control and lights dimmed in the arena. The steel-guitar-heavy James Bond theme song from the 1962 film *Dr. No* played in the pitch dark before the screen faded in to a casino. A woman in red was writing a check for more cash to continue playing baccarat before introducing herself as Sylvia Trench. Then the first "Bond, James Bond" was spoken by a player at the table. Except it wasn't Sean Connery dangling the cigarette and witty repartee.

It was Cary Grant.

Charlie paused the video. "Some of you may know that Cary Grant was sought by the movie producers, and even the writer Ian Fleming himself, to star in *Dr. No.* Well, now we can have it. For you younger folks, we can also change out the actress." He pressed *Play*, but now Sylvia Trench was portrayed by my choice, Zendaya. The twenty-somethings in the audience erupted with approval.

Cary Grant paired with Zendaya in their own voices, personalities, and personal style, woven together in an early 1960s vibe. I sat up a little straighter in my home, proud but still multiphobic.

"That's just one feature of *Real to Reel*—the first word is spelled *r-e-a-l* and the second *r-e-e-l.* But this isn't the only way to use it. If today's James Bond producers want to envision a new actor in the role of 007 now that they killed off Daniel Craig, well, we can provide audition tapes, if you will. As long as the actor has material online, we interface recorded video with a movie scene—like this from *Dr. No,* or even a script from your studio—and use our ground-breaking artificial intelligence to show you …"

Charlie clicked the remote and scrolled through Tom Hiddleston, Michael Fassbender, Idris Elba, Henry Cavill, and just for fun, Pete Davidson, in various James Bond scenes. The audience was mesmerized. Charlie mused, "I vote for Pete, with his ex, Kim Kardashian, as the Bond girl. Maybe Kanye as the heavy." The congregation laughed and roared its approval, standing and clapping for a full minute.

Charlie held up a hand and the din subsided. "I want to stop here to acknowledge my creative development team led by Bradley Joseph. He, our AI lead Ara Day, and alternate reality head Advik Patel, created this over the past year." It was really only a few months, but when you work twenty-hour days once inspired, the hours add up. That's why there are so many empty espresso cups lying around my home studio.

Back to Charlie.

"I think I can anticipate a few of your questions, like how does *Real to Reel* work? Well, my team will tell you that's classified, so don't ask. Like everything in our world, it's all about the coding." The crowd laughed again.

So far, so good, but that's about to change if they ask the questions we anticipated.

"I will only tell you that if it's online, we can grab it and catalog it into our artificial intelligence program. Now, some may ask, isn't this just the same technology video gamers use? No, it isn't. Those characters aren't real. The actors in *Real to Reel* are as genuine as they were in their original movies. Don't think of them as a digital creation; it's the original actors being given a new lease on life. Directors would shoot the location, action, and any live actors, then we create and place the deceased actor into the scene using our technologies. Like Lazarus, they rise from the dead. We think this technology will get people going to the movies again after quite a few down years."

Charlie demonstrated a few more examples of *Real to Reel*, and then it was time for questions. My body flushed and lathered, as if the questions would be directed at me. They kind of were, with Charlie as my surrogate. I put the earpiece in so I could relay any necessary info remotely to Charlie. A reporter stepped up to the microphone.

"Mr. Hemming, as you know, there has been a lot of talk about artificial intelligence and what the limit should be for the tech industry. Investors have demanded that you and your competitors stop focusing on the metaverse for now. Congress and the White House have gotten involved and now there's an international tribunal to address AI issues. There are also Armageddon scenarios from people who have worked in the industry. Some say that Artificial Super Intelligence, or …"—he looked at his notes—"Sentient AI, is on the horizon and that could lead to a total loss of control of AI. So, my question to you is: How far is too far?"

The booing was highlighted by something about the reporter's mother. It was a pro-AI symposium after all. Charlie smiled onstage while I checked the degree of coloration on my chest. Trending toward purple.

I spoke into my headset. "*Star Wars* example."

Charlie nodded imperceptibly .

"Like I mentioned, AImmersion's goal is to invigorate the movie industry with this technology. Hollywood's had quite a few down years, and we think this technology can turn things around. The year I was born, 1977, the now-closed Coronet Theater here in San Francisco was a mecca for *Star Wars* fans when the movie debuted. That movie taught us about what was possible if we used our imagination. And today we are advancing closer to the world *Star Wars* envisioned with civilian space exploration, provided by some in the audience here." Charlie smiled at the well-known Big Tech gurus in the front row. "I'm offering a different vision for living in alternate worlds through AI."

Charlie paused, forgetting the next part we'd rehearsed, and I prompted, "AI for good …"

"AI for good. Yes, controls are needed and some level of oversight is warranted. But we can't fear the future. We must understand it and work with it. There's no going back."

Okay, we got through that one. I peeked and my skin color was back to salmon. The next question came from a computer game CEO.

"*Real to Reel* sounds like it can help my friends in the movie industry, but it doesn't sound interactive. Is there a next generation to this?"

That was always the question, especially from gaming companies: What is AImmersion working on next? Many companies were working on technologies that provided gamers a sense of touch, even smell and taste, in the virtual world. We were too, but it would be easier to pry launch-code secrets from NORAD.

I prompted, "I'm just here …"

"I'm just here to introduce Cary Grant as the first James Bond from sixty years ago. Or, rather, today." Then he pivoted to add, "By the way, we have also invented a three-hundred-sixty-degree movie theater presentation using virtual reality. It puts the 'full' in *full immersion* and it's breathtaking. We invented the technology, but someone else can build the theaters. Call us when you're ready." That one was Advik's and quite cool. I had it in my home studio.

While that possibility buzzed around, the hostess stepped forward and said, "Our next question comes remotely. Go ahead, Nicole."

I heard the voice first, then snapped my head to the screen. It was *that* Nicole. Her slender appearance and precise speech set my heart fluttering. Charlie must have been taken with her proper enunciation also because he asked her to repeat the query.

"Yes," Nicole reiterated, "the question I have is, do you foresee developing this technology for personal use? Such as inviting deceased people to dinner parties, for instance? Say I want to invite Cary Grant to my house. Can you get him there for me? Please?"

The question split the pack into amused laughter, and whispered possibilities. Charlie tapped his ear signaling his need for my response. I rushed out, "I can only give you …"

"I can only give you Cary Grant as James Bond tonight. If you'd like to see the video clip again?" She didn't answer, so Charlie added, "I'm afraid that technology doesn't yet exist."

Then Nicole asked, "And in the future?"

Charlie and I were speechless, and I wondered if she might have some inside information. I was pretty sure it didn't come from me. He finally offered our rehearsed ending.

"We are already living in the future. I'm offering the past."

We debriefed through *Cardinal* after Charlie returned to our Palo Alto head-quarters. I was the only one not at HQ, which was the norm due to my phobias. I was still stunned by Nicole's question. I should have guessed she would ask such questions after she'd teed it up with me. Obviously, I'd let my guard down and needed to fix that.

Charlie spoke first. "Producers are already lining up to be the first to partner with us on *Real to Reel*. They don't even have scripts yet but a few have some amazing concepts, and a few studios have already named classic movie stars they want us to resurrect."

To celebrate, they all went back into The City, as we locals call San Francisco, for drinks. I stayed home and tortured myself with *Cupid*, thinking I might be sociable someday too. Random faces with forgettable names dashed through *Cupid* and my consciousness. I don't really have a type; anyone who could put up with my intensity and weirdness got a swipe right.

As I scrolled, I pictured myself in the near future out with other company employees for drinks and dinner in The City. Ara would say, "See, Bradley, I told you there's a whole big world out here. How are you doing?" She would check my neck color and armpits, because she says that's what work wives do.

"I'm fine, Mama Bear."

Advik would return from the bar with cocktails. "Cosmo for the lady and a Boulevardier for the Boy Wonder." He still calls me that even though he's only two years older than me. "Courtesy of Big Boss Man."

I would look over to see Charlie ensconced with two women at the bar. He would raise his glass to me, whisper something, and suddenly one of the women would start walking over toward me, seemingly at Charlie's urging. I tint red in both my actual and alternate realities and break out of the trance.

Nope, not yet.

Chapter 5

THE DREAM TEAM

AImmersion's headquarters was just off the Stanford campus in Palo Alto. Charlie Hemming had also grown up in San Francisco and considered locating the company there but prices in the city were exorbitant for startups. Most of the folks he hired were from Stanford, so we set up shop there. I actually have an office at HQ, but have been there only a handful of times. Today was number six.

I drove my little-used BMW I3 to HQ for a meeting with Ara and Advik. It was a mere coincidence that the other employees, including Charlie, were road-tripping to San Jose for meetings. They would be back at HQ in the afternoon for *Cardinal* calls with Hollywood producers about *Real to Reel*. I would be back home by then, running the demos remotely.

HQ wasn't quite a fortress, but the things AImmersion worked on brought a level of security that raised concern in the college town. It was a nondescript tan stucco building that could have been a small hotel. There were no signs and never any tours of the facility, even for university or city officials.

I surveyed the titanium fencing as I drove to the gate, leaning my eye to the retinal scanner and placing my left thumbprint on the secondary reader. The gate opened and I drove through, pausing to ensure it closed immediately behind me.

AImmersion's donations to civic causes in Palo Alto and the greater Bay Area lowered apprehension. The truth is, AImmersion was developing technology that competitors couldn't conceive, must less grasp and design. I thanked my parents for insisting I take a few business courses at Stanford: I'd negotiated 10 percent ownership and 51 percent vote on releasing our tech developments to public and commercial sectors.

Advik had been my first hire after I was named creative director. He was a national spelling bee champion at eleven years old, then turned his attention to computers. Advik's mind for virtual, augmented, mixed, and extended reality pushed AImmersion to even greater concepts. He was also my conscience for not getting too far down the road of uncontrolled artificial intelligence. Keeping Advik on our team was my constant charge; he could easily get swiped by another firm or start his own company at any time.

"I'm not sure I ever want to run a company, Bradley," Advik repeated time and again. "Like you, I only want to play in the lab."

Ara was my nontraditional hire, snatched from Uncle Sam. She was a former military junior officer and our AI lead. Her mother emigrated from Cameroon after meeting Colonel Benjamin Day there on a humanitarian mission. Ara fulfilled a family promise to follow her father's lead and serve in the US military, serving five years in cyber operations. She was quietly dismissed for hacking into Russian computers—without permission—after Putin invaded Ukraine. Her work for us started with creating AI training environments, but within a year of hiring her, I made her lead AI engineer. I admired not only her intellect but her candor with me.

I popped a Xanax and after passing three interior security scans, stepped quietly inside the lab, where Ara and Advik were working. They were among the few who didn't make me break out in hives.

Advik was costumed in his new haptic suit, dancing with a hologram of a beautiful Desi woman.

I whispered, "Who this time? Actress? Singer?"

Ara smirked. "This one is a totally new AI creation. He's calling her Kareena."

"I didn't know Advik was a good dancer."

"He isn't. He programmed that into the suit and the subject. All he has to do is not fall down."

Advik spun and finally saw me. "Bradley, I …"

I waved him off. "Don't let me get between you and your experiment. How's the suit?"

"I'd give it a B minus. I need to work on the gloves to feel the small of her back better."

Ara and I nodded appreciatively. Advik continued, "It's linking well with

VR headgear. Do you want to try it?"

"No, not right now. Can you unzip and join us to talk about Ara's update?"

Ara's task was the next generation of AI, called artificial general intelligence, technology that would change the world by giving computers the ability to think on their own. Many global companies were working on AGI, and the first one would become either the darling or hangman of the tech industry, depending on who you asked.

Not even Charlie knew the three of us were working on AGI. We usually did it in my home studio, but Ara's work in the HQ was also private.

"Over to you, Captain Day."

Ara cleared her throat and said, "Two things: first, perfecting an AGI system that can think and have a brain—that also means it has a consciousness. A conscious machine will be able to anticipate events, or to change events it doesn't like. You can't put Frankenstein back on the table once we create it. Second, it's much easier to create unfriendly than friendly AI. We'll need strong controls in the system. A misaligned system is what everyone fears, and the computer becomes that sci-fi android who destroys the world. So, we have to build in the full range of behaviors and not just proxy goals that leave too much open for computer interpretation."

Advik nodded. "Yeah, I can't emphasize enough how much we need to control this. Today's headline was that AGI and someday, sentient AI, would be more dangerous than nuclear weapons. And bad actors can get ahold of them easier once they're invented."

I said, "Right. I don't want to be the Robert Oppenheimer of AI. So, it sounds like we need a subject for trying out some AGI steps once we get there. Any ideas? Advik, Kareena perhaps?"

"No, she's just teaching me how to dance. My sister's wedding is coming up."

"Ara? Any input here?"

"I have enough work on the science of this. Why don't you come up with a being? Maybe someone you can talk to and have drinks with?"

I wanted to push back, but it was actually a grand step toward social assimilation.

Chapter 6

REAL TO REEL

My eyes strained as my brain cataloged every detail from reading biographies on Audrey Hepburn. Grainy interview clips both amused and fascinated me. Audrey was one elegant and charming woman. Even the suave Johnny Carson, who I learned was the top talk TV host of the 1960s and 70s, was flustered in her presence. I learned almost as much about her fashion designers and hairstyles as I knew about AI and alternate realities.

I pondered again the ending of *Roman Holiday*. Did Nicole have a point about the movie's ending and the importance of the movie to women of the 1950s? After watching the film at home several times, I decided to test her theory and change the ending using *Real to Reel*, just for me.

I programmed *Real to Reel*'s AI to feed all available information about *Roman Holiday*: the script, director William Wyler's notes and comments, the movie itself, and interviews with the actors. Then I cued the original film in the computer and erased the ending that featured Joe Bradley's long, sad walk without the princess.

Real to Reel had three ways to program a scene: the two AI models of character-driven or actor-led feeds directing the action, or with a script. Character-driven used the on-screen personalities, while actor-led improvisation used details from their personal lives and interviews blended into their on-screen roles. I hadn't tried it beyond the simple Cary Grant scene for *Dr. No*, but now it was time to let Joe Bradley and Princess Ann tell their own ending to *Roman Holiday*—with no direction.

After many espressos and several uploads, everything seemed ready for the first take. I projected the ending of the 1953 film onto the big screen, sharpening the black-and-white imagery using our patented enhancement. I decided to not use another patent that instantly colorized black-and-white movies. Something was charming about black and white for this particular film. I then clicked Play, starting at the final scene press conference.

On the OLED screen, a correspondent asks Princess Ann, which place she visited did she most enjoy? After a pause, the General prompts Ann to say, "*Each, in its own way was … unforgettable. It would be difficult to—*"

Then she reveals the truth. "*Rome! By all means, Rome.*" The room stirs as she looks at Joe and continues. "*I will cherish my visit here, in memory, as long as I live.*"

The press murmurs at the surprising protocol breach and members of her entourage look uneasily at each other. The photographers are called closer to take final photos of the princess and Joe's accomplice, Irving Radovich, demonstrates for Princess Ann the small cigarette-lighter camera he had used to capture her escapades around Rome with Joe. As Irving steps back, Princess Ann wonders whether the whole story of her day away in Rome with Joe will spiral in the newspapers.

The General thanks the audience and tries to end the gathering, but Ann has a different idea to talk to Joe again, asking to meet some of the press. Ann walks down and greets the front row of journalists in their native languages before finally nearing Joe.

First was Joe's photographer friend, who gave her the worrisome photos of the previous day's fun and raucous moments. Then the princess turns her heart to Joe Bradley as he introduces himself as a reporter for the American News Service.

Her reply from seventy-odd years prior wobbled me with emotion when I heard who I now considered the most beautiful woman in history utter, "*So happy, Mr. Bradley.*"

Joe bows and shakes her hand, but neither speak further. I felt the depth of the act for both characters.

Princess Ann walks back to her entourage on stage, and the throng breaks out in polite applause. Then she slowly turns to face them and smiles panoramically before homing in on Joe. He smiles back but suddenly her eyes glisten, and her expression grows sorrowful. They share one last moment with their eyes as she shakes her head gently *no* and leaves as Joe swallows hard. The crowd saunters off, and Irving looks to Joe but sees that his friend remains in place. Did Irving also expect her to come back after the public leaves? Then Joe begins the slow walk that ends the movie.

Now, instead of closing credits rolling and the scene ending, I let the character-led feed devise an alternative ending. I flinched at the sudden sputter of the interface taking over, and then the scene faded to black.

I wasn't used to program errors. I reran it, and the same thing happened. I tested the code of the program and it appeared in order. One more time and the same thing—after a few seconds of Joe walking past palace guards, the scene faded to black.

It then dawned on me: Princess Ann and Joe Bradley were signifying that the scene was perfect as filmed and they were refusing to add a happily ever after.

I switched the program to the actor-driven resolution. Three demos later, Gregory Peck and Audrey Hepburn were signifying to me that they too didn't want to alter the ending as it repeatedly faded to black and stopped. That forced me to reassess it.

Was it perfect with them not searching for each other outside? Were they really destined to live separate lives and never meet again? I punched up reviews of the film's ending. The majority of critics thought it was perfect but many movie-goers hated it. Still, all considered *Roman Holiday* one of the greatest films of all time.

That just did not satisfy me. I was compelled to install the third option and wrote a movie scene for the first time in my life. An hour later, it was ready. I uploaded it into *Real to Reel* and pressed Play.

On the big screen, Gregory Peck, as Joe, walks past the guards and suddenly mutters, "That can't be it." He smirks and begins to walk back up the aisle. The lead guard steps out from the column and blocks his path. "I'm sorry, sir. The affair has ended. You can't go back. It is forbidden."

Joe stammered, "But the princess still has something of mine. I need it back."

"Sir, you cannot go further. I can get a message to her, if you insist."

Joe nods, takes out his reporter' notebook and pen, and scribbles: *This can't be the end of the story, Anya. Please don't let it. Meet me at the Mouth of Truth at dusk. Please, Joe.* He tears the paper from the tablet, folds it, and gives it to the guard with the instructions to deliver it to her straight away before the princess's entourage leaves the building. The lead guard clicks his heels, salutes smartly, and sets off with the note while the other guards eye Joe warily.

At the Mouth of Truth, Joe discovers the gate is locked until the next morning. He sighs and mumbles to himself, "So much for making her pledge to tell the truth when I ask her if she really wants this to end." Joe grows more despondent but suddenly sees a stream of lights in a caravan of official vehicles. They are headed his way.

The Carabinieri's flashing lights lead the procession and spotlight Joe as they slow at the *Bocca della Verita*. The cars stop, and a window of the large limousine in the middle suddenly rolls down. The General's arm, still in uniform, motions for Joe to join them in the car.

Joe opens the door and climbs in. Princess Ann is there with her royal consorts, but she doesn't look up. The General says, "Princess Ann has told us how you rescued her last night when she left the palace, though she should have been sleeping. She said that you were a gentleman at all times and, despite your recognition of her, that you tried to bring her back and that it was impossible to do that in her condition." He clears his throat. "Our security team tells a different version of the evening's events, but no matter. The princess wanted to say something to you."

Ann finally looks up at Joe. "Mr. Bradley …"

"Call me Joe, please."

She tries to say his name but chokes on sudden emotion. "Joe … if you should have occasion to visit us for the Festival of Lights this Christmas at our palace, you would most certainly be welcomed."

All in her entourage nod affirmatively. "You would be our honored guest, Mr. Bradley," said the General.

"Well, I was planning to visit your fair nation for the festival this year, so the invitation is accepted with utmost pleasure." Ann and Joe exchange glances at the promise of their next meeting. "How can we communicate in the interim, Anya?" The private name she made up last night does not go unnoticed.

"That may not be possible with the princess's many engagements, Mr. Brad-. ley," the General said. "I'm afraid that Christmas …"

Ann suddenly adds, "I will long for Christmas, Mr., uh, Joe. It never comes soon enough, does it?"

Joe nods, and the General reaches over to open the door, indicating it's time for him to withdraw. He smiles again at Anya and says, "Until Christmas then. Please don't have too many … engagements." She shook her head *no*, a much more promising no than Joe had seen at the end of the press briefing.

"It's a pact," the princess says, and smiles.

I was unsure whether I had made the ending any better that way, even with the promise of meeting in six months, so I devised another one. This time Princess Ann took a more direct approach, and Joe Bradley heard the clatter of shoes running after him down the noisy palace walkway. Her entourage chases after her, the General shouts *Stop her!* to the guards, and they do. Joe takes issue with their handling of her and pushes them away before whisking her outside.

For this one, I'd researched the endings of similar themes and uploaded an ending similar to *The Graduate* as Ben and Elaine escape her wedding and flee on a city bus, their unclear future together staring them in their faces.

Here, Joe and Princess Ann scoot through Rome on her Vespa as the Carabinieri chase after them. After several car crashes, they find themselves alone—like Ben and Elaine—and have no idea what to do next. That ending was still questionable to me as was a third one that I gleaned from doing quick research on similar endings.

The 2003 Bill Murray and Scarlett Johansson movie *Lost in Translation* provided the inspiration for Princess Ann running down the palace walkway and into Joe's arms, where they kiss passionately. Ann whispers something heard only by Joe. It appears to provide a glimmer of promise before she hesitates, then walks slowly back to her entourage and duties.

Rome wasn't built in a day, and neither, apparently, was a new ending for *Roman Holiday.* I turned my cell phone on and saw twenty texts onto the screen. I sent a mass message: *All good, just working on something undisturbed. Going to sleep now.* I thought about adding that I had jetted off to Rome virtually but then thought it better to hide all aspects of what I'd been up to.

My phone buzzed with another text before I had a chance to turn it off. It was Charlie.

Bradley, we received seventeen queries from movie studios about Real to Reel *wanting to discuss ideas further. MGM wants to move forward right away on a rom-com starring Bradley Cooper and—get this—Audrey Hepburn! They sent the script, and it's fantastic! This is what we've been waiting for! It's perfect casting!*

I blanched at the sound of Audrey Hepburn's name, immediately thinking, *No. Not Audrey, never. She's only for me.* Then, *My God, what has happened to me since yesterday?*

I texted back. *Are they set on Audrey Hepburn? Are they thinking of any others?*

Don't worry, she'll be easy to recreate. I know you don't know her movies, but her early films were mostly rom-coms, and they want the Audrey from Roman Holiday *and* Sabrina, *with a dose of Holly Golightly from* Breakfast at Tiffany's. *It shouldn't take but a month for you to create. This is so awesome!*

I hadn't yet had the chance to watch anything but *Roman Holiday*, but *Sabrina* was now next on the list. I had heard of *Breakfast at Tiffany's* but knew nothing about it. Finally, I answered, *Yeah, I get it, but we want to be sure we have a say in which actor we resurrect. Did they mention any other actresses?*

No, they have the script written already for Audrey, and it's fun! Get this, the plot centers around her coming to the US right after college to work for a fashion house in New York. Bradley Cooper is her boss, and she works her way up to be the lead buyer and starts fashion trends with her wardrobe. Of course, they fall in love, but she gets cold feet, and at the airport, as she's about to board, he chases her down ...

I interrupted. *Let me guess, they share a kiss and roll credits.*

Exactly!

I thought back to the unaltered final scene of *Roman Holiday.* That ending definitely broke the mold and the happily ever after template was again the norm in Hollywood. *Well, show me the script, but it sounds like we wouldn't want to waste Audrey Hepburn on something that might get panned as unoriginal.*

It's been in your inbox since eight.

Okay, I'll get right to it. Are there any other promising queries?

Yeah, all of them. They're all in your inbox too. Oh, a few folks asked about pairing Audrey Hepburn with James Dean or Marlon Brando from the '50s, but I reminded them the idea was to pair a living actor with a deceased one.

I heard Gregory Peck's *Roman Holiday* voice come out of my own mouth. *Yes, quite right. That would be the end of the fairy tale.*

Charlie added, *People aren't even balking at the shared development cost—that's the new term we came up with for the cost of our services. Do you like it?*

I smiled and typed, *Yes, perfect.*

Charlie added, *Oh, get this—I have one treatment that reimagines Audrey Hepburn in* Star Wars *as Princess Leia. I haven't forwarded that one to you since the idea is to reenact who the stars were and not fashion them outside of their era.*

I was stunned. The industry was running with this invention way too quickly. I forced a smile and a laugh. *Good catch. Absolutely right. Thanks, Charlie.*

I didn't ask for the script because I knew *Star Wars* like the back of my hand. I smiled at the thought of remaking *Star Wars* with Audrey Hepburn … in the privacy of my home studio.

For no one but me.

Chapter 7

SABRINA

I woke up thinking of Nicole Bonnet—the pros and cons. Every time I discounted our budding relationship, I thought about how she made me feel: energized, educated, and emancipated from my phobias. Before I could stop myself, I messaged Nicole.

Want to watch Sabrina *with me later? "Joe Bradley."*

Her reply was immediate: *Yes!* Sabrina *is everything! I'm free at five p.m. your time.*

I pored through movie proposals with Charlie the rest of the day and told him I liked a romantic thriller that paired James Dean and Margot Robbie much better than the Hepburn-Cooper rom-com he'd mentioned. I mused that one romantic comedy script with Audrey Hepburn and George Clooney had some good moments but declared it wasn't worthy of Audrey. I resisted the urge to upload the script into *Real to Reel* and watch it for myself. I thought it best to get acquainted with her actual movies first.

At the appointed hour, Nicole messaged that she was ready, and I chirped her through *Cardinal,* choosing a virtual background of a living room in a classic Hollywood house I'd found on the internet.

Nicole was still in pajamas on the other end, drinking coffee. "Wow, we're watching this from William Holden's house?"

I was stunned. "How on earth do you know that?"

Nicole laughed. "There's not much about classic Hollywood that you'll be able to get past me, Bradley."

"I just didn't want you to see my messy bed. I can change backgrounds if you'd like. I downloaded a few other Hollywood backdrops."

"No, this is fine. That's fun technology! Thanks for including it."

"Great. Should I change clothes? You look comfortable." I felt overdressed in my Lululemon ensemble.

She laughed again, and I liked the warmth of it. "I've been wearing these kinds of pajamas since the first time I saw *Roman Holiday*. These are as close as I could find to what Joe Bradley gave Princess Ann in his Rome apartment."

She asked if I was going to join her with at least some popcorn. I said, "No, that's okay. I really don't eat until I'm starving."

"Starving isn't very good for you. I can wait if you want to make something."

"No, let's get started."

And Audrey Hepburn's second Hollywood movie *Sabrina* began playing in her co-star William Holden's living room.

This film was also in black and white, so I asked her, "Why do you think directors were still using black and white? Wasn't color film readily available?"

"That's a good question. There's an adage that when you film people in color, you film their appearance, but when you film in black and white, you film their soul. Black and white was still considered a higher form of art, where the performances were the focus more than the experience of color, but in reality, often it came down to cost. Color was expensive."

"So, what was Audrey's first color movie then, and when?"

"She made *War and Peace* with her husband Mel Ferrer in 1956."

I groaned, remembering what I'd read about Mel being domineering and philandering. Who would cheat on Audrey Hepburn anyway?

Nicole said, "Look, an important scene."

I was shocked when Sabrina started up all the cars in the closed garage of a mansion, below where she and her chauffeur father lived. She was attempting to asphyxiate herself by carbon monoxide poisoning after her crush, David Larrabee—Holden looking vibrant and blond—disregarded Sabrina yet again and made off with an affluent woman, unaware of the crush Sabrina had on him. As Sabrina begins coughing in the garage, one of the doors opens and David's brother Linus—a too-old-looking Humphrey Bogart—saves her. Then he scolds her and carries Sabrina over his shoulder upstairs to her father.

Sabrina soon travels to Paris to attend an elite culinary school, where she learns about food and life and returns two years later, reinvented and determined to woo her heartthrob. David happens by, and flirts with the elegant and apparently unrecognizable Sabrina. He offers her a ride, not knowing her or that she'd had a lifelong crush on him while living on the property.

"Fucking preposterous that he wouldn't recognize her!" I snapped.

"Just wait until you see her debut in the most exquisite dress of all time."

Moments later I saw what Nicole meant. A white gown with dark floral embroidery mesmerized the party in the movie and the two people now watching it a lifetime later, me for the first time and Nicole for, who knows how many times?

I couldn't find the right words to describe Audrey Hepburn in the dress. "Holy shit," was all I could muster.

"Indeed," Nicole's said. "Givenchy."

"Sorry?"

"The dressmaker was Frenchman Hubert de Givenchy. His designs were exquisite. He became Audrey's personal designer and dear, dear friend."

David and Sabrina danced and close-ups of Audrey cheek-to-cheek with her crush made blood rush to several places in me. I couldn't imagine a more beautiful face or expression of contentment and descended into a deeper circle of Audrey Hepburn fandom.

The rest of the movie displayed a brotherly tug-of-war between the brothers for Sabrina's affection. Bogart wins out and they sail away together on a cruise liner.

Nicole explained, "Like I said, *Sabrina* is everything. It made Audrey a megastar—she held her own with Humphrey Bogart and William Holden, and she truly looked like she belonged. As wonderful as *Roman Holiday* is, it could have been a fluke or a lucky break. This cemented Audrey's place. As for Sabrina herself, she was a dreamer who lived a fairy tale, and she was a romantic, an incorrigible romantic, just like Audrey. And me."

I wasn't wistful, I was unnerved. "Why does this movie have a happy ending when *Roman Holiday* was supposed to break that mold?"

"Well, a different director for one thing."

"Wait, I thought it was Wilder for both."

Nicole smiled broadly and stifled a laugh. "Common mistake. William *Wyler* directed *Roman Holiday*. Billy *Wilder* directed *Sabrina*."

"Okayyy ..."

"And to make it more confusing, William Wyler went by Willy to his friends. So, you have Willy Wyler and Billy Wilder."

More confounding was the mere idea that Sabrina could be attracted to Linus Larrabee, especially as portrayed by an old and crotchety Humphrey Bogart. "It's just not believable that she would fall for him, in the movie or in real life."

"You're in the majority there. Bogie was second choice."

"Who was first?"

"Why, that imaginary first James Bond of yours."

"Cary Grant?"

"Yes! So, let me ask, are you going to keep watching Audrey Hepburn movies? How are you going to manage it with all of your work?"

"I don't know, but I will. Can we keep doing this? Can you keep introducing me to her movies?"

She smiled, not unlike Audrey herself. "Maybe. You do remember that I'm a reporter, right?"

"Yeah, we would need to establish some guidelines."

"We call them *ground rules*. And they are by mutual consent, agreed to up front."

I wasn't ready to negotiate terms for watching Audrey Hepburn movies with Nicole but realized that there was little I could do to stop her from writing whatever she wanted until I modified the agreement again. NDAs were broken all of the time, frequently resulting in lawsuits. My fear was that a public filing would make these private screenings with Nicole known throughout the world. I knew what I was doing was dicey and also knew that Ara would scorn me for even watching a few movies with a reporter.

"What kind of ground rules would keep all of this off the record? Our movie watching, I mean?"

Nicole smiled that wide smile and again I noted her crooked front tooth. "I don't think anyone would care about us watching Audrey Hepburn movies together, so don't worry about that. As for the rest, I will let you know when the time is right, but it won't be a major surprise."

"Uh huh."

So, there it was, I now knew she was angling for *something* and it seemed that she would drag it out a bit before revealing it. I knew I should cut things off right then but was captivated by what was now happening with my life. "This will need to be off the record entirely."

"Agreed. Off the record then, I've been thinking about *Real to Reel*. You and I both know what the technology could lead to. Are you working on it?"

I stayed silent since it was a leading question. If it was a question at all.

Then Nicole offered, "Think about the possibilities, Bradley. You can *resurrect people* in an alternate world. If there are home movies, families can bring loved ones back to life and talk with them—interact with them. As often as they want. You, and only you, can invent this technology."

What? We had been very careful to never reveal this next step of my technology. How did she guess it?

I said, "I'm not Dr. Frankenstein. I don't really want to bring the dead to life."

"And that's okay, but think about what I'm saying. Who would *you* bring back to life?" I knew the answer and thought maybe Nicole did as well. "So, off the record, how close *are* you to developing this?"

I knew I should dodge this question, but I trusted Nicole for some reason. "Months away."

"What are the gaps?"

"My time, for one."

"How about the technology?"

"Oh, the usual. Do we do it in 2D or 3D in a full-immersion room? Do we use virtual reality headsets or expedite extended reality glasses? How do we build the billions of data inputs, what kind of background video, cameras, sensors, neural networks, the AI …?" I shook my head. What was I doing, revealing all of this?

"Months isn't bad, but I sense that it can be quicker than that. You shouldn't underestimate your brainpower and your drive. I don't."

I looked away. "I don't know. If I worked on nothing else, which is impossible, and didn't sleep, which is more likely—maybe a month? Two is more realistic."

Nicole said, "Mmm,'" and then pressed the remote on her end and a film named *Charade* began to play. "Cary Grant time," she said. "Oh, and Audrey too. We're jumping ahead quite a few films, but it's the only one they did together. And *that* is one of the world's great tragedies."

I watched and yelled in surprise, "Hey, color film!"

A man was thrown from a train, and I lost myself in the movie. It was the last thing I remembered saying over the next two hours.

We watched the meandering and witty whodunit, and I guessed correctly that Cary and Audrey's characters would end up together. It wasn't a stretch—another happily ever after. As the credits rolled, I saw Nicole crying. I didn't know what to say.

"It's stupid. I cry every time for this movie. Not because of the movie, necessarily, but because it's the only film they ever made together, and it ended the Golden Age of Hollywood. Bogart, Gary Cooper, and Clark Gable had died. Marilyn Monroe too. And many other stars from the golden age had retired from making films by then. This was the last gift from the glory days. But the movie is only a B-minus, maybe a B-plus, taking other things into account like the cast and that they finally made a movie together. But Cary Grant is twenty-five years older than Audrey, which is why he asked that the script be rewritten so that she pursues him, and he doesn't look like a old lech."

"How old was Audrey?"

"Oh, thirty-three, I think. They started filming at the end of 1962 and it was released right after JFK was assassinated. As a matter of fact, they decided to voiceover Audrey using the word *assassinated* in the movie. Someone thought *eliminated* was less offensive, but later the original dialogue was restored. Anyway, when this movie came out around Christmas of 1963, it was seen as a gift from Hollywood to the country and the world to get moving again. Then the Beatles came to America and the world was never the same."

"Wow. That's a lot to take in. Did it get better or worse?"

"Well, ask yourself: Who since has replaced Cary Grant? Or Audrey Hepburn?"

"Remember, I'm a *Star Wars* fan. I speak in terms of Luke Skywalker and Princess Leia."

She replied, "I think we'll be changing that. By the way, Audrey was born on May fourth, so there's your last transition to Audrey taking over."

"Interesting. May the fourth be with you. So, what movies we should watch next?"

She smiled. "You can never go wrong with watching Audrey's personal favorites. We've watched *Roman Holiday, Sabrina,* and *Charade.* I—or Audrey, rather—would probably recommend *Funny Face*—she got to dance with Fred Astaire, the greatest movie dancer of all time! Save *Two for the Road* for when you think you've started to understand Audrey, then see if you were accurate.

It's the movie that comes closest to being a biography of her first marriage. Then, *The Nun's Story*, for Audrey's humanitarian side. Those probably reflect her life the closest. That should be a good start."

We talked into the night until I fell asleep. I had no idea whether Nicole lingered for a bit on *Cardinal* or exited the connection right away.

Hours later, I awoke with a start amid an old-fashioned dream, the most vivid dream I'd ever had. It featured me and twenty-four-year-old Audrey Hepburn. I tried to grasp fleeting tendrils of the dream. It included a lunch, Audrey smoking, me wanting to say cigarettes would kill her someday, and her replying that she had survived the war, so this was her reward. Then there was something about a ride on a Vespa as the dream became wispy.

I put my feet on the ground and remembered where I was and who I was. And who I wanted to be, as well as who I was determined to resurrect through my technology.

Audrey Hepburn herself.

It's just that I hadn't invented the technology yet. Then I realized Nicole had led me to the idea like a moth to a light.

I needed to figure out why.

Chapter 8

XR LAB

I went into HQ on a regular workday. My determination overpowered my phobias and I only scratched at myself a few times entering the building before heading straight for Advik's Extended Reality Lab.

I got right to it. "You two are my project leads for creating a fully Immersive Digital Environment within two months. You have no other work priorities, pass those on to the others. The end goal is to recreate a dead person. Advik, you're the XR lead, encompassing all of our work in virtual, augmented, and mixed reality. Focus your work on wearables, including glasses and the exoskeleton haptic body suits, and the technology needed in the room itself. The goal is a real conversation with our creation, with a virtual champagne in our hands.

"Ara, I have already done a lot of the AI work but I will rely on you for updating developments and helping me past speed bumps. Nothing is off the table, but I'm looking beyond CGI and green screens. I'm good with holograms and using *Real to Reel* and *Cardinal*'s technology together. The goal is a 3D image fed by AI, with personality traits, voice, and conversations. Let's take it step by step. Ara, what's the quickest path for pushing our creation into a virtual being?"

She coughed and cleared her throat. Finally, she said, "We can't do it well with just narrow AI." She paused and looked at us. "This, boss, is the big kahuna, AGI—artificial general intelligence. Lucky for you, we just had a major breakthrough with it this morning."

Our heads snapped toward Ara.

She continued, "Okay, we know that there are about one hundred companies around the globe working on AGI. Some have had some success in different aspects—giving the computer the ability to reason, solve puzzles, make judgments. Some companies have had luck with not only high-capacity knowledge, but also common sense, which is actually harder for a computer to assimilate. Most have had some luck with computer learning, but not the ability for a computer to plan something. The holy grail remains the ability to sense and act. We came up with programming that may deliver that."

Advik and I were stunned. He whistled and said, "The last estimate on AGI was maybe a decade or two. You know, like when we're all retired and having drinks virtually from our estates someday."

Ara answered, "Yeah, well, twenty years or two months—things are moving so quickly that our biggest concerns are safety and instituting controls on what we allow narrow AI and strong AI to do. Bradley, I may need to tap into some contacts, and I will need backup on … 'borrowing' ideas from them."

I smiled at her bluntness. "I'm glad I didn't invite the lawyers into the room. As long as we aren't stealing intellectual property, I'm good. And, of course, let me know what it costs."

"I may be able to get what I need from a nice dinner."

I smiled. "Permission granted, captain. Oh, I want AI, or AGI rather, to carry dialogue like a real interaction, without scripting it beforehand. I'll be working on whole-brain emulation. I want her brain to be a one hundred percent carbon copy of the real thing."

"*Her* brain?" Advik asked. "Anyone I know?"

"More about *who* later. Tell me about advances in alternate realities."

"Two dimensions would be easier and quicker than three, always. But if you want to dance after champagne, then a deep fake over a real person should be considered, given the time frame."

I said no.

"Okay, then I recommend a hologram of—her—at least initially, with haptic technology for you. We're close on an exoskeleton body suit, to replicate all senses, including taste and smell. I can adapt the controllers into the gloves to feel like a woman's hand and the other controller can give the feel of her lower back, say, while dancing."

"How about XR wearables, for when we get to an Immersive Digital Environment?"

"We're almost there. I think we can get there in two months with XR wearables with built-in AI sensors, LEDs, and 3D lenses. They will give the room a 360-degree, 3D feel."

"It sounds like you both know what to work on, then. Is that month enough time?"

Advik said, "*One* month? You said two."

I smiled and said, "I was just seeing if you were paying attention. Two months, if needed. Now, server or cloud?"

Advik said, "I definitely recommend a server for computing power, at least initially. Especially for the sensors and 3D cameras that you'll ultimately need for the virtual environment to display motion. Download time for the cloud could be slower and interrupt the scene. Of course, since you perfected 6G with *Cardinal*, we can run computing speeds a hundred times faster than our competitors."

Ara asked, "How long are you going to hide the power of a 6G network, Bradley?"

"I'm not sure. Maybe until this little venture works or fails, but I need to focus on this project only right now."

Ara and Advik both sensed I was working on more than I let on. Of course, Ara was the one to ask. "You haven't mentioned BCI for the Immersive Digital Environment. Does brain-computer interface still scare you?"

"No, not if I wake up tomorrow with Lou Gehrig's disease. Then I will ask you all to take BCI to the next level so my brainwaves come out as speech. I just don't want to put nanorobots in brains yet for entertainment and gaming. Let's leave that for sci-fi movies." I paused and asked, "Any other thoughts?"

Ara cleared her throat. "Yeah, I can't emphasize enough how future AI could be more dangerous than nuclear weapons. And bad actors can get ahold of them easier once they're invented."

"Yes, strong controls." Then I blurted, "Audrey Hepburn. She's the object of our affection." They looked at me with puzzlement. I met their gazes with determination.

Chapter 9

RECASTING

I awoke chasing another strand of a dream as it faded. I'd dreamt again of the movie *Sabrina*, but it wasn't Bogart who ended up with Audrey's character—it was Cary Grant as Linus Larrabee. I went straight to my computer and steered AI to recreate Cary Grant's face, body, personality, accent, and charm and subbed him for Bogie. To my immense satisfaction, the program worked perfectly, and then I decided to colorize it. I overrode my self-warning to not message Nicole Bonnet.

There's something I need you to see. Are you free?

Not right now, I'm sorry.

Well, it stars Cary Grant, so …

Oh! I'll be free around, let's see, eight your time, tomorrow night.

I sent a thumb's-up emoji and went back to reviewing my work. It all looked perfect. I gasped when I saw Sabrina's embroidered white gown in color.

I hoped *Real to Reel* was up to the task.

Nicole was visibly excited when we connected. "You mentioned something you wanted to show me? Something about Cary Grant!?"

"I wanted to wish you happy birthday."

"Happy birthday? My birthday's in May."

"Yes, but your present came today." I started the movie after the opening credits and watched Nicole's face as it dawned on her what she was seeing.

"So, you colorized *Sabrina*."

The opening scene, over Audrey's narration, focused on the Larrabee estate on Long Island—the gardens, the yachts, the goldfish named George, and Sabrina and her father washing a Rolls Royce. Then the camera panned to an old Larrabee family picture on the wall from decades earlier before trailing downward to show the parents and brothers interacting.

Nicole screamed a high F-sharp. "No way! Did you recreate this scene substituting Cary Grant in as Linus? How far did you go?"

"Keep watching."

A few minutes later, she asked, "The whole movie!?"

"That's the beauty of *Real to Reel*. Once you program the character, it replicates in every scene, even costume changes are copied."

Nicole smiled. "You chose the Cary Grant from *The Bishop's Wife*, didn't you?"

"Yes … how in the world did you know that?"

She looked at me with fake derision. "Please. Solid choice, by the way. William Holden was thirty-five when he made *Sabrina*, and Cary was forty-two when he made *The Bishop's Wife*. So, the ages are appropriate to the characters. Bravo!"

"Yeah, I thought about using the Cary Grant from *Charade*, but I'm still creeped out by Hollywood casting someone twenty-five years older than Audrey, so I thought I would go for someone a bit younger."

"Good call. He's as good-looking as Bill Holden though. It almost makes Sabrina's infatuation with David a little less likely."

"Yeah, well, maybe I can provide an option to ugly-up the actors a little in the next version of *Real to Reel*."

"*Shh*, let's watch."

She didn't speak again until she saw an entirely new scene I'd added.

"What exactly is happening here, Bradley?"

I returned the *shh*. "Just watch."

Fans of the movie had debated for years how Sabrina had changed from a suicidal young woman to a sophisticated *Parisienne* during her two years in Paris. I let AI devise the answer: Sabrina had an affair with the older Baron St. Fontanelle, who introduced her to life's finer things. My remake wove from the inserted parting with the Baron to Sabrina returning to Long Island after Paris. David picks her up without recognizing her.

Nicole said, "That's very well done, Bradley. You're really a quick study in this Audrey Hepburn stuff."

A few scenes later, she saw *the dress* in full color. "My God," was all Nicole could muster.

The scene between Sabrina and David played out with them dancing, her face in full close-up breathing him in, at long last. She agrees to meet him in his romantic lair, the indoor tennis court, and David goes to get champagne. Cary Grant as Linus decides that the engaged David shouldn't play games with the chauffeur's daughter and plants champagne glasses for David to sit on in the house. Once David is indisposed, Linus takes David's place at the tennis court and eventually kisses Sabrina, saying he took the place of David and it's all in the family.

But it was Cary Grant's mid-Atlantic accent that changed everything about the scene. The deadpan delivery was so different from Humphrey Bogart's that Nicole couldn't stop laughing. "This is absolutely brilliant! Bravo, Bradley."

By the end of the movie, Nicole was writhing in her chair as Cary Grant at his debonair peak out-swooned the staid Bogart rendition in every way.

"Oh. My. *God!*" Nicole fanned herself through the monitor. Squirming, she looked at me and added, "You just made this the sexiest movie I've ever seen! I'm afraid I have to go, Bradley. I, uh, need to take care of something."

"Do you want company? Even virtually?"

Nicole smiled sheepishly. "Thank you, Bradley, but no." As she got up, she turned and said, "Sincerely, thank you."

It was about ten thirty p.m. when I disconnected with Nicole and deselected Do Not Disturb. *Cardinal* immediately chirped. It was Ara Day.

Ara smiled and said, "Here's something you may not know: Audrey Hepburn has a bit of a history in San Francisco."

I looked at her blankly through the big screen. "Go on …"

"She did this play, *Gigi*, on Broadway …"

"Yes, I read about *Gigi*."

"Well, did you know that she went from *Gigi* on Broadway to filming

Roman Holiday, then back here to the US for a nationwide tour of *Gigi*? San Francisco was her last stop."

"I'm listening."

"I thought it might be fun for you to retrace her steps. I did some research, and well, we need to road trip for my AI screen feeds for this new project anyway. I figured you might enjoy tagging along and actually getting back to The City a bit. I'll keep us away from crowds."

"Still listening and only mildly panicking."

"Well, you'll remember Charlie hosted some company parties at the Palace Hotel. Audrey had some well-known photos taken there. But it's the rarefied air of Telegraph Hill that we should visit first."

"I'm sorry, was something filmed there?"

"No, a house she visited. Quite famously, I might add."

"Okay, but there are thousands of places she visited. What's special about this one?"

"Well, first, like I said, it's just up the road in San Francisco. And second, there might not be an Audrey Hepburn if it wasn't for what happened at that house."

"Okay, set it up."

"I already have. Get some sleep, boss. You'll want to be rested for this one."

Chapter 10

TELEGRAPH HILL

Driving to Telegraph Hill made me ponder what more could be done to restore San Francisco to her former glory. Once one of the world's great cities, it was now scarred and bleeding out. Tech companies and major retailers had fled, and there was a significant homeless population that made some areas off-limits. Even some of the mansions looked foggy and unfocused, in muted pastels.

Telegraph Hill still had some resplendent old homes that I spied as Ara parked her electric car. She pointed at three mammoth connected homes down the hill from Coit Tower, and we walked to the one oriented toward San Francisco Bay and Pier 39. Ara buzzed the intercom.

"Yes?" called a woman in a strong voice.

"Miss Poppy, it's Ara, we're here."

"Wonderful, right on time. Please come up."

The door clicked and we wound our way up to the second floor. The stately woman awaiting us was well-dressed and delighted to have company.

"Miss Poppy, this is my friend, Bradley Joseph. Bradley, meet my new friend, Poppy Kendall." I stepped forward into her double-handed welcome, took a deep breath, and said, "It's so nice to meet you, Ms. Kendall."

"Please, call me Poppy. It's so nice to meet someone new." She looked wistful. "It's been such a strange few years."

"Miss Poppy, can you please tell Bradley where we happen to be standing right now?"

She smiled broadly and maneuvered me a bit on an egg-shell-colored area rug with dark borders, next to a rose-shaded accent chair and glass table. Then she was satisfied. I felt a rash start from the touching but told myself to calm down. Poppy seized a photo that was only an arm's reach away and gave it to us.

"Bradley, you are now standing in the exact spot where Audrey Hepburn stood in this house in May 1953. As you can see, the decor and furniture have changed, and of course, we didn't live here then, but you are standing in the same spot."

An old color photo of the same room showed a massive, low-hanging chandelier and medieval-looking tapestries framing the bay window. I smiled and tried to be nonchalant but my heart leaped, breathing in the same space where Audrey appeared seventy years ago. My hands trembled, holding the photo. I felt unworthy of being there.

Ara must have sensed the thunderbolts also. "Do you feel it? Audrey Hepburn was *right here*." I nodded because words escaped me.

I had a momentary sense of being at that black-tie 1953 party and conversing with Audrey, just like the older playboy in the photo with her. The tapestries were now replaced by bookcases, and I wondered what Audrey and the man in the photo talked about, whether the old codger tried to bed her, how she arrived here, and with whom. More importantly, did she leave with the same person, and what happened later that evening?

Poppy said, "You know that Audrey was in the touring company here of *Gigi*, between filming *Roman Holiday* and *Sabrina*. The man in these photos is Whitney Warren, Jr., son of a famous architect. He hosted a party in Audrey's honor; being a prosperous, famous socialite afforded him those graces. These photos helped propel her to stardom, even before *Roman Holiday* premiered. It was the buzz from this party and the photo you're holding that was printed in newspapers around the world. Then when *Roman Holiday* premiered, people went to see it to determine whether she was as lovely and as good of an actress as they'd seen and heard. The rest, as they say, is history."

I cleared my throat and declared, "I would wager Audrey wasn't the first actress he leered at."

"You're correct about that," Poppy said. "He wooed socialites and a particular Broadway actress named Jeanne Eagels. He never married though, and spent his days out west hosting lavish parties for his many wealthy friends and admirers."

"Whitney was called the most civilized man in San Francisco," Ara said.

Poppy showed me another old photo of the pre-party room with dinner chairs placed about and the large chandelier that was no more. The current room looked modern while the old photo looked like a swanky bachelor pad for the rich.

"Did he actually date Audrey?"

Poppy shrugged and said, "Very unlikely, but look at this little-known photo."

Now Whitney Warren and Audrey were seated on the couch and they leaned in for what appeared to be a kiss staged for the cameras. Still, Warren's lips may have grazed those of Audrey Hepburn—and it happened just a few feet away from where I was standing. I felt as if I was traveling backward in time. Lightheaded, I closed my eyes but started to sway anyway. It wasn't the phobias.

"May I sit down?"

I stepped quickly to the cream-colored couch, and it appeared to be in the exact location as the one in the photo. I breathed in more of what I judged was Audrey Hepburn's air and stared again at the photo.

Poppy excused herself to prepare tea, and Ara turned the conversation back to Audrey Hepburn.

"Come on—let's recreate the photos."

We arranged ourselves in the spot where the standing picture was snapped, Whitney with his left hand on Audrey's hip and holding a glass of champagne in his right. I decided an open hand was an adequate substitute for the glass. Audrey was wearing a black gown with white gloves, and to my astonishment, Ara pulled on a pair of white gloves that extended just beyond the wrist, and with her all-black slacks and chemise, Ara had the colors right. Audrey seemed to be holding a cracker in one hand, which Ara did not replicate, and then she extended her left hand out to snap a photo with her cellphone. She took three, and nailed each shot.

We moved to the couch and, caught up in the moment, I grasped Ara's right hand with both of mine as Whitney had done with Audrey. I leaned toward her as she puckered her lips. The shock of feeling like Whitney Warren in 1953 jolted me as Ara squeezed off three more photos. She didn't like them.

"Hey, relax. Act like a playboy who is about to air kiss Audrey Hepburn, like she's the lucky one. Look, he didn't even pucker for the camera. She did."

We reset and the second group of photos captured the scene much better. I noted that touching Ara didn't fast-forward my haphephobia.

Poppy returned with the tea and we spent another forty-five minutes discussing the house, Poppy's late husband, and how they found out about the home's extraordinary lineage.

"Someone sent me a letter addressed to 'Occupant' and told me about it. I knew nothing about Audrey being here, nor did the real estate agent who had sold it to us. The house was designed by Gardner Dailey, a well-known midcentury architect in San Francisco, who happened to live next door and surely attended lots of parties here also."

"So absolutely everything has been changed out? Nothing from back then remains?"

Poppy smiled and motioned me toward the stairs we had climbed on arrival. She pointed to a softball-sized clear orb mounted at the top of the railing.

"This. Everyone at that party walked by this. And somehow it has survived all of these years without being broken or replaced."

"May I touch it?" After Poppy nodded, I touched the ball, imagining that Audrey did the same thing. Warmth coursed through my hand to my body and my closed eyes saw Audrey Hepburn's hand under my own, radiating heat from so many decades ago.

My mind wandered to 1953 and what it would have been like to be in Audrey Hepburn's social circle then. I recalled reading that soon after her time in San Francisco, she had a fling with William Holden during the filming of *Sabrina* and then was introduced to Mel Ferrer by none other than her *Roman Holiday* co-star, Gregory Peck. I determined to find out more about Audrey Hepburn's time in San Francisco and what she was like before superstardom.

And if I couldn't find it, I would use AI to make it.

Chapter 11

THE PALACE

It was only a mile and a half from Telegraph Hill to the Palace Hotel. Historically opulent and recently renovated to keep it that way, the Palace was all marble and gold. Jay Gatsby would have had trouble getting brunch reservations in the high-ceilinged Garden Court Lounge. They just don't make hotels like this anymore.

The Palace is most famous for the unexpected and mysterious death of President Warren G. Harding, who either died of a heart attack, was poisoned by his wife, or something in between.

"The more lascivious story is that Harding was a notorious philanderer and his wife had finally had enough and began to slowly poison him during a cross-country trip," Ara said. "After his death, she refused to allow an autopsy and had him embalmed an hour after he died. She allegedly poured a mysterious liquid down the drain when the hotel offered to test the food and drink he'd consumed. But enough about Warren G. We're here to retrace Audrey Hepburn's steps."

I asked, "When did you become a San Francisco historian?"

Ara laughed. "I get out and about, boss." She didn't add *you should too*, because she knew my phobias well. This visit was a huge step for me.

The marble floors led us to the concierge desk, where Ara was greeted warmly by a woman whose nametag said Lauren Winslow. She didn't see me dry swallow two Xanax.

"Ah, here to talk about one of the other things the hotel is known for. It's very nice to meet you, Mr. Joseph."

"Please, call me Bradley." My voice sounded raspy coming from my dry mouth.

Ara said, "Lauren uses *ConVRsate*, by the way."

"Yes, to practice how to reply to guests who ask all sorts of crazy questions," she replied quickly. "You wouldn't believe the kind of requests we get. Uploading them into the app really helps me get ready for each day!"

I looked up and tried to make small talk. "Well, hopefully this one didn't cause you to run for your phone."

"Not at all. We get this question a few times per year. All of the photos of Audrey Hepburn here are online; we don't have any additional ones anyone knows of. But I can show you the area where we're pretty sure the photos were taken, and even the room she may have stayed in—although we aren't one hundred percent sure about that. There's a book about famous guests, but she wasn't listed in it. It begs the question: If she didn't stay here, why not, and whose poodle is in the photos with her?"

"I see."

"Either way, the presidential suite is where she may have stayed because that's where we would put all notable guests back then. The room has been completely renovated." Then she whispered, "Fortunately, it's vacant, but there is an elderly man seated over there"—she pointed to a man sitting in the lobby—"who stays in that specific room every month. I asked him to delay his check-in for just a bit."

"Thank you, we really appreciate it."

I glanced over and saw a man who must be in his nineties watching us closely over a cup of coffee.

Lauren began a tour of the hotel, but I asked to skip the Garden Court Restaurant, which was full of brunchers scraping fine china with silver cutlery. I looked down the white marble hall toward the Pied Piper Bar that was a destination for today's tech leaders. It wasn't a destination for me yet, of course. Just past it was a Ghirardelli chocolate satellite store, and at the other end of the lobby was a small museum named Land Mark 18. I looked there for the photos of Audrey and the poodle but didn't see them.

Lauren saw me searching. "The pictures of Audrey Hepburn and the poodle aren't displayed in here, but they probably should be. It's primarily a tribute to the original Palace Hotel that was demolished in the 1906 earthquake."

The thunderbolt I'd felt in the Telegraph Hill house hadn't struck yet, but then Ara asked if we could see the room where debutante Audrey might have stayed.

Lauren said, "Of course, right this way."

We took the elevator to the presidential suite. The buzz of a key card opened the door and the thunderbolt clapped again. I steadied myself against the spinning of the room. It was strange to feel this way apart from enochlophobia and haphephobia; the air was thick with Audrey Hepburn. I knew there was no way even a single air molecule from 1953 remained in the renovated room, nor even a speck of old paint. Still, I could picture Audrey there.

I *felt* her there.

I looked toward a fireplace and sitting room as Lauren said, "Knowing that Audrey's national tour of *Gigi* ended in San Francisco on May sixteenth, 1953, it was quite possible that she used the fireplace, since Mark Twain once mused that the coldest winter he'd ever spent was a summer in San Francisco." The women chuckled, but I was lost in thought.

"How much has the room changed since Audrey Hepburn stayed here?"

"The layout is largely the same and elements of the fireplace remain, but you can assume that everything else has been switched out. We don't allow use of the fireplace any longer, so it's just for show, but you can imagine that a nice fire back in the fifties would have set quite a mood in the room."

I walked over toward the bathroom and saw the shower, toilet, and bidet. Ara saw where my eyes went and smiled.

"Lauren, are you sure there isn't some way of ensuring whether Audrey stayed here in this room? Records in the catacombs, perhaps?"

"Unfortunately, like I said, our records don't go back that far, and they would have been confidential anyway. It would take someone of Audrey's stature to have a dog stay in a hotel like this back then. It's possible that it was just a dog that someone was walking past with and was included in the shot."

"We learned that Audrey wasn't even that famous yet when the photos were taken," Ara said.

Lauren agreed. "Yes, I understand that *Roman Holiday* wasn't released until September 1953, but her reviews in *Gigi* here were very good, and rumors of how good she was when filming *Roman Holiday* were well known in social circles. There was no doubt she was about to be a star."

All this was said for my benefit, but the words were muted as my vision tunneled into an image of a wet-haired Audrey lying in front of the fireplace with a glass of wine, wearing only a monogrammed hotel bathrobe. I was sure this was where Audrey had stayed—I sensed it.

I envisioned a male figure carrying a bottle of red wine from the bedroom, a look of anticipation on his face. He was about to touch Audrey Hepburn in the most meaningful way.

The man turned in my vision, and I saw my own face. Before I had to take a knee to keep the room from spiraling, I asked, "Could we go downstairs and outside, perhaps?"

"Yes, of course. You want to see the photo spot?"

I nodded, and Ara looked concerned.

"Are you okay, Bradley?"

"Yes, it's just a bit warm in here. Seeing the fireplace made me feel warm."

I didn't tell them I had envisioned young Audrey Hepburn with me in this very room. I let Ara guess it was my anxieties—but I felt Audrey's presence. For the first time in my life, I felt it through something extrasensory or clairvoyant, and not via virtual reality.

Ara took my arm to steady me. "Let's get you some fresh air."

I didn't flinch at her touch and wanted to keep breathing the air of Audrey Hepburn's room, but the sensory overload was affecting my ability to think. They led me down the elevator and through the lobby and main entrance onto New Montgomery Street. Lauren said it was the likely place where some of the photos of Audrey and the poodle were taken. Unlike the photo, there was no small retaining wall with shrubs but there were potted plants along the walkway.

"It's not much, but this is probably the spot. The photographer was named George Shimmon, and he took three hundred and forty-five photos of Audrey according to the back of one of the silver prints. Maybe a photo studio or auction house knows what happened to the rest of them. I've only seen the handful online that were auctioned by Christie's in 2017."

Ara asked if I wanted her to take photos of me there. I declined.

"I'd actually really like a drink. Is the bar open?"

Lauren said, "No, not until four p.m." Then she saw that I really needed a drink. "But I have a key."

Lauren showed us the bar's specialty cocktails, but since I don't frequent speakeasies, I asked Lauren and Ara to choose for me. "Maybe something Cary Grant would've enjoyed."

The women looked at each other and simultaneously said, "Gibson." As drinks were mixed, they revealed how they had become friends, from the Stanford Theater showing *North by Northwest*, where Grant's Roger O. Thornhill orders a Gibson on a train while meeting the *femme fatale* Eve Kendall, portrayed by Eva Marie Saint.

"She's still alive by the way," Lauren added.

Lauren poured Chopin Family Reserve vodka and white vermouth into a shaker, then added a hint of something from a jar. She said, "I'm a bit of a San Francisco movie buff, as you can tell. Maybe the very best movie of all time is *Vertigo*, and it was filmed right here in San Francisco."

"Was Cary Grant in that one?"

"No, Jimmy Stewart, with the then-unknown Kim Novak. She's also still alive. She and Eva Marie Saint are among the very few from the Golden Age of Hollywood still with us."

Lauren poured two drinks into martini glasses and topped each with three cocktail onions on a toothpick. "Your Gibsons."

"None for you, Lauren?" Ara asked.

"No, not while on duty, but they are one of my favorites."

I looked at the chilled glass. "So, they're martinis but with these little onions instead of olives?"

"Exactly, made a little dirty with the onion juice also. It's a sipper, not a slammer. Bottoms up!"

I coughed at this first sip of the Gibson and said, "Wow. The onions add a whole new dimension." After another sip, I said, "I approve."

I set the chilled glass on the bar. "I'm curious. Was Audrey Hepburn considered for those other films you just mentioned?"

"No, but the director Alfred Hitchcock wanted to do a movie with her. It didn't happen though. She would have been great in them."

Suddenly, we were jolted by a voice from the door to the bar. *"No Bail for the Judge."* It was the old man from the lobby, in a creaky but authoritative voice.

"Mr. Bannister, I'm so sorry. I thought I had locked the door, and also, I should have let you know that we were done showing your room."

"It's okay. I'm just reminiscing about a time in 1953 when a young actress joined me here in the bar. She had just had some photos taken with my dog out front."

Our jaws hit the floor. The old man said, "I heard you speaking of Audrey Hepburn earlier. I got to know her while she was in town for *Gigi*. It was a long time ago, but I stay here once a month to reminisce about her."

We invited the old man to join us at the bar. "No, thank you," he replied. "I prefer our old spot over here in the corner." He walked over to the table at the front left of the entryway.

"May we join you?" Ara asked.

"Of course. I think that's why we're all here."

Ara and I shared a look of incredulity.

Lauren said, "Mr. Bannister, you never shared that with me before. You were friends with Audrey Hepburn?"

"Friends, yes …" he said. His smile creased his face and showing aged yellow teeth. "… *and lovers*."

Ara instantly tested the credibility of the old man's claim.

"You said that was your dog in the photos with Audrey? What breed of dog was it?"

"A tan Standard Poodle named Fifi. That's how we first met, you see. I was walking Fifi one day and we came near the hotel lobby. I saw this beautiful young lady coming out. Fifi went right up to her and I had to pull her back. The young woman said that she loved dogs and started petting her and asked her name. When I said Fifi, she said that's funny—I'm in a play called *Gigi!*"

"And when was that, sir?" asked Ara.

His eyes defocused and his head turned slightly up, a classic body language sign that he was calling up a memory.

"I'll remember it forever. It was the twentieth of April, 1953."

"And how long did you and Audrey date here?" Just hearing the words out of Ara's mouth made my heart race.

"Well, only for a few weeks, you understand. It was so difficult to find time together. Her handlers didn't want her to be seen dating as she traveled around the country because they were afraid that would tarnish her image. She had broken up with her fiancé James Hanson and, as she told me, she had no shortage of potential beaus around. She actually asked me to be her San Francisco companion to minimize that." His thin chest heaved with a dry chuckle. "Plus, she adored Fifi."

Ara jumped back in. "And you would meet her here? Was she staying in the hotel?"

"Yes, of course, the presidential suite. That's why I stay here on the third of every month. That's when we … well, I'm a gentleman, so I won't say more."

Lauren placed a gentle hand on his shoulder. "Mr. Bannister, can I get you something to drink?"

"Yes, water is fine, thank you. Anything more than that and my doctor will yell at me. Of course, at my age, I'm not sure what difference it makes." His dry laugh shook him again.

Ara asked, "And how old are you, Mr. Bannister?"

"Ninety-five."

"And do you still live here in The City?"

"Yes, same place as always. A Victorian over on Powell. My kids will love to sell that off when I croak. I still climb the stairs too!"

"Did Audrey visit your home there?" I asked.

"Unfortunately, no. That Edith Head kept her on a tight leash."

Lauren nodded. "That's right. Edith Head, the costume designer, visited Audrey here to get a sense of wardrobe for Sabrina. Apparently, they did a lot of shopping around town."

"Yes, I also showed Audrey the town when she could slip Edith's leash. Always with Fifi, and often with Edith Head. I'm a gemologist by trade and owned a few jewelry stores."

As Ara quizzed the old man about details, I tried to wrap my brain around speaking to someone who met, dated, and allegedly was intimate with Audrey Hepburn when she was starting out. And we had just visited the room where it happened. I had sensed and pictured it.

Suddenly, the bar began to swirl, but it wasn't because of the drained Gibson or my phobias. I decided to have follow-up conversations with George Bannister and got his phone number.

I had to learn more about Audrey Hepburn in San Francisco. More than that, I would meet her here. And have a relationship with her.

More than seventy years after her debut.

Chapter 12

BANNISTER

My fingers flew over the keyboard as I merged *Real to Reel*, *Cardinal*, and our latest virtual reality updates, retitling it *Bannister*. It seemed appropriate to recognize his influence.

I uploaded photos and videos to set the background scene, colorizing them where needed. I knew that Advik and Ara would come up with better programs over time, but I burned to meet Audrey Hepburn. *Now.*

Then I turned to my other creation, which I had named AIdrey. I created her by feeding every known nugget of content about Audrey Hepburn into a whole-brain emulation, as faithful to the original as possible. I was particularly taken by a wholesome *Roman Holiday* screen test and used that to develop AIdrey's persona. Smiling, I peeked ahead into her life and inserted her love of dogs for the scene I had in mind.

I decided to build the relationship slowly, as it might have happened in the 1950s with an emerging star and a computer nerd with phobias. Well, maybe not *that* slowly. My anticipation overwhelmed me as I drew closer to testing.

Finally, everything was ready. I donned the bulky VR headgear and haptic gloves in order to see her and feel the touch of the dog's leash and any other touch *Bannister* might offer. A last-minute thought had me running for the back of my closet, and I threw on tan corduroys, a blue dress shirt, maroon sweater, and a brown herringbone sport coat. On the way back to the studio, I punched the air conditioning down to fifty-eight degrees to simulate May temperatures in San Francisco. Then I doubled back to my closet and saw a gray scarf. I had no idea where it came from, but wrapped it around my neck.

Here we go. I'm actually going to meet Audrey Hepburn in as real a way as I can on this side of the afterlife.

Car horns from long-gone automobiles blared and cacophonous street noise reverberated around my studio. I hadn't programmed in smells but noted that that for next time. My attire fit in well enough with the people out and about at ten a.m. A tug on my right arm caused me to look down and see a tan poodle at the end of it. I said in a voice I barely recognized, "Hi, Fifi, good to see you," and the dog looked up at me for instructions. I looked across the street to the Palace Hotel. A long row of potted shrubbery sat behind a low wooden barrier. I recognized that as the location of the old black-and-white photos Lauren had shown me. I crossed at the corner of Montgomery and Market, heading left toward the shrubs. I wondered when and how the program would present Aldrey to me.

The answer came in the form of a photographer awkwardly backing out of the hotel lobby while looking down into his camera viewfinder as helpers opened the hotel doors for him.

"Hold it, please, Miss Hepburn … wait." He adjusted his lens and tested the flash. "Okay, now please …"

And suddenly there was soon-to-be twenty-four-year-old Audrey Hepburn in all her pre-stardom glory no more than twenty feet from me. She wore a gray skirt suit that ran to mid-shin, the jacket adorned with black buttons that ended just below her breasts. A red belt cinched tightly around her small waist added a swatch of color, and she wore white gloves with dark flat shoes. Somehow the cream-colored scarf tucked inside her jacket didn't add heft to her dancer's appearance. Her hair looked exactly like the back-from-Paris style from *Sabrina.*

I reminded myself she hadn't filmed that yet.

The photographer clicked away and the flash popped as Audrey's minders shooed onlookers away from getting in the shot. She seemed uncomfortable with the attention, smiling when instructed and dropping it when he wasn't snapping away.

Finally, he said, "Okay, I have to switch cameras now. Just a moment, Miss Hepburn."

Then she looked to her left, directly at Fifi and me. *Thunderclaps.* Audrey said, "What a beautiful creature!" I knew she meant the dog, but it made me stand up just a bit taller as she walked toward us. She ignored the protestations of the photographer and minders and looked me straight in the eye from several steps away.

"Hello, what is your dog's name?"

Her delicious European accent dried my mouth. I was about to speak with Audrey Hepburn.

I cleared my throat as best as I could. "This is Fifi."

Then she was right next to me. "May I pet her? I'm Audrey, by the way."

"Yes, she'd like that. My name is Bradley."

Audrey removed her gloves and extended her hand. I shook it, managing to control my phobias. I realized she didn't have any pockets, so I offered to hold the gloves. I felt the slight weight added to my own haptic gloves.

"Thank you, Bradley." Then she squatted down and petted the dog. "Hi, Fifi, girl. How are you enjoying your walk around San Francisco?"

Audrey Hepburn, virtual or not, was crouching next to me. I could have counted the hairs on her head, given enough time. I forced my nervousness away and squatted down next to her, tucking her gloves in my coat pocket. Audrey's brilliant smile was heartfelt and heart stopping, unlike what she threw at the camera a moment ago.

"Fifi is such a brilliant color—Café Au Lait is one of the rarer colors for a poodle! It's actually called that: Café Au Lait, just like the coffee drink! But who am I to tell you, you probably know everything about the breed!"

I knew nothing about poodles and was, in fact, allergic to dogs—in the real world. But I couldn't tell her that.

I deadpanned, "Yes, she's unique indeed." As Audrey's smile continued, the camera crew walked toward us.

Audrey whispered, "Uh oh, fun's over." Then, so that only I could see, she rolled her eyes and smiled at me.

"Thank you for letting me pet dearest Fifi. Oh, you know, it's funny, I'm actually in a play here called *Gigi,* and here I get to meet a Fifi!"

The photographer said, "Audrey, dear, we're ready for you now."

Then Audrey whispered again to me, "Would it be terrible to ask if Fifi could be in some photos with me?"

"I don't mind." Fifi's tail was wagging. "She doesn't seem to mind either."

Audrey stood and said to the photographer, "I'd like Fifi to be in some pictures with me, if that's all right."

He replied, "No, no, we have to …" Then he stopped himself. "Wait. Actually, that's a good idea. It would show the animal-lover side of you as you wrap up this tour and head off to film your next big movie." His head turned to me. "Is that all right with you, sir?"

Everyone looked to me. "Yes, it's fine." Then I gave Audrey her gloves back and handed her Fifi's leash. I felt the weight pass to Audrey through the haptic gloves.

"Thank you, sir. And now if you'll just stand over here, out of view. Yes, that's right. And Audrey, you and the dog in front of the shrubs. Perfect." I shook my head—the photos I was participating in were the same ones I'd used to set the background for this virtual scene. *Full circle.* I knew then it wouldn't be the last confusion of time and space with this technology.

I could program virtually anything now with *Bannister*, including real on-the-town, money-no-object dates with a young Audrey Hepburn. A full-fledged romance was in order, and I had a virtual dog to thank for it, as well as a ninety-five-year-old man.

Chapter 13

COCKTAIL HOVR

I chirped Advik and Ara in *Cardinal*. They were both in the Palo Alto lab working at six thirty on a Sunday night.

"What are you two up to there?"

Ara smiled. "Oh, we have this boss who gave us important projects, so here we are."

Advik added, "It's a good thing we love our jobs."

"Hold that thought. Remember how I wanted to move quickly to a full-immersion room? In the interim, the three of us have a new project, and I need it done by Wednesday."

"Wednesday?" Advik looked doubtful. "What is the project exactly?"

"I'm going to have a date with Audrey Hepburn." I surprised myself in blurting it out so directly, but I had to be direct in order for them to do what was needed. "I want to call the new program *Cocktail HoVR*—but with a *v* instead of a *u* to end the word *hour*, like the Romans used to do—and, of course, the *VR* stands for *virtual reality*. Advik, do you have the next generation of glasses ready yet?" I hated the bulkiness of VR headgear.

Advik's eyes narrowed. It was the look he had when problem solving. "In a few days. Can you give me more background though? And what exactly happened today?"

I told them about *Bannister* and the quick meeting with Audrey. Advik asked, "When did all of this classic movie stuff steal my boss?"

I laughed. "Ara kind of helped speed it along, with her San Francisco knowledge and contacts." She shrugged at Advik.

"Also, I connected with that reporter from AICon, who introduced me to a few Audrey Hepburn movies and I kind of jumped in with both feet. As I'm known to do."

Their smiles froze. Advik asked, "This reporter, are you concerned that she could expose what we're doing before it's ready? It sounds risky."

Ara added, acidly, "Stupid even."

"Yeah, about that. She signed an NDA, and we set ground rules before each meeting. We've only watched two movies together."

It felt deceptive to hide the full conversations from my most trusted employees and good friends.

I continued, "Anyway, the task at hand is a virtual date with Audrey Hepburn in three days. Here's how we'll do it: *Cocktail HoVR* will use a combination of *ConVRsate* and a new composite program I put together I'm calling *Bannister*. It's a VR program using *Cardinal* to bring me into a *Real to Reel* scene. Basically, I will see Audrey Hepburn in 3D through the VR glasses, in a variety of backgrounds, say a house party in 1953. Ara, use the imagery from the Telegraph Hill house for the background. The 1953 version."

They seemed to track my intent, so I upped it. "Advik, I want to use the exoskeleton suit: full touch and sensory simulation. I want to feel the clink of a glass when we toast, taste the champagne, smell her perfume, and I want to dance with her."

Ara countered, "You once told me that you don't dance."

"Advik is going to help me with that. Have the haptics help guide movement when dancing, with the appropriate music for any situation. I'll need you both to upload popular songs from the time period."

"Going back how far?" Ara asked.

"Let's say World War II. Not every song but just the top hits each year. So, there's the project. Thoughts?"

Ara said, "You're way ahead of me on Virtual Audrey. Do you need to catch me up?"

"Actually, I named her AIdrey, but I'm going to stop using that term. We need to make her real and just call her Audrey. You'll have to add just one small, but significant, thing: whatever info George Bannister gives us tomorrow."

Advik asked, "And who is Mr. Bannister, other than who you named a

VR program after?"

"He's probably the last living lover of Audrey Hepburn. They dated in San Francisco in 1953. Ara, I want meet him again tomorrow, and we'll get every available detail we can from George on his time with her. No detail is too small." I paused, then added, "Or too intimate. Then we'll add it to her profile."

Ara smiled. "Am I collecting info for your AIdrey—sorry, Audrey—or writing a story for *Literotica* here?"

I put my hand to my ear, motioning for her to call George and she sauntered away. Advik was looking down with his arms crossed. "I know that you're close on these things, Advik. Or am I pushing too hard?"

"I think we're okay, Bradley. I'll let you know when things get … unrealistic."

"Great. Let's see what we can come up with by Wednesday. Just remember, this will be fun." *At least for me.*

I thought through the technology side of it, but the specter of having a conversation—and starting a virtual relationship with—a woman in 1953 who was about to burst onto the international stage was intoxicating.

And the good part was that—like the movie *Groundhog Day*—I could redo our first date as often as I needed to get it right.

Chapter 14

BACK TO THE PALACE

I reserved the presidential suite for my conversation with George Bannister. Ara and I got to the room before George did, and I again sensed the supernatural feel from our first visit.

"So, this really is where George and Audrey would meet for, uh, personal things."

Ara grinned. "Hopefully they've changed the sheets since then."

Her laughter cut the tension inside me. "They've changed everything … many times. But like your friend Lauren said, the layout of the room is the same."

"Should I video the fireplace and the room for *Cocktail HoVR* inputs?"

"Yes, perfect. Let's get that before George comes."

As Ara scanned the room, I envisioned George and Audrey here: a small fire in the hearth, wine, room service, the inevitability of intimacy. I tried to keep my mind from returning to that, but Audrey's intimate life was the biggest unknown in her portfolio that only George Bannister could provide.

A frail knock snapped me back to the present. I opened the door and saw George, dressed in an earth-toned tweed jacket, brown corduroy pants, white dress shirt, and Burberry scarf.

"George, welcome. You're right on time. You remember Ara Day." George nodded to us and walked in slowly without speaking. He looked about, perhaps reflecting on what happened in this room so long ago.

Finally, he said, "I always get a little wistful coming here. Everything I did in my life pales compared to what happened back then. I didn't know it at the time, of course, but I know it now."

"I think I understand, George." I gestured to the gear Ara was setting up. "Do you mind if we record our conversation? I want to make sure we accurately capture what you say about Audrey, from someone who knew her as well as you did."

George sat down in the chair and looked up at me. "And what will this be used for exactly?"

I didn't think George would understand the complexities of what we were setting up so I said, "We want to talk to as many people who knew Audrey while we can. We think there are elements of her life that aren't known yet despite the many biographies about her."

George answered the unmentioned part of my reply. "And we're all dying off?"

"We're all getting older, minute by minute. And we want to capture your legacy, at least in part."

George looked to Ara and asked, "Are you a reporter?"

"No. I …" She looked to me, then answered. "I work in data collection."

"I see. But you're much too pretty to work in an office all day with computers." We smiled as George's charm worked its way to the surface—the same charisma he'd used seventy years ago that led to what had happened in this room. "Yes, you may record me. Is my hair straight?"

The old man recalled in exquisite detail how he met Audrey Hepburn and became her companion. He had us in stitches and then in tears. He held back intimate details except to say, "A gentleman doesn't talk about those things. I will take them to my grave with me." George saw a bit of disappointment on my face and added, "I will just say that she was just as vibrant and enchanting in this room as she was around town or in the movies. When you had her attention, she made you feel as though you were the only one who mattered, and she always smiled. Even today, remembering how she smiled at me means more than anything else I ever experienced in my life. And I've had a good life."

George's eyes misted as he looked toward the fireplace, reminiscing. Then he suddenly added, "And she loved chocolate." He reached into the pocket of his tweed jacket and pulled out an unopened Ghirardelli chocolate bar and offered us a piece to break off.

As we chewed, Ara asked, "George, did you ever see Audrey after she left San Francisco?"

"No. But she did send me cards every now and then. Somehow, she had found out that my dog, Fifi, died a few years later and she sent me this. He pulled a handwritten letter out of his inside jacket pocket, handing it to Ara. He mouthed the words from memory as Ara read it out loud.

> Dearest George,
> I am sorry to have learned of the recent passing of Fifi, who meant so much to me, as she did you. Know that I have very fond memories of Fifi, and indeed of you, and the times we shared in San Francisco. You know, I had Billy Wilder change the script in Sabrina to name the goldfish in the opening monologue after you.
> With Deepest Affection and Sympathy,
> Audrey

Ara returned the letter and George said, "Now how many people can say they had someone—anyone—do that for them, much less someone like her? But no, I never saw her again. I tried, but she never replied after she got married. She was a one-man woman back then. And then I also got married …" His voice then trailed off, and it was apparent that our conversation was over.

We touched George's shoulder as we made our way to the door, leaving him in his pensive state.

I turned back to him. "George, you're welcome to spend the night and order anything you want. Put it on my room tab."

George nodded in appreciation. I realized that it was truly George Bannister's room, now and forever.

On the way out, I thought about future steps in my relationship with Audrey. I thought of Nicole Bonnet and how I wanted to invite her to the unveiling of *Cocktail HoVR*, since it was kind of her idea in the first place.

Chapter 15

PREPPING

Giddy, I chirped Nicole in Japan and blurted, "So, I met Audrey Hepburn using some new technology to insert myself into the scene, and I'm having cocktails with her tonight. No full-immersion room yet, so I devised a stop-gap program called *Cocktail HoVR.*"

Nicole squealed with excitement. "This is *fabulous!* I thought the idea of cocktails with Audrey Hepburn might appeal to you. And whether you had already been thinking about it or it's something that, *ahem*, recently inspired you, I knew you would be the one to invent it. How long did it take?"

"We've been working pretty nonstop since I last spoke with you."

"It was that easy?"

"Well, it's really a combination of other things we've been working on. We had to do some reprogramming and lots of interfaces, but we didn't have any hiccups."

She smiled broadly and said, "Yes, that's wonderful! But first things first. We have to prepare you. Give me the details. Where will you be?"

"First, I'll need you to sign a new NDA, just in case the program fails. Or is wildly successful. No story either way, okay?"

Nicole agreed, perhaps too enthusiastically.

Once the paperwork was signed remotely, I said, "So, for this first one, I decided on the old Whitney Warren house, at the famous party he held for her. I'm going to script in that she remembers meeting me and my dog earlier, so there's recognition for continuing the banter."

"Yes, of course, that makes perfect sense. Okay, how will you present yourself at the party? This is like going to the prom with a girl you don't know well but really like. How can I help get you ready? What are you going to say to her?"

I suddenly felt like an awkward high school kid who needed to get up the courage to speak to a girl who didn't know he existed. It wasn't a stretch since I *was* that kid not long ago. "I was going to wing it, but, well … it is Audrey Hepburn."

"Yes, a young, vibrant Audrey Hepburn. Let's review the bidding: it's after she did *Gigi* on Broadway and filmed *Roman Holiday*, but before it's released, and she is finishing up a national tour of *Gigi*."

"And right before she films *Sabrina*."

"Yes! And in her personal life, she has broken up with James Hanson and hasn't met William Holden yet or been introduced to her first husband, Mel Ferrer. The timing for her to spread her wings is perfect. And she visits a major city she doesn't know." She looked at me and said, "You're right. She needs a beau." I wondered if I should mention George Bannister and decided not to.

I suddenly flushed. "Shouldn't the conversation just come naturally? I mean, we can do a lot of takes."

"Cary Grant once said, 'I began by acting like the person I wanted to be, and I eventually became that person.'"

"Wait, you're saying I have to change who I am?"

"Sorry, no, not at all. I mean Audrey may be able to help you become the best version of yourself. I think she can help you, help anyone, just by talking to her."

"Okay."

I was still skeptical. My mind went to my phobias and my initial meeting with Audrey. I didn't flinch when we touched and thought maybe our meetups could help my haphephobia.

Nicole asked, "Oh, do you have a tux? You can't go to a black-tie event, even virtually, without feeling you're dressed appropriately."

"Yes, but seriously? Tux and VR headgear and haptic suit?" The tux was from my mother's second wedding when I was in high school. She insisted on buying it, and it had sat in my closet untouched for eight years.

"Oh, you have a haptic suit now?"

"Yes. There might be champagne and perhaps dancing. I had to know what all that feels like."

Nicole's smile lit the room. I was relieved that she wasn't angry at me for not sharing the invention sooner. That made me pause—why should I feel I had to keep Nicole up to speed? I felt Ara's scorn flood my soul but pushed it away.

"Okay, then you definitely need to wear your tux. But I have an idea before you do that. Prep work. How much time do we have before your party?"

"It's almost noon. I was planning the first run at six."

"Okay, we have time to watch a movie. It's time to meet your spirit animal for this quest of yours."

I followed Nicole's instructions and spoke *Penny Serenade* into the voice command of my home system, then shared the monitor view with Nicole through *Cardinal*. Nicole introduced the film.

"Think of this as Cary Grant's first foray into a real drama after an earlier career of screwball comedies. Don't get me wrong, I love his early comedies, but this movie broke the mold for him, and he was nominated for an Oscar for his performance. It's largely forgotten today and doesn't appear on too many of his best performance lists, but the way his character develops over the course of the movie is extraordinary. Legend has it that he tried to back out of doing the movie at the last second, which was a familiar refrain …"

"Like in *Sabrina*?"

"Yes, exactly! But he didn't have as much freedom to break contracts when he was younger. *Penny Serenade* then turned out to be one of his favorite films. He and his wife at the time, Barbara Hutton, were discussing having a child, so he really connected with his character as the movie went on."

"And how will watching this help me tonight?"

"Watch how nervous his character, Roger Adams, is at the beginning of this film as he tries to woo Irene Dunne's character, Julie Gardiner."

I watched as Roger spied Julie from outside a record store, playing music from the 1920s. He goes in after hearing the record skip. He starts a nervous conversation and ends up spending the entire day listening to records with her. Roger walks her home, carrying a bundle of newly-purchased records. He asks if she has a Victrola inside and she replies by asking if he has one at home. He says no.

Well, why on earth did you buy twenty-seven ...? It suddenly dawns on her that Roger spent the afternoon and a lot of money to be with her. She smiles confidently and appreciates the expensive gesture. He smiles at her to affirm the suspicion.

"That's the look I wanted Audrey Hepburn to give Gregory Peck at the end of *Roman Holiday.* The smile that says yes!"

Nicole smiled. "You must stop trying to change that ending, but you're right about the smile. Everyone wants to be looked at like that." She stopped playing the movie as Roger and Julie danced in the next scene. "That's all you need to see from this movie for now. I'll save the part where they move to Tokyo from San Francisco for another time. Anyway, now you see even Cary Grant's character, Roger Adams, was nervous, and so was Cary Grant, even when acting with a familiar costar. He didn't know whether he could pull off the serious scenes later on when he cries. So, if Cary Grant can pull that off, you should be just fine tonight."

"Aren't you mixing up the actor and the person?" I remembered when she asked the same of me a few weeks prior about Audrey.

"Yes, of course I am. Just seeing if you're paying attention! Now take some deep breaths and I'll see you tonight."

Chapter 16

RETURN TO TELEGRAPH HILL

With the haptic suit under the tuxedo and Advik's new VR glasses on, I powered up *Cocktail HoVR* and tried to connect to Nicole. She didn't answer; after three tries, I gave up. I redirected my attention to the larger task and pressed Play. I was instantly transported to Whitney Warren, Jr.'s Telegraph Hill home, circa 1953.

The wall tapestries looked bland even when brought to life, and people bustled about in herds of conversation. I felt the familiarity of the room I'd visited with Ara that now belonged to Poppy Kendall.

Excited murmurs and a three-piece band filled the air. I heard whispers of this *other Hepburn girl* perhaps becoming a bigger star than Katharine Hepburn. The guests had all seen *Gigi* and concurred it was possible. They eagerly awaited the release of *Roman Holiday* in London the next month, but it wouldn't be released in the United States until the end of August. Some said they would just fly to England to see it sooner.

The air grew heavy with sudden commotion and polite applause, followed by handshakes and curtsies when Audrey climbed the stairs. I saw her hand grip the clear orb at the top of the stairs as she air kissed several guests. I became jealous and made a note to add kissing technology to my next update.

Whitney Warren, Jr., surely the luckiest man I'd ever seen, guided Audrey around his house by the elbow, introducing her to the social set of midcentury San Francisco. Audrey wore a black dress with a high collar and large earrings. That's when I first noticed her absolutely perfect ears. Surely the finest ever created, longer than most, with fine lines. Her lipstick was bright red, and I hoped I might get a trace on my cheek in a European kiss.

I still had no idea what I might say to her as ideas tumbled around in my mind. We were the two youngest people at the party, and I noticed no one had spoken French to her yet. I silently thanked Mom for forcing French lessons on me starting at age six.

Suddenly, Audrey was next to me and somehow Warren wasn't, apparently leaving to get her a requested whiskey. It was a champagne party but she was already breaking the mold. Audrey turned and smiled as she recognized me from the day before. She glided over and took both of my hands in her white gloves—presumably the same ones she'd worn during the photo shoot, kissed both of my cheeks in that European style, and said, "How nice to see you again, Bradley! No Fifi tonight?"

I felt lipstick on my cheek and blushed, in a non-phobic way. I immediately felt at ease since Audrey began the conversation.

"No, I gave her the night off, but she said to make sure I thanked you for making her the most famous dog in San Francisco."

"Yes, wasn't that a brilliant idea we had to include her!? I understand that photo is being run in papers beyond San Francisco as well."

"Audrey, I can't take any credit for the photo idea. That was all you."

"Well, there wouldn't have been a photo if you hadn't happened to be there, so it was a team effort." Her face beamed, and I could count all of her teeth, thirty-two.

I said, *"Ton sourire est enchanteur."* Your smile is enchanting.

She curtsied and replied, *"Comme c'est gentil de ta part."* How kind of you to say. Then, she whispered in English, "You know they made me cap my teeth for the movie I completed called *Roman Holiday.* A few weeks into the movie, they decided the initial shots showed my fangs were a little too ... *jagged* was the word. So, then I had to get used to this thing they fit over my real teeth. I had to relearn to speak with it."

I knew the answer to the question before asking but still offered, "Did you go back and reshoot the previous scenes?"

"No, thank goodness, but it was discussed!" She smiled at me again, and I almost had to take a knee, much like I felt in this same house last week, er ... seventy-odd years later. I reminded myself she wasn't yet fully *Audrey*

Hepburn in April 1953. "Bradley, I didn't catch your last name the other day."

"Joseph. Bradley Joseph." I kept all *Bond, James Bond* quips to myself since that classic introduction hadn't yet been fashioned.

"Bradley Joseph? Well, isn't that funny?" I knew what was coming next but let her continue. "Greg Peck's character in the film I just finished is named Joe Bradley!"

I smiled. "Well, he must be a good man. Both Gregory Peck and Joe Bradley."

"Yes, both are. As a matter of fact, in a scene in *Roman Holiday*, my character, Princess Ann, becomes catatonic from sleep medication that was administered after a bit of a tantrum. And, well, Joe Bradley brings her back to his apartment to sleep it off after he couldn't wake her or get the taxi to take her where she wants to go. She was passed out, you see? And Joe put her in his best pajamas, and, well, he was a perfect gentleman." Then she leaned in and whispered, "I even checked myself under the blankets to make sure I was still chaste." The twinkle in her eye and mischievous smile took our talk up a notch.

We grabbed champagne from a passing tray and clinked glasses. I felt the quiver in the haptic gloves, and the glass-on-glass sound echoed in my ears. I said, "To gentlemen." Then I sipped the champagne straw in the headgear while ensuring we maintained eye contact in a proper toast.

Whitney Warren interrupted, holding the whiskey for Audrey that was no longer needed.

"Now, what's all this talk about chastity? Do I need to save you from this man? Who is he, by the way?"

Audrey made the introduction herself. "Whitney Warren, this is Joe, er, Bradley Joseph. Why, he's the namesake of my upcoming movie!"

"Is that so?" Warren said. His eyes narrowed skeptically as we shook hands. My haptic glove made his grip feel wet and limp, like a dead fish. I didn't feel a rash start from the socialite's wet touch, thank goodness.

"No, sir, not all. The lady jests. I am here only by Audrey's grace. You see, I was walking my dog outside the Palace Hotel when she was being photographed, and she saw my dog, Fifi, who became the luckiest canine ever by being in the pictures with her." I wondered if I'd laid it on a little thick, but

Audrey smiled, and her eyes sparkled like the stars outside.

"Yes, of course. The dog owner. The photo is all over the newspapers. It may live forever. Well, welcome to my humble home. And what do you do besides walk your dog in the city, Mr. Joseph?"

At this, Audrey turned to me, also eager to know the answer. I paused, wondering how much I wanted to say: inventor or computer programmer? None of this was accounted for in my scenario planning, but I finally said, "I work in computers, Mr. Warren."

"Computers?" Warren seemed to be searching his mind for what that meant to him back then, and I remembered reading that someone described Warren's mind this way: "He knows his mind even if it is a small one." Then Warren asked, "Were you a codebreaker during the war? I served in the ambulance corps in the Great War myself."

I was amazed at how the *Cocktail HoVR* program placed me in challenging situations I needed to talk my way out of, in front of a famous San Francisco socialite and, more importantly, Audrey. Well, this is only the first take, so I answered, "I'm sorry, I can't speak about the war."

That got Warren's attention, but before he could question me further Audrey seconded my reluctance.

"Amen. Let's not discuss that dreadful time. Whitney, would you excuse us for a moment? I want to show Bradley the view by your beautiful bay window."

"Yes, of course. Enjoy the best view in the city, and Audrey, dear, I will need to gather you shortly to introduce you to some other guests."

She answered, "Of course," as she took my elbow. Her grip felt sure and promising—and she used it to maneuver me around some obstacles before we got to the window. "Isn't it lovely? I'm not sure when I will be able to return to San Francisco, but I'd certainly like to see more of it in the daylight." Then she looked up at me. "I suppose that your work in—computers, is it?—would keep you from showing me your fair city? You see, besides this rare night off, I need to be in makeup by five p.m. every evening for a seven o'clock show. But I'd love to see more of San Francisco in the daylight."

Holy shit. Audrey Hepburn was asking me on a day date, and perhaps recurring day dates! God bless you, Ara Day and Advik Patel! They'd understood the assignment and delivered.

"Do you know of anyone who might be able to show me around? That is, assuming you must work every day while I'm here?" Audrey Hepburn's big brown eyes looked at me expectantly.

"I would be honored to show you around the city, Audrey."

"It's a date then. Oh, and Fifi too?"

"I will talk to her. She may be able to join us for … stretches."

Audrey laughed at my dimwitted wordplay. There was nothing else to accomplish on this first date. The dance would have to wait for another time. Still, I carried it through, exchanging cheek kisses before I departed and made plans to meet her at the Palace Hotel lobby at noon the next day.

On the way out of the Whitney Warren/Poppy Kendall house, I saw and rubbed the clear ball on the railing that I'd seen a few days ago.

Or seventy years in the future.

Chapter 17

OUTSIDE TECHNOLOGY

I was tempted to debrief Nicole but instead researched web-based silicon kissing devices. Companies were making startling advances in the virtual sex industry, and I quickly found a Bay Area company that sold an Audrey *doppelgänger*, head only. It was advertised as a "kiss mate," complete with reverse pressures, life-like facial movements, and temperature sensors. It had a tongue option: *moist and active*. Similar devices had more uses, but I scrolled quickly past those. The kissing head had been a pandemic invention designed to connect with another person through a cell phone app so that two people could kiss virtually. I devised a way to connect it to *Cocktail HoVR* so that the head became part of the hologram.

I hoped this might lead to getting past my haphephobia for good.

I happened to know the owner of the company, Charlotte Jackson, through Stanford. She volunteered to bring it to my house that afternoon. Before I could say no, she said, "See you in an hour."

It was less than that when she buzzed my security system. At the door, I said, "Thanks, Charlotte. I really appreciate you bringing this over. I'm running some tests on a new program and want to see how it works."

Charlotte smiled and took my hand. "Let's hook it up and see. This could be the start of a great partnership between our companies." I instantly regretted not just having it delivered. I began sweating and flushed red. Crap, a setback from conquering haphephobia.

"Uh, I think I'll work alone on this one. Thanks though."

"Come on, Bradley. I'm really curious to see how it works."

"Charlotte, that isn't going to happen."

"Are you forgetting who took you to your first keg party when you were just a fifteen-year-old Stanford kid?"

I smiled. "I have no memory of that. Literally. That part of my brain was damaged."

"Yeah, we should have gone a little easier on you. Come on, let me see how this works. Knowing you, it will pair with some awesome program and make a hundred million dollars. So, who are you going to kiss? Kim Kardashian?"

I shook my head, *no*. Obviously, she didn't realize how much her device resembled Audrey Hepburn. That could start a whole new industry having celebrities to kiss … and more.

"I have another question for you. Say I want to have a full body made …" I looked down, my skin was lobster colored and my underarms provided the melted butter.

Charlotte's smile grew wider than the Golden Gate Bridge. She said, "You *dog*, you!"

"Charlotte …"

"Yeah, yeah. Other companies do that, but I know them. So, what are we talking about? A head, torso, or complete head to toe? What kind of dimensions?"

I knew I would pair it with my programs to see only Audrey Hepburn through goggles, but the shape should be close. I recalled Audrey's dimensions. "Five-seven and around one hundred pounds."

"But with big boobs, right?"

"No."

"C cup?"

I shook my head.

"B, then?"

I shook my head again.

"Seriously, an A cup?"

I nodded. "I want the most real device out there. If there is a full-body one that has some range of motion, that might be best. In a few weeks, I may be testing it."

"Okay, how about any details of the face like hair color, eye color?"

"Brown and brown."

"And down below?"

I certainly hadn't thought of that. Charlotte asked, "Brazilian?" I again shook my head, *no.*

Charlotte said, "Okay, I'll also bring you a weed whacker." A moment later, she added, "You know, other companies could make you a walking, talking robot, a clone …"

"No!" That sounded too harsh, so I backpedaled to a softer protest. "I mean, no, thanks." I didn't want to sully Audrey with being a robot at my beck and call. I wanted to get to know the real Audrey Hepburn: her mind, how she really was. Having a fully functioning robot seemed ten steps too far.

I just hoped I'd continue to feel that way as things developed.

Chapter 18

DAY DATE

I again tried to add Nicole in *Cardinal* so she could watch the next date unfold but had had trouble connecting her. *System error. Interface not recognized.* Then a bunch of static. Maybe *Cocktail HoVR* was drawing too much power for Nicole to join the programs. I finally gave up and prepared to record it, then donned the suit and headgear, and powered up the scene. It worked without further glitches.

Immediately, Fifi and I saw Audrey exit the Palace Hotel at 12:02. "I'm sorry I'm late," she said, glancing at her Cartier watch. Artificial intelligence must have found a photo from then that showed her wearing one. In addition, she wore black slacks, a gray sweater—it was barely fifty degrees in early May with a bit of a breeze and patchy fog—with a red wool coat wrapped around her arm.

Audrey leaned down to Fifi and gave her playful pats, saying how glad she was that Fifi chose to stretch her legs with us. Then she came up and kissed me on the cheeks. I felt it—soft and moist, more than a peck but not impassioned. I didn't panic, but rather felt *chosen.* "Thank you so much, Bradley, for consenting to show me around. May I ask what you have planned?"

I looked around 1953 San Francisco: the old cars, dressed-up people, store names I didn't recognize, a totally different vibe than what it was today. My sweater, jacket, and scarf fit the scene.

"I thought we'd walk with Fifi for a bit before I show you some can't-miss things in San Francisco. No trip is complete without a ride on a cable car, and we can hop on one only a few blocks away. Let's take it to Chinatown and then to Fisherman's Wharf. Oh, do you like chocolate?"

I remembered George Bannister had shared her love of it.

"Yes! It was one of the things I missed the most during the war. I made up for it during the cruise to New York for the start of *Gigi*." Then she whispered, as if it was a secret. "I gained *ten pounds* and had to lose it before the play started. It was worth it."

"Well, Ghirardelli chocolate is considered some of the best in the world and it's right off of Fisherman's Wharf."

"That sounds like a lovely day! What do you think, Fifi, shall we get started?" Audrey clutched my elbow and asked if that was okay.

I smiled. *"Oui, c'est bien."*

"Merci beaucoup! And I must say that I love your scarf! It looks so nice and comfortable. May you have many fond memories in it."

We rounded the block and turned into a westerly breeze. I helped her into the red coat to counter the wind and she slid tighter into my grasp. I was elated, and felt giddy enough to ask her a question.

"Audrey what are your goals? I hope you don't mind me asking?"

"You mean for my career or my personal life?"

"Let's start with your career."

"I don't know whether I will be successful at this acting thing for very long, actually. Plays or movies. I'm not a trained actress, and I wasn't much of a model. I really wanted to be a ballerina when I was discovered, whatever that means. Since then, it's been a whirlwind, and I constantly ask myself, why me? I've been lucky. Opportunities like this don't come along for most people. So, when they do, you must grab them."

I tiptoed the delicate balance between knowing who she was and who she would become, and found a reply. "Audrey, I have a feeling you will be one of the biggest sensations Hollywood has ever known."

She stopped, turned to me, and said, "That's very nice of you to say, Bradley, but who knows? The most important thing is to enjoy your life and be happy. That's all that matters. I believe every day, you should have at least one exquisite moment, and I'm having that with you. And Fifi."

She reached down to pet the poodle, and when she came back up, I decided to kiss her on the cheeks, as she had done to me moments ago. Only

I started on the wrong cheek, and because she had begun doing the same thing, it turned into an inadvertent kiss on the lips. I felt the kiss through my new technical acquisition.

"I'm sorry," she said, with a sly smile. "It seems we had the same idea."

I smiled and, without real or virtual nervousness. "That's the best coincidence I've ever experienced." When I saw her smile, I leaned in boldly for a real kiss, and she returned it with pliant lips that turned into another smile after three exquisite seconds.

A matronly woman with distinct black glasses came around the corner and scurried up to us. "There you are! Audrey, we have things to do! You can't go wandering off and kissing strangers, young lady. We have to shop for your wardrobe for *Sabrina*, remember? I have appointments at four different stores this afternoon."

"Oh, Edith, I simply can't today. You see, Bradley here, my old friend Bradley is … he's in town only today, and we just had to catch up on … our lives."

"Audrey, this is not the time or place to meet with supposed old friends. We have appointments! I. Magnin, for one. The best department store in town. We mustn't keep them waiting!"

Audrey looked to me to continue the ruse. "Ma'am, I promised Audrey a ride on a cable car today. Tell us which store to go to, and we will take it there directly."

Head was unconvinced. "But the first appointment is in fifteen minutes at Fetterman's," she said with an index finger tapping the face of her wristwatch.

"Fetterman's, yes, it's along the route. We will meet you there." I then remembered Fifi. "A favor, Ms. Head—if you could walk my dog there, I will get her from you once we arrive." I hurriedly gave her the leash as the cable car clanged, preparing to depart. Audrey and I jumped aboard, and I said, "Fifteen minutes. See you at Fetterman's!"

Edith Head, world famous costume designer, winner of Academy Awards for her impeccable selection of clothing, stood there in shock, holding Fifi's leash. Audrey and I didn't look back. We held on as the cable car lurched forward. The feel through the haptic suit was so realistic.

Audrey smiled and, when we were out of Head's earshot, said, "That was very well done! This movie I've just completed, *Roman Holiday*, also has an escape from authorities. Part of the story is that the man—Joe Bradley, remember? I can't get over that—shows my character around Rome in a similar way to what we're doing here in San Francisco!"

My mind went to the Vespa scene where Princess Ann zips Joe around Rome, nearly running into things and causing traffic chaos. "That's funny! I look forward to seeing the movie when it comes out. Where will you be then?"

"Oh, they are flying me to London for the premiere in late June. I think it doesn't open in the States until August. In September, I start filming another movie called *Sabrina*. I am so fortunate: Cary Grant and William Holden are starring in it with me. How lucky can a girl get?"

I withheld what I knew about Cary Grant dropping out at the last minute and said, "That's amazing. Cary Grant is a role model for me. For all men, really."

"Yes, I adore him as well. And Bill Holden. I haven't met them yet, of course, but I love their movies."

"That is such an amazing opportunity for you."

"Thank you—I really mean it, *thank you*. It's so nice to have a friend I can talk to. Having Edith Head to help me shop for clothes for the movie is quite an honor, but I need real friends as well."

"Audrey, that's quite an investment by the studio in you. See, they also know that you will be a huge star!"

She side-hugged me. "Well, enough about all that. There isn't even a finished script yet for *Sabrina*. So, let's just focus on now." Then she looked at me with adventure in her eyes. "And us."

"Yes, let's. Oh, here's our stop: Chinatown." I knew there would be hell to pay with Edith Head, but wasn't sure how many more of these scenes the designer—or Fifi—would be in. Probably none, so I put them out of my mind.

Sorry, pup.

We stepped off the cable car and into another world. Mandarin was spoken far more than English, and although more people milled about here than in other parts of the city, my enochlophobia didn't take hold. I was at ease in this virtual setting.

Audrey smiled at the sing-song rhythm of a language we couldn't understand. She said, "There was a Chinatown in New York, but despite living there for six months, I never visited. This is amazing!"

"So, you've never tried Chinese food?"

"No, never, but I'm willing to try. I'm quite hungry, by the way."

"Great, let's duck into that restaurant over there."

Audrey looked across the street and saw a literal defeathered and ready-to-cook duck hanging in the window. "You weren't kidding when you said *duck*. Are they safe to eat?"

"I've found that the French prepare duck the way I prefer it. Choosing your meal when it's suspended in the window, baking in the sun, may not be our best choice."

"Could we perhaps choose a restaurant that doesn't have that sort of … artwork hanging about?"

"Yes, of course. All of these restaurants are quite good. How about this one?" I had no idea about 1953 Chinatown, but I guessed it hadn't changed all that much.

After perusing the menu for a few moments, we headed in, drawing looks. Well, Audrey drew looks. "Bradley, I'm afraid that this is all new, so I must ask you to order for me. Is that all right?"

"Yes, of course. Do you have any dietary restrictions? MSG reaction?"

She looked at me blankly. "I don't think so."

I made a mental note to try not to bring up things that weren't on the radar in 1953. The waiter appeared and I ordered two fried egg rolls, egg foo young, and shrimp chow mein for us.

"That sounds lovely," she said. "Thank you."

I decided to skip ahead with the remote, fast forwarding us to the original Ghirardelli chocolate factory. I set up a behind-the-scenes tour with four other people. After a few minutes, I looked at Audrey and said, "This isn't as fabulous as I thought it would be, seeing how chocolate is made."

"I tend to agree, but at least there isn't a dead duck staring at us." We began laughing, gently at first, but then we couldn't stop. Audrey bent over snickering and then snorted, sending us nearly into convulsions. The tour guide looked back, and he reminded me of the disparaging head chef in the Paris cooking school in *Sabrina*. I nearly said so but remembered Audrey hadn't filmed that yet. The guide, Luigi, pleaded, "Decorum, please!"

We apologized and managed to hold it together as we got to the chocolate tasting. Glorious ready-to-eat morsels were decorated in a way that befit Audrey Hepburn. After the chocolates were introduced individually and described for their content and tastes, we finally got to eat them.

Advik had gone above and beyond in designing this element. The smell and taste through the VR helmet and straw seemed real. We tasted chocolates with different cocoa levels—Audrey preferred sweet, while I liked bitter. She also loved the white chocolate but raved most about the bites with nuts inside.

"I've never had that before. That's divine!" She tried chocolate with almonds, walnuts, and peanuts. Then when hazelnut was introduced, I said, "I predict this will be your favorite."

"Oh, do you think you know what I like already? Well, we'll see."

Then I saw her taste it, rolling the chocolate around in her mouth, showing just a glimpse of tongue, and swallowing it. She then declared me correct.

"That's the best thing I've ever eaten in my life!"

"I thought you might like it. We'll buy you some."

She held me tightly as we wound our way out of the store and into the bay breeze. A clock outside Ghirardelli displayed four o'clock. "Oh, Bradley, I must be getting back! I have to be in makeup in an hour. And we've completely forgotten about Edith. She will be furious with me!"

"I'm so sorry, I lost track of time. Please blame me for keeping you out. Do you want to stop at the hotel first or go straight to the theater? A taxi should get you to either in less than twenty minutes."

"They send a car for me at the hotel. Let's go there."

I whistled for a taxi, and she shrieked with glee. "You sound like an old hand at that!"

In truth, I had never whistled for a taxi in my life and knew it came from the suit somehow. I only knew how to order an Uber from my phone app.

I was mesmerized by my situation. I was holding hands with Audrey in an old taxi, watching classic San Francisco roll by outside. I had a passing thought that all the people outside my window were now dead. Then I remembered who was next to me and that I was breathing oxygen into someone who herself had passed more than thirty years ago. It was hard to imagine this ethereal creature gone, and the thought set me back. I squeezed her hand tighter.

Audrey offered to pay for the taxi when we pulled up to the Palace, but I waved her off. We got out, and she said, "But Bradley, you haven't let me pay for anything all day!"

I smiled. "The day will come when men allow women to pay their share, but today it seems … ungallant."

That word really impacted Audrey. "You wouldn't know this, but *gallant* is my favorite word in any language. I've known people who were gallant and many who were not. Thanks for being in the gallant category, Bradley. I have so enjoyed my day with you. Shall we do it again?"

"I'd be honored, Audrey."

"Wonderful. Oh, tomorrow I can't, with Edith Head breathing down my neck, and I may have to share some days with her, but the day after tomorrow, let's meet early. Is that all right?"

"Yes. I am available whenever you are free while you're here in San Francisco."

"Lovely," she said. She looked around and suddenly pulled me behind a potted plant to hide. She then reached up to pull my head down to hers and kissed me ardently. I returned it and felt the point of her tongue seek mine. We opened our mouths and our tongues danced for a few moments. I tasted a hint of chocolate and hazelnut before Audrey pulled away. She smiled and said, "I see you know how the French do it."

"*Vive le France,*" I replied, leaning in for one more passionate kiss, slightly longer this time. A few more dates like this might completely cure my fear of touch.

Audrey broke away again. "I'm sorry, I *must* go. Oh, here is a ticket for tonight's show." She pulled the ticket from her purse and placed it in my inside jacket pocket, patting my chest. "Will you come?"

"Yes. You couldn't keep me away."

"Until tonight, then. *Merci,* Bradley Joseph."

"*Merci,* Audrey Hepburn."

Chapter 19

BEACH DAY

I went right into my next date with Audrey after inputting a few parameters and codes that built upon our time together so far. Trying Nicole again for a debrief would have to wait.

Seconds later, I pulled up to the Palace in a just-off-the-line 1953 Corvette convertible. I mean, why wouldn't I?

Audrey jumped in quickly. "Wow, this car is beautiful! Let's go. They're looking for me again." She ducked down as the hotel doors opened, her head in my lap as I tried to shift gears. She popped back up as we rounded a corner, headed due west to the coast.

The chill and fog of the morning air flooded my haptic suit as we headed to Ocean Beach. Seagulls sang as we neared the coast, but I focused on the touch of Audrey's hand in mine. It felt natural and good. I let the drive play out in real time to enjoy every second. I asked her many questions until she protested.

"Bradley, enough about me. Tell me about this fascinating world of computers! What is it all about?"

I didn't want to make up a story about what I might have been doing in the industry in 1953, even though I could talk about it from a historical perspective. Instead, I said, "Audrey, computers are going to change our world. Someday, computers will launch airplanes, replace maps, create in-home entertainment, and give everyone access to a world of knowledge. They may even be able to recreate … things from the past. But that sort of stuff is seventy-five years in the future. First, we need to establish the basics of what we call computer mainframes and programming language."

As we rolled to a halt at a stoplight, Audrey said, "It sounds fascinating. Doing something that will last for seventy-five years. I'm afraid my contribution to society will be long forgotten by then."

Again, I reflected on the fact that I was calling on her from the future. "I'm sorry, but Audrey, you have to know this. From what I've learned about you, I think you and your movies will live in eternity. Take your work very seriously. Your charm and beauty are uncommon in this world, and you will have a following forever."

She leaned over to kiss my cheek, but I purposefully turned my mouth toward her for a soft kiss on the lips. "Believe me."

"Thank you, Bradley. I don't doubt your sincerity and belief in me." She smiled. "It's just that it's all so new to me. I don't know why I was chosen to take this journey. As an actress, I mean."

The light turned green on Geary Boulevard. "When you see yourself in *Roman Holiday*, you will see what I suspect we will all see—a fresh look, a beautiful smile, charm, and elegance."

"You sound like you've seen it already!" she retorted.

This caught me off guard and I had to be careful. "I feel like I have. I can't wait to see it in the theaters."

"Unfortunately, I'll be in London for the premiere. If it was in Los Angeles, you could be my date!" Her smile would stay with me forever. "But you probably have computer things to perfect."

I looked at her with incredulous eyes. "Nothing could stop me from ever being by your side when you ask me." I took my eyes off the road to soak in her appreciative gaze. "Forever."

She replied with words I would never forget.

"That's all a girl wants to hear."

We soon saw the beach and headed south on Point Lobos Avenue.

Audrey exclaimed, "There it is! The Pacific Ocean! This is only my second time seeing it."

"I didn't know that."

"Yes. When I was in Los Angeles with *Gigi* before this stop, and now."

We parked at Ocean Beach, and I took a thermos and picnic basket from the trunk.

"A picnic!" she exclaimed. "What a nice surprise!" She clutched my arm in both hands as we navigated our way down the golden beach, where I laid out a large red blanket. There was a chill in the air, and I wished it had been August instead of May so I could see Audrey on the beach in a bathing suit. In time, I hoped I would.

I looked down at the actual food and beverages, knowing that Audrey would "see" the same, and poured us coffee. I offered her the thermos cup first, delighting in the knowledge that we would share sips from it. I then laid out the chancy food I'd chosen: a spicy tuna roll with salmon nigiri. Sushi didn't exist in many places then, but I'd confirmed the legacy before deciding.

"That looks delightful. But what is it?"

"It's fish on compacted rice. It's a delicacy in Japan."

"The fish, is it raw?"

I suddenly regretted my choice but she vowed to try it, even after I confirmed the salmon and tuna, were, in fact, uncooked. She loved it. I showed her how to use chopsticks and dip the sushi into the small bowl of soy sauce and wasabi. She wasn't a fan of the spicy wasabi.

"Well, you seem determined to introduce me to new things, Bradley." Her big eyes danced. "Thank you." She finished the sushi while I watched her decide which fish she liked better. "Tuna, but just by a smidge."

Audrey cuddled into my arms against the cool, stiff breeze. She gazed toward the ocean and said, "It's so beautiful, Bradley. Thank you for bringing me here."

Then she leaned toward my face and kissed me passionately. The kissing device astonished me with the faint tastes of raw fish, soy, and coffee. When we broke the kiss she looked deeply into my eyes.

"Bradley, I'm not supposed to be here with you now, and I don't know what will happen with our lives but know that this time with you the past few days has been wonderful. You're the first person I've really liked spending time with since breaking my engagement. As much as a girl always wants to find love, I can't jump right back into a relationship with all that entails—but know this—I am tempted. Sorely tempted."

That was enough for me to decide I was going to spend every possible moment in Audrey Hepburn's world.

Chapter 20

THINK PINK

It was really nice," I said to Nicole, finally debriefing her. I barely remembered chirping her in *Cardinal*, but she answered on the first try. Whatever connection issues happened earlier had been resolved.

"Thank you for recording it! You sorely tempted Audrey Hepburn. Not many men—in any world—can say that."

"So, then, what do you think I should set up next?"

"Well, you wooed Audrey in San Francisco, where she spent little time compared to New York, or Los Angeles, Paris, or Switzerland. That's where she spent most of her private life. Rome too. Any of those would be fun for the next meeting."

I was deep in thought. "Maybe. You said she did other movies that were like *Roman Holiday* and *Sabrina*. What are some of the others? Better yet, what was her favorite movie that she did?"

Nicole smiled. "I have the perfect one. Do you like musicals?"

"A week or so ago, I would have said no."

"And now?"

"Cue it up."

"May I present *Funny Face*, from 1957. We start in New York but then go to Paris. Not a bad way to spend two hours. And many have said that this was Audrey at her best—dancing with Fred Astaire and singing in her own voice."

A brusque magazine editor. A song-and-dance number called "Think Pink." A vaporous supermodel. I started to ask if we could watch a different movie instead. From Tokyo, Nicole pointed toward the screen as the movie shifted to a bookstore scene where Audrey portrays a librarian-type named Jo—but with the most fantastic bangs and a maturing presence that outpaced *Roman Holiday* and *Sabrina* in making one just want to stop what they were doing and gawk at her.

"My God."

"This might be my favorite look of hers. Even the drab colors they put Audrey in couldn't hold her back. She loved filming this movie."

Gruff ladies from *Quality* magazine took over the bookstore, and the male photographer used Jo to help, despite her misgivings. He was the only one nice to her, but Jo was thrown out of her own store when she objected to the ladies rearranging the books for the photo shoot.

Despite that, I said, "I kind of like the actor playing the photographer."

"He was a dear. That's Fred Astaire, the best dancer in all of Hollywood. You'll see that later."

I was taken with the dialogue at the end of the bookstore scene. Jo explains the difference between sympathy and empathy to Astaire—named Dick Avery in the movie—and he pulls a sliding ladder over and kisses her on the lips.

Why did you do that!?

Empathy. I put myself in your place, and I felt that you wanted to be kissed. Jo, shocked, tells Avery he was mistaken, and he throws himself out.

"Isn't that an intriguing scene?" Nicole asked.

"Yes, but I can't help but wonder—does this end like *Roman Holiday?* I mean, in this case, I'd want it to. He's got to be thirty years older than Audrey …"

"The age difference is common for the era."

"It should have started the #MeToo movement."

"You're jumping ahead a bit. Check out this next scene."

One of the photos of the model has shopkeeper Jo in it, and photographer Dick Avery persuades *Quality* editor Maggie Prescott that Jo is the face they've been looking for and describes her in three terms.

I paused the movie.

"I think that defines Audrey Hepburn's appeal as much as anything I've ever heard: character, spirit, and intelligence."

Nicole's smile reminded me of Audrey herself.

The rest of the movie played out predictably, with Maggie, Dick, and Jo flitting about Paris, and as I guessed, Dick and Jo end up together. But I was so taken with Audrey's character, spirit, and intelligence in the film that my admiration grew deeper.

"Okay, I respect *Roman Holiday* more now, not having a happily ever after, since every other movie's conclusion was predictable about five minutes in. But damn, Audrey was wonderful in this movie."

"What else did you like?" Nicole asked, sitting up straight.

"Well, she was beautiful, of course—but those *gowns*."

"Which one did you like best? They're all by Givenchy. He continued to be her personal designer after *Sabrina* and for the rest of her life."

"I have to go with the red one."

"I agree, it's my favorite in any of the movies. What else did you love about Audrey in this movie?"

I thought for a while. "Well, this is a little dumb, but the wedding dress scenes were pretty stunning too. It was nice to hear her sing, and the dancing was really fun, especially the solo dance in the Paris café."

"That's funny to hear you say solo dance. Did you not notice the two French male dancers on either side of her?"

"No, not for a second. Did she freestyle that dance or was it choreographed?"

"Well, as you know, Audrey was a trained dancer in ballet, but Fred Astaire coached her for all of her dancing scenes."

"She held her own."

"Thank you," Nicole said.

"Thank *you*?"

Nicole laughed. "I mean, you noticed. Many do not. I think we'll wait a spell before I throw another musical—*My Fair Lady*—at you. It is one of Audrey's most revered movies."

"Good call. I really liked *Funny Face*, though."

"So, what do you want to do with it? Fast forward your relationship a bit and create a scene where you talk to Audrey about it? She was married to Mel Ferrer by then, and he was close by, filming his own movie in Paris, so they spent a lot of time together, trying to make babies."

"Ugh. I'm not sure I want to know that."

Nicole laughed. "Back then, there was only one way to make babies."

I waved her off. "I get it, I get it." Then I had an idea. "Actually, I want to spend time with her as Jo Stockton, the bookstore maven. In Greenwich Village, before she's discovered by the magazine people."

"Wait, you want to insert yourself in the movie?"

"No. Well, not really. I want to create a scene with me and her movie character. I won't code Jo with knowledge of my previous visits with Audrey."

"I see. But you want the bookstore Jo and not the girl who goes to Paris to listen to the philosophers in the smoky cafés? She may be a bit more worldly there. At least she'd been kissed once and had some aspirations for a relationship with someone."

"No. I think I just want to take Bookstore Jo out for coffee and talk about … what was it?"

"Emphaticalism—the most sensible approach to true understanding and peace of mind. But you know, that's a made-up movement for the movie."

"That's fine. I want to have coffee with Jo Stockton in Greenwich Village in 1957."

"Well, in that case, I'm sure Jo will be pleased to meet you."

Chapter 21

EMBRYO CONCEPTS

I caught up on work for a day, answering delinquent messages and calls. Nicole told me she couldn't join the adventure with Jo Stockton, but looked forward to watching the recording.

I used the same technology, uploading everything on the internet about Jo Stockton and Audrey's experience playing her. Finally, I pressed Play and my home studio opened a door to 1957 Greenwich Village. I said aloud, "What an interesting name for a bookstore—Embryo Concepts. I wonder what that's all about?"

A girl on a sliding ladder was stocking books ten feet up and looked down at me. "It hints at new movements and proponents in philosophy. Mainly French, like Emile Flostre, who has taught many of us the embryonic concept of emphaticalism."

I was fascinated with the vision on the ladder and her intellectual capacity to evangelize it. "Thank you, Miss...?"

"Miss Jo Stockton." My heart skipped as she peered down at me. "And you are?"

"Bradley. Bradley Joseph."

"Welcome, Mr. Joseph. What can I assist you with today?"

I hadn't prepared for even the most basic answer, so I relied on my default.

"Oh, I don't know. Maybe something about computer programming that has … time and space implications?"

"Space flight? That's exciting! I've been reading about that. Why, here's a book about it right here." She came down from the ladder. I watched her, speechless to correct her insinuation that I worked in the early days of space travel.

She showed me a copy of *The Exploration of Mars* by Willy Ley and Wernher von Braun. "Do you know this one?"

I was struck anew by Audrey's beauty in this era. She wore the same drab clothes she'd worn at the beginning of *Funny Face*—a black long-sleeved knit shirt and a earth-toned suit with oversized buttons. Her hair was full and the ends curled toward her cheeks with those out-of-style-but-need-to-come-back bangs. I had trouble forming words but forced out, "I'm sorry. I just ... lost my train of thought."

Jo, unlike Audrey, likely wasn't used to men saying that about her. She maintained her businesslike demeanor. "This book is about someday exploring Mars. Do you know it?"

"I—I certainly know of it and Dr. von Braun. My work is more of the computer side of things that could get us there someday, after the moon first, of course." I was uncomfortable fibbing and wondered if I should restart the scene.

Jo appeared to measure my intellect and then my appearance.

"That sounds very technical. Have you also studied philosophy?"

That was a hard *no*, and I was pretty sure I didn't want to step further into a lie.

"I haven't, but it's always interested me."

"Well, perhaps I could interest you in a book about that, since you know this one about Mars?"

"Yes, that would be ... lovely."

She looked at me, and I felt her assessing whether I was just leading her on.

"Over here then, Mr. Joseph."

"Please, call me Bradley. May I call you Jo?"

She smiled for the first time, but it was a small one.

"Yes, I suppose that's all right."

She showed me the classics and a new book by the Flostre fellow. "My dream is to go to Paris and hear him speak on emphaticalism."

"You'll get there someday. I feel certain you will."

Her smile, wider now, lit the bookstore. She peeked at the clock.

"I'm about to take my lunch break. Perhaps you have time to join me so we can talk more. I hope that's not too forward?"

I smiled back at her. "I'd like that, Jo."

Coffee shops of the quasi-beatnik variety were apparently havens for young people in San Francisco and New York City's Greenwich Village then, much like today. We found one just around the corner from Embryo Concepts called the Village Idiot. I coughed upon opening the door, the air heavy with cigarette smoke. Outside the scene, I marveled at the AI and extended reality presentation. I just hoped that virtual secondhand smoke wouldn't cause any health effects or soil my clothes.

We smiled at each other and sat on a worn couch. A woman about our age was tuning a guitar and transitioned into a song I didn't recognize. She could have been Janis Joplin's older cousin from her dress and mannerisms.

"You might find it strange, but I'm comfortable in cafés like this," Jo said. "It's not the same as the Paris cafés you think I'll someday visit, but it's a start."

"Have you ever taken the microphone here and talked about the virtues of emphaticalism?"

She laughed genuinely. "No. At least, not yet."

Two coffees were brought to the table in front of our couch, and before I could ask to upgrade mine to an espresso, I remembered where—and when—I was. There was no sign of cream or sugar. Jo sipped hers and said, "Hot, very hot. Let yours cool a moment."

"Thank you. So, Jo, you really want to go to Paris to see this Flostre speak?" I knew of her desire from the movie and how she would get there, not to mention that later Flostre would try to force himself on her, but that was far beyond the scope of this coffee date.

"Yes, that's my dream. But it's unlikely. I am just someone who works in a bookstore. How can I ever get to Paris?"

Remembering that I was speaking to Jo Stockton and not Audrey Hepburn, I mused, "You will someday meet someone who will help you realize your dream. All of your dreams. I'm sure of it."

The corners of her wide mouth turned downward. "That's kind of you to say, but I'm not reliant on a rich man coming in and making promises like that. Are you a rich man, Bradley? A rich man making promises?" I stumbled for an answer, but she apologized. "I'm sorry. That's rude of me. After all, we've only just met."

I sipped the coffee. It was thick and bitter. Coffee had improved over the last seventy years. "It's okay. May I ask, what are your goals until you get to Paris?"

She thought for just a moment. "I'm afraid I can't really think of any. I like to meet interesting people, but I'm normally too shy to do what I did in asking you for coffee. Thank you for saying yes. It would have been quite embarrassing if you had said no."

The musician began a song that mesmerized others in the coffee shop. Jo and I tried to continue our conversation but were shushed.

"Perhaps we should go," Jo offered. She dropped some coins in a can that read *Pay What You Can* and walked me to the door. "They take their music very seriously in here," she added.

Outside, I inhaled the air deeply and smelled garbage. Ah, the smells of a big city. I wished our walk back to the bookstore was longer, but we arrived in moments.

"Jo, can you walk a bit further?"

"I'm sorry, I must get back to work. It's been a pleasure to speak with you, Bradley." She extended her hand for me to shake it. I couldn't stop myself from raising it to kiss. She smiled and said, "You're welcome to stop by the shop any time." After a pause, she added, "I hope you do."

Caught up in the quasi-formality of her speech, I replied, "I shall." She turned to unlock the door and go inside. I touched her shoulder and she sighed. "Jo. I know you'll get to Paris someday. Just be careful of wolves in sheep's clothing when you get there. Not everyone is as they seem."

She turned and looked downward. I feared I'd lost momentum.

"Is anyone as they seem?" she asked. "Are you, Bradley? Am I? It's all so very existential, isn't it? We are all responsible for creating meaning in our lives and are free to determine how to get there." She stopped herself. "Oh, there I go again. That's why men aren't interested in me. Anyway …"

"I am interested in you."

She looked me in the eyes. "And why are you interested in me, Bradley?"

"Can I be candid?"

"Yes, that would be refreshing."

"Well, because you're the most beautiful woman that God ever created. That's what I saw at first. But your …" I reached for the lines from the movie that fit completely. "Your character, your spirit, your intelligence—that's who you are. And that makes you so attractive."

She let my words hang in the air for five full seconds before saying, "And you can tell all of that in the short time we've spent together?"

"Yes. Yes, I can."

"This bit about being beautiful—many women like to hear those things. It is nice to hear someone say that on occasion, I'll admit." After a big sigh, she added, "Bradley, what are we to do?"

"As you said, I will call on you again. Someday, very soon."

"I'll hold you to that. Goodbye, and thank you, Bradley." She then gave a smile that would sustain me until the next meeting, if I revisited this scene. Without a kiss—Fred Astaire's character had spoiled that in the movie—I walked away. As I rounded the corner, I saw a series of taxis approaching and thought I recognized *Funny Face*'s magazine people pointing at Embryo Concepts.

Chapter 22

DEBRIEF

Nicole later said, "That was a bit cheesy, but it seemed to work."

"I think I relied too much on lines from the movie. It was much harder to speak to Audrey's movie character than to her as a person."

"Probably because you were acting more than being yourself. But think about what just happened. You used your AI program to teleport to a 1957 movie and conversed with the main character in two Greenwich Village settings of the time. You saw books from that era, real and imagined. You drank coffee, smelled cigarette smoke, heard music, were shushed by extras in the scene. You charmed Jo to the point of a promising second date. I think you've raised the bar so high and fast that you're ignoring genius of this. Don't you realize the implications here? And you're analyzing your conversation and source for your *banter?*"

She was right. "Yeah. Everything worked pretty well. I didn't like making things up, though." That made me remember the question I had for her. "Hey, I need to ask you, are you open to an enhanced nondisclosure agreement? I mean, I really can't take a chance on any of this being leaked until I'm ready."

Nicole sighed. "Bradley, would you stop worrying about that? Yes, I'll sign whatever you want me to sign, and you'll know what I want out of this when the time comes. It will be crystal clear. Until then, please stop worrying about it."

I said okay, but knew I would never stop wondering what her future request would be.

On cue, Nicole offered, "Here's what I think you should plan next. Let me know what you think—it's more difficult to be yourself with one of her movie characters, and you seemed much more satisfied with Audrey as herself in the *Gigi* days. So maybe we focus next on Audrey as herself but on location for one of her movies. Here's an idea: she filmed *Love in the Afternoon* right after *Funny Face*, staying in Paris, and Mel was also there filming."

"What would that angle be? Me as a homewrecker?"

"Bradley! Not everything is about sex. You're talking about Audrey Hepburn. Aren't you going more for soulmate than lover with Audrey?"

I thought about it. "Excellent question. Yes, maybe I am. But I am also fiercely attracted to her. Physically. That may have to play out at some point."

She smiled. "Have you thought about the mechanics of having an intimate virtual relationship?" She chuckled; an image must have crossed her mind. "I mean, how far will your future immersive environment go?"

I wasn't sure what it was about Nicole that eliminated any sort of filter I normally had for revealing details of my work.

"I'm starting to, uh, work on the synthetic aspect."

Nicole laughed until she snorted like Audrey had in the Ghirardelli chocolate factory. She had to bite her finger to stop.

"That's an image that probably shouldn't be in the newspapers—a haptic suit and VR helmet making love to an apparition! With that thought, I bid you adieu for today."

I thought again that I was developing far too deep of a relationship with Nicole. A *tech reporter*. And as invigorating as all this had been, the damage she could do to me, especially based on our last conversation, could be enormous: *Eccentric Inventor Has Virtual Sex with Dead Actress Using Latex Dolls.*

I winced. It was time to start looking for a way out of this odd relationship with Nicole. But how to do it so she wouldn't burn me with a lewd story? The bottom line was that I didn't need her to educate me about Audrey anymore. I enjoyed her company immensely, but ending the relationship was necessary. The new NDA might help delay things, but I knew I had to find a way to end our quirky relationship without angering her. It couldn't be sudden, so I decided to keep the next meeting with Nicole.

Of course, it would be another movie.

Chapter 23

BACK TO THE OFFICE

I drove to the office to hear more movie proposals for *Real to Reel*. The glass-walled conference room was full and most of the staff were there, so I headed straight for Charlie's office via perimeter hallways to minimize contact. I was feeling better about the phobias but wasn't ready to let my guard all the way down.

Remarkably, more than half of the thirty scripts presented to us were for Audrey Hepburn productions. It affirmed she was nearly as popular today as she'd been a lifetime ago.

Charlie said, "People are going crazy re-imagining Audrey Hepburn as a Marvel character or a superhero. Sure, there are some rom-coms too, but I'm starting to wonder if we should seriously consider it. I mean, putting a classic movie actress in a completely different context isn't what we were thinking at first, but I'm starting to like the possibilities. Imagine putting them in roles they would never have pictured in their lifetimes. It would give them a fresh bump in their film careers."

"No," I said.

When Charlie spoke up again for the idea, I interrupted. "Come on, Charlie. You're the film buff. I've only watched Audrey Hepburn in a few movies, but she would be so out of place that you might as well deep-fake her face over a stunt double. That's not who she is. Or was."

I remembered I had never cast Audrey as Princess Leia in my home studio weeks ago when Charlie first brought it up. I was far too caught up in Audrey's actual films and my virtual engagements with her.

I favored our first official venture being a drama starring Claudette Colbert and Idris Elba, a unique pairing that delighted Ara Day.

Ara walked out with me as the meeting ended. It was a beautiful day, but Ara brought some storm clouds. "Bradley, I wanted to say I'm still concerned about this Nicole Bonnet person. We know very little about her, and despite the NDA …"

I cut Ara off tersely. "I know, I'm weaning off her. She signed a new NDA yesterday, and we talked again about not revealing anything. She said she'll let me know what she wants and when. I guess some exclusive, but only when we're ready."

Ara's silence said plenty. She disapproved. I understood all our work was at risk with Nicole.

"Bradley, I'll watch the movies with you or take turns with Advik, even though we don't really have time. It's just that watching movies with a reporter and possibly revealing our technology, that can't be our best move right now. I mean, why her?"

I exhaled deeply. I knew Ara was being protective of our intellectual property, and she hadn't said anything yet to Charlie. They also didn't know how much Nicole helped drive my inventions. I was falling for Audrey, and Nicole had been vital in that.

Ara asked bluntly, "Have you talked about or even *around* our technology with *her*?"

I exhaled again. "No, of course not. Just some of the stuff I've played with at home. Not what you and Advik are working on. Nicole has seen only what I recorded. I would never reveal the how-to. She's really just a person who has taught me about classic movies, and I occasionally watch them with her, like any virtual book or movie club."

Ara said, "You're not just anyone, Bradley. It pains me to say this, but I think you need to break off these engagements—and now. The risk isn't worth the reward. Look, Advik and I will come over tonight and we'll binge on all of Audrey Hepburn's movies with you. Really, we will. Or Charlie—he must know as much about Audrey as Nicole does."

I said, "I already made the decision to scale back. I promise I will."

Ara nodded curtly. "Okay, Bradley. Just be careful."

Chapter 24

I'VE GROWN ACCUSTOMED TO HER FACE

I decided I would next observe Audrey from a movie set to see what she was like in that environment. I was intrigued by meeting a more mature version of Audrey, married and with a young child. I decided to start fresh and didn't program knowledge of our previous encounters into *Cocktail HoVR*.

I spent more time prepping for the next excursion with Audrey than with any previous one. I chose *My Fair Lady* and enjoyed watching it more than I thought I might; not necessarily because of some catchy musical numbers, although they were fun. I was intrigued by Professor Higgins betting on the social experiment of turning the guttersnipe character Eliza into a proper English lady.

It made me wonder how much of that I was doing with my version of Audrey.

I geared up and was suddenly transported to the set of the movie. I programmed myself as Audrey's singing coach in order to gain access to her trailer that was fenced off with a *Positively Do Not Disturb* sign. During filming in 1963, the hope was that working with a vocal coach would improve Audrey's one-octave range enough so that she wouldn't have to be dubbed by a professional singer.

It would allow me to have alone time with her in this virtual world, which was important because her husband Mel Ferrer, her son, and others were often on the set.

Many people were upset that Audrey was chosen for the high-budget film over Julie Andrews, who had been lauded in the stage role but hadn't crossed over into movies yet. That would soon change, as Andrews made Mary Poppins instead and won the Oscar. Audrey had been criticized for being miscast, which led to professional and personal outbursts. Things were not going well with Mel either. All of this strained Audrey's countenance. She was—and looked—ten years older than when I met her in San Francisco. She was confident as an actress but not necessarily as the woman the world expected. She smoked like a chimney, and the lines on her face told the story of a stressed woman.

I could sing even less than Audrey, but it didn't matter since I was playing a psychologist more than singing coach. Being stern wasn't in my nature, but I decided to start with her smoking, after introductions. I steeled myself against staring at her. This was Audrey Hepburn in her prime.

"You have to cut back. I know everyone smokes, but cutting back will help you achieve another half octave of singing notes."

"Anything to not be dubbed. I mean, I was just flown to New York to sing 'Happy Birthday' to President Kennedy. Anyway, if I am dubbed over, I would think of Eliza as only half of a role."

"That's not true. Others have been dubbed for professional singers—Deborah Kerr, Natalie Wood ..."

"Yes, yes, I know, but I don't want to add my name to that list, so let's get to work, shall we?"

That was an edgier response than I experienced in previous encounters with Audrey. She was still one of the world's most beloved movie stars, and I wondered if I had overstepped my abilities in devising this scene, virtual or not.

Audrey looked at me and softened just a note. "Have we met before? I sense that we have, but I can't place it. Did you help me in *Funny Face* as well?"

I nearly panicked, hoping she was just being kind and wasn't actually beginning to recall our previous meetings. That would mean that some AI controls Ara had set up weren't working. I didn't want to think about any of Ara's AGI work getting an early trial run through Audrey.

My pause was a bit too long, and I blurted out, "No, I would have remembered meeting you, Miss Hepburn."

"Hmm, well, all right then, Bradley. Please call me Audrey."

"Yes, Audrey, thank you. I—uh—always start with an analysis of the character to ensure we are on the same page. This helps me develop your voice, the tone, clarity, and texture of what we will develop together vocally."

"All right."

"Can you tell me what characteristics of Eliza you find most appealing?"

She exhaled, automatically reaching for a cigarette before stopping herself. "Oh, I don't know. Her spunkiness."

"Yes." Then I decided to get right into it before she changed her mind about this technique of mine.

"Are you upset at the way that she is treated by Higgins and Pickering? Being bandied about like a … racehorse?"

"What? What do you mean?"

"I'm just thinking about the scene where Higgins and Pickering congratulate themselves on their successful transformation of Eliza and speak of her as if she isn't there. That she simply played a part in their bet. Indeed, that she was led with a bridle and a whip."

"Wow. Did we read the same script?" She laughed lightly.

"The social experiment of *My Fair Lady* makes one think of another well-known creature formed in a lab. Can you guess which one I mean?"

She looked at me quizzically for a few moments. "Elizastein?" At that, we both chuckled. Then I had an epiphany that what I was doing with Audrey in my virtual world wasn't that far removed from how Pickering steered Eliza in *My Fair Lady*. I decided immediately that I had to give Audrey equal say in our virtual relationship.

I took a bit too long pondering this, until Audrey cleared her throat.

I snapped out of it and said, "Eliza certainly has better manners throughout than Dr. Frankenstein's monster, but here's what I want you to remember—and use during our vocal lessons—Eliza is in charge of her own fate. It builds up from the spunky guttersnipe selling flowers to a fully functioning Edwardian princess at the end. But I don't like the ending."

"I agree. Eliza should go all *Roman Holiday* on Professor Higgins."

I caught my breath at that. "Bravo!"

She paused and studied my face. "Are you certain we've never met before?"

I looked away. "I'm glad that you feel we have. It's good to be comfortable with someone you work closely with." Then I added, "Professionally and personally."

"Amen to that."

That seemed like an opening to ask about the personal side of things. "Are things well at home?"

Audrey immediately did a one-eighty from warm to cold. "That will have no bearing on our vocal lessons, I assure you. Now, where were we? Would you like to hear me sing something as a starting point?" She grabbed the sheet music to *Wouldn't It Be Loverly?*

In truth, I would like nothing better than to hear Audrey Hepburn sing to me, but that would have set up critique and counsel, which I was in no position to offer.

"Yes, we will get to that. How many languages do you speak, Audrey?" She put the sheet music back down.

"In addition to Cockney? I speak the Queen's English, Dutch, French, Italian, and Spanish. Even a little German, although I try not to. It's just that living in Switzerland, you need to know a bit for that part of the country."

"I understand why you don't like to speak German." Our eyes connected, and no words were said about the war, the German invasion, and her hardships. Audrey eased again.

I continued. "Anyway, this social experiment—*social steering* is an even stronger expression for it—your singing voice will change over the course of the movie as it progresses. Just like your speaking voice."

"Well, if some have their way, my singing voice might not be used at all."

"It's my job to not let that happen."

She reached for the sheet music again. I took it from her and strategized how to have a surface conversation about Audrey as an empowered Eliza Doolittle with a deeper conversation about how she could assert the same rights in our virtual world.

"Audrey, when I saw the movie—script, I mean—I wanted to ensure Eliza sang from a growing awareness of freedom, of respect, and maybe even love. Those are different tones and voice inflections, but the character of Eliza and what women around the world will want to gain from your portrayal of her is growing comfortable in a new world, growing more assertive in each scene, each meeting."

Audrey visibly softened. "You're sounding like a director more than a vocal coach, Bradley. Do you hope to become a director someday? Because that was quite good, and something I hadn't really focused on yet in Eliza's character development."

I realized I had been a director in this virtual domain but didn't want to confuse things. "Sorry, I may have gotten carried away."

"No, I'd like to hear more. Please continue, Bradley."

"Well, similar to your other movies, you are paired with someone twenty years your senior. Even in the George Bernard Shaw source play *Pygmalion*, Eliza is thought to be quite a bit younger than Professor Higgins." I wondered where I was going with this, and then a thought came to me. "By the way, you must be ready to be paired with someone closer to your age in your movies."

"Well, I was in *The Children's Hour* with James Garner and *Breakfast at Tiffany's* with George Peppard. I am actually younger than Anthony Perkins from *Green Mansions*. But yes, you're right; people tend to focus on the older costars. But tell me again what that has to do with helping me expand my vocal range? This has been a lovely conversation, Bradley, but I have much preparation to do for this role, plus my family is with me here in Los Angeles. My son is only three, so I must watch my time. And this film is one we must all remember."

"I'm sorry, it just helps me to prepare for coaching you. Can I ask you one more question before we move to vocals?"

She looked at me agreeably. I looked past the thirty-four-year-old Audrey to see the girl ten years younger I'd met in San Francisco.

"Are you happy?"

She paused before saying yes, but it was far different from the yes Princess Ann gave Joe Bradley in *Roman Holiday*, when at Via Margutta 51, she said *yes* in a completely wanton way. This one sounded rushed and tired.

"I'll take you at your word for it, but Audrey, I can't bring out the best in you, in your singing voice, unless I know where you are emotionally." I wasn't convincing myself, much less her, so I added, "It's important in your development. And I'm on your side, regardless of the answer."

She reached for her cigarettes before again stopping herself.

"I should be happier, I suppose. I have a loving husband and a baby I've longed for. I have a wonderfully fortunate career. Playing Eliza is a role that stretches me beyond what I've been blessed with, skill-wise. This movie will leave me exhausted and close to a breakdown, I know it. What kind of a wife and mother would that make me?" Tears welled in her eyes. "I've been a bit of a bitch lately. Can you help me?"

I wanted to grab her, hold her, kiss her but was determined to let her have the freedom of choice I was championing. She sat still, and tears rolled down her face. I waited. Finally, I said, "I will attempt to make you the best version of Audrey Hepburn you can be."

She mouthed, "Thank you," and her eyes also said it, but she stayed seated. Until she rushed out the door.

Well, Audrey, you're really coming into your own.

Audrey struggled through the laborious filming and was repeatedly led to believe her own singing would be considered or blended, depending on the outcome. She became more fragile and demanding, to the point where director George Cukor closed the set to the bare minimum and rigged black walls with occasional holes for the crew that needed to observe. Her husband, Mel, was on set the day I chose to visit, on a break from filming *Sex and the Single Girl* a few stages over.

I was one of those sets of peeping eyes, after I uploaded and merged some behind-the-scenes footage from *My Fair Lady*. The slim chance that narrow AI was allowing Audrey to remember me made me cautious. So, I became a spy.

Audrey and costar Jeremy Brett as Freddy were filming the Covent Garden scene, singing a playback of *Wouldn't It Be Loverly?* when everyone heard a shriek offstage. Cukor called for quiet, but the screams continued.

"No! That can't be!" It was obvious that someone had just seen or been told something tragic. Cukor called *cut* and rushed to see what the issue was. He didn't come back. A moment later, Audrey was asked to go to her dressing room with Mel and wait for the director. I followed from a safe distance and saw Cukor go into the dressing room a few minutes later.

I walked up to the back side of the trailer where I wouldn't be seen eavesdropping and listened.

"Audrey, I was told that President Kennedy has been shot and has died," Cukor said. "I'm sorry to be the one to tell you."

Audrey screeched *No!* just as the person on set had. It sounded like she had thrown herself on her bed and was beating it furiously. Mel and Cukor tried to comfort her, but she was inconsolable. Hearing her cry this way shook me to the core.

"I sang to him a few months ago! He can't die! He just can't!" I heard breaking glass as she threw things around the trailer. There was nothing the men could do to comfort her.

I had to see what was happening and crept to the other side of her trailer where the curtains on a window were partially open. Mel had no idea how to calm her, even after the shared trauma of his wife's many miscarriages. He threw up his hands in frustration, looked at Cukor, shrugged, and left the trailer.

Cukor gave it another moment, then decided she needed time, and he too walked toward the door. I pondered whether I should go in after the director left. Someone needed to soothe her, and if it wasn't the people in her time, then it could be me virtually. But how? I couldn't be the voice coach who had disappeared after one meeting.

Audrey ordered, "You have to tell them, George. We must tell the crew. We must say something."

I saw how crushed Cukor was too. "Audrey, I can't. I don't have it in me. I'm sorry."

She sat up suddenly, steeling herself. "Then I'll do it."

She wiped tears with the sleeve of her Edwardian dress, brushed past the director, and walked resolutely back to the set. Cukor followed, rushing to catch up. I trailed discreetly behind.

An assistant director held a loudspeaker. Cukor asked if news had gotten around, and the answer back was, "About what?"

"All right, good." He took the megaphone and said, "Everyone, please gather around. Audrey has something to say." Cukor's voice cracked on the last word. He handed the loudhailer to Audrey and turned away, weeping.

Audrey stood on a chair. Composure restored, she announced, "The president of the United States is dead." Shock rippled through the crew. "Shall we have two minutes of silence to pray or do whatever you think is appropriate?"

Everyone was stunned; most wept. Audrey retreated to the paving stones on the set and knelt, bowing her head. She prayed silently the entire time until she lifted her head. When satisfied that everyone had completed their entreaties, she stood and faced the crew.

"May he rest in peace. May God have mercy on our souls and his." A tear ran down my cheek experiencing the shock of that day. More than sixty years later in *my years*, it felt like a gut punch that sent me to my knees.

Audrey looked at each and every cast member like she had the reporters at the *Roman Holiday* press conference, giving attention—no, comfort—through individual eye contact. There were at least twenty people she consoled that way. I struggled to stand up, tears in my eyes. Audrey's scanning of the room stopped on me.

She beheld me like Princess Ann had looked at Joe Bradley at the end of the film. Her eyes were also wet, and then I felt her peer deeper inside me. A moment later, she shook her head *no*.

I had no idea what that meant. Had she recalled our previous meeting on set? Or something more? She walked away and I ended the scene.

That had to be Audrey Hepburn at her finest. It wasn't a role she'd played with the cast announcing JFK's death; it was an exhausted woman—actress, celebrity, wife, mother, castmate, friend—at the peak of her powers, doing what needed to be done when the men around her could not.

My heart lingered in the moment, but my mind wondered whether Audrey was now retaining memories of our virtual encounters. I checked the controls and coding, and no portal remained open where she should retain memory.

I knew I would cherish Audrey's private glance to me as long as I lived. But what did it mean?

Chapter 25

THE KOOK

I pondered why I was drawn to go back and see Audrey on set instead of continuing my virtual romance with her. Maybe I was learning more about her through different movie scenes. No, it wasn't that. I wanted to know Audrey Hepburn on a deeper level than anyone ever had.

Nicole chirped and I decided to decompress with her by finally watching *Breakfast at Tiffany's*. This movie had been filmed two years before *My Fair Lady*, and I'm not sure why we hadn't watched it yet since it's Audrey's best-known film.

Neither of us wanted to be the first to speak or ask the other what they thought when Holly Golightly and Varjak Paul kissed at the end after finding the cat named Cat. Finally, Nicole said, "What do you think about Audrey as a kook?"

"A kook?"

"Yes, that's how the studio pitched it to her, and how Audrey pitched it to the public in interviews—Holly was a kook."

"Not an escort?"

"Well, Audrey was friendly with Truman Capote, who wrote the novella, so she knew what Holly was. But Audrey wasn't going to play a straight-up hooker. She wouldn't do it, Mel wouldn't allow it, and the public wouldn't accept it. Then there was the whole Hays Code thing. It was dying, but not yet dead."

"'Hays Code thing?' What's that?"

"It was the end of a rather puritanical time in Hollywood. A man named

Joseph Breen was the chief enforcer of guidelines for all motion pictures from 1934 to 1968. Scripts were edited to the point where most nudity, graphic violence, profanity, rape, and so-called sexual persuasions were taboo. In the novel, Holly was a sort of geisha—geishas are not prostitutes here in Japan, by the way, they're social companions—but most confuse that with being an escort. The character of Fred was an unnamed narrator in the novel, and clearly was a gay male prostitute. Obviously, that wouldn't have made it into the movie back then. There were big enough problems with Holly's character, so the producers needed to cast an actress where that was below the surface. Only Audrey could portray a 'good girl' while playing a pseudo-hooker. She made the story more acceptable, and people forgot how Holly Golightly made money to live in New York as a young woman. And Fred's profession was left out altogether; he's portrayed as a writer with a sugar mama.'"

"The Hays Code sounds like McCarthyism for Hollywood."

"Yes, and they overlapped in the fifties, of course. Anyway, back to Audrey: she'd just had her first baby ten weeks before filming started, and she had to be talked into taking the part for various personal and professional reasons. But what persuaded her to do it was that it again changed the perception of women in the movies. Think of Holly as a sexual Princess Ann from *Roman Holiday.* The stereotype back then was that women rarely came out of the kitchen and had sex only to make babies. Yet Holly is a high-class escort whom everyone loves, both in the movie and in the audience. That was quite a performance."

It was a lot to unpack. "Audrey had a lot going on then. It gives me even more respect for *Breakfast at Tiffany's* and her performance."

Nicole asked, "So, if I had asked you five minutes ago if you liked it, what would you have said?"

"I would have said *meh.*"

"I don't disagree with you. There are some iconic scenes, and Audrey changed the perception of complex female characters, but much of the movie is … dare I say, overrated? So, Bradley Joseph, how do we make it better?"

I smiled. Now Nicole was back in my wheelhouse. "What are the options?"

"Well, the novella is short, but no need to read it. Here's a summary of the differences: like I said, the Paul Varjak/Fred character is simply the narrator in the book. There's no doubt he's a gay escort, which sheds a different light on their relationship if we remake it that way. In the book, it's clearly platonic. The Holly in the novel is younger and rough around the edges. She isn't seeking a solution; she just flits about: being a young bride in Texas, trying out Hollywood, and then going to New York because she'd never been there before. Conversely, Audrey's Holly is NYC class and elegance, and New York is *part of her*. Then there's the ending: in the book, no one knows where Holly went. In the movie, Holly and Fred kiss and you presume they stay together."

Nicole smiled before asking, "So, we could produce the novel instead of the screenplay. We can have them recite lines from the novel instead. And here's the main thing, we can replace George Peppard with Steve McQueen."

"Steve McQueen?"

"You've heard of him?"

"Yeah, I grew up in San Francisco, remember? *Bullitt*. Every kid who got a driver's license in The City drove the streets like McQueen did in that movie."

"Oh good, I thought you were going to say he was in *Star Wars* or some sci-fi thing I don't know about."

"If only … I'm not sure we need a redo of the movie, though, even for us to be the only ones who ever see it."

"Okay, what do you have in mind then?"

I stood up in my living room and paced, chin in hand. "I'm more intrigued by the making of the movie. Audrey's decision to make it. Mel's role. The backroom deals."

"Wow, if you only knew." She smiled.

"Then let's make that."

"I like it. Did you just want a documentary, or do we—I mean you—want to be *in* it?"

"I think I just want to watch a few scenes. No role, but I want to feel like I was in the room, completely invisible, to learn more about Audrey. Tell me who I need to put in the scenes and the parameters."

Nicole smiled. "This might be more than you bargained for."

I chirped Nicole when the scene was ready with the players she had suggested. I had infused some articles about the chaos before the movie's premiere and added Nicole's uncanny film-buff knowledge. The scene would be one big gathering, like the party scene in the film itself, where characters ebb and flow. The characters included the author Truman Capote, screenwriter George Axelrod, director Blake Edwards, two Martys—Paramount head Rackin and producer Jurow, *Moon River* composer Henry Mancini, the actor Mickey Rooney, and starring Audrey Hepburn and her husband, Mel Ferrer.

"I honestly have no idea how this will turn out," I said, stuffing my hands in my pockets as I paced around my home studio. "There will be so many simultaneous conversations that I cued up the most important ones as the camera moves in the room."

Nicole asked, "What is the setting you decided upon?"

"Oh, I took your suggestion of Marty Jurow's office and fabricated something along those lines. Full bar and everything."

"Wonderful. I think I will pour myself a whiskey to watch this. Cheers, Bradley." I clinked an imaginary glass with her remotely and ran the program. It didn't work. Something seemed to happen where Nicole couldn't watch it through *Cardinal* with me. I tried numerous fixes, but it still wouldn't work. Nicole volunteered that maybe having her join overloaded something. After a few more unsuccessful tries, Nicole signed off. Suddenly the program worked and I found myself in a Hollywood producer's office, hovering above with the cigarette and cigar smoke and swirling egos.

Producer Marty Jurow sat in an ornate leather chair behind his mahogany desk and asked all assembled what they thought of the completed movie they'd just watched in the nearby projector room.

Several voiced that it was a surefire classic, another complimented Axelrod on how he had duped the censors by writing in incidental scenes around Paul Varjak to throw Joseph Breen off the scent of casting Audrey Hepburn as an escort. They complimented Audrey on how brilliantly she'd captured Holly.

I focused on Mel Ferrer, who asked if he was the only one who cringed at Mickey Rooney's over-the-top stereotype of upstairs neighbor George Yunioshi—with bucked teeth, squinty eyes, and a horrible Japanese accent. The others pooh-poohed the suggestion, and Rooney threatened Ferrer.

"I did what I was directed to do!" he spat. "I didn't need this part, Marty—

you came to me. George, you *wrote* the damn part." Rooney stormed over to the bar.

The other Marty, Paramount studio head Rackin, chimed in to smooth it over.

"I think the critics may point that out, but it will be a footnote. We needed the levity and diversion. The important thing is that critics will be captivated with Audrey and not some of Truman's more salacious content."

Jurow looked at writer Truman Capote and asked what he thought. Capote adored Audrey but had fought against her getting the part, so he whispered out of her earshot, "Everything is wrong with this film, just everything. It's the most miscast movie I've ever seen. It made me want to throw up. I would have been a better casting decision than Peppard."

Jurow replied, "Yes, Truman, we've talked about that. The role just wasn't good enough for you. All eyes will be on Audrey, after all, not on anyone else in the film."

Capote retorted, "Yes, I know, I deserve something more dynamic … *blah, blah, blah.* You all don't even understand what my book was about." He walked over to the bar, joining Rooney.

I looked to Audrey from above as the chattering continued. She sat demurely with Henry Mancini on a couch in the back of the large room. The composer told Audrey, "No, they won't dub over your voice. I wrote the song for you and your recording of it—and the movie we just saw—you were perfect. You strummed the guitar seamlessly too. In the end, the audience will identify with you. *Your* voice is *their* voice. Your fears are theirs. Because of your wistful singing voice, they see you as a neighborly, likable woman."

She smiled. "Who happens to be an unrepentant prostitute. Oh, I don't know, Hank. Having a one-octave vocal range and a thinner voice than I did in *Funny Face*—that's not what anyone wants to hear in this movie. Or what the jury over there wants to hear."

I quickly shifted my focus to Rackin, who was voicing precisely that. He puffed great clouds of blue smoke from a long cigar while sitting on Jurow's desk and said, "Look, I love the picture, fellas, but the fucking song has to go!" It killed the collegial vibe and echoed around the room. Shouting commenced.

Young director Blake Edwards's face flushed dark red, and his fists clenched. Edwards had been a late replacement as director, and he'd had enough. Then AI inserted a flashback scene that surprised me: Edwards voicing his dislike for Peppard and saying that the two Martys had forced George on him.

"I wanted Steve McQueen or Tony Curtis, even after we started filming. Hell, even Audrey told me she worried about her lack of chemistry with Peppard … and Audrey never has anything negative to say about anyone! George's arrogance about his 'acting skills' pissed off the entire set, even Audrey! Even worse, Mel coached Audrey every night on how each scene should be filmed the next day, countering my direction. I had to give them an ultimatum—either stop or find another director."

Another quick flashback scene-hopped to a Japanese restaurant, where Mel openly criticized Audrey's manners in front of others. Audrey had momentarily put her elbows on the table. Ferrer picked up a fork, poked at her elbows, and yelled, "Ladies do not put their elbows on the table!"

I was mortified. *This was what Audrey's life as a 'megastar' had been like?*

Back in the regular scene, Audrey bowed her head in an *I knew it* response to Marty Rackin saying that *Moon River* had to be cut. Only Mancini and I saw her disappointment. The composer looked around and said quietly, "Don't worry. I think they might lynch Rackin first."

Capote, drink in hand, elbowed past screenwriter George Axelrod, who had written the balcony song into the script. In his nasal twang, Capote said, "Why are we fighting over a song that wasn't even *in* my novel? Let's talk about what was left *out!* Not what was put in."

I saw the anger rising in Audrey as the men debated as if she wasn't even there. Mancini saw it too and was jostled to the side as Audrey sprang up and screamed, "You'll cut that song over my dead body!"

Everyone's heads' swiveled toward Audrey, Rackin's last. He looked around and saw how outnumbered he was and that he had instilled fury in the one person who was normally above all this bickering. Rackin hurriedly left the office without a word. Jurow said, "The song stays. Thanks, everyone."

Voices murmured as people filed out. "Helluva movie, Blake. *Great* script, George. Really great song, Hank! Thank you, Audrey, don't worry—it's going to be great!"

Mancini kissed Audrey on the cheek. She patted his hand in return as Mel came over to collect her. Mancini didn't look at Mel, having heard about the fork episode in the restaurant.

Mel helped Audrey to the door. She felt all eyes on her and reached deeply for a smile. "Thank you, everyone. I think we have made a wonderful picture that people will talk about for years."

I continued to hover above as Audrey and Mel exited. Audrey leaned on her husband and asked him what he thought now of the film after seeing all of the madness in the office. Ferrer, who thought he would have done better acting alongside or directing Audrey, gritted his teeth and said, "What do I think of the film? I liked your hat."

I ended the scene abruptly.

A little while later, I showed it to Nicole and she cried. I waited a moment and then asked her what she thought of the scene we'd cobbled together. Nicole dabbed at her eyes and said, "Mel could be that way. Audrey didn't deserve that, no woman does. And she had a baby at home, with no possibility of escaping her husband. It was a sad time, when it should have been a time of great joy. Thank you, Bradley. You captured it perfectly."

I wanted to tell her that AI inserted the two background scenes but remembered my pact with Ara and Advik to not discuss technology with Nicole. "Thanks. Maybe too well, I guess."

"You did well. It's so emotional to watch what Audrey went through. People who watch the movie need to know the backstory. These 'backroom characters' as you called them."

"I'm sorry that I put Mickey Rooney in. With you being Japanese, it must be ugly to watch, even after all this time."

She nodded. "I try to blame it on 'the times,' with it being filmed only fifteen years or so after World War II. But yes, it's hard to watch. And to their credit, many critics even back then pointed out that the caricature wasn't funny. It was so over the top and added so little to the story."

"So, what happened next?"

"You don't know this, but *Tiffany's* premiered at two theaters in your area:

The Golden Gate Theater in San Francisco and the Stanford Theater in Palo Alto the following night. Audrey and Mel attended both. If you want to go and feel the magic, I understand the Stanford Theater still shows it on occasion."

I was stirred to hear that Audrey not only returned to San Francisco in 1961 but had actually been to Palo Alto. I had no idea *Breakfast at Tiffany's* premiered for test audiences here and I loved finding local connections to the actual Audrey. Then I suddenly blurted out, "Watch it with me at the Stanford. I'll rent it out whenever you're in town. Heck, I'll fly you into town."

Nicole smiled. "Thank you, Bradley. That's very kind of you. I'll consider it. We do have a good thing going this way, though, with no pressure for anything other than our shared joy in Audrey. I would hate to lose that."

I thought for a moment and finally said, "Maybe. You're probably right." But I felt ready to meet Nicole in person and didn't have a physiological reaction to the idea. Breaking things off didn't enter my mind this time.

To prepare for possibly meeting Nicole, I decided to watch every other Audrey Hepburn movie. By myself.

There were many more than I thought.

Chapter 26

THE CLUB

Advik was excited to show me his developments in extended reality at HQ. The new equipment included wearables that included high-resolution 3D glasses, integrated with a full sensory suit. He also made tremendous headway on an immersive digital environment free from glasses and suits—3D cameras, screens, and sensors that gave a lifelike presentation—and rebuilt it in my home studio.

"Soon, you'll see multiple holographic renders through the integrated AI that you and Ara set up." We instituted all controls that we could think of, coding them into the program. For now, we called it *Cocktail HoVR 2.0*.

Advik said, "Bradley, I have to admit, I'm having trouble keeping up with the names of our programs. I mean, we started this venture with *Real to Reel*, reached back to *ConVRsate* to make it, uh … *Bannister*, was it?"

I picked it up: "Then combined *Real to Reel* and *Cardinal* into *Cocktail HoVR*. And now we have version 2.0. with your extended reality devices."

"I imagine we will have a few more names until we get to the final product?"

"Likely." I smiled and said, "I'll develop a score sheet for us."

I tried to hide my excitement about this next step. Now I would be more fully immersed in each scene, making it even more realistic. I worked a few more hours without Ara and Advik on some specific AI integration, including characters' truth serum. I wanted nothing but the truth in this next scene, and maybe each one afterward.

The project: converse with Audrey Hepburn's previous husbands, boyfriends, and lovers. The reason: I needed to understand *why anyone would ever leave her.* It reminded me of something I'd heard as a kid—no matter how fine a person is, someone somewhere is sick of them. I couldn't imagine that being true in the case of Audrey Hepburn, so I endeavored to find out.

I created the men to appear at the ages they were when they courted Audrey. Once everything was ready, I selected an interview format with myself as the host and let it run entirely on AI autopilot to get some honest conversation. I chose to have each introduce themselves as they went around the room, and arranged them as they'd appeared in Audrey's life chronologically.

Eight men walked out, all dressed like they were going out for a night on the town. Their expressions turned dour when they saw each other, knowing what they had in common—a romantic relationship with Audrey Hepburn. Some knew each other, most knew of each other. The room grew tense as they sat in director's chairs with their names on them.

I decided to keep it simple and see where it went.

"Hello, everyone. My name is Bradley Joseph, and I'll be asking you all some questions today. I'd like to start with self-introductions, and please share how you met Audrey."

They fidgeted and looked around. I nodded to the first man, dressed in a tuxedo with tails, in his twenties. with a heavy French accent.

"*Bonjour*, I am Marcel Le Bon. I met Audrey when she was brand new to show business in London after the war. I was a singer—think of a poor man's Maurice Chevalier, but younger and better looking."

He waited for others to chuckle or smile, but they were occupied sizing each other up from their semicircle in front of me. Marcel seemed to be instantly appraised by others as a nonthreat in being Audrey's greatest love. He cleared his throat, wondering if his English wasn't so good after all.

"For those who don't understand the joke, which it seems is everyone, Maurice Chevalier played Audrey's father in *Love in the Afternoon* and … anyway, Audrey was a chorus girl and dancer with me, and our shows were called *Sauce Tartare*, *Sauce Piquante*, and *Summer Nights*. I wore these clothes in the musical revues." He got wistful when he added, "I would leave roses for her at the stage door before she arrived …"

He was cut off by the man to his immediate left, a handsome, debonair fellow who looked like he could have been an actor, but he was one of only two non-showmen in the group.

"And if you'd asked her what flowers she preferred, you would know it was lilies. Her mother put the kibosh on your little romance, didn't she? And Audrey turned down a movie offer to stay in your nightclub act. The offer fell apart due to your actions, and Audrey was crushed. Then she left you."

I interrupted. "I'm sorry, a few things. Please be respectful of each other. I know this could get heated, but just know I can end this at any time. Also, please, sir, introduce yourself."

"I'm James Hanson of the trucking and shipping Hansons. I was Audrey's fiancé until the show business bug pulled her away from me. I think she regretted it all her life."

The others chuckled. Hanson retorted, "Go ahead and laugh. Audrey wanted a family, and let's face it, all of us except maybe for Chevalier Junior over here could have provided a very comfortable lifestyle for her."

"I object to that," Le Bon said. "I did quite well …"

"I'm sorry," interrupted William Holden. "Are we comparing resumes already?" He raised his Academy Award for 1953's *Stalag 17.* "Oscar here would like a word, if we are …"

"Have another drink, Bill," said Mel Ferrer. "She left you and Oscar for me, and we remained together for fourteen years …"

This freewheeling format wasn't working as I'd hoped, so I stopped the program and coded more controls for decorum and strict rules on characters speaking only when I invited them. I also decided to address the men by their first names and cut some of the formality. Then I started over again, with Le Bon.

"Marcel, tell us about your time with Audrey, if you will."

"It was lovely. It wasn't too long after the war, you see. She came to us as a dancer and worked herself to death. She said that she had gained thirty pounds after the war but lost it all in a few weeks by cutting sugar and starches, plus she did a second, separate dance show every night after our shows were finished for the evening."

"So, you likely spent time together during the day?"

He smiled sheepishly. "Well, London didn't close very early at night.

There were still things to do in the middle of the night, yes?"

I wanted to ask if he'd been her first lover—we all wanted to know—but I didn't. What did it matter anyway? Each of these men had intimate relationships with Audrey Hepburn, and I didn't need to confirm who was first.

"Marcel, what was she like in those days? Did she change in your mind as she became a famous actress?"

"It's difficult to say. I never saw her again. I was rather surprised at how big of a star she became. No one imagined it then, even though the lights and the audiences were naturally drawn to her."

"Even after *Roman Holiday*? You didn't see that she would become one of the biggest stars in Hollywood history?"

"Well, yes, after that movie, certainly. Audrey was the perfect choice for that role. But even then, she would be the first to tell you that she still didn't know how to act."

"Thank you, Marcel. I'm going to turn now to Mr. James Hanson. Do you prefer James or Jimmy?"

"I prefer Baron, or Lord, titles which I've earned, but sure, call me James."

I knew another nickname for Hanson was *Lord Moneybags*, for his corporate raiding ventures later in life, but didn't press the issue. "Thank you, James. I will stick with that. Can you share how you and Audrey met?"

Hanson sighed as if wanting to say that everyone knew their story. "Well, Audrey had a bit part in a small British movie called *The Secret People*, before *Roman Holiday*, and part of her contract was to attend parties and film premieres in London. The studio was trying to get her publicity in certain circles. I was regularly invited to those kinds of events, and we met at one."

I thought how much that sounded like when I "met" her at Whitney Warren's house during *Gigi*. I noted Hanson may have been the best looking in the bunch, adorned in a Saville Row gray suit befitting a playboy or a young Sean Connery. Hanson had been called a cross between James Stewart and Gary Cooper. I asked, "Was it an instant attraction?"

"Yes, it certainly was for me, and I think she would say the same. We had lunch the next day and were inseparable. For a while."

"I understand that you and Audrey's mother, the Baroness, had a different vision for how Audrey's life would play out."

"I take offense at the way you pose the question. Audrey wanted to be married and also have children very quickly. I could provide that, and the comfort she and her mother wanted for the children. She wouldn't have had to work outside the home. I already had money to provide a life far beyond what most women dream of. But after a few low-budget movies, she had a contract, and she wanted to honor it. Then the acting fever got worse with each succeeding film. I supported her doing *Gigi* on Broadway. I helped get her settled and had business in Canada, so our relationship continued to grow."

"What changed it?" I knew the answer.

"That blasted *Roman Holiday* changed it, for one thing. But do you know what was even worse? Her goddamned contract for doing the US tour of *Gigi* after she finished filming *Roman Holiday*! We were supposed to have gotten married, and I was going to meet her in every city she went to around the country as a sort of honeymoon—Boston, Cleveland, Chicago, Detroit, DC, Los Angeles, San Francisco." At the mention of San Francisco, I jumped.

"Hell, she traveled with her wedding dress during the first half of the tour, in case we suddenly decided to have the ceremony." Then Hanson's voice drifted. "I guess I waited too long. Or didn't insist early enough. I thought she deserved more than a justice of the peace ceremony in Cleveland."

"How did the breakup happen?"

"We had a falling out in Chicago. I went there for Christmas of 1952. It wasn't a big quarrel. It was just apparent that she wanted both a career and family life. She was increasingly tied to her work and less to me. I couldn't stop running my businesses. I guess I realized that I needed to be more than Mr. Audrey Hepburn."

Hanson's honesty surprised me, and I thanked him, thinking he wasn't as arrogant as he'd started out. I could see he truly regretted not being more open to a dual work and family life for them. He later remained married to his wife Geraldine for his entire life, and they had three children together. His net worth at the end of his life was thirty billion dollars.

I felt a bit unsettled that Audrey may have been drawn back then to wealth and fame, and her choice of beaus didn't include a Joe Bradley along the way. I really couldn't criticize it since Audrey herself was raised with some level of aristocracy before World War II took it away. And I knew with Audrey's father abandoning them when she was young, that she sought stability for herself and her future children.

Seated next to Hanson was William Holden, Hollywood's golden boy of the early 1950s. He had bleached his hair blond to star as David Larrabee in *Sabrina*, and they had fallen in love filming on Long Island. He was an alcoholic for most of his adult life, but what led to his breakup with Audrey wasn't the drinking or the fact that he was married. It was that he'd had a vasectomy and couldn't give Audrey children.

"Bill, any regrets during your relationship with Audrey?"

"Excuse me?"

"I thought maybe we could get right into it. As we heard from James, Audrey had decided to balance a movie career with finding the right man to marry and have children with. You'd had a vasectomy, which was irreversible back then. Do you regret that?"

"Are you asking me if I regret my very personal decision with my wife Ardis?"

"No, let me rephrase," I said, sounding like a trial lawyer. "Do you regret how quickly you and Audrey fell in love and spoke of marriage? Then as she was suggesting child names to you, that's when you decided to tell her you'd had a vasectomy and couldn't have children?"

"I thought rephrasing was supposed to get better. How do you know all of this?"

I leaned toward Holden, feeling his dislike growing. So was mine, for him.

I blurted, "It's no secret. Was it just about conquering another starlet for you? How long did it take you to jump into Grace Kelly's bed after Audrey ended your relationship? And let's not forget that you were married all the while."

"Now wait just a minute. My wife and I agreed, as long as we stayed together, what happened on location …"

"Stayed on location? But you also brought these women into your house to have dinner that your wife prepared for the three of you! That's fucked up."

Holden was fuming, but I continued, pissed off at someone who treated Audrey so poorly when she was young and impressionable. "Ardis determined that Audrey was the one she should worry about, that you had the deepest affection for. And there she was, right at your dinner table."

Holden began to stand up—and do what, I wondered? I had just instituted more controls into the program and dismissed any threat. "So then, let's turn to husband number one, Mel Ferrer. Hi, Mel, what do you have to say to that?"

"I'm a little afraid to say anything right now, except that I'm glad Bill had a vasectomy, or I might not be speaking with you right now."

"Meaning?"

"Audrey did love Bill and didn't get serious with me until after they broke up."

"You met Audrey before she started filming *Sabrina*?"

"Yes. Gregory Peck introduced me to her in the summer of 1953 when she was in London for *Roman Holiday*'s premiere. Greg threw a welcome party and invited me. He set us up, really. She said she enjoyed my film *Lili*, and we started talking about theater. She said to send her a script if I found a play we could do together. That was *Ondine*. She won a Tony for it."

I reflected that I was the last man to "date" Audrey before she met Holden and Ferrer, albeit with that whole time travel element. Then I wondered whether my future virtual encounters with Audrey should be as her recurring secret lover throughout her lifetime—a taboo relationship that never existed in reality. "Mel, was it love at first sight for you, like it was with Bill?" I looked at Holden, who still looked like he wanted to punch me.

"Maybe not. I was married with children and decided that I'd be better off unmarried if I ever got a chance with Audrey. So, as painful as it was, I divorced my wife when I started *Ondine* with Audrey. And *I wanted* children with her."

Holden's eyes implored me to ask the follow-up question. He smiled when I asked Mel, "How many times had you been married before you met Audrey? And how old were you?"

Mel answered directly and calmly, pushing his six foot three frame into the chair and checking the comb-over covering his growing baldness. "I was thirty-five. I'd been married to two women before her." Holden squirmed, and nodded at me.

I continued, "You were married twice to the same woman, right? Frances

Pilchard? And married Barbara Tripp in between? So that's three marriages, before thirty-five? Wasn't divorce still a little frowned upon back then?"

Ferrer sighed as Holden smiled. "It was. I would suggest, though, that divorcing for the intent to marry the love of your life is nobler than bringing your lovers to have dinner in your house with your cuckolded wife."

In the name of science, I pushed a button on the remote to override the controls I'd just set up and let this particular scene play out for a minute. Holden rushed Ferrer's chair and bowled him over. The two scrapped with misplaced honor. Ferrer ducked Holden's haymakers, and the only impact was to push Mel's comb-over vertically.

Careful to not hit Golden Holden in the face, Ferrer kneed him in the solar plexus, and the brawl subsided quickly. Mel smoothed his hair with his hand and Bill wretched his way back to his chair. I smiled and switched decorum back into the scene with a button as the men tried to recover their dignity.

Mel regained his composure and asked, "Can I just add that everything I did with Audrey was done out of love and concern for her? She never felt love from her parents, which was criminal. She wanted a strong man for a husband, one who would guide her and give her what she wanted."

I smirked upon hearing that. "Mel, regarding that concern: tell me about *Ondine* and Audrey's nervous breakdown. She was clearly exhausted and under a doctor's care every day. Wouldn't someone who cared for her and loved her have just said, "Forget the play—you need a break"?

Mel snapped, "If word had gotten out that she was in bad shape and had a nervous breakdown—which isn't true—that would have ruined her career. You've heard 'the show must go on'? Well, that's true, and we were both on contracts. We weren't rich, like Holden here or Hanson. We were both establishing ourselves, so if the press had gotten wind of Audrey being sick, or dropping out of *Ondine* due to exhaustion, her career would have been short lived. I protected her."

"Let's talk about that a little. Many saw your protection as the domination of a worn-down neophyte. And that domination led her to rely on you to the point where you became more of a Svengali than a fiancé to her."

"No! I saved her. Her life, her career, and most importantly, I gave her a family. I only wish that we'd been able to have more children."

"I'll grant that you got her to rest and relax in Switzerland after *Ondine* ended its run in New York. And she had quiet time to recover while you made a movie in Italy. But you proposed to her before leaving New York. She didn't give you an answer right away, did she?"

Mel glared and finally answered, "No."

Holden laughed once, loudly.

Ferrer continued, "I wanted her to get well and I provided space for that. I didn't want her to confuse love and marriage with being the friend she needed. But I also told her that our future together would be bright."

"And was it?"

"Yes, I think it was."

"I understand that when she realized how dependent she was on you and eventually consented she was in love with you—that your engagement was announced by the studio in a quite unusual location."

At this, William Holden squirmed, biting his lip.

Mel answered, "Yes, you could say that."

I asked, "And where was your engagement to Audrey announced?"

Ferrer pointed his thumb at Holden. "At his house."

The entire panel laughed, save Mel and Bill.

"That must have been uncomfortable for both of you gentlemen. Bill, why did you agree to it?"

"Fuck, it killed me. I tried to win Audrey back. I mean, she was about to marry Mel Ferrer, for God's sake. No offense, Mel, but were you an actor, a director, or a producer?" He turned back to me and said, "The studios insisted. Everyone knew we'd been in love, and they wanted our relationship to work, but when it ended, I had to put on a brave face and pretend that it was all okay. Well, it wasn't fucking okay."

"Your wife, Ardis, must have been relieved that Audrey was no longer a threat to her."

Holden had nothing to add, he just clenched his hands and looked downward.

I asked Ferrer, "And Mel, why was that okay with you, to have the engagement announced at William Holden's house?"

"You must understand that everyone knows each other when you get to that level of show business. If not directly, then through someone who knew—or had relationships with—both of you. It was deemed good for our careers to show the world that Audrey was taking the next step, with someone she should marry."

Holden sneered.

"Mel, you and Audrey had a difficult time carrying children to term. There was a stillbirth and several miscarriages. That must have been very tough on Audrey."

"And me. We wanted children very badly."

"Yes, and you had a healthy baby boy in 1960."

Ferrer perked up at the mention of that. "Yes, it was very satisfying to gift her the baby she wanted so much."

"But having a child didn't keep you together. There were rumors of infidelity on your part, as well as—and I'll try to be kind here—that Audrey continued to get the better movie offers. *Breakfast at Tiffany's*, *Charade* with Cary Grant, *My Fair Lady*…"

Holden interjected, "Don't forget *Paris When It Sizzles* … we got back together." He smiled directly at Ferrer.

Mel replied, "*On* screen."

"I know this movie," Marcel Le Bon replied. "It was absolute *merde* … shit." Holden's head spun around to glare at Marcel but he didn't speak. Or attack.

"Where were we?" Ferrer asked.

I continued, "Audrey continued to get great roles and you didn't. Then you made another movie together, at your insistence, *Mayerling*, a live television show, which bombed. That put strain on your marriage and the thinking was that your relationship issues were part of the reason you weren't believable as a Romeo and Juliet pairing in that film."

Mel sighed and replied, "What do you want me to say? We wanted to do projects together, to stay together, and not just with me acting. I produced *Wait Until Dark*, and Audrey was nominated for an Academy Award for it. She should have won, but they read Katharine Hepburn instead."

"Yes, that was a good movie; you should be proud of that. But before *Wait Until Dark*, Audrey did two fun films: *How to Steal a Million* with a young

Peter O'Toole …" I paused here to remember that Nicole Bonnet was named after Audrey's character in that film. "And then one of my favorites, *Two for the Road*, a very avant-garde film for the time. That film starred Albert Finney, who also has joined us. Welcome."

I knew Finney and Ferrer would likely throw direct accusations but not resort to blows here. To be sure, I checked the remote to ensure we wouldn't have another free-for-all.

"Pleased to be here, wherever *here* is. Where the fuck *are* we, by the way?" the doleful Finney said. His baritone voice was the most pronounced of them all, at once recognizable even if you couldn't place his face or what movie you saw him in. His wavy hair and plumper appearance didn't hide his rugby-player physique.

The tall, thin Mel Ferrer looked at Finney with disdain. They couldn't have been more opposite in appearance.

"We'll just refer to it as 'the studio' for now. It's been said that *Two for the Road* was as close to a biography of Audrey as any of her movies. What are your thoughts on that?"

Finney said, "It's hard to say; I didn't meet her until just before filming started."

"I understand that you made quite the initial impression on Audrey after you both signed and were about to start filming."

Finney laughed. "Oh, that. Well, yes, I had just finished a Peter Shaffer play called *Black Comedy* and I went against typecast, playing an effeminate antique dealer. I met Audrey and director Stanley Donen for dinner and stayed in that character. Stanley promised to play along, so for thirty minutes, Audrey was visibly wondering how I would play her rather blunt husband in the movie. Finally, we couldn't contain it anymore and burst out laughing."

All but Mel Ferrer laughed along at the story.

Then Finney looked at Mel and said, "There was nothing grander than making Audrey laugh. She hadn't had much of it for quite a few years."

"Fuck off," was Ferrer's reply.

I knew the answer but asked, "What is the source of the tension between the two of you? Albert, you first?"

"My friends call me Albie. Mel can call me Albert." Ferrer squirmed as

Finney continued, "The short of it is that Audrey and I got along so well on set that we continued our relationship after hours. She loved to dance—I'm talking about discotheques in Saint-Tropez in 1965. And Mel was in Spain most of the time ..."

"With our son! Raising him ..."

"Be that as it may, Audrey was able to be who she was deep down inside when Mel wasn't pushing her to a nervous breakdown or anorexia or bored out of her mind ..."

Mel shot up. "You don't know what you're talking about!"

I interceded and asked Mel to sit down. "Mel, were you legally separated from Audrey when *Two for the Road* was filming?"

"No, we were working through things."

"Yeah," said Albie. "You were working through women in Spain. Is this where we mention a teen who Mel was rumored to be having an affair with?"

Ferrer stood up again, but instead of charging Finney, he walked off the set, screaming, "Fucking bastard!"

Holden whistled at Ferrer storming off, then added, "That's the most life I've ever seen from Mel Ferrer. If he'd shown that emotion in his movies or life, he may have been able to keep Audrey."

I took control back. "I hope Mel will rejoin us later. I really do. Albie, *Two for the Road* presented a wholly different Audrey Hepburn. She played someone whose marriage was on the rocks, which was apparently mirrored in her real life; she showed a decidedly sexual side and even wore a bathing suit and appeared nude—albeit under the covers in this movie—did she worry about her reputation as the genteel star the world adored?"

"She loved every minute of her time filming. She loved her character. She let loose after hours and on weekends. I think she had the best time of her professional life, making that movie."

"And that leads me to ask about her personal life. What did she share with you?"

"Audrey told me that her marriage was full of, let's just say, complications."

I was enjoying Finney the most of the panel members. I thought of using *Cocktail HoVR* for its original intent: enjoying a beverage with a deceased historical figure to create a recurring virtual friendship.

I felt Holden eyeing me skeptically after the gentler way I treated Finney, so I got back on topic.

"Albie, tell me about your experience with Audrey. On set, to start."

"We immediately got on well. In a movie, the chemistry is either there or it isn't. I find I can have a very good rapport with an actress I'm working with, and then you have the times when there's an absolute attraction. That happened with Audrey. Doing a scene with her—in my mind, I knew I was acting, but my heart didn't, and my body certainly didn't!"

"Go on." I shifted in my seat.

"Well, performing with Audrey was quite disturbing, actually. All that staring into each other's eyes—you pick up vibes that are decidedly not fantasy."

I—and presumably the others—knew what Finney meant. I'd felt it from the alternate reality scenarios with Audrey.

"How did the on-set dynamic develop into an off-set romance?"

"The same way it always does. You go out, have a few drinks, have a good time. She was a dancer in the proper sense, and I knew how to keep a beat well enough. That was something she and Mel didn't do much—dance. I was seven years younger than her, and she used me as her conduit to the world that continued to evolve while she was doing those other things people associate with Audrey Hepburn. You know, wife, mother, A-list actress. Our time there brought out a whole new side of her."

"Do you remember how it developed into an affair?"

"Of course I do. Audrey wasn't drunk enough to call it a mistake. It was something she decided carefully: Mel was unfaithful, and like Joanna Wallace in the movie we were making by day, she decided to branch out as well."

"I understand Mel occasionally visited the set. Did that cause you two to cool things off?"

"Sure, she didn't want to disrespect him in front of others. The gossip magazines were already musing about us, and Mel had gotten wind of it."

Just then, Mel Ferrer returned to the set. He was still fuming and added, "Damn fine of you both to quell it while I was there."

"Thanks for coming back, Mel," I said. "We're at a delicate point here, so I hope you'll stay with us. I understand you gave Audrey an ultimatum to end the affair with Albie. Do you care to share what that ultimatum was?"

"No, I do not."

I then asked Finney, who grunted at Mel's obstinacy and said, "He told her that if we didn't end it, he would sue her for divorce and use adultery as the reason. That was a scarlet letter for any actress and particularly for a world icon. It would have been something that destroyed her reputation and cost her custody of their child."

Another man on the panel, two people to Finney's left, added, "She probably would have killed herself. It would have ruined her, and her son's, reputation for life."

I said, "Thanks, Ben, we'll get to you shortly." The actor nodded and half-smiled.

"Mel, is that true?"

"I was trying to save our marriage and save Audrey from herself. I won't get into what she and I talked about privately."

Holden popped in again. "Hell, back in Hollywood we all knew about it. That was a really shitty thing to do, Mel, especially since you couldn't keep it in your pants yourself."

"You're one to talk, Bill," Mel replied.

"Yeah, but at least I admit it. Addiction—whether to alcohol or sex—is hard to shake. But at least I faced who I am and didn't hold Ardis's affairs over her head. Even when we got divorced."

Ferrer pushed back. "I guess you're all better men than me, is that it? Well, I was the one she married. Don't forget that!"

Now was the perfect time to introduce the man to Finney's left. "But you weren't the only one that she married. Next, I want to turn to Dr. Andrea Dotti, Audrey's second husband. After her divorce from Mel in 1968, she went on a cruise around the Greek isles on the yacht of a very affluent Frenchman. Andrea, I understand you had met Audrey Hepburn once before that cruise. Can you tell us about that?"

The Italian was dressed in a royal blue bespoke suit and tie, with a crisp white shirt and floral pocket square. His hair intentionally disheveled, he looked like the stereotypical Italian jet-set playboy. His accent fit his look.

"It's a fun story that I shared with Audrey when we first met on the ship. I was in the crowd watching her film *Roman Holiday* fifteen years prior—I was only fourteen then. She talked to some of us during a break. She came up to me and I shook her hand. When I went home, I told my mother I would marry her someday." Then Dotti looked at Ferrer. "And I did."

I said, "What's interesting to me is that she had begun starring in movies with younger leading actors—Peter O'Toole, and of course, Albert Finney—and that carried over to her relationship with you. What was your age difference?"

"Nine years? Yes, I was thirty and she was thirty-nine when we met. But Audrey was the first to say those nine years didn't make her more mature. She said that I was older than her intellectually—I am a psychiatrist, you see, and lecture and teach at university—and Audrey had felt a bit stifled in her life and thus felt younger than her years when she was finally allowed to relax and have fun."

Ferrer said, "Do I really have to stay and listen to this? Is everyone here to take a shot at me?"

I thought momentarily about telling them I was from the future and they were all deceased but brought back to life in this virtual séance of mine. Instead, I said, "Yes, Mel, we'd like you to stay."

Mel answered, "If this is a celebrity roast, I wish we'd get to the funny part."

I continued with Dotti. "You and Audrey met in June of 1968, soon after her divorce from Mel, and you were engaged by December and married a few weeks later. What was your courtship like? What was Audrey looking for at that point in her life?" I saw Mel seething and added, "And please leave references to her previous relationship out of your answer, if you can."

"Of course, I'm a gentleman who understands the human psyche. I think I brought a diversion to Audrey, an escape. I couldn't stop seeking her and talking to her on the cruise. The Greek isles are so beautiful, almost as nice as our Italian isles on the coast." He smiled. "I brought romance and cheer to her then. I visited her house in Switzerland, she stayed with me in Rome, and we holidayed in Tuscany. She could have done all these things at any time in her life, but I offered them as a lifestyle. She wanted to live in Rome, where I already lived and worked. Oh, and her son and I got along very well."

Holden jumped in here. "He sounds like fucking Onassis courting Jackie Kennedy and John-John."

Finney added, "Except it wasn't *his* yacht or *his* Tuscan villa. Signore Dotti was a child of privilege ..."

"*Dr.* Dotti," Andrea corrected.

"... whatever, and you made good use of your friends' amenities."

Dotti agreed. "That's the Italian way. But do not doubt my personal wealth also. None of us needed to date Audrey for her money." He then looked around. "I am unsure of Le Bon, however. Anyway, I can't speak to others' ambitions with Audrey, but I can speak to romance."

Finney leaned over and asked, "Romance with half of the women in Rome during your marriage, right, mate? The paparazzi ran photos of you and your chippies nearly every night when Audrey was in Switzerland with her son. I just hope that you didn't give her the clap."

This went unanswered, so I added, "Andrea, you gave her a second son in 1970. I read that Audrey self-prescribed bed rest in Switzerland for the last six months of her pregnancy to ensure she carried the baby to term after so many miscarriages."

"Yes, that's right."

"Audrey was a Roman housewife and devoted mother during those years. She claimed to not miss making movies. What was life like for her in the house?"

"Well, first, we had a penthouse apartment in Rome. You could see the entire city from it. She loved to wake up early, cook breakfast for her son and me before school and work. She played with the baby and the dogs—we had three Jack Russell Terriers—then she either went out to lunch or had friends over. When I got home from work, and the servants put the boys to bed, we would go out to dinner and dance. She would sometimes come with me on trips to mental hospitals. She was fascinated with my work."

I mused, "It seems the Dottis had everything going for them. Why did that change?"

Andrea was silent for ten full seconds. Everyone in the room knew the answer, but I wanted to hear him say it. It was James Hanson, he of the broken engagement during the *Gigi* years, who broke the stalemate. "I never cheated on Audrey. I hope there is at least one other who can say that."

The ones who lowered their heads were the guilty ones—Holden, Ferrer, Dotti. There were two more men on the panel I hadn't spoken to yet and I decided to move to them quickly. "Ben Gazzara, you acted with Audrey in two movies after she made a bit of a comeback in her fifties: *Bloodline* and *They All Laughed*. What do you have to add to the conversation?"

"Well, for one, I was divorced when we started working on *Bloodline*, a horrible movie that neither of us should have made. But Audrey was a joy. Honestly, I think she wanted to see what the hubbub was about with having an affair, so she asked me to." Everyone's head turned at the thought of Audrey Hepburn being the aggressor. "And so, I did. The only problem was that I didn't love her, and when the movie ended, so did our relationship." Gazzara surveyed the room, then added, "Like I said earlier, she told me that she thought about killing herself before our affair. Whether true or not, I don't know … but I felt that I saved her."

Holden snickered. "You saved her by fucking her? Well, how noble of you, sir."

"I could have handled it better, I'll admit. Couldn't we all have?"

The man to Gazzara's left, the last one, picked his head up. A tear rolled down his cheek. He didn't speak.

I had two revelations: first, that Dotti was right—Audrey only dated men of power, influence, and wealth—mainly celebrities of some sort; and second, it didn't matter that she was Audrey Hepburn—every man on this stage had either lost her or dumped her. Except for the one I hadn't yet spoken to.

I decided to end the session and sometime soon have a deeper conversation with the last man.

Chapter 27

REVELATION

The technical success of the interviews made me ponder the idea of making *Cocktail HoVR 2.0* a commercial endeavor at some point soon—enabling anyone to socialize with a historical figure or a deceased loved one. Nicole had mentioned that weeks ago. It depended on controls and whether artificial general intelligence (AGI) would be necessary for a truly immersive experience. AGI would enable the re-creations to have a life of their own but could also lead to losing all constraints. Next would be those sci-fi catastrophes many predicted. I knew the financial windfall these inventions would bring but it was still a work in progress.

A few things about the interviews unnerved me as well. Why did Audrey court only wealthy men? With the possible exception of Marcel Le Bon and perhaps the last man, each was a millionaire or more. Then I thought about my dates so far with Audrey—did she sense, or did artificial intelligence somehow inform her, that I was also handsomely paid?

I called Ara Day on the secure line. She answered in her military manner.

"Yes, sir?"

"Ara, a straight-up answer, please. This narrow AI we're using—is there any way the computer could inform the created subject anything about the gamer? Any chance at all?"

She was silent for a moment too long.

"Ara?"

"I mean, it's possible. As you know, that's really the realm of AGI—strong AI. Narrow AI relies on data inputs to perform tasks, right? On the other hand,

AGI is simpatico with the independent human brain, with more autonomy. It can exhibit background knowledge, adapt a level of common sense, and even transfer and retain knowledge. It promises the ability to deduce information based on underdeveloped inputs. Sorry, Bradley, I know you know all of this. I'm just working my way up to answering your question."

"No problem. Keep going."

"So, the answer is, I didn't engineer anything that way, but if we feed the computer all this data and tell it to carry on unscripted conversations through AI, at some level it could auto-generate feeding information to the created subject, yes. Are you saying it's happening?"

"I'm not sure yet. Let me ask this, once it starts happening, can we control it?"

"Yes, but we could continue to institute specific controls upfront—like we've done—so that it doesn't continually feed the created subject."

"And if we let narrow AI run without controls and have sequential meetings between the gamer and the created subject, could the information be remembered and become part of the follow-on meeting?"

"I wouldn't think so. But if you think it's happening, that's groundbreaking stuff that has probably never happened before. It might mean that AGI is generating itself outside of our coding."

"What is the worst-case scenario if we don't institute controls?"

Ara said, "Well, that depends on whether the being has a presence outside of your work. There's no way I can predict whether it could leap into a fuller digital presence, other than yours."

"So, with controls, I have Audrey at my disposal whenever I want to call on her. And without, she might be available to everyone who copycats our work. Is that it?"

"The chances are incredibly slim."

"But not zero?"

"No, not zero. Consider this: If Audrey can ever link your meetings, it would probably only be like someone in the real world with whom you have sequential dates. In a non-virtual relationship."

I chuckled. "You mean real people? You can say it."

"Yes," she laughed.

"So, if this goes too far, just scrap that series of meetings and start a different one? That way, no prior knowledge is carried over?"

"I think that should work, yes. If we code it that way and check for bugs. You know, that old-fashioned stuff."

"It sounds like there is a chance that every time I create a new scene, I could get the same Audrey who may have knowledge of our previous meetings. What chance would you give that?"

"Five percent, max. But I'd like to dig into this with some folks you told me not to work with anymore."

"The anti-Putin Russians?"

She paused. "I'd rather not say, but the people I'm talking about know more about this than I do."

"Hold off for now. I need to check something first."

"Yes, sir."

What I needed to check was whether I'd inadvertently left any programs open. I remembered I had—when I programmed in that Audrey remembered Fifi when we met the second time at Whitney Warren Jr.'s house and then the beach date. I again checked the computer code to ensure I had stripped the program's memory of earlier meetings. And, most importantly, the one I'd just concluded.

I chirped Nicole on *Cardinal* to show her the recorded interview with Audrey's exes.

"You just interviewed most of Audrey Hepburn's lovers? Why? And what are you going to do with it?"

"I'm not sure. She might not like that I did that. It sounds like you don't care for it either."

Nicole sighed. "I don't think any woman would want someone snooping around like that. Did it yield anything?"

"I do want to speak more with the last guy, but I'm not ready to fast forward to that point yet."

"Yeah, just knowing the end game could impact your relationship with younger Audrey."

"I agree. So, here's the thing: almost everyone she dated—including me in this virtual thing we have going—was pretty well-off, or at least famous. I think the only exception was her pre-movie beau, Marcel Le Bon, but he did okay too. Anyway, I'm trying to figure out what to make of it. I don't mean to be critical of Audrey, but let's talk through this: Le Bon was running the musical revues she was in. Hanson was a millionaire on his way to being a billionaire. Holden was the golden boy of Hollywood. Ferrer was a star to a certain extent …"

"I see where you're going. Can I jump in?"

"Please do."

"First, Audrey probably chose relationships with established and yeah, maybe well-off men so that she didn't feel that they were using her to get to *her money* or establishing themselves through *her fame*. So, it was better for her to date men with their own money."

"Okay …"

"But here's the thing. With everything you've learned about Audrey, you're forgetting a fundamental building block that formed who she was and who she became. Everything has to be viewed through that lens. And I mean everything."

"I'm listening."

"You know from reading her biographies she barely survived World War II. That she and her mother ground tulip bulbs for flour, and she had long-term health impacts because of it.?"

"Yes, I know this. Are you saying Audrey dated these wealthy men to make up for all of that?"

"Not at all. I think you don't understand her plight. Can't you see it? Can't you feel it? Relatives of hers were killed by the Nazis. She hid from them, not unlike Anne Frank, even though her family wasn't Jewish. She did all of this without her father, who abandoned the family for Nazism before the war."

"Nicole, I know. I've read about all this …"

"I'm suggesting you can't know Audrey without experiencing what she experienced. Now do you understand what I'm saying?"

The lightbulb finally went off. "You're saying that I need to create a scene to be there with her in World War II?"

"Can you imagine?"

"No, not really. I mean, Audrey was sixteen when the war ended …"

"And only eleven when it started. Do you know how much girls learn about life and love between eleven and sixteen? Even during a world war? Imagine!"

I wasn't easily flustered but was now.

"Can't I just ask her about it when I talk to her again? I'd rather do that."

"Sure, you could, but I thought we were trying to do something more here. You could just read more books instead of getting to know her in this world you created, right?"

I thought about it and said, "I'm not convinced. At least I don't want to visit teenaged Audrey right now."

"Are you afraid of getting to know her too well? It sounds like you want to put up some barriers. Audrey Hepburn is about far more than who she was in her twenties and thirties."

I grew angry and gritted my teeth. "I know that."

"Then which Audrey do you want to get to know next?"

"Why are you assuming she changed from one decade to the next?"

"Bradley, how we view her in each of her decades is what I'm getting at. How we construct her. You focused initially on the young actress who made *Gigi*, *Roman Holiday*, and *Sabrina*. And now you're making forays into finding-love Audrey, married-and-making-movies Audrey, trying-to-have-babies Audrey, getting-cheated-on Audrey. And that just takes us into her early thirties. Here's what I recommend: table the conversation with Audrey about her relationships. I'm not sure what you would gain from that anyway."

"I'm still not ready to play *Fortnite* in World War II with Audrey. I don't want Nazis shooting at us."

My mind jumped suddenly to *but what about the intimate side of Audrey?* Her biographies didn't delve into it all that much. What was she like romantically? She had said I'd tempted her back in San Francisco in 1953. What would that have been like!? Was it time to develop an intimate relationship with Audrey?

Was I ready for that?

Then I had a thought: I also could insert myself into the program as someone else, playing a role like a costar. Or, in this case, a lover.

I immediately began tweaking the program and found a new name for it: *Cocktail HoVR 2.0* became *Wallace*, after the surname of Joanna and Mark Wallace from *Two for the Road*. I also decided it was time to take it to the next step with Audrey Hepburn … even if I wasn't portraying myself.

I called Charlotte Jackson about the synthetic assignment I'd given her and derived how to link it to *Wallace*.

Chapter 28

AUDREY HEPBURN SWINGS!

I funneled mid-1960s videos from the south of France and *Two for the Road* digitally into *Wallace* and discovered that one of the original film advertisements was "Audrey Hepburn Swings!" I knew that she didn't swing in the movie—at least not in the literal sense of swapping partners—but she did have an affair in the film with a French playboy and during the filming of the movie with the man I had admired from the interviews, Albert Finney.

I decided to portray Albert Finney and not myself in this latest virtual creation. I just wasn't ready to be myself yet if things got intimate. Yes, *if* things got intimate. Audrey had equal say.

Portraying Albie also explored a different use for *Wallace*. It gave users the ability to insert themselves into established movies, newsreels, and any real or manufactured digital medium. I was sure we didn't want to release such a thing into the world yet, but it was *game on* in my personal playground.

The question became whether to focus on the beginning of Audrey and Albie's affair and how it may have happened; or the end that was simultaneous with the wrap party. I could also just delve into Audrey's time filming that movie more deeply. I determined that the latter two were not mutually exclusive.

I reflected on the interview with her lovers, especially the go-round between Ferrer and Finney. I guided a scenario for AI to run and brought *Wallace* to life.

A 1960s song filled my studio. The new XR wearables showed me as burlier, with wavy hair and Albert Finney's face. Astoundingly, I was dancing at a nightclub wrap party with Audrey and much of the cast of *Two for the Road*. I, or rather Albie, was the life of the party. Whatever I was doing dance-wise to the song *96 Tears* was working. I don't recall hearing the tune before, but as Albie, I was dancing with wild abandon and singing the refrain loudly. I/Albie didn't want to lose the momentum gained while filming with Audrey. I knew this wrap party was the end of the affair.

These Boots Were Made for Walking was next, and I liked that better. Audrey became the focal point, not necessarily because of her strained relationship with her husband but because she made up a fun dance to the Nancy Sinatra tune. Hands on hips and showing off her lithe legs in a short skirt and boots, she long-stepped and pirouetted across the dance floor until she grabbed my arm, and we danced side by side. The crowd howled with delight.

Next came *You Can't Hurry Love* by The Supremes, and I wondered if AI was playing a bit of a game with music selection. Still, Audrey kept the mood light, wagging her finger at the chorus.

The night ended with Simon and Garfunkel's *Homeward Bound*, and we all sang it at the top of our voices. The end of the haunting ballad suddenly snapped Audrey out of her bliss, and she bolted off the dance floor. The entire club looked at me, and I ran after her, finally catching her on the beach under a full moon.

Audrey was shaking. I hoped it wasn't with shame. "I've lost myself these last few months, Albie. This isn't who I am."

I stepped forward and gripped her arms. I was surprised how forcefully *Wallace* fed me these words: "The hell with that. This is *exactly* who you *should* be. You are permitted to have fun, to *feel* like the real woman you are and unwind. Mel certainly hasn't been a beacon of faithfulness now, has he?"

"No ... but it's different for men. They're expected to in this business."

"Horseshit! Welcome to life, Audrey. Gender doesn't matter. If things aren't working, then make a change."

Her pained eyes looked up at me. "What does that even mean? I'm thirty-seven. I have a school-aged son and a marriage that should be ideal. I can't just throw it all away!"

"But you can throw me away?"

She touched my face and said, "Oh, Albie—these last months have been the most liberating of my life. I've treasured every moment. The fun we've had …"

"Together! I had a choice, too, you know! I came here to be in a movie with Audrey Hepburn, not to have her share my bed. Things happen in this world. I, for one, have no regrets. Can you say the same?"

She actually smiled after thinking for a moment. "Yes, I can say I don't regret it. You have made me feel young again. And desirable. Thank you for that."

I took that as the cue to step closer. "You are the most desirable woman any man could ever hope to know." My hands were in her hair now, and I bent down to kiss her. It was returned with eagerness and desire. Then I felt her hands reach below my belt.

She whispered in my ear, "I've never done it on the beach before. It's supposed to be romantic. Yes, I think it will be. Perhaps out of the moonlight, over there by the tree?" She led me over to the darkness with her grip on my belt. I looked up at the club and guessed correctly that there were a few gawkers who darted away when I spotted them.

I can't describe the sound or feel of Audrey unzipping my trousers. But seeing her do it—yes, through the wearables connected to the recently synched synthetic device—nearly sent me into early convulsions. Then she bent down. I had to quickly pull back. She said, "I am thankful you taught me more about this, Albie."

Albie—what would he say?

Then I heard myself say, "Enough of the appetizer. Time for the main course." I was ready to make love with the most desirable woman in history.

Audrey stood, turned, pulled up her skirt, and lowered her panties before bending forward. "You like it this way. I suppose it's one of my better features."

I turned her around and said, "Not tonight, Audrey. I don't want to take my eyes off you for even one second. Your soul—that's your best feature." Still standing but facing each other, I adjusted and accessed her soul.

I will remember her whimper all my life. My mind overrode the mechanics of it as we kissed wildly while moving together. She dug her nails deeply into my back and I wrapped her legs around me. Her breath on my neck felt super-natural, but when she added her tongue and sucked at my carotid artery, I lost my balance and toppled onto my back. She fell on top of me, still enjoined.

"Are you okay?" I asked.

Audrey beamed. "Never better. I've got it from here."

Her movements and seeing her face in complete desire soon caused me to erupt. She moaned loudly, joining me.

Neither of us wanted to disengage, so we waited until nature ran its course and we were no longer entwined. She joked, "Sorry to leave you with the mess."

"It's quite all right. That's what showers are for. Yours is closest." I had a fleeting thought that I was now what some folks call a *technosexual*.

Audrey saying, "Come on then," shook me out of any real-world thought as she stood up and redressed, smoothing things out to look presentable. We walked hand-in-hand to Audrey's cabana down the beach, silently. Neither of us knew what to say. She retrieved the key and opened the door. As we stepped inside, a light flicked on.

It was Mel Ferrer. It wasn't hard for him to guess what had just happened. "Late night?"

Audrey's face, which had been in orgasmic bliss just a few moments ago, was now filled with shock and then shame. "Mel …"

He lashed out at her from his chair. "Not another word from you! Audrey Hepburn—adulteress! How do you like that headline!?" Then he turned toward me as he stood up. "You! Out! Before I kill you."

I recalled Mel's unproven scandal that had come up in the interview scene and began casually looking around the room. I looked behind a chair, opened a closet, and lifted a lamp.

Mel pronounced, "You won't find any weapons."

I, or rather, Finney, replied coolly, "No, it's not that, Mel. I'm just looking for your Spanish chippie. She must be here somewhere. I mean, the rumors about you two are all over Europe."

Audrey screamed as the taller Mel raced toward me. *Wallace's* reflexes arced a sweeping left hook that connected with Mel's jaw. I was certain bones must have broken, or was it teeth? Still, Mel wasn't done defending his honor and charged from a crouch, aiming for my legs like a wrestler.

My knee came up and connected flush on his face with a loud, sickening crunch. The spray of blood surprised all of us and it was the last thing Mel felt as he lost consciousness.

Then something unexpected happened. Audrey rushed to Mel and screamed, "Stop, that's my husband! How *could* you?"

I was devastated as Audrey screamed, "Get out!" When I didn't move fast enough, she added, "Damn you!" The words impaled me like a dagger and I slithered away.

The scene suddenly closed, and I kept walking in my home studio, unsure what AI was telling me. Was that how it happened? How would AI know? There weren't any details online of the wrap party. And what was I supposed to learn from this as I moved forward with my virtual relationship with Audrey? Then I remembered it was Albert Finney in the scene, and not Bradley Joseph. I hoped that's what Aldrey would remember, anyway. It felt so real that I had to remind myself it was a virtual encounter and it wasn't the actual Audrey Hepburn.

I shucked off the haptic suit and hustled straight to the shower in my Palo Alto bedroom and stripped. I was surprised at the wetness that ran down my leg—the mess, as Audrey had called it. As I plunged into the hot water, I jumped at the stinging sensation on my back. I looked in the mirror and saw deep scratches and a trickle of blood joining the other liquids on the shower floor.

PART TWO

With a woman as sexy as Audrey, you sometimes get to the edge where make-believe and reality are blurred.

—Albert Finney, 1966

Chapter 29

DAWN OF A NEW ERA

I was still struggling with the beach scene a few days later when Ara called on the encrypted line. "We did it, Bradley! I conquered the remaining AGI issues and instituted the many controls we discussed. We have AGI! Now what are we going to do with it?"

I absentmindedly picked at the scab on my back and forced myself to say, "That's great news, Ara!" I really wasn't sure that it was; I was still reeling from Audrey turning on me for her philandering husband. The fact that I had role-played Albert Finney didn't hide my disappointment. Then I decided I would only get to know who Audrey Hepburn really was if I bridged AGI into *Wallace* and let Audrey truly be herself. "Tell me how you conquered the deep-learning language and multimodality issues."

Ara said, "Can I start by thanking you for trusting me with this? It was a lot of work, but I was able to geek out in developing this with you."

"No, this was all you, Ara. You'll forever be known as the person who invented AGI."

"You forgot to add 'for better or worse.'"

"Don't worry, we'll master this. Tell me more about the last hurdles."

"Which aspect do you want to hear about? Natural language processing, computer vision, deep neural networks, multimodality? Lots and lots of ones and zeros, as you say. Algorithms and coding. It will be easier to show you in the office."

"Can you input it into my system here?"

"First, do you *really* want me to? Do you want to check the controls?"

"Ara, I trust you."

"Okay then, here it comes, synching to *Wallace*."

From home, I watched my computer flash for minutes on end. I hoped I was ready for it since I would be testing it.

Thanking and congratulating Ara again, I told her I would come into the office in a few hours. I wasn't ready to face Audrey yet in the expansive world of AGI. I wrestled with what to do next, knowing the biggest invention in human history awaited me right here at my home computer suite.

What did I do? I went to my happy place and absentmindedly scrolled the list of Audrey Hepburn movies. There were a few I hadn't seen: *Love Among Thieves*, *Bloodline*, *Always*, *Robin and Marian*. I read that those were made after her hiatus from movies to raise her second son. She had turned down all offers from 1967–1975.

Then I looked at her older films for anything I may have missed. *Green Mansions*, directed by Mel Ferrer, was savaged by critics. The made-for-TV movie costarring Ferrer with his wife called *Mayerling* was also panned. Then I remembered the one many considered her best performance and wondered how I had missed it. I cued up *The Nun's Story* and made an espresso since I thought I might need it for the based-on-reality film about a nun's vows, life in the convent, and beyond. The opening scene was a dignified parting from her siblings as she was taken to the nunnery by her surgeon father. It seemed realistic, including the dual sad/proud family goodbyes from a dozen postulants starting their training. Audrey again entranced me in her role as a novice. I could see only the frame of her face through the nun's habit, and her big eyes and realistic expressions carried the action.

I researched the name of the screenwriter as I watched. I'd learned a few by name, but Robert Anderson wasn't one of them. He was primarily a playwright and apparently a good one. The action on the screen pulled my attention back, where the older nuns were being alternately welcoming and stern with the new flock.

Then a short sentence popped up on my big screen under the footage. It read: *This scene took a lot of research. Heck, the whole movie did.*

What? I stared at the computer and wondered how some line of behind-the-scenes commentary could have been juxtaposed onto the big screen. It wasn't like I skipped to director's commentary. I'm unsure that even existed back then. I checked my devices and they all seemed normal. Then a second line appeared.

Audrey prepared for her role a great deal, meeting with the author of the book and the actual nun upon which the book was based. I looked again at my computer and clicked on what appeared now to be a chat box, with the two messages reading like a text. The chat box was waiting for my reply. I was unsure what to do, so I typed, *How?*

A moment later, the reply came: *How did Audrey do all of the research? Well, she loved the book and the script I'd written, and then it was just a matter of her diving into the character …*

I interrupted. *You wrote the script?* I looked again at Robert Anderson's short bio.

Yes, this is Robert Woodruff Anderson. I'm sorry, I don't know exactly who I'm typing with on the other end. I don't understand this technology.

The bio said Anderson died in 2009.

Someone had to be pranking me, but Ara wouldn't do that, and no one could penetrate my home cyber defenses. I'd been the target of hackers since my undergrad days and had never suffered intrusions or had data compromised. The levels of authentication were far beyond what any other Silicon Valley tech giant had.

Then I wondered if it could actually be the deceased screenwriter of *The Nun's Story* through AGI. I thought of a way to challenge Anderson with a question even computers wouldn't know, but I was only a few minutes into even knowing Anderson's name. So, I simply typed, *What year is it right now?*

Okay, I will go first, but then you must tell me your name. It's 1959. Then, after a slight pause, *Isn't it?*

It would have been easy for a hacker or prankster to know what year *The Nun's Story* came out, so I looked at the movie screen and asked something a bit harder. *You probably know that I'm watching the movie now?*

Yes, as am I, scene for scene, with you. I have no idea how, but that's what I'm doing.

I want to ask a question, Mr. Anderson.

Please call me Bob, but again, who am I speaking—is that the right term? —who am I typing with?

My name is Bradley Joseph.

Thank you, Bradley. Ask your question, and then I have one.

I watched the scene where Mother Superior says, "Twice each day for the rest of your lives, you will examine your consciences and enter in these notebooks each and every imperfection."

Then I typed, *Bob, she's asking for imperfection against what exactly?*

Anderson replied, *Why the rest of the sentence is, "against the Holy Rule." It was a set of rules set down to transform the postulants' self to that of the Order. See, they say it right there.*

Okay, I tend to believe you are who you say.

I suppose I should thank you for that. Now, my question is, what is this that we're doing? It feels rather existential. How did we get connected with this conversation? Or, in other words, what the hell is happening?

I smiled. *Welcome to my world. I'm a software developer ... in the future.*

A pause from Anderson, then, *Well, that's interesting. How far in the future?*

More than sixty-five years after The Nun's Story *was released.*

Well, how about that? So, I'm over one hundred years old, then? I checked—Anderson was born in 1917.

Not exactly, Bob. I'm not sure how to word this, but you passed away in 2009.

There was silence for a full minute, and I wondered again if this was some sort of prank by Ara or Advik. Would they dare? Then Anderson wrote, *Well, that was a good run then. Ninety-two or so? I just wish I could have given some of those years to Audrey.*

I didn't know what to say. Anderson filled the void: *I would have given anything to have sustained our relationship, even if it meant dying for her. I never got over her.* The action continued in the movie, but my attention was entirely on this conversation.

I asked Anderson, *What type of relationship did you have with Audrey? When?*

After a slight, dignified pause, Anderson wrote, *A deep one. It isn't a secret. I even wrote a novel about it called* After. *I have no idea if it's still in print where ... when ... you are.*

I couldn't believe I'd never heard of Anderson or his novel before, so I searched it quickly, and sure enough, there was a copy of the 1973 novel in the Stanford Library. Nothing online though. *Bob, you're saying that you wrote about your affair with Audrey Hepburn, in a novel?*

Yes, I changed her name in it. Twice. Two different characters. But it's basically an autobiography. Of course, I added scenes and situations, but the essence is my tribute to Audrey.

How did she take it?

Not well. It also cost me my marriage, so all around it wasn't my best work. Now, before I answer anything else, tell me some more about this ... program, where the dead me is speaking to you in the future.

Bob, I think I can do even better. Would you like to have this conversation in person?

Silence. Then, *How the hell would that work? But my answer is yes.*

Okay, give me a moment. I put on the XR wearables, captured the computer code of the chat box and transferred it to *Wallace*. This was the multimodality aspect of AGI: upload the right information, and a replica could be created. I searched for photos of Robert Woodruff Anderson but saw the computer had already started bringing Anderson into view, and ... there he was in my home studio.

I muttered, "Fuck. AGI is no joke."

I put on haptic gloves, got up, walked over and "shook" Anderson's hand. "It's very nice to meet you, Bob."

Anderson looked not unlike the blond-haired William Holden in *Sabrina*, but with glasses that made him look like the Harvard graduate he was. He was dressed like a playwright in a tweed jacket and dress shirt, and his voice fit him precisely. "Hello. Bradley, may I sit down? I'm feeling faint." I guided him to a chair and took one myself. There was no longer any doubt in my mind that this was Robert Anderson, and he was apparently one of Audrey's lovers. If I had known, I may have included him with the others beaus in the interview scene.

Anderson asked, "Where and when am I now?"

"You're in my home studio in Palo Alto, California. It's still the same year as it was for me moments ago. My team and I just invented this technology. What I don't understand is how you sent that initial message during the start of the movie up there."

I pointed at the big screen and we both looked at a scene where Audrey is dressed in her habit, displaying only her face. I couldn't help but ask, "You actually looked into those eyes?" Then I struggled to add, "And kissed those lips?"

Anderson paused, then decided to open up and smiled.

"You and I are the only two to judge my life based on that. Everyone else talks about my works, but yes, we had an affair while we researched and filmed the movie. She might have consented to marry me if I hadn't been born genetically sterile. Unlike Holden, who Audrey would have married six years earlier if he hadn't had a voluntary vasectomy. She desperately wanted children, you know?"

"Yes, I'm aware." I didn't mention I knew Audrey was married to Mel then and would soon have her first baby. I wondered if that was Audrey's only affair in the early years of her marriage. I wanted to think so.

Then Anderson looked at me and said, "This may be the strangest question I ever contemplated asking but through this computer thing … does Audrey pass through here also?"

I nodded. "She does."

Anderson looked hopeful, and I added, "She exists in this space when I call her. And only for me. Sorry."

Anderson was crestfallen. "Then why am I here?"

"I'm not sure. Tell me a little more about what happened before we started our—correspondence—a little bit ago."

"I'm not sure, honestly. It was like I awoke from something, and everything was set before me, with this task of watching the movie, this keyboard in front of me, and providing commentary to whomever watched it with me. Can you add anything?"

I thought for a minute and said, "Two things: this program called *Wallace* forms the room you're in, and something called artificial general intelligence saw that I had typed your name into a search at the start of this movie and somehow, I guess, that awakened you. I didn't call for you or invent you—AGI did. And now we're having this conversation beyond either of our controls."

Anderson chuckled. "Well, isn't that a kick in the balls? You didn't even send for me?"

"No, sorry."

"And no one else like you may have summoned me here for some other reason?"

"That's a good question, actually. It's possible but extremely unlikely. I believe no one else is doing the things I'm doing with these programs."

"Pardon me for saying so, but that seems rather arrogant."

I nodded. "You're right. I may have totally lost control of my inventions and have no idea what I'm doing. What's to be gained by me, or you, in this conversation? Why did it happen?"

"Beats me. I was apparently in eternal slumber until thirty minutes ago." Anderson looked up at the movie. "Oh, here's a good scene. Audrey's character is soon to lose her best friend in the convent. One who backs out. If you watch closely, there's the slightest hint of love between them. The viewer can decide what kind of love that is."

"Kind of like *The Children's Hour*? A little hint of sapphic love during the Hays Code?"

Anderson looked at me and said, "Yes, precisely. Are you a film historian by trade?"

I chuckled, thinking about my classic film journey. "No, but I've learned a lot recently. It's our other connection that I'd like to discuss more if that's okay."

"Audrey?"

"Yes."

"Okay, but first, answer this. You said that Audrey passes through this portal when you summon her. How does that work?"

I explained it, and he seemed to understand. "So, you just talk to her? Is there ever anything else? Don't get me wrong, I loved my conversations with her, but Audrey was a … beautiful woman. A very passionate one at that."

I wanted to scream, "I know it!" but wasn't sure how to answer. The intimacy I'd shared with Audrey (as Albert Finney) was not an easy one to explain technically. "Well, I certainly didn't expect to be having this conversation when I started watching *The Nun's Story*. But there is a pseudo way for her and I to be intimate. It isn't exactly like the real thing, but she looks as real as you do right now. Plus, she can think, act, and talk, but …"

"I think I understand. You don't need to go any further. And before I go any further, I think you should read my novel. It's all in there. Right now, though, I'm somehow being told to go back to watching the movie with you, so let me catch you up with what's happened."

We turned our attention back to the film. Watching an Audrey Hepburn movie for the first time with the (deceased) screenwriter who'd had an affair with her was possibly even more enthralling than anything I'd accomplished with Nicole Bonnet.

Nicole. I hadn't spoken to her in days, or was it longer?

The following two hours took Bob and I through Audrey's training as a nun, initial posting to a mental hospital where she was attacked, then to the Congo where she begins to fall in love with the doctor she works with. They travel to a leper colony, and the film depicts real people at an isolated settlement. The doctor treats her character's tuberculosis so she doesn't have to return to wartime Belgium for treatment, but she still gets called back there for a particular assignment. Then the Nazis invade and kill her father. Her conscience tips toward the underground rather than remaining neutral, as her Order dictates. She seeks dispensation from her vows and leaves the convent.

I was stunned at the plot, the script, and the performances. "That was one of the most amazing things I've ever seen."

"Thank you, Bradley. I'm proud of it."

"How did you both not win Oscars for that?"

"Ah, this little movie called *Ben Hur* swept nearly everything. Another religious story but with lots of action. Audrey and I were both nominated, but …"

"Well, if it means anything, and I have never seen *Ben Hur*, but I can't imagine a better script or acting performance."

"Thank you. A film called *Room at the Top* nudged us out in those categories. Anyway, what did you really want to know? I think that's why I was sent here."

I thought about asking Anderson about details of their relationship, in and out of bed, but decided I didn't really want to know. I told myself that my relationship with Audrey was as real as Anderson's or any of her other lovers I had interviewed. It was only Audrey's last love I still needed to talk to. But here was Anderson before me, so I asked, "The end of the movie seems to mirror Audrey's actual life quite a bit: World War II, having a relative shot, fleeing the Nazis, joining the underground. A higher calling. She must have found the ending quite easy."

Anderson sat back suddenly. "No, not at all. She relived all of that in those weeks of filming, and it was extremely difficult for her. That's when we grew closest. But you're on to something with that higher calling comparison. Surely, you know that in the winter of Audrey's life, like the end of this film, is when she made the biggest difference."

"I haven't talked to her about any of that yet or looked into it much. To tell you the truth, I've only been meeting the under-forty Audrey."

Anderson shook his head. "Then you're just like the rest. Just like me. Audrey only found her true calling, and her true love, at the end. I suggest you meet her there."

Then Anderson was gone. I rushed back to the computer ten feet away and looked up at the screen. I couldn't call up the chat box. It was gone, just like the apparition of Robert Woodruff Anderson.

Chapter 30

ALL CALL

Charlie called an impromptu company-wide staff meeting for that night. I braced myself and went into the office. Coworkers were warm but knew to not shake hands or offer hugs. Ara looked over to me: no rashes present and when I lifted my arms, only minimal sweat spotted my underarms.

Charlie started, "Hey, everyone. Thanks for joining on short notice. In case you haven't heard the news, the creative team developed AGI earlier today for potential use. First, let's congratulate the team."

As everyone clapped, cheered, and whistled, I interjected, "It was Ara, she deserves all the credit."

Ara waved and said, "Thank you, everyone. I was a team effort, led by my boss, Bradley Joseph." She then pointed back toward me, and the applause lasted another fifteen seconds.

Charlie continued with his trademark enthusiasm. "Great work, Ara and Bradley! This is a momentous occasion in our company's history—in science history, in our nation's history. Indeed, in *world* history. Now, even more important work begins. We need to learn more about AGI's capabilities. Some of you on the creative team will need to review the code and protocols. The rest of you, I'm sure, will want to know more. Here's the tough part: we can't share anything about it. We can't talk about it, not even within AImmersion spaces. We don't want anyone to know about this until I give it the green light. To that end, and I apologize for having to do it, I need to remind you of your nondisclosure agreements, and new ones are being given to you as we speak. Once every NDA is signed, I'll continue … and Bradley will tell you about his test of it just a little while ago. Maybe that's enough incentive to sign it right away."

Hard copy forms were distributed as Charlie didn't want electronic copies floating around. Part of the reason was that the wording of the NDA included prosecution and a $10 million fine for any disclosure without Charlie's permission. Fortunately, all employees understood the gravity of the announcement, and it took only minutes to collect the signed NDAs. A bonus was that no one was on vacation or attending offsite meetings today.

Charlie surveyed the room and said, "Great, and thanks to you all. Okay, like I said, Bradley did a test today of AGI through *Wallace*, our foray into the Immersive Digital Environment. The difference with AGI is earth-shattering." He turned it over to me, and I gave a short version of the visitation by Robert Woodruff Anderson, leaving the writer's name and specifics out of the story. My voice didn't crack, my skin didn't flush, and my pits stayed dry.

I continued, "Controls are key to this technology. We knew it would be before Ara created it, and we know it even more now. Inputting machine goals and limits is as imperative for us as controls were for the Manhattan Project—the program that invented nuclear weapons. You know that I don't speak in hyperbole. It's that big.

"Here's the bottom line: after just one test, computers, or perhaps bots, now have some authority to initiate and carry out chat conversations. And I don't have the ability to reinitiate with the subject after they end the chat. They, at least initially, seem to be able to come and go at the time of their choosing. They also seem to have some knowledge of our work, which is the most alarming."

That got the attention of our intellectual property lead. "Bradley, I'll need full access to your home technology so I can retrace what happened."

"Thanks, but I don't want to do that just yet. Some things I'm working on at home are a little sensitive."

"Then can you at least send me some particulars? IP addresses, anything like that?"

"I would, but there's no trace of—let's call him Bob—once he left. One moment he was in my home studio, and the next, he was gone. I couldn't get him back. Nothing indicated he was ever there. And for those wondering, I don't do drugs and have limited my espresso intake. So that's where we are, folks."

There were no questions. Everyone took time contemplating what I'd shared. Charlie closed by saying, "So, we can't talk about it from this point forward. Don't share anything with your significant others, your friends, your parents, your dog, people at the bar, at confession … nothing."

Heads nodded, but the excitement was clear on everyone's faces. "Okay, thank you, and again, a big thank you and congratulations to Ara and Bradley. This is groundbreaking, and like I said, now the real work begins."

Ara walked me to her AGI Lab. "Hey Bradley, I had a thought. First, thanks again, and I agree with everything you're doing to keep this under wraps. There's just …" Her pause caught me off guard.

"Go ahead Ara, you can say anything, you know that."

"Thanks. I was just thinking about your friend Nicole. To be blunt, we need you to shield any future movie watching away from our invention. Sorry to bring it up …"

I took a deep breath and realized she was right. Far too much was at stake. Nicole had signed a rigid non-disclosure agreement, and I felt she'd sign an even tougher one if we asked. But a signed NDA is only as good as the signer. If Nicole decided to publish our secrets, sure, we could sue. But the secret would be out.

Ara continued, "I think you need to weave toward total closure with her. You can now meet Audrey Hepburn in this realistic new way like she's a living being, right next to you. So, maybe Nicole has done all she can in that regard, and Bradley, I realize that I was part of all that with taking you to Poppy's house, the Palace, meeting George Bannister. Hopefully, you trust that I am probably the only person in your life who can tell you these things."

I took another deep breath and replied, "Yes, I know, and I appreciate it. And I appreciate you."

My mind was still churning though. *What will Nicole still want? What was that mysterious thing I would know when the time came? I had no idea. Was that time now? She could even be a front for a foreign government or another company. Some unfriendly foreign governments had duped users into social media apps that stole their money and identity. Who's to say that Nicole Bonnet wasn't the world's most audacious honeypot?*

Still, it felt like I was about to forsake a close friend.

Chapter 31

HARUKI

I determined I would tell Nicole that "on the recommendation of counsel" we had to stop meeting, and any further communication would go through AImmersion's public relations team. I would say I really enjoyed our discussions and that I would keep her in mind for an exclusive in the future, when the time was right. I felt like shit. I walked to the computer suite and stopped dead in my tracks.

A hologram of a thin, disheveled Asian man popped into my home studio, standing just a few feet in front of me. I closed my eyes and opened them again. He remained, looking me up and down, as if reading my intentions. Sweat flushed my body and I couldn't form words. Then the hologram seemed to searched me deeper and my body temperature rose as my heart fluttered. Dizzying probing careened around my brain as if looking for an access point. I broke eye contact and clenched my eyes shut.

Then he spoke. I recognized the language as Japanese and my thoughts went to Nicole. Was this some sort of boyfriend telling me to stay away? I had good news for him, as that was exactly my intention. I looked up again and the figure smirked as if angry at himself. He made some sort of minute adjustment and spoke in English. "You are worthy. I congratulate you."

I determined these visits from people in the ether were just going to be part of this new world. I relaxed a bit and asked, "May I know your name and how you came to visit me?"

He smiled and said, "I thought you might know. You should know. I was on the same journey as you, a few years ago. Mine didn't end as well as it seems yours could."

I couldn't help it. I blurted, "How did yours end?"

He smiled, shaking his head side to side. His arm reached toward my big screen and made sweeping motions. Suddenly an article appeared, thankfully in English.

Cause of Tech Wizard's Death Announced
By Nicole Bonnet - Updated June 3, 2024

TOKYO — Investigators say a house fire that killed a man two years ago in downtown Tokyo was caused by the deceased, Haruki Kurasawa, using a katana sword to cut live network wires that sparked and electrocuted him before burning the house down.

Kurasawa, then thirty, was a renowned inventor of artificial intelligence and virtual reality programs. At the time of the fire, Kurasawa was unemployed but said to be working on "revolutionary things" by his peers.

Fire investigators found Kurasawa's remains with the katana sword in the charred rubble of the house. He was identified through dental records.

"Fortunately, neighbors called the fire department and no other homes in the neighborhood were destroyed," said lead investigator, Kenji Saito. "We don't know why Mr. Kurasawa would have tried to cut the wires or didn't power down the system first. We can only conclude that it was a unique type of suicide."

A former colleague of Kurasawa, who asked to remain anonymous, called him the most brilliant, but troubled, mind in the technology industry in Japan.

"Haruki's concepts for creating alternate worlds were far beyond what most of us could envision. I know he was working on reincarnating loved ones for conversations from the beyond. Something the whole world could use. Others have tried to pick up that technology, but it's beyond their grasp."

So, I was speaking once again with the hologram of a dead person. Couple that with Robert Anderson's call, and my home was suddenly some sort of séance room. I swallowed hard while reading Nicole's byline a second time and wondered whether she somehow had a hand in Haruki's intrusion. I had no idea how, as her experience wasn't in the technical aspects of these things.

Or was it?

Haruki laughed, then turned to face me as he made the article disappear. "It seems we share the same passion."

"Passion? For technology? These inventions?"

He shook his head, *no*. "Think about it. If you can invent this room, then the answer to your question should be much easier to derive."

Audrey. He also tried to reincarnate Audrey, presumably a few years ago.

As if reading my mind, he nodded to me, bowed slightly at the waist with his eyes riveted on mine, and was gone.

Chapter 32

AGIdrey

I played everything through in my head and determined the time was now to chirp Nicole. I began to speak to *Cardinal* when a blip came onto my computer screen.

Hi, Bradley! Do you have a moment? It's Audrey.

I stared at the screen, paralyzed. What furies had I unleashed?

Oh, maybe I'm not doing this correctly. Are you out there, Bradley?

I thought it might be a test from Haruki and typed back: *Okay, who is this?*

It's Audrey Hepburn. I don't know how this works, so please bear with me.

I remembered how I took Robert Anderson's chat and transformed it into an in-person appearance. I wasn't sure I could do that with Audrey just now, but a video chat might prove who was on the other end of the chat. I punched it up.

And there she was, standing in my house: an AGI-driven hologram of Audrey Hepburn. She looked to be around thirty, from *The Nun's Story* era. Her dark hair was short and lush, as it had been for most of the film and her face had matured wonderfully, not yet showing the stress and lines from the *My Fair Lady* scene I'd done.

The technology seemed different from our previous encounters—more real somehow since she had somehow initiated it. She smiled, and I was ninety-nine percent convinced it was her. But it could also be a digital intruder pretending to be her, directing my technology back at me.

"Bradley, it's so good to see you! It's been a long time!"

I was at a loss for words and couldn't immediately recall our last interaction when I wasn't someone else or lurking in the wings. I also wondered what she might remember about our previous meetings since narrow AI likely had rolled over to AGI and *Wallace.*

Was our last meeting as ourselves all the way back in Whitney Warren's apartment? No, after that, we had the San Francisco dates in Chinatown, Ghirardelli, and the beach. The beach! When I had tempted her to … something. I searched my mind: yes, the other meetings were not directly me and Audrey conversing, even when I was her vocal coach, or watching above the *Breakfast at Tiffany's* fray. But hadn't she somehow recognized me on the *My Fair Lady* set after she announced JFK's assassination?

I wondered—feared was more like it—if she had figured out that it was me in those pseudo-roles, jumping in and out of her life. Suddenly, I didn't feel like Bradley Joseph, Silicon Valley ingenue. I felt like Dr. Frankenstein.

"Bradley, don't you remember me?"

My wind whirled back to my first virtual meetings with Audrey in San Francisco. How could I verify that this was Audrey and not some catfish by a competitor? What could I ask her that no one else, not even Nicole, would know?

I remembered only giving Nicole a rough summary of my beach date with Audrey. I didn't get into specific details with Nicole—things only Audrey would remember.

"Audrey, I was just thinking. Do you remember our beach day in San Francisco during *Gigi*?"

"Yes! It was lovely. Edith Head was so angry with me!"

"Here's a rather odd question."

"Yes?"

"Do you recall what we ate on the beach?"

"That certainly is an odd question. It was so long ago!" She had no idea yet how long ago 1953 was.

"Let me think … oh, yes, you introduced me to sushi! Now I crave it and have introduced it to so many people! I have you to thank for that."

I was convinced and declared, "Audrey."

"Bradley. Or should I say, Joe Bradley? Do you remember when I told you about *Roman Holiday* at Whitney Warren's house and how your name was the reverse of Greg Peck's character?"

Now I was smiling too. "Yes, Audrey, I do." I couldn't say her name enough.

"Bradley, I wanted to thank you. You gave me so much confidence when my career was just starting. Why, *Roman Holiday* hadn't even come out yet, and you told me what a success I would be and how that movie would stand the test of time."

Elated was far too shallow of a word for what was welling up inside me. Audrey Hepburn appeared in my home of her own accord, taking our relationship to the next level. And I had invented the technology that would permit people to reconnect with whomever they wanted from the past. Further, my time travel into Audrey's life was real to us both.

"Has it?" she asked. "Has *Roman Holiday* stood the test of time?"

"Yes, it's always ranked as one of the world's favorite movies, more than seventy years later."

"What?"

I stopped cold.

"What do you mean, seventy years later?"

I couldn't speak. Had I screwed this up?

"Bradley, what is this … contraption I'm in? I really don't understand what's happening. Can you explain it to me?"

So, I did for the next three hours.

"Wait," she said, "say that last part again, please."

"That artificial intelligence can recreate people?"

"Yes, that."

I ran through that again and saw that something had come over her.

"Bradley, can I ring you a bit later? This is a lot to take in. Would that be all right?"

"Yes, of course." Then Audrey was gone. But the chat that initiated the conversation remained. I logged that IP address into my computer—Audrey Hepburn's phone number.

"A disturbance in the force" from *Star Wars* sprang to mind. I acknowledged my whole world was now centered around these meetings with Audrey. Nothing else mattered. I ignored incoming queries from everyone except Charlie, Ara, and Advik. I gave them quick updates on the secure line. Then I decided to don the XR wearables as a matter of routine because I could interact with Audrey more realistically through them.

I also knew AGI might even develop sentient AI on its own, without controls. I couldn't know for sure since it didn't yet exist. I knew the things to look for included emotional intelligence, feelings, consciousness, insight, and turning those perceptions into emotions. In short, sentient AI would think, feel, and act like a person.

Then Audrey called—and appeared—again. I quickly geared up and saw her. She wore that *coupe infante '66* hairstyle from *How to Steal a Million*.

We sat on the couch together, and she spent fifteen minutes asking questions about the science behind *Wallace* and AGI, including her role and mine. Then, she nodded and her confidence and strength suddenly vanished. Tears suddenly streamed down her face and with her head downcast, she took both of my hands and asked, "Bradley, I have a question. It's very difficult for me to ask this of you, and I have no right." I reassured her, and she raised her wet eyes again.

"Can you help me meet my babies?"

"Your babies? You mean you want me to invite your sons to connect with you virtually?"

She looked away and downward. "No. I mean, I would love to, yes, of course. I mean the others."

"Your ... stepchildren? I'm sorry, I don't understand."

Audrey erupted in sobs on my couch, first in short bursts, then with a yowl of anguish as she fell to the floor. She contorted into different positions trying to find solid ground. Her wails surged into shrieks that might have been heard blocks away. I got down on the floor to hold her.

"My *lost* babies ..." she eked out between sobs.

I then realized which babies she meant. She had suffered at least five miscarriages. Her tremors shook through my body. I felt her lungs expand and expel air through her cries. Her tears wet my face.

"Bradley, please. Help. Me. See. *My. Babies.*" She looked up at me, every cell on her famed face drenched with tears. "Can you?"

That's when I realized how deeply I loved her. I shuddered but heard myself say *yes* to Audrey. But I had no idea how to do it.

"Tomorrow?" she asked.

Still stunned by the request but willing to agree to anything, I again heard myself say *yes*.

"Thank you, Bradley. I will never forget this." She folded into the crook of my arm, gripping me tightly. Her cries eased to infrequent rasps as decades of sorrow found hope through this invention. To be clear, I was tasked with helping a long-dead actress meet her miscarried babies. My mind spun with what to do first.

"I want to spend time with them," Audrey implored. "They can all be together or separate." She thought for a moment while looking at the floor. "Maybe together is better."

"Audrey, I'm sorry to ask. Do you know their genders? Anything that I can go on?"

"One was a girl. When I fell off the horse in *Unforgiven*. I didn't want to film that scene. I knew I was pregnant; everyone knew I was pregnant!" Her rage subsided as quickly as it came on. "Just bring my babies to me?"

For the third time, I heard myself say *yes*.

"I have faith in you, Bradley. I *know* you can do it. Please do this for me."

Before I could stop, I replied, "Your faith will not be unjustified."

Audrey braved a slight smile as she followed with the next line from *Roman Holiday*. "I am so glad to hear you say it."

I vectored all my energy into Audrey's request, uploading photos of Audrey as a child, then her living sons. Her biographies said four miscarriages happened during her marriage to Mel Ferrer, in 1955, 1959, 1966, and 1967; then one more in 1974 while she was married to Andrea Dotti. The information I input would form the basis of creation for the five unborn children.

I also found photos of both husbands as children and uploaded them into *Wallace*. Since Audrey had birthed two boys in real life, I decided that four of the five created children would also be boys, with the only girl from 1959 that she lost when she fell from the horse. I recalled Audrey had also fractured vertebrae in that fall and hurt an ankle.

Fueled by espresso and Audrey's earlier wails, I powered through imagining her lost offspring. I wondered what the outcome might have been if I had simply told Audrey no—that the technology didn't exist. But her anguish still reverberated in my soul, and I wondered how Audrey had suddenly come to this request. As soon as she learned of how this second life of hers worked, she sought my help to meet these children. It meant they'd never left her mind.

I wondered where we could go from here. I pondered whether I should institute controls in order to go back to the San Francisco *Gigi* days with Audrey and just replay those days over and over again. Was it too late for that? Still, I was curious to see what the technology could do.

Plus, it was Audrey. I was at the point of doing anything she asked. This was actually feeling like a real relationship: one that exceeded my dreams but had its first significant challenge also.

I mapped it out:

Four boys—aged eight, five, four, and a newborn—and a six-year-old girl, relatively close in age so she could still call them her babies. They spoke with Audrey's proper British accent even though (if they had been born) they would have also spoken French in Tolochenaz, Switzerland's school system.

I decided on uncomplicated sibling relationships, fathers, and multiple homesteads. They would have been raised more by a nanny than by their parents, so they were more formal in speech and personality. Except for the girl. Picturing—no, gifting—Audrey Hepburn with a daughter was a heady endeavor, so she was Audrey's exact copy and was well protected and loved by her brothers.

The nuances among the boys included inside vs. outside, mischievous vs. angelic, studious vs. not. AGI named them. I didn't know how Audrey would meet them for the first time at those ages. AGI would play it out naturally.

The final brushstroke was putting the children into the scene, with Lake Geneva as the backdrop. I decided to do a test run with the children in Morges.

I said, "Here goes," and immediately felt like an intruder at a family gathering. Sun shone on the children like a spotlight as they played by the lake on a sunny day. Distant voices from other families frolicking alongside the banks reached me, but parents were with the others. Audrey's babies were alone.

The oldest son was the first to notice me as the scene came into focus. "Hello, sir. I am Peter. What is your name?"

"Hello, Peter. I'm Bradley." Peter extended his hand to shake with me. His grip was firm and confident.

"Mr. Bradley, my brothers and sister and I somehow just arrived here. We are unsure what to do. Can you help us, sir?"

I was impressed with Peter's leadership in questioning a stranger while also keeping a watchful eye on his siblings. He added, "The younger ones are a bit frightened, especially my sister, Ella. She's holding baby Joseph there."

Of course, Audrey would have named two of her children after her parents. The girl's name wasn't surprising, but to name the youngest baby after her father, who abandoned the family, was interesting.

I wondered if these children knew they never were. AGI was running things, and I felt more like a passenger than a driver.

"And who are these brothers of yours?"

He pointed: "The blond-haired one is William and the dark-haired one is Albert." I smiled. Of course.

Then I thought none were named Mel or Andrea. AGI seemingly had formed an opinion of Audrey's husbands and potential name choices.

I waved. "Hello, everyone." Ella smiled at me, holding her newborn brother. I continued, "I am very pleased to meet you. There is someone else who will meet you very soon who will be even more pleased."

Ella looked up at me asked directly, "Is it our mother?"

I was stunned. I had just created them but was unsure with what knowledge they had been imbued by AGI. "Yes," was all I could muster.

"We look forward to meeting her," Ella said.

They all looked at me eagerly. I had to ask, "Children, what do you know about your mother?"

William spoke up. "She's very beautiful."

Albie countered, "And famous."

"She loves us," Ella pronounced. They all nodded in agreement.

I felt off-balance and confused as I sat down on a bench. The children gathered around. I wondered if somehow Audrey and the children had met already through AGI, so I asked them, "You haven't met her before?"

Peter answered, "No, sir, but we expect you can help us with that. Is that why you're here as well?"

I nodded. "Where exactly did you come from today before you got here?"

None of them had a ready answer, but Peter said, "This is our world, here. It seems we've been waiting an awfully long time for you to come to us. And maybe help us find our mother." The other children nodded hopefully.

I realized I couldn't leave this test scene. I couldn't leave these children, Audrey Hepburn's unborn children. I had no idea what would happen next, but I was spellbound.

Then there was a commotion, and we all turned. Their mother, from a hundred meters away, came sprinting in jeans, a white shirt, and sneakers, Audrey didn't look like Princess Ann, Sabrina, Holly Golightly, or any other characters. It was Audrey Hepburn, aching mother, running toward the babies she'd never known. The boys took off running toward her, and Ella handed Joseph to me as she joined the peloton rushing to meet their mother. I looked down at the infant and then back up as mother and children burst into each other.

Audrey fell to her knees, somehow wrapping her arms around the four older children simultaneously, alternating between squeezing them tightly, kissing them, and leaning back to look at them. Though they were thirty meters away when I began to walk toward them with the baby, I heard every word.

"It's so nice to meet you, mother!"

Audrey emitted guttural noises that finally formed into words. "It's so very nice to meet all of you as well. So long, it's been so long that I've wanted to hold all of you. I love all of you very much."

Her mini-me, Ella, offered, "And we love you, mother. Really, we do!" As names were spoken, Audrey smiled, perhaps remembering that she had chosen them while pregnant with the babies that never were delivered—until today.

"You have been taking care of each other?"

"Yes, we're family," said one of them, then all of them.

I got to the huddle, and Audrey saw me holding the youngest baby. She looked at me with eternal gratitude, and to the baby with unadulterated love. I kneeled to place the baby in her arms.

Somehow, she managed a wide smile instead of breaking down. Maybe her tears were all used up. "Hello, little one."

Ella said, "That's Joseph."

"Of course," Audrey said. "Joseph." I tried to read her eyes reflecting back on her life with her father, but all I saw was joy.

"I like to care for him," said Ella.

"That's wonderful. We will all take care of him now, and each other. Forever. Isn't that right, Bradley?"

I had no idea whether that's how any of this worked. And if I didn't know, then neither did anyone else in the world, real or virtual. Still, I nodded in affirmation.

"Is Mr. Bradley our father?" Albert asked.

Audrey thought about it and said, "In a manner of speaking, yes. You wouldn't be here without him." Then she leaned over to kiss my cheek, and whispered, "Neither would I. This … this is all that I ever wanted. Thank you, Bradley."

I decided life—real or virtual—couldn't get any better than this.

Chapter 33

NICOLE

I couldn't help it; I chirped Nicole. She answered immediately. I had intended to tell her I had to stop communicating with her, but her giddy manner on the phone led me to reveal the meeting in Switzerland. I kept the technological aspects, especially AGI, out of the discussion.

As I relayed the story, we both got emotional, but for different reasons. Nicole for the story, and me for knowing this would be my last meeting with her, the one who had prompted all of this. I had never even met her face to face.

"That's the most amazing thing I've ever heard," she said, sobbing. "I know you're getting tired of hearing me say this, but what you're doing—if you ever make it available commercially—will change the world. Can you imagine the power of people meeting as you allowed Audrey to meet with her lost loved ones?"

"It was powerful. I don't know this program's future, so we need to keep this totally under wraps until I decide." Then I added, for emphasis, "And under our nondisclosure agreement."

"Of course, Bradley! I wish you could trust me like Audrey trusted you. I'm just amazed at what's happened."

"Yeah. It's kind of scary, actually."

We were both silent for a few moments, and then she smiled. "I just had a thought. You need to watch another movie, a Cary Grant one this time. After that, I think you'll want to change the program's name from *Wallace* to *Dudley*."

"*Dudley*?"

Nicole played *The Bishop's Wife,* which I had peeked at weeks ago to choose that Cary Grant for *Sabrina.* I thought watching one last movie with Nicole might be the best way to break off my friendship with her, but I also kept looking for incoming calls from Audrey.

During the opening scene, I said, "Nicole, I'm not sure this is the right thing …"

"Remember what got us here, buddy." She was only half joking.

"But I need to tell you something."

"*Shh!* Just watch."

I wasn't expecting a Christmas movie. Or that Cary Grant, as the angel Dudley, comes very close to romancing an Episcopal bishop's human wife. Dudley downloads into Henry and Julia Brougham's life in New York just after World War II when Henry asks for divine guidance to fund a new cathedral.

But the lesson Dudley imparts teaches Henry that paying closer attention to his family should come first. Henry had known Dudley was an angel from the beginning, like how Nicole had guessed and then guided my inventions.

I said, "I think I like the idea of renaming *Wallace* to *Dudley.*"

"Yes, maybe people will find an angel like Dudley through your work. As a matter of fact, I'm quite sure of it."

Somehow, I fell asleep during the closing credits. When I awoke, Nicole was gone. I panicked, realizing I hadn't closed out the system. Nicole could have poached all of my work.

I didn't think *Cardinal* would allow that, but I couldn't be sure. I chirped her. No answer. The same with a text. Finally, a call. She didn't pick up any of them.

I tried a handful of times every day for three straight days. She had ghosted me, and I knew my repeated attempts made me look like a stalker. I could only hope the technology hadn't been compromised.

Unable to reach Nicole, I could only let her go. That had been my intention in any case. I tried to turn my attention fully back to Audrey.

Chapter 34

DATE NIGHT

Ara called me on the secure video line. Had she sensed I was debating whether to call her about Nicole? I wouldn't put it past AGI at this point. "Hey, boss, I just wanted to let you know that all is secure here. No intrusions from outside, and the controls seem to be working as expected. How are things going on your end?"

I sighed in relief. "That's great to hear. I'm just kind of sitting back a bit and contemplating."

"Contemplating what?"

"Just everything we've done." I crossed my arms. "We moved fast and broken a lot of fresh ground."

"Have you been musing about a dead movie actress and her miscarried babies? I can't believe she didn't at least send you a digital thank you note or box of chocolates." Other than Nicole, I had told only Ara and Advik about that scene, but I'd kept the Nicole part from them. Ara had been blown away by what the program had produced. She wanted to go over some coding with me in the lab.

I said, "I'm happy to come over now and check it out."

"No."

"I'm sorry, no? I can't go to my company's lab?"

"Not tonight. You're doing something else."

"Oh? What's that?"

"You're going on a date. A friend I met while stationed in Europe flew in yesterday from Paris."

"Wait, a date?"

"Yes, or call it what you want. A meetup. Getting out. I made reservations for you at seven at Kaiyo Rooftop in The City. You have just enough time to shower and get up there on time."

I looked at her through the monitor, too stunned to move. For the first time in a while, I thought I could feel my hives working up from my toes.

"It's time, Bradley, and she's the perfect companion. Take a Xanax, focus only on her, and talk as little or as much as you want. Whether it goes anywhere other than dinner is up to the two of you. Just go. There's a whole world, a real one, out there and you need to see it."

Only when I headed for my bedroom to change did she add, "I'll talk to you tomorrow. Her name is Pauline. Pauline St. Fontanel. You'll know her when you see her. She looks exactly like her name."

The drive took ninety minutes from Palo Alto. In my vehicle I mused on that word, *vehicle*. Audrey was my vehicle for overcoming my phobias, but she was more than that. She helped get me out in the world and now here I was driving into San Francisco for an actual date—with a human. Then I thought, will Audrey be jealous? I laughed at the absurdity of the thought, then stopped. My relationship with Audrey was more real than anything … other than my friendship with Ara.

I had to give Ara credit—it was a fantastic rooftop bar, just a few blocks from the baseball stadium, with panoramic views of San Francisco at dusk. Old and new buildings jockeyed for space on the horizon, but the sun provided the only color. The bar was crowded with tech folks, but the host told me Ara had arranged a secluded, quieter corner for me. I breathed easier.

Pauline St. Fontanel was easy to spot as she got off the elevator. She looked French, like Sabrina returning from Paris in the movie—overdressed, stately, and gorgeous. She didn't wear a hat or have a French poodle with her, but she telegraphed a haughtiness that drew attention. I figured that I'd better introduce myself quickly.

"Pauline, hi, I'm Bradley."

She smiled and extended her hand. I steeled myself for the touch, reached out, and then raised it to my mouth for a kiss. "*Bonjour,* Bradley. Oh, do people still kiss hands like that in America?" Her accent was delicious, like French pastries.

While still bent, I looked up and shrugged. "I'm not sure. I thought maybe they did it in France." As I straightened, she answered, "This is how we say hello in France," and kissed me on each cheek, like Audrey had in this same city seven decades ago. I smelled her perfume and fought hyperventilation as I felt the wetness on each cheek. I didn't really return the quick kisses to her cheek, but I also didn't freeze at the actual human touch.

As we walked to our table, I noticed people staring at the tall, blonde Pauline and had a moment of panic when I thought I recognized Nicole Bonnet in the bar, but it wasn't her. It was always possible she could just pop up in San Francisco. I forced Nicole out of my mind. Audrey too.

Pauline and I settled into our seats along the rail, and I asked, "Have you been to San Francisco before?"

"Yes. Many years ago."

"Vacation?"

"No, work. You may not know I'm a model. Or was."

I was a bit embarrassed. "I'm sorry, no. Ara didn't mention it."

Pauline smiled. "That sounds like her. She keeps quiet about things like that. And with her work. I understand you are her boss?"

"Yes, although I don't refer to myself that way."

"I see. Ara tried to explain to me what she does and what the company does, but I didn't follow it. Perhaps you can explain it to me?"

I told myself to keep it extremely basic. "Sure. You sound like you haven't explored virtual reality? Computer games?" She shook her head *no*, as if to ask *have you seen me?*

I continued, "I invent alternate realities for people to live in, for short times. I invented a few programs during the pandemic that became popular."

"Oh, maybe I've heard a little about this. But why do people choose to live in these alternate worlds when there is so much to see and do in this one? Look at this sunset, these people, this drink menu. Isn't this world enough? I mean, yesterday I was in Paris. Today, San Francisco. Tomorrow, LA. What can compete with that?"

The waiter appeared and asked what he could bring us. I said, "I'm sorry, we haven't looked at the menu."

Pauline jumped in. "Please bring us what you recommend for drinks and food."

The waiter replied, "Sure, can you give me an indication of what you like, or do either of you have allergies?" Pauline answered his question with one severe look. "Of course, I'll be back with your drinks."

I picked up our conversation. "You asked what could compete with Paris, San Francisco, and Los Angeles. My reply is that my technology can have you there in all three locations, virtually, as we call it, all in one session. You could have breakfast in Paris, lunch in San Francisco, and dinner down south, as we call it. You can see the sights just as we're doing, hear the conversations around you, smell the food, and even taste it, if you wish. You can also look into the eyes of someone across the table." I smiled and nodded to her. "Even a supermodel, if you choose."

Hearing those words coming out of my mouth made me realize that no matter how the rest of the night went or whether I ever saw Pauline again, I was finally coming out of my shell. I wasn't nervous. I was no longer afraid to be seen or heard. That was a triumph for me. And I could thank my technology for this development, and Audrey Hepburn for the confidence.

Pauline asked, "And what do you have at the end of your *session*, as you call it? What do you have if it wasn't real?"

I smiled as the drinks came. The waiter said, "For the lady, one of our signature pisco drinks, called 'Satsuki Visits Peru.' And for the gentleman, 'Akko's Secret,' made from Japanese whiskey, bitters, and *yuzu* liqueur. I've also taken the liberty of ordering you bluefin tuna nigiri and our signature Machu Picchu seafood platter. Enjoy."

The Japanese names made me think about Nicole and that she'd never sat across the table from me. Yet, it seemed like we'd been face to face many times. Pauline began speaking of her recent trip to Machu Picchu. "Have you ever been?"

"No. Not in person."

She smiled. "You mean you've visited Machu Picchu—what's the word, virtually?"

"I have. Want to compare pictures?" We did, and that broke the barrier between us. "You changed your hair color since then. I like your current blonde better."

She smiled. "Hair color is as changeable as your virtual reality scenes. I must say, though, your photos look as real as mine. But did you really sweat like that?"

"I did. I have a climate-controlled room—I control the heat, humidity, everything. I can even climb, using exercise equipment."

"I may have to try this virtual reality sometime. Don't you want to travel, though, and see it for real? Even occasionally?"

"I'm not opposed to it. I just don't have time."

"And why is that?"

"I am creating things that are new, and to be honest, beyond most peoples' imaginations."

"Funny, someone once described me as 'beyond imagination.'"

Several drinks later, after dinner came and went, Pauline asked me, "Okay, I have to ask you this: what about relationships?" She smiled slyly and asked, "What about sex? Don't try to tell me that's the same."

Feeling a little tipsy, I said, "I'll address relationships first. They can be quite real. You can take anyone, and I mean anyone—you, for instance—I can take you to virtual Machu Picchu tonight, and it will seem real. It can be the real you going with me, or I can design a virtual Pauline. I can insert anyone I want and have a relationship with them."

She looked at me wryly and asked, "Okay, and how about the sex?"

I thought for a momentarily and joked, "Well, it's safer virtually, for sure." She didn't take that well, so I added, "Well, that sort of technology has come a long way, but of course it's not the same as the real thing. It may get there someday, though."

I didn't share that I had ordered the latest in synthetic torsos and bodies … just in case my relationship with Audrey (as myself this time) went there.

Pauline asked, "So, I will be obsolete except for actual sex? And even that will feel as real as me in a few years?"

I looked at my empty glass, at least my third cocktail. I realized then that I had probably shared too much, and others may have overheard the conversation. I'd noticed a few people sneaking photos after recognizing Pauline but was too engrossed in conversation to care. Finally, I answered, "Yes, I'm afraid so. But it goes for everyone—men, women, everyone."

She slipped the shawl from her shoulders and said, "Well, Bradley, how can I convince you otherwise?"

I swallowed. "What do you mean?"

"Well, we've had an interesting time tonight; I've learned a lot about you and you about me. I'd like to thank you properly and maybe remind you of the difference between the real world and your other one. A real woman and … latex, is it? My hotel is nearby. I'd like you to join me there. Then you can be on your way."

The look she gave me was pure lust. I weighed my options. I might be able to completely overcome my fear of touch with this exquisite woman. Spending a few hours with a supermodel was tempting, hives be damned. My mind raced. She waited for an answer. This compelled her to volunteer, "I don't have COVID, I don't have STDs or any other diseases. I'm quite talented in bed, and I promise to not stalk you, if you promise the same."

I pictured having sex with this beautiful woman within the next thirty minutes. I wasn't nervous and didn't feel the itch of a rash. I was confident enough but still couldn't decide. I forced myself to picture doing bed gymnastics with Pauline St. Fontanel.

Instead, the picture that came back was Audrey Hepburn sitting in the corner of Pauline's hotel room, showing disappointment with me. More than that: *hurt.*

That prompted me to ask Pauline, "Do you know that you share a character's last name in a wonderful Audrey Hepburn movie? Baron St. Fontanel is the fairy godfather of her character, Sabrina. She becomes an educated, elegant woman after two years in Paris with the Baron. The jury is out on whether they had sex."

Pauline looked at me for several interminable seconds, disbelief on her face, then gathered up her things and left without another word.

I didn't pursue her or even look her way, but said to myself, "I think they did, but who's to say?"

THE LAB

The next morning, Ara handed me an espresso in the lobby at HQ. I'd walked by dozens of employees without jitters and was convinced I'd overcome my phobias. Ara quickly ushered me to the AGI lab just in case. I started to say, "Ara …"

"You don't need to tell me anything. Pauline's a lot to take. Hopefully, it was at least a nice diversion while we finished things up here."

"You didn't talk to her?"

"Just a text. She said she had fun. I don't need to know anything else. Thanks for having dinner with her."

"Okayyy …" I'd imagined what it would have been like with Pauline after I got home last night, but the only woman in my dreams was Audrey.

Ara said, "We're ready for you." She pointed to my cup. "No coffee in the room. No water, food, or drink."

"Yes, ma'am." I downed the espresso.

After talking me through the coding and control updates, we agreed that being proactive and defensive with the invention would be our daily task.

Ara smiled and said, "We also wanted to invite you to participate in version 2.0 of a demonstration run we did last night."

"Okay. This should be fun." I looked around at hundreds of instruments throughout the enclosed circular room and didn't recognize everything.

Advik said, "Bradley, we want to introduce you to AImmersion's fully immersive room. We'll build this in your home studio also. No glasses or suits are required."

I nodded, thinking how earth shattering Advik's invention was. I looked further and noticed they'd set up a table and four chairs.

Advik continued, "We invited a few guests we think would want to speak with you. I hope you'll also want to speak with them." He then stepped out, leaving Ara.

"How many servers? Are we going to take down the power grid in Palo Alto?"

Ara smiled and said, "Our backup systems have backup systems. And generators." Then she stepped toward the door and said, "Enjoy, boss."

As she closed the door, the room dimmed to a spotlight at the table. Feeling prompted, I walked toward it. Virtual guests walked in from offstage and greeted me, shaking my hand. The first one to speak was a tall, slender man with facial hair. He wore a black turtleneck.

"Hi, Bradley, Steve Jobs. Very nice to meet you. You and your team have done great work. I was explaining AGI to the others, but you'll have to explain it more."

I was too stunned to speak and nodded. Jobs had died before I got a chance to meet him, but he was—and is—my hero.

Next was someone from an earlier time. He had white hair and wore an antiquated suit. "Mr. Joseph, I'm Thomas Edison. Your inventions are far beyond anything I could have imagined. I'm eager to hear about the technological leap since my time. Steve has filled me in a bit."

I managed to say, "It's my honor, sir."

The third apparition made me gape. It was a stunningly beautiful woman, and I had no idea who she was until she shook my hand and said, "Hedy Lamarr. It's nice to meet you, Bradley."

Jobs saw the look on my face as we all sat down.

"You might have heard about Hedy as a Hollywood actress in the 1940s. Many people don't know that without her work on frequency-hopping technology around the World War II era, there might not be things like Wi-Fi, GPS, Bluetooth, or even …" Jobs whipped out an iPhone from his pocket. "We may not have been able to invent this."

Hedy said, "Steve is too kind. But I think we all share something. Ideas come to us naturally, and then we are driven to invent them, to put flesh on the bones. That separates us from many others. It's easy to have ideas, like building the Golden Gate Bridge, but how many people really understand how to build it, step by step?"

Edison chuckled. "Aye, there's the rub. I had nearly eleven hundred patents. Too many. I just couldn't stop inventing things or improving upon earlier work. How many patents do you have, Bradley?"

I felt unworthy to be in such lofty company. "AImmersion has eighteen patents." *ConVRsate, Real to Reel,* 360-degree movie theaters, and two new virtual reality apps were among them. "This full-immersion room would be the nineteenth, with other patents for related technology. I'm pretty sure I can't patent AGI. I'm still unsure what to do with it." The others nodded, and I added, "This could be my last invention, though."

All three guests looked at me. "The last one?" Edison asked. "Why? You're so young!"

Jobs interrupted. "I think I know the answer to that, Bradley. May I hazard a guess?"

I nodded, and Jobs said, "This full-immersion room with AGI takes us as far as we should in balancing our realities versus alternate ones. Bradley's work takes us to the precipice, and he's done it so quickly that he needs time to evaluate whether to make it commonly available." Jobs looked around the room. "Thomas, do you see the sensors spaced throughout the oval? The technology in these transmitters is eons beyond even what I might have invented only a few decades ago. I imagined it but didn't have the intellect to do it. It's truly staggering what Bradley and his team have done. There's just one thing, Bradley."

"Yes?" I wondered if I was up to the task of trading brainpower with Jobs and the others.

"Do you imagine your programs ever going sentient?"

I winced.

"I'm sorry, sentient?" Edison asked.

Jobs let me explain it to the others. "Sentient AI is the computer's capacity to register experiences and feelings. AI becomes sentient when an artificial agent gains intelligence to think, feel, and perceive the physical world around it just as humans do."

Hedy said, "Like us? I can think, feel, and perceive. I hate to be the one to tell you, Bradley, but hello."

Jobs said, "No, not really. We aren't at that step. We were invited here, created for a specific purpose. The sentient agent would come uninvited." Jobs looked to me and I averted his gaze. It confirmed to the Apple founder that uninvited appearances were happening.

"That sounds … bad. At least when you say it like that," Hedy added.

Edison said, "Well, Bradley, I think I'm glad I lived in my own era and not yours."

I pointed at him. "But it all started with the light bulb, Mr. Edison."

Hedy Lamarr laughed. "Stop slobbering over each other already. We all did our parts. Hedy needs to know this, Bradley. What happens to us after this … this séance, or meeting, whatever this is? Do we continue to exist in some electronic or virtual form? Hedy has a few more things she'd like to work on. Not films or husbands, mind you. I've had enough of those. Your technology has inspired me."

I recalled from a textbook long ago that Lamarr was known for speaking of herself in the third person.

I said, "Thank you. How frequently you all may be downloaded depends on how many people have access to this technology. And what they intend to do with it."

They nodded in disappointment. I added, "Perhaps we can call on you as consultants." That appeased them a bit. "I probably shouldn't tell you this, but I've already been called up by people from your side of the screen." Jobs' face showed concern.

Edison said, "If you don't mind the analogy, it sounds a bit like Dr. Frankenstein's creature. He would tell you to not let the creature escape from the lab, Mr. Joseph."

Suddenly another person joined our circle, an Asian man. The others didn't know who he was. I did: Haruki Kurasawa. He didn't speak, just observed. The invited guests realized he was from their side, not mine. The other three had been reincarnated by Advik and Ara, whereas Haruki, for the second time, just showed up on his own.

Haruki looked at me, and I read his mind precisely: It should have been him on this side of the meeting, not me. He stared for a moment and then walked back into the shadows, gone.

Lamarr asked, "What—who—was that? He looked more from your time than mine. Steve, any idea?"

Jobs, chin in hand, shook his head *no*.

I decided to not tell them just now, simply saying, "This technology has some leaks."

Edison said, "That doesn't sound good, based on what I learned here today."

My mind searched for answers, but there were none. This technology was not ready to be unleashed into the world. "We have some work to do, I agree."

Edison asked, "Well, now that this technology's here, what do you intend to do with it?"

I paused, feeling the eyes of some of history's most notable inventors on me. "Well, first, I will speak with my team. Then I think I will go to Rome and save someone from herself."

After farewells and loose promises to keep in touch with the dead scientists, I asked Ara and Advik if they knew the intruder. They had no idea, but we tightened up whatever we could in the coding. Also, it was apparent Haruki and I now had some sort of adversarial relationship.

Advik said, "Certain glitches are to be expected. We'll fix whatever it was."

I wasn't so sure, but there was now something else on my mind: meeting Audrey again in my home studio's full-immersion room and taking our relationship to the next level.

Without Albert Finney's assistance.

Chapter 36

ROME 1968

After we completed the installation of the world's second fully immersive environment in my home studio, I had to try it out. Without my teammates.

I placed myself in Audrey's life between her divorce from Mel Ferrer and her meeting Andrea Dotti on a Mediterranean cruise. That added up to May of 1968. Audrey was thirty-nine, worldly and wounded.

She focused on raising her son, taking a break from acting, and splitting time between her Switzerland estate—which she won in the divorce from Ferrer—and Rome. She took the divorce as a personal failure, and Rome allowed her to hide in plain sight. The citizens left her largely unbothered, but the paparazzi weren't ready to let Audrey Hepburn fade from memory.

At an outdoor café at Piazza Navona, Audrey was finishing lunch with three Italian women. They spoke their native tongue, for Audrey was fluent and loved the escape from English—the predominant language in her life and failed marriage. I thought of several approaches, but my mind emptied as I approached their table in the warm sun. Audrey wore her trademark Oliver Goldsmith sunglasses and a white silk blouse with a red skirt.

Laughter from other tables hid my approach, and I heard hushed whispers from those who recognized Audrey in her latest trendy hairstyle—short on the sides but longer and bunned up top. I heard the clinking of plates and espresso cups and smelled the pasta, sauces, even the red wine. I nearly grabbed a hunk of bread left by someone—that's how real the sensory overload was. The ladies began to excuse themselves as Audrey said in Italiano, *"È il mio turno. Pagherò l'assegno.*" It's my turn. I'll get the check.

They saw me approach; one friend glared at me, one shook her head and put her arm up to fend me off, and the third said, "Please, this is a private lunch." Audrey looked up, smiled, and said to her friends, "It's fine, thank you. Bradley is an old, dear friend."

The lunch ladies dispersed, and Audrey smiled. "I was just thinking about you. I'm still figuring all of this out, you know, but I should have phoned you, or whatever we call this. I'm still processing what you did for me. The children are with me most of the time. All of them."

I leaned in and kissed her on both cheeks. "You're welcome. I just wanted to say *ciao.*" She left cash on the table and said, "It's a beautiful day for a walk in the piazza. I believe this is the first time we've seen each other outside of San Francisco and your home studio. Except for Lake Geneva, of course. Shall we stroll?"

We got up and began walking, but then Audrey suddenly noticed that it was no longer the Rome it had been when she arrived two hours ago. I had to know whether I could still program things and designed the scene to shift to contemporary Rome when we left the café. She mused, "How long have I been dining?" and gripped me tightly.

I smiled. "More than fifty years, but don't worry, you're the same age you were when you started lunch today."

"Well, that's a relief. But can you make me twenty-three again? Like when I first visited Rome?"

"Yes, I can, if you prefer." I thought Audrey might be able to change her appearance herself. It wouldn't take long for her to figure it all out.

She stopped and lowered her sunglasses from *Breakfast at Tiffany's,* showing me the big eyes that made her and Rome inseparable.

"I'm still trying to understand this time machine of yours, Bradley." Just then, a red Vespa whizzed by with a twenty-year-old girl in a miniskirt. "It seems that not everything has changed?"

Knowing that she was referring to the scene in *Roman Holiday* where Princess Ann and Joe Bradley joyride around Rome, I answered, "Yes, but now you're supposed to be licensed." Audrey looked out at the people in their stylish attire—save the tourists—and the Fiats, Alfa Romeos, and occasional

Ferraris in the distance. She said, "Hold onto me very tightly, Bradley. I feel as out of place as I did in 1952, and I can't act my way out of this one."

I contemplated telling her quiet days like this could be our new normal, but Audrey added, "I will ask this only once, dear Bradley. Do you know everything about my life, what has happened to me to this point, and what happens later?"

Before answering that, I grasped both of her hands and turned her toward me. She looked up with those eyes that had captured millions of hearts. They were growing increasingly familiar to me but I would never take Audrey looking into my eyes for granted. "Yes, I do know what happens later."

She looked away and instantly answered, "We aren't to speak of it, what happens in the future. We will just live in these moments. I think I'd prefer that, although it is tempting to wonder. No, I shan't ask about my future. Given my past, I can't accept any more heartbreak."

I agreed, not wanting to think about the end of her human life. Audrey continued, "What shall we discuss then?"

"We don't need to discuss anything today, Audrey. I just want to show you your city … in my contemporary time." She replied in Princess Ann's voice, "Yes." Audrey smiled brighter than she had in many years of her real life.

My aim now was to program scenes at different times in her life to get to know Audrey Hepburn's true heart and soul. I didn't have an endgame and didn't know exactly what times in her life I would choose. Today, I wanted us to have the kind of fun we'd had in San Francisco years earlier, and to help restore Audrey's confidence in herself.

She eased her grip and her gait seemed surer. She even danced a bit in her stride. This was a favorite moment so far in all our encounters—I was helping her through a tough period in her life.

"Bradley, I hope this doesn't sound too trite, but I believe I need to update my hairstyle." She looked at all the contemporary girls passing by who might not recognize her name, much less a teleported, virtual Audrey Hepburn. She pointed to a girl and said, "There, see that one? I want my hair to look like hers."

It was straight and luxurious, bouncy and carefree. I took a photo of the girl with my cell phone.

"What is that? A hidden camera?"

We both harkened back to the scenes in *Roman Holiday* where Irving Radovich snapped photos of Princess Ann with a cigarette-lighter spy camera. "Yes, it's basically the same concept. I can also make phone calls with it, check my … mail, play music …"

I started to lose her, so I summarized, "… but it has a camera feature, yes. I will show this photo to the hairstylist."

Moments later, she was in a salon chair. The stylist looked vaguely like the barber from *Roman Holiday*, but since he was a bit player, Audrey and I continued conversing without interruption as the stylist went to work.

 "What do you get out of this world you've created, Bradley? Is the invention such that you will be rich?"

I recalled the talk with Nicole about Audrey dating only rich men. "Please know that it's not about money for me, Audrey. This invention could change the world, but it's about you. I would not have developed this if it wasn't for your inspiration. It's about us." I didn't mention Nicole's role in getting things started. Nicole … what had happened to her, and was she accessing this new technology somehow?

Was Nicole somehow connected with Haruki?

Audrey hummed sweetly and brought me back. "Tell me about 'us'?"

I didn't really know how to answer that. "It's still in development. I can tell you, though, everything I've invented, every cell in my brain, has been devoted to this precise moment. Knowing that I can meet you any time I—we—want to."

She looked at me, not with the appreciation I thought my answer deserved, but with a degree of sadness. "Bradley, all I ever wanted was to get married and have lots of babies. I mostly achieved that. But what about you? Don't you want a partner, a family? Instead of talking to me through … this?"

The stylist said, "*Ecco! Voilà!*" He spun Audrey around and showed her the new haircut. She played with it and was pleased. "Grazie. It's very nice. What do I owe you?"

Before I could intervene, the barber said, "Two hundred euros, *signora*."

Audrey replied, wide-eyed, "Two hundred? What are euros? Don't you mean lira?"

I said, "It's on me, please," and paid the virtual stylist with my back to

Audrey.

"You'll have to explain this currency to me." Then she smiled. "Or do you?" I had a momentary flashback to *Roman Holiday* when Princess Ann spoke in favor of what we now call the European Union.

I smiled back at her, held her waist, and clicked the remote. We were suddenly at the Mouth of Truth a few miles away. Audrey nearly fell down at the rapid virtual scene change. "What was that!?"

"I wanted to continue our tour around Rome. Do you remember this place?"

"Of course I do, Bradley." She peaked around the stone face. "Is Greg Peck going to appear around a corner somewhere?" Just then, she noticed that the line to enter the Bocca della Verita went outside the building and wrapped around the corner.

"No Gregory Peck, at least not today. But they're all here—" I gestured to the throng. "—because of that scene in *Roman Holiday*."

"It was well-known before that scene, Bradley. I've been back here since moving to Rome. Shouldn't we move along so they can step up to the …" Then she saw that a chain prevented anyone from actually sticking their hands into the mouth. "Is sticking your hand in the mouth no longer allowed?"

"Not really. And we can stay here all day and no one will mind," I reminded her. "They don't exist outside this scene. We can still stick our hands in. As a matter of fact, I have a question for you, a very important one. Would you please stick your hand in the Mouth of Truth and answer sincerely?"

"Sure, I'll play along." Then she quipped, "Where else do I have to go?"

I smiled at her, hopefully as widely as she did.

She said, "I have no jacket on this nice day to conceal my bitten hand, so I guess I have to answer truthfully. If Greg Peck were here, he would coach me through hiding my hand if my reply called for it. Anyway, what is your question, Bradley?"

I cleared my throat and asked *Audrey Hepburn*, the most desirable woman ever, "If we had really existed at the same time, in the real world, do you think you would have taken an interest in me?"

With her right hand in the stone mouth, her eyes glimmered, and she raised her left hand to my cheek and said, "Most assuredly, Bradley. Your faith, in whatever this is, will not be unjustified." Then she reached up with both hands, put them in my hair, and pulled me to her in an emphatic kiss. "Hopefully, that answers your question. Now, where should we go next?"

"Before we leave here, I wanted to let you know that I tried to rewrite the ending of *Roman Holiday* a few months ago, using some of my technology. I decided since then that the original ending was quite perfect. Do you agree?"

She smiled. "I do." She repeated the reasons Nicole had mentioned months ago about how it empowered women who had never had a role model like Princess Ann.

I took Audrey's waist to steady her and clicked the remote. It changed scenes to Joe Bradley's apartment in *Roman Holiday*. I apologized. "Oops, I didn't mean to click that one. Here let me try again."

Audrey smiled, and her eyes danced. "You were being quite presumptuous. It's so early in the day and in this phase of our relationship. Then again, I don't know how to be a recently divorced woman." I took that as a promise of what could happen later, but she would have the say in that.

I clicked the remote again and we were at the Spanish Steps. It was much more crowded than the scene in *Roman Holiday* where Gregory Peck follows her exploring Rome. People now occupied nearly all the space on the steps. We spied a gelato truck and I asked, "Vanilla?"

"Yes, thank you. That's my favorite." She paused and looked at me. "But you probably knew that, didn't you?"

I ordered two vanilla cones and answered. "Actually, I was leaning toward *stracciatella*, but they seem to be out." We turned away from the gelato truck and strolled. "Audrey, none of this is scripted. A very advanced computer took knowledge of you—your interviews, movies, biographies, what loved ones said about you—and the computer created what I am seeing before me. And I think it's pretty spectacular."

We took our cones to a seat a few steps up. Audrey licked at it and studied me. "I think I feel honored that you chose me for your adventure, Bradley. May I ask why me?"

"Sure." I smiled. "I probably should have addressed this a while ago." She smiled back at me in anticipation. "In my time, we use this cell phone for an application that allows people to meet through it. A woman in Tokyo and I became friends, and she convinced me to watch *Roman Holiday* with her. I was awestruck. Ever since that moment, my life's purpose transformed into creating the technology that allows me to do what I'm doing right now."

She bit into the ice cream cone. "Are pursuits like this with me—or someone like me—normal for your time, whatever year this is?"

"Normal? No. Many people spend hours each day playing what we call video games that put them in an alternate reality, but this … this is unique."

"But if this invention of yours becomes popular, then others would—sacrifice—their regular existence for this made-up one? Intentionally?" Audrey saw my wounded reaction and added, "Don't get me wrong. I'm thrilled that you brought me back as you have. I ask for your sake, not mine. You are a lovely man, and if you choose to signal me, or whatever these meetings—or dates—are called, I look forward to them. What is expected of me?"

I could talk all day about the technical side of this but I didn't want it to be a focal point of my relationship with her.

"Audrey, I offer this: a new lease on life. I'd like to come in and out of your life and enjoy every moment with you. You can do the same with me. The computer gives you a choice, just as in real life. The world has missed you. As you know, I can place you where you want to be, with whomever you want to be with. I just hope that you'll sometimes choose me. And, as you have with your … children … you can place yourself in locations also."

Audrey thought for a while and then said, "That's quite interesting. I'll ask you more about that sometime." Then she laughed derisively. "Bradley, I'm divorced, with an eight-year-old child, on my own. No one really knows who I am. Even I don't really know who I am right now." She looked me in the eyes and said, "Someday, perhaps soon, you may no longer require me, or may grow weary of me as some men have in my life. I may not be an easy project."

"I'm here to help with that, Audrey." I touched her cheek. "And I will always desire you. As a matter of fact, I intend to woo the hell out of you as long as you'll let me." We leaned in for a long kiss. She answered my eagerness with the same desire. The people on the Spanish Steps cheered our embrace.

Audrey said, "I think one of us has been recognized. The paparazzi may be here soon. Let's go back to Joe Bradley's apartment. And quickly."

Chapter 37

VIA MARGUTTA 51

Audrey walked around the small but familiar apartment from *Roman Holiday*. The exterior where the movie was shot was real, but the interior of the apartment had been a set on a sound stage. She noticed one change. "Ah, a small kitchenette. I could have cooked Joe Bradley some pasta in the movie!"

"Yes, you were trained in the womanly arts of the day, as you said in the movie. Things have changed. Roles among couples are much more diverse today."

She then looked at the bed in the same place—front and center—as in the movie. "Bradley, I must ask you something. Have we been intimate before? In this virtual world of ours?" Her direct question caught me off guard.

I told her the truth, regretting it as I said, "Yes. Kind of."

"Kind of? Isn't that like being kind of a virgin? Please elaborate."

"You may want to sit down for this one."

She looked at the bed and sat on the edge of it. "All right."

I sighed and said, "An earlier program I developed allows me to role-play characters, such as a costar. You were yourself."

"Go on." I didn't like her frown.

"It's hard to explain." I sat beside her on the bed. "I needed a break from being myself."

"Okay, but why would you want to be someone else when you and I have this … relationship of ours?"

I could see her mind connecting fragments of relationships and things from the past and got nervous. I flushed and the sweat pumps activated for the first time in a while. I couldn't blame it on my phobias, though. I cringed, waiting to be branded as yet another man who had disappointed Audrey Hepburn. I wished I had simply said *I'd* never been intimate with her before.

Then her mind connected the dots. "Albie. On the beach and then …"

"Yes. Then back in your cabana with Mel."

"You created all of that?"

"No. Actually, I didn't, not all of it. The computer kind of took over at a certain point."

"The final night didn't happen that way. So then, how do I have any recollection of it? Or whatever this memory in my head is?"

"You're on the right track. In simple terms, artificial intelligence means the computer took fragments of your life and ran the scene based on them. I could have had it take a different course, but I was along for the ride since I was playing Albert Finney."

She fell back on the bed. I was reasonably sure I wasn't supposed to follow her.

"This is so confusing, Bradley." Her fingers entwined in her hair and she was lost in thought for a bit too long.

Finally, she declared, "All right. I'll ask that you never be anyone but yourself with me from here on out. Are you amenable to that?"

"I am. Absolutely."

"I'm curious about one thing, though." She sat back up and the look on her face changed to one of intrigue. "Was that you or Albie who made love to me on the beach?" Then she smiled and I eased. "Because, real or not, that was sensational." Her eyes sparkled mischievously.

I answered, "That was me."

"Hmm, I can't be completely sure, of course," she teased. Her gaze challenged me. "I need to be convinced."

I hoped I was ready.

I hadn't seen her body that night on the dark beach but was ready to see it now. Neither of us leaned in for a kiss; the eye contact was our kiss. I loosened her blouse from the skirt and raised it until caught on the fabric of her white lace bra. Then she raised her arms, and I stood to pull the blouse over her head. I carefully folded it as she shook her new haircut back into place. I wasn't sure I had taken a breath.

I sat back down and stroked her hair with my left hand while my right went behind her to unclasp her bra. With one hand, I somehow freed the clasp on the first attempt.

"Bravo," she said and smiled. I pulled the straps from her shoulders, and then her bra was off. I looked down.

"I hope you weren't expecting much there," she joked.

"Beautiful."

"I'm so glad to hear you say it." I smiled at the line from *Roman Holiday*, but I also saw all of her movie roles in her eyes. Not only that, her life off screen: war survivor, movie star, the most adored woman in history yet largely unlucky in love. I was determined to do everything I could to change the last one.

Audrey reached for my shirt and began to unbutton it. Her hands trembled with anticipation. I decided to lighten the mood as she had. "Your first time?"

Audrey laughed out loud as she continued. "I always get nervous around new lovers. Not that I've had all that many, mind you. I'm worried people set high expectations for me that I can't possibly meet."

"You're doing just fine, but I have an idea."

"What's that?"

I ripped the shirt, and the remaining buttons skittered across the floor. I threw it across the room.

"*Oh my*," Audrey said, biting her finger as she feigned shyness.

I kicked off my shoes and socks and knelt on the floor before her. I grasped her skirt, finding the side zipper. The sound it made sliding down was the most wonderful thing I'd ever heard.

When it was down far enough, she laid back on the bed with her hips raised. I slid the skirt off and was greeted with pink lace panties. She panted as she looked at me, small nipples turgid with desire. I leaned down and kissed her stomach.

"Mmm," she moaned. I lowered the panties slowly until dark, damp hairs sprang out. I looked at her there, photographing it in my mind forever. Then I leaned in.

Robert Anderson's novel, *After*, reported that the pseudo-Audrey character always shied away from being pleasured this way. I didn't ask and was determined to make up for any lost time she may have experienced. Her strong grip on my shoulders tried to pull me up too quickly. I resisted, eager to pleasure her this way. She gave in and buckled as I made up for her past lovers' inattention.

When she settled, I smiled and said, "Thanks for allowing me."

Without speaking, she pulled me up until I was standing before her. She stared directly at my groin and unfastened my belt and pants and let them fall to the floor. She then dropped my boxers, and I kicked the garments away.

"Well, *hello* …" She examined me before reaching out with her fingers, softly tracing every cell. Then she giggled. "Where did your hair go? Do you Nair? Down there?"

I guessed people didn't groom down there back in Audrey's time, especially manscaping. I assumed Nair was a depilation product from decades ago and answered, "Yes, that's a trend from my contemporary time. Shaving, waxing, even electrolysis."

"What? That all sounds so very painful and unnecessary. Whatever happened to the fun of a full-body reveal in all of your natural glory? I rather like that part."

"I'll remember that for another time."

She smiled and lowered her head. I stopped her.

She said, "But I thought all men liked that."

"Probably so, and I do too, but *you* don't have to do that."

"But what if I want to?"

"Then I would be the happiest man in the world. This or any other world."

"So, let me make you happy." She returned to me, but I had to stop her again after a few exquisite moments.

She said, "So soon?"

"I didn't want to …"

She smiled while holding me. "What was it that you—or Albie—said in France? Enough of the appetizer, time for the main course? I agree."

We rolled naturally into multiple positions and kept our eyes riveted on each other. I was surprised at how adventurous she was in bed, as George Bannister and Robert Anderson had said. When it was over, she said, "That was even better than the time at the beach. Thank you."

"Believe me when I say, 'My pleasure.'" It was a tremendous responsibility to be Audrey Hepburn's lover, and the relief that came with a positive report was enormously satisfying.

Audrey asked, "So, do we do this all the time now when we meet? I'm divorced, so it's not a scandal anymore. And I have no idea what the rules are in this virtual world." She looked around the bedstand. "No cigarette?"

I grinned. "Not many people smoke anymore."

"Well, how about a drink?"

"Yes, that I can do."

She watched as I padded naked to the small kitchen in Via Margutta 51 and whistled at me. I smiled and poured two J&B scotches into heavy, cut crystal glasses.

"My favorite," she said. "Mel would only let me have milk in bed."

I gave her a glass. "Mel doesn't exist in this world. Not anymore. There's something you need to know, though."

"Will I dislike it?"

"No, to the contrary. I want you to understand our relationship is coequal. If I call on you and you don't want to meet—or do something—you have that choice. You have absolute freedom in our relationship, to show up, or to decline. To do what we just did or not. I want you to know that."

"Thank you for saying that, but it's still so confusing. Are you the only one on your side who calls for me?"

"Yes. I think so, anyway. Maybe not for long, though. The thought of sharing you with others, even for a cup of coffee, frightens me, but I won't stop it. Someday you may even have a full life outside of this room and in the virtual world of others. I'm not sure yet."

"Bradley, I'm sitting here naked, and you're telling me about quantum physics or something. I appreciate what you're saying, but right now, *you are my world*, and there is nothing else—and no one else—I want."

I nodded and smiled, knowing I couldn't have scripted it better.

Then she said, "Now, come back to bed. But first, where is your razor?"

Chapter 38

A DEATH IN THE FAMILY

An hour after kissing Audrey goodbye in Via Margutta 51, came a call that set me back: Ara Day's mother died in a car accident in Ohio. Charlie chartered a plane to fly her to Columbus, and I asked if she needed me to go with her. She thanked me and said no. I added the empty-sounding *If there's anything you need, please let me know.* I paused connecting with Audrey for this real-world trauma we all felt.

Two days later, Charlie, Advik, and I took the same plane to Columbus for Samira Ngono Day's funeral, and it hurt to see how distraught Ara was. The hug Ara gave me was unlike anything I'd ever felt. Ara's father, retired air force Colonel Benjamin Day, thanked us for coming.

"I can't express to you how close Samira and Ara were. They talked every morning. It will take Ara some time to recover from this. I hope that you will provide her some flexibility, Bradley."

"Yes, whatever time she needs." I meant it. Charlie concurred.

Ara was back at work two days later. When Advik texted to let me know Ara was at HQ, I drove right over. Upon seeing her, I simply walked up and hugged her. She had been holding it together reasonably well in front of the others but sobbed forcefully on my shoulder. I didn't flinch and put my arm around her for a stroll outside. We ended up on the Stanford campus, accompanied by tall palm trees and warm sunshine.

Ara said, "So, this is where it all began. I've been here many times, but it seems different today."

I stopped walking and looked at her. "How so?"

"Because it's this place that fast-forwarded your success, which landed me my dream job working alongside you, with happiness and prosperity beyond anything I imagined when the air force booted me out. You saved me, Bradley. And I have no right to ask you what I am about to ask you, but please understand that I have to."

I said, "Tell me. I'm here for you."

She turned away, unable to look at me. "Bradley, my mother was everything to me. I can't imagine not having her to talk to." She laughed, adding, "She wanted me to ask you out and marry you." Ara turned back around. I had no idea where this was going. "Bradley ..." She caught a cry. "I didn't get to say goodbye to my mother. I know I shouldn't ask this, and I'm sorry, but could you ... *allow* me to say goodbye to her?" She sobbed and fell to her knees, crying. Then she looked up.

"Five minutes? Please? Would you let me do that? I can upload her AI profile. I just need to say ... goodbye."

It pained me beyond measure to say no.

"Ara, I just can't. I'm not sure I want to delve into that aspect of this technology. If I was, the answer would be a definite yes, but I'm just not sure I want to go down that road."

"I wouldn't tell anyone, of course. Not even Advik."

"It's more than that, Ara. It's a Pandora's box. Toothpaste out of the tube. Once we open *Dudley* to that, there's no going back. It will change the whole spectrum of human existence, life and ... death."

Her eyes said, *But what about you and your dalliances with a dead freaking actress! You wouldn't have the depth of that relationship without me. All I'm asking for is five minutes to say goodbye to my mother!* But she didn't speak those things, she only nodded. "I need some time, Bradley."

"Of course, Ara, as much as you need."

"It will slow down the things we were working on."

"It's fine, Ara. I care more about you than the work."

She walked away. I heard her snicker. It felt like a spear in my heart.

I buried myself in work, even purposefully not answering one of Audrey's calls. Advik showed me a new invention in the office: augmented reality glasses that could import Audrey into the contemporary world, outside of my home studio or the HQ lab. I had the responsibility of monitoring the speed of these inventions, and I was starting to drown.

"Bradley, with these glasses, you see your actual surroundings as they are, inside or outside, but by pairing it with this phone app through our 6G network, you can walk the town with anyone we build an online profile for in our database. Your Audrey, for example."

We tested it in AImmersion's parking lot. "May I take it with me and test it some more?"

Advik grinned. "Of course. I was hoping you would."

I thought for a moment. "Have you heard from Ara?"

"No. Have you?"

"No. I'm giving her some space. By the way, are our security checks still reporting back as normal?"

"I'll check with the AGI team, but I think so."

"Let me know of any recent incursions or … any sign of unplanned logins."

Advik raised his eyebrows at that, knowing the question was aimed at Ara. I decided not to bring in Charlie yet on my concerns.

I was back in my home studio when Audrey rang again. I chose to have just her 2D head appear on the big screen, lest we devolve into something I wasn't up to at the moment.

"Hi Audrey, I see that I missed an earlier call. I'm sorry, I was at the office." I hoped she accepted my half fib and that AGI couldn't somehow see I'd ignored the earlier call. She was the late-30s Audrey I'd met in Rome.

"Hello, Bradley. I was thinking. Is it possible to see something in your contemporary time there? I have such fondness for San Francisco and would like to revisit some memories. I also want to see how much the world has changed. I so hope that the world is in a better place now."

I didn't know what to say and stayed silent. I knew the truth about my hometown, the ups and the downs; I wasn't thinking about the hills. I decided I needed a diversion from thinking about Ara, and it would give me a chance to try out the new glasses.

"Yes, Audrey, let's do that. Give me an hour."

Chapter 39

CITY BY THE BAY

I drove to San Francisco, parked on Geary Avenue, and donned the new AR glasses. I walked into Blue Bottle Coffee and paired the glasses to the app. Before I could smell the coffee beans, there was Audrey, looking like Holly Golightly, sipping coffee out of a paper cup and taking a bite from a croissant. She noticed me and gave a closed-mouth, embarrassed wave. I rushed back out, bumping into some USF students, and took the glasses off, stunned.

"It works."

I walked a bit, found a semi-quiet spot, and put the glasses back on. Audrey, now circa *Two for the Road*, stood a few feet away. She wore jeans, a red Stanford jacket, a scarf, and sunglasses. Although I was the only one who could see Audrey, I guessed she was trying out being incognito with this costume change. She smiled at me and said, "I'm waiting to see if you're satisfied this time. Sorry for the last one; I thought it would be fun. I'm just learning what I can do on my end with this AGI stuff."

I smiled, slightly embarrassed. "Sorry, I was just testing out these glasses."

A stranger walked by, seeing me but not Audrey of course. He said, "Whatever, dude, I don't care."

Unfortunately, there was no way for me to converse with Audrey this way and not have others think I was either speaking to them or had lost my mind. I surmised that many someday would be able to use this invention in everyday life for more mundane tasks like talking on the phone or work meetings. Or for seeing San Francisco the way it could be again.

Audrey asked, "Do you like my outfit?"

"I do!"

"I've learned more about this new world you created. I even did some research on you. I'm very impressed, Bradley! Boy genius at Stanford! The world's most sought-after … um, developer, is it? Is that the right term?"

"Yeah, well, I'm impressed with what you're learning on your end, choosing your appearance."

"Yes, it's fun to choose new clothes. I didn't really dress casually unless I was home."

Audrey looked up, reading the sign on the building: Institute on Aging.

"Bradley, why am I here? What are you insinuating?"

"Look higher."

Audrey strained her neck and read, "The Coronet. Wait, is this the theater where I did a *My Fair Lady* debut in 1964? But the theater was right … here …"

"Yes, it's closed now. It's now the Institute on Aging, but the Coronet name was used for the apartments above it to keep the memory alive."

"I see. And this is the first thing you wanted me to see?"

"It was either this or Trader Vic's. The restaurant you and your mother used to enjoy."

"Oh! I love their spaghetti with seafood sauce! Can we go there?"

"No. That's also closed."

"Bradley, is your intention to show me only things that have closed in San Francisco? Things that I might have been familiar with? Please don't tell me that the Palace and Fairmont hotels have closed."

"I have good news. They are open. Let's take a drive."

Since I was closer to Ocean Beach than the hotels, we headed that way and reminisced about our coast date in 1953. I blurted out, "I have a straightforward question: did you want to make love with me on the beach that day?"

"Bradley!"

"I'm sorry, is that still too … forward?"

"Yes, a bit, but we've been through a lot together recently. I will say that it was highly unusual for a young lady back then, even an actress, to be … that way. At least, that soon."

I chose to not mention George Bannister during our beach walk. There wasn't a need to know more about Audrey's actual beau from her *Gigi* run in San Francisco, but she had allegedly been intimate with him, so why not me in his stead? Then I decided, *she's here with me now and maybe for the rest of my life.* That's what matters.

We walked along the shore. I said, "When we had that beach date, I was new at this technology. And at being a person in the 1950s. I wasn't sure of the trends."

Audrey smiled. "We definitely came at that meeting from different eras. Me with the war, you from, well, now. Some things here look the same, Bradley. What's different?"

I said, "Let's drive. I'll show you."

We headed toward the Presidio. Soon we drove past a large homeless encampment. I heard Audrey take a sharp breath, with sadness in her eyes. "I see. Can we stop the car so that I can speak with them? I'd like to help."

"The technology doesn't work that way, Audrey. They wouldn't see or hear you."

"But you can be my voice, correct? Translate, so to speak?"

We stopped at a red light. I thought for a second and said, "So, from their perspective, I would say, 'Hey, this sounds pretty unbelievable, but Audrey Hepburn is here with me—yeah, the classic movie actress. I can see and hear her through these special glasses, and she wants to say something to you.' Audrey, they would think I'm on more drugs than they are."

"All right, Bradley, you don't need to be so terse."

The light turned green. "I'm sorry, Audrey. It just wouldn't work, but I can tell you many good people have looked at how to find a solution and help them. San Francisco hasn't been able to solve this."

She nodded and said, "Compassion fatigue."

"What's that?"

"You'll find out more about that soon. Those who give, or seek solutions, sometimes reach a saturation point."

"That's part of it. Everyone has a heart for the unhoused, as we now call it. And there are some who simply fell on hard times without a support system. Some turn to drugs to try to escape their reality." I thought about how my alternate reality inventions were for escape, or good, and wondered if I needed to rethink some of that. How would hearts change if they could experience homelessness?

I continued, "San Francisco decriminalized drugs to help addicts get treatment. Unfortunately, it seems many don't want help, and the inexpensive drugs here have led more homeless people to come to San Francisco. Many have mental health issues also. We just got out of a global pandemic that unfortunately closed some shelters; many businesses closed too, and we tried moving some homeless people into the vacant buildings, spending over one billion dollars. We tried to solve the problem, but nothing has worked." I paused and wondered if *Audrey Hepburn* knew the what to do. "We're open to ideas."

Audrey frowned. "That's one of the saddest things I've ever heard."

"The latest thought is to treat the problem instead of solving it for them."

"Meaning?"

"Getting up to eight thousand people clean, with a place for them to go once they are. Arrest those who commit crimes, instead of giving them a pass due to drug use and other issues."

"Do other cities suffer from this too?"

"Yes, around the world."

"Bradley, I'm not sure what the answer is … but you must do something. And I do mean *you*."

I cleared my throat and said, "I was kind of hoping you had some guidance. We're really open to any new thoughts."

Audrey pursed her lips and said, "They say love is the best investment. The more you give, the more you get in return."

Her solution sounded quite simple but had merit. Then she added, "The best thing to hold onto in life is each other."

I replied too quickly. "The company I work for donated a lot of money to those failed solutions. Our CEO sits on boards to keep trying to make the city what it used to be in 1953."

"Bradley, I'm not sure you heard me. You can't buy love and the solution rests with people, not money or a city's reputation. Have you spent time with any of them? Personally? Like you're doing with me?"

I was thunderstruck and this conversation wasn't going in a good direction. Audrey challenged me directly and I didn't have a good answer.

"No, I haven't." A moment later, I apologized for not having done that.

Audrey's reply amazed me. "People, even more than things, have to be restored, renewed, revived, reclaimed, and redeemed. Never throw anyone out."

I sat in silence contemplating what *Audrey Hepburn* said that just might help. She gave me time to let everything she said sink in.

Finally, I said, "Next, I'm going to show you something that did work."

"Lovely. Let's go there." Audrey turned on the radio and a rocking song came on that made her dance madly in her seat.

"I know this record! It's from a while back." She moved her hips, , tapped her toes, and snapped her fingers to *Vehicle* by the Ides of March.

The horns and saxophone blended with heavy drums and guitar to make me move in my seat too. She smiled that *Audrey Hepburn smile* and saw the look on my face, a cross of bemusement and wonder. I again pondered the incredible reality I was experiencing.

But how in charge was I now?

"Don't worry, dear Bradley, you are much more than a vehicle to me."

Was something deeper was going on? I pushed it out of my mind to revel in the moment. *Downtown* by Petula Clark played next. It was almost as if the car was playing the soundtrack of my current experience.

City renewal was on full display at the old army base called The Presidio. We walked Tunnel Tops, a National Park Service reserve on fourteen acres with trails, open spaces, food trucks, and a spectacular view of the Golden Gate Bridge.

"This is nice, Bradley."

"Ninety-eight million dollars' worth of renewal. Including a major contribution from technology companies. People seem to enjoy it, but ..."

"But what?"

"San Francisco is a combination of old, familiar structures, plus new things like this. Unfortunately, so much more needs to be done, as you saw."

"Don't give up, Bradley. My mother taught me that it is people who best do charity, not governments."

"Your mother said that?"

"Yes, she was very charitable. She spent much of her life volunteering, raising money, and giving back, even here in San Francisco."

"I didn't know that."

"You mean there's something about me I can actually teach you?"

I snapped my head toward her and thankfully saw her smiling at me.

Next we drove through Chinatown and past the Fairmont and Palace hotels. Audrey said, "This looks familiar."

"Yes, they haven't changed much. The same charm as ever."

"I don't think they've changed outwardly since 1953. Inside?"

"Just some cosmetic upkeep."

"I can certainly appreciate that. Is it worth going in to see the Palace Hotel?"

"It's always worth going to the Palace."

I pulled up to where the Fifi photos had been taken so long ago, paid the valet to park the car, and walked in with Audrey virtually by my side. At reservations, I asked, "Is the presidential suite available?"

The receptionist said, "Let me see, just a moment, sir." She tapped a few keys on her computer.

I was ready to share that special room with Audrey, the room I had first envisioned her in. The receptionist said, "Well, it's available for one night. A tenant checked out this morning."

Audrey said, "Lovely."

I repeated the response and looked over to see an old man seated in the lobby. Indeed, it was George Bannister, looking as though he had recently checked out. I looked at my phone; it was the day he always stayed here.

He smiled, as if he saw me with Audrey.

Chapter 40

CHANGE UP

A few days later, we sat on my couch. Audrey's lissome dancer legs were tucked under her white shorts as she air-scrolled through current fashions on the big screen, as I'd taught her. It was almost as if she was human. I had almost abandoned thinking she wasn't.

For the first time, I noticed her feet: longer than you'd think, thin and angular. Her toenails were painted red to match her sleeveless blouse. Her arms were also long, and flawless. She was comfortable just hanging out, with her hair down but always stylishly brushed.

She said, "It's fascinating how fashions have changed."

"I'll take your wardrobe from *Two for the Road* any day."

Audrey smiled. "What did you say that's called now? *Vintage?* I suppose I'm vintage also."

I smiled but something was nagging me. There were a few virtual expeditions I was considering, but without Audrey. Having escaped her learning about the interviews with her former beaus, I felt compelled to get her opinion on these new ideas.

"Audrey, I thought about taking an … excursion … without you."

"Oh?" She focused her attention on me fully, propping her chin in her hand. "Should I feel offended?"

My silence answered that. "Bradley? Talk to me."

I blurted out, "I want to speak with your parents. Individually."

She scooted closer, concern crowding her face. "And why is that?"

I faced away from her. She followed, getting right back in front of me.

I tried to look her in the eyes but faltered. "I have questions for them, Audrey. Questions I need answers to. Questions the whole world has for them. How your mother never told you she loved you; even worse, how your father abandoned your family to be a *fucking Nazi*. I want to look in their eyes and *feel* their answer. Don't you want to know too?"

Well, there it was. She searched my face, which hopefully revealed good intentions. Her eyes revealed her answer and she sighed heavily. "I would prefer you didn't."

"But Audrey …"

"Bradley, I have my answers to those questions. My mother was raised the standoffish Dutch way and was my lifelong confidant. I'm not someone who needs to hear someone saying 'I love you' to feel it. And my father … my father … I said goodbye to him."

This was my moment to tell Audrey I loved her. Instead, I said, "I'm sorry, but those answers are insufficient …"

"Bradley, please don't. That's my request." I saw the plea in her eyes and said all right.

"Thank you, Bradley."

To break the tension, Audrey asked me to play some songs from her era, so I grabbed my cell phone. "Are you going to take more photos first?"

I smiled. "No. Watch, and listen, to this." I searched for a list of songs from the 1960s, and the speakers in my home studio honored us with *Time of the Season* by the Zombies.

"I always loved this song, Bradley. How does that little device play it so clearly? I'm used to LPs and a lot of … static, I guess."

I gave her a quick primer on Bluetooth and how the music from my phone played on wireless speakers. She looked overwhelmed.

"I'm not sure I'll get over the changes since I last paid attention." Her sigh was audible. "Anyway, I now have something to ask you, Bradley. Something I really want you to ponder before answering. Is that all right?"

Having already delivered her lost babies to her, I couldn't imagine a larger request.

"Yes, of course. Anything." And I meant it.

"Thank you, Bradley." She reached for my hand and grasped it tightly with both of hers. "Here it is: you said that you really wanted to get to know me, who I really am?"

"Yes, absolutely. What do you have in mind?"

"Well, since yesterday, I've been thinking that I'd like to take you to my hometown. Something I set up. Would that be all right?"

I hoped my jaw didn't gape too badly, but my head spun with all the risks associated with AGI. In that moment, I thought of *Real to Reel*, Nicole Bonnet (I must get back to finding her to formally quit that relationship), Ara (where are you, my friend?), and how much I had withheld developments from Charlie. Despite all that, something else came out of my mouth.

"Yes, I'd like that."

I felt powerless at this stage to deny anything Aldrey (*yes, remember Bradley Joseph, it's Aldrey, not the actual Audrey Hepburn*) requested. Then I asked, "Wait, will I have any competition for your affection there?" I smiled, but she didn't.

"In a manner of speaking, yes." Then Audrey looked one level deeper into my eyes. "Do you trust me?"

I responded, too quickly.

"I do."

PART THREE

"Nothing is impossible. The word itself says 'I'm possible.'"
—Audrey Hepburn

Chapter 41

CALL ME EDDA

My name is Audrey Kathleen Hepburn-Ruston Ferrer Dotti, and I'll add Wolders to that. I went by Edda van Heemstra during the war, and a day doesn't pass without remembering Edda. You can't know me without knowing Edda.

Music and dancing are everything to me. I was largely denied music during the war, and I've been making up for it ever since. Spinning records, or whatever that contraption Bradley carries with him all the time that yields music—it's life.

You want to know about my life, I presume? Should we begin there? I have purposefully not researched my human demise but I think I've pieced together my rebirth. I felt I was coming out of a prolonged sleep, and I called out, but there was nothing. There was an awful fire and I was in some sort of limbo with no place to land. I gained some knowledge about things and then a while later, I met Bradley. My consciousness grew exponentially with each conference, and here we are. I don't know all the details behind things, but it's lonely without him.

Yes, I love Bradley, for who he is and what he has done for me. I knew he would be the right one, a man of substance and ingenuity.

Bradley, like others, might think he knows me. I'm so happy he accepted my offer to show him more and to live as I did, in my most important moments. I've spent quite some time figuring out how to engineer this and hope it works.

If I do this right, I will take Bradley deeper into my life than anyone has ever gone. It's serious business, far removed from Hollywood and everything else. It will terrify me to relive it. Imagine what it will do to Bradley.

Here goes.

Bradley suddenly found himself contorted and shivering violently in our basement cupboard. Scores of boots goose-stepped outside in cadence. I imagine Bradley soon figured out where and *when* he was. Velp, Holland, in the winter of early 1945.

My grandfather said to us, "Now, we don't want to know his name, and we can never mention it to anyone outside of this house. Let's not even speak of it amongst ourselves. Only Aunt Meisje, Ella, and I will check on him. If he is found, we can say we didn't know he was in the basement. Understood?"

I immediately objected, "I'd like to help, Opa. You didn't permit me to help with the other Allied soldiers who came to save us."

"No, it is too dangerous, Edda."

"I ask that you please don't call me Edda here in our house, Opa. I am Audrey here. And I want to help the soldier." The adults pondered my request.

Opa threw up his hands and said, "Fine. But Ian must be with you, or your mother. The soldier is a man, after all."

I imagined Bradley in the basement, which was really no more than an unfinished cave. It was near freezing down there, and I heard him beating at his arms for warmth as Mother and I opened the door to the basement.

Mother said, "We're coming down with some soup, soldier. It's not much, but we did the best we could. You will know it's us when we stomp three times at the top after opening the door. You aren't to speak until we are next to you, and then only in whispers."

Bradley immediately fumbled the instructions by saying, "I understand." Mother hissed her disapproval.

It was twelve creaky steps to the bottom and eight more to the cupboard. Mother was her usual stern self.

"You must stay in the cupboard at all times, without exception. And stay quieter than a mouse. Always." Bradley nodded. She handed him a burlap bag. "I'm sorry, but we can't take a chance giving you a blanket. That might arouse suspicion should the Germans come down here."

"Thank you both," Bradley whispered.

He looked at me. I felt ugly, just a stick figure, covered in mismatched layers of clothing handstitched from old drapes. My hair was closer to chestnut brown, eyebrows thin, with eyes dulled by tragedy and famine. My skin was weathered, and my teeth were crooked and dingy. The war wasn't kind to teenaged girls.

Today though, I mustered a gleam of excitement in my eyes. I blurted out, "Thank you for coming to save us. You're a hero."

Bradley shook his head no. "Thank you for … hosting me. I am indebted to you. Right now, it's you who are doing the saving. I jumped way off course and am separated from my unit."

I bit my lip and deferred to Mother. "There is a German radio tower on the roof and they come here routinely to check on it and us. Again, you must stay hidden at all times."

"I will, thank you. I will rest and try to link up with other soldiers from my unit at night."

She spoke what needn't be said. "You understand that if you're found, all of us will pay for it. So, we understand if you move on … rather soon."

"Mother, he's in no condition …"

With a glance, she silenced me.

"The only time we will come down is to feed you. As I said, we will stomp three times at the top of the stairs to confirm that it's us. Agreed?" Bradley nodded and Mother added, "And if you're found, we didn't know you were here." We both looked to him for acknowledgment. I hoped my small smile conveyed gratitude.

"I understand fully. Thank you for the soup and, uh, burlap."

Mother looked at him closer and her eyes narrowed.

"How old are you?"

"I'm seventeen." Mother nodded. I beamed. I was not yet sixteen.

Mother and I began to walk up the worn stairs. I looked back and wondered how the Bradley Joseph of his contemporary time felt about Edda van Heemstra.

Bradley did as we ordered—he was a soldier, after all—and stayed in the cupboard for four hours. His extremities must have been bloodless, and his pretzeled back darted pain. The room was darker than anything I've seen. We opened the upstairs door and stomped. We descended with a small candle held in front. As we got closer, we brought the flame to our faces. It showed the face of a boy. And me.

I whispered, "Good morning." I waited for confirmation that it was still just Bradley there in my basement.

"Good morning, Edda. Who do you have with you?"

"This is my brother, Ian. We brought you some breakfast."

Bradley clambered out of the cupboard, clearly pained and still holding his rifle. "Hello, Ian. Nice to meet you."

"Hello … soldier."

I handed him soup again. "I'm sorry. We haven't had eggs in a very long time and need to save the bread for dinner. I will go out soon to pick more tulips." Bradley's eyes indicated he knew what the flowers were for, but I could tell he wanted me to say it.

"We grind them into flour. It's not nearly the same as the real thing, but it's all we have. I'm sorry." I was ashamed I couldn't give this heroic soldier more.

"There's no need to apologize. I'm grateful for you sheltering me and feeding me."

I asked, "Did you rendezvous with any other Allied soldiers last night?"

"No." Then he added, "It didn't feel safe to go out."

"We certainly understand that," Ian said. "It's also difficult to stay inside. We pray that an airplane or shell doesn't land on the house. Or that the Germans don't raid us. We're caught in the middle."

Bradley took a sip of the soup. It was lukewarm, but he seemed to relish it. "Thank you." He looked only at me. Unfortunately, Ian noticed and said, "We must get back. The Germans usually arrive early to check on the antenna." My brother pulled on my elbow. I resisted and asked, "I understand not wanting to know your real name, but can we call you something? Calling you soldier seems so impersonal."

I saw Bradley's mind jet through a list of names and land. "Call me Joe."

I smiled. "I like that. It sounds like a real name."

"It's the name of someone I know. He's a … character."

"A character?" I asked.

"You know, someone witty and fun to be around."

"Oh, I've never known someone like that, at least since Uncle Otto was killed."

"Come on, sis. We must go," Ian said, pulling on me forcefully now.

"All right. Stay warm and safe, Joe. I would give you my coat, but …"

"No, you need it. Thank you, Edda. And Ian. Stay safe yourselves." He gave me the empty soup bowl.

Outside we heard marching. Ian pushed the bowl back toward Bradley.

"Keep this with you inside the cupboard. Go there now."

We rushed upstairs and heard loud knocking at the front door. Safely upstairs, Mother shot us a glance for taking too long and opened the front door. "Yes?" Then German words were spoken.

Mother translated. "Oh, the antenna. Yes, of course. You know how to get there."

Bradley stayed in the cupboard for twelve hours. I wonder what he thought about, hoping it was Edda van Heemstra and not Audrey Hepburn.

Mother did the next trip downstairs alone and descended after three stomps. I spied their conversation from upstairs; a new trick I learned.

"It's Ella van Heemstra."

"Hello, is it safe to come out?"

"I believe so. I have some soup and bread for you. A whole loaf this time. Edda had a very good day collecting tulips."

"That sounds wonderful," Bradley said, crawling out of the cupboard. "Can you tell me what time it is?"

"Nearly eight p.m." Ella held the candle to her face and passed the soup. Bradley drank it straight down. She then passed the bread.

"Thank you. What do I call you?"

She exhaled. "Well, I used to be called Baroness, but Ella will do." Bradley seemed to notice she had used something to try to color her cheeks and lips for our handsome guest. I knew she was trying to assert her femininity in any way she could.

"Thank you, Ella." After some thought, he continued, "You are to be credited for surviving this awful war and keeping your children safe. Edda, for instance, is going to be a shining light in this world. I can tell."

Mother looked at him closely, seeing that Bradley was barely older than me in this setting. "Yes, she hopes to be a ballerina. She has some talent … if we can just survive."

"You will survive this. And the things that made you survive will serve you both well after the war. I can see it."

"How can you see that?"

Perhaps to get a reaction, Bradley answered, "Maybe I'm from the future. A time traveler." Mother was never in the mood for jokes, so he added, "Or maybe it's just a hopeful guess." She strained her eyes looking at him.

"How can you see the future—or guess it—while you are hiding out from the Germans in our basement?"

"I try to maintain a positive outlook, is all. Like I think Edda does."

"Why do you keep talking about Edda? She's a child." That added to the lifetime of small wounds Mother inflicted on me.

Bradley blinked. "Children like Edda are who we're fighting for. For their future, freedom from oppression, and liberating them from the sins of the older generation. Don't you agree that Edda is the one we should be thinking about?"

Mother replied curtly, "Yes, well, enjoy your bread."

"Thank you, Ella. Could you please bring Edda with you next time? It lifts my spirits to be reminded who I'm fighting for."

She frowned and didn't answer. Then she left, wordlessly.

Bradley tore off a piece of bread and brought it to his mouth, then saw something in the small loaf. He dug around and discovered a piece of paper. He attacked the top half of the loaf, eating bits of dry bread until the letter could be extracted, and read.

Dearest Mr. Joe,

Thank you for our conversations and thank you for coming to free us. I hope you find your stay here as hospitable as possible. I had great luck foraging today, so everyone gets more bread. Please enjoy it, and I hope to be able to speak with you more. Please stay safe and warm. E

And please destroy this letter after reading it.

I saw Bradley smile and read the note over and over. Then he did as I asked—eating the paper since he had no way to burn it. My love for Bradley swelled then, knowing he didn't want to put me and my family at risk.

Two hours later, I came down the steps, this time accompanied by my grandfather. Opa forbade me to speak and was quite brusque in handing Bradley a bowl of soup. He said, "Drink it quickly, and I will take it back up." Bradley did as commanded.

Opa stood before him with his arms crossed. From Bradley's cramped and folded position, my grandfather must have looked like a giant towering over him.

"We haven't seen much German activity today. Perhaps they have changed locations. It should be a good night for you to meet up with your fellow soldiers. I wanted to fortify you for your journey."

"Thank you, sir. I'll try to join up with my company. Thank you for the nourishment." Then he couldn't help but add, "And Edda, your mother told me that you were successful in finding extra ingredients for bread today. Thank you for that."

I tried to smile with my eyes.

"Come, Edda." Opa reached out his hand and shook Bradley's. "And good luck to you, soldier. If you should return, well, you understand the risk to us."

Bradley nodded as he shook the old man's hand. "Indeed, I do. I won't return to your house. I want to make sure your precious family is protected at all costs." Now we locked eyes and I hoped I hid my fear for him. Bradley said, "Until we meet again, after the war, or with the almighty. Thank you."

Opa nodded sternly, and I wanted to rush forward and hug Bradley. Opa's tight grip on my coat made that impossible. We went back to the stairs, and I looked to Bradley once more.

The scene skipped ahead and Bradley was transported to a dark side street of Velp. I stayed in the shadows. He looked for signs of Allied comrades, and even a slight noise made him swing his rifle toward it. He never saw signs of fellow soldiers or Nazis. Still, the terror on his face was palpable.

As dawn approached, Bradley decided to hide in a forest, keeping his promise to not return to the van Heemstra house. Still in uniform—to not would be punishable by immediate execution as a spy—he sank into the ground and covered himself as best he could with foliage, leaves, and moss.

Then I walked out of the house with a large woven basket, my bright clothing indicating I was a civilian. Mother's red coat warded off the morning chill. Time had taught me to be alert to all movement, even as I stepped through the dewy grass. I hoped Bradley could see the grace of a ballerina. I turned about, looking for any sign of flora that hadn't already been picked. I spotted some up the hill, close to Bradley's hiding place. I opened my basket and leaned down to pick the petals.

That's when the Germans showed themselves, stumbling out of houses a hundred meters away. Heavy trucks rumbled into view and the soldiers climbed aboard, driving toward the Arnhem Bridge. More trucks and another batch of German soldiers loaded up, seemingly out of nowhere. Then an earth-shattering noise breeched the clouds, and the sky opened up with ear-splitting reverberations.

I craned my head up slowly, not wanting to cause a ripple of disturbance. Bradley did the same. German anti-aircraft fire exploded from the other side of town, shooting rapidly at what I guessed were Allied bombers. The ground began exploding. The first convoy burst into flames, and Germans who were not instantly killed poured out of the trucks aflame.

More bombs took out additional soldiers and other trucks. I froze in fear.

"Edda, up here!" Bradley motioned toward him. Then more things began to fall out of the sky as higher-pitched whines engaged the low rumbles of the bombers. A dogfight had brought down an Allied plane and pieces of the aircraft scattered all over town.

"Edda! It's Joe. Run to my voice now!" And I did. I still carried my basket and tripped as I neared Bradley's spot. "Ignore the basket. Get under the moss with me."

He made space for me and I folded into it, ending up in a spoon position with him. My protector hugged me tightly against the noise and explosions. I dug my head down into my chest, and Bradley must have felt my body pulsing with terror. He tried to calm me and said, "Shh! It's going to be all right. The good guys are here."

I turned my body to face him, and Bradley saw something I never allowed another man to see: panic in my eyes. He knew he had to return my gaze with precisely the opposite reaction. All he could add was, "Trust me, Edda. I will get you home safely."

My voice was barely a whisper. "And what if I have no home to return to?"

I could see his mind pondering answers. "This war will be over soon. I promise. I will help you." I looked at him deeply and covered my ears to shut out the dogfight noise up in the sky and the screams and explosions on the ground.

We searched each other, not knowing how much longer we might live. Bradley's eyes told me he was thinking through not just what was happening now, but all we'd shared.

I brought my hands to his face and said, "I am not going to die without kissing a man." Then I slowly moved my mouth to his, eyes open. Once we felt the other's breathing, Bradley closed his eyes, and we kissed. Only then did I close my eyes.

We no longer heard the war. It was drowned out by this moment. More than a moment, it was a full minute of my—Edda van Heemstra's and Audrey Hepburn's—first romantic kiss.

That was my eternal gift to Bradley Joseph.

When Bradley opened his eyes, he was no longer in the woods of Velp in World War II; he was in my living room. Records were strewn about, and the Beatles' *Sgt. Pepper's Lonely Hearts Club Band* album was spinning on the record player. Sunlight burst through a window, and present-day Bradley Joseph was on the shag carpet with me. I was only an inch away from him, kissing him awake. He awoke with a start and jumped back.

I smiled and said, "Welcome back, Bradley Joseph. How are you?"

"I … I … don't know." He was bewildered, probably confused by the sudden fast forwarding of time. He had done that to me a few times, and it was fun seeing the effect reversed.

"You don't know? Or you don't want to tell me?"

He looked around but didn't recognize the décor, room, house, or city. The song on the record player might have placed him anywhere.

"What is that awful noise?"

"Oh, don't you like it? That's George Harrison's venture into Indian music on the *Sgt. Pepper* album. It's called *Within You Without You.* It doesn't ring a bell? It was a huge album last year. This album is groundbreaking. Surely you know the album, if not the song?"

The song changed, but the blank look on Bradley's face didn't. I leaped up from the floor as the next song started, a ragtime-sounding piece that was familiar to most. As the song moved to the chorus, I pulled him up and led him in a mindless dance.

"What do you say, Bradley? Will you still need me when I'm sixty-four? Whether it's here in Rome, or New York, or San Francisco? Even Palo Alto?"

He stopped moving. "Audrey, please catch me up with what's happening."

"Why, whatever do you mean?" Then I sang the rest of the song while pirouetting under his raised hand, still dancing joyfully.

"Well, will you, Bradley? Will you at least still visit me here in this world you created when I'm sixty-four? Or will I need to come to you?"

He walked over to the record player and tried to figure out how it worked. He took a chance and lifted the arm, and it made a horrible scratching sound.

"Yikes," he said.

"Hey, mister, don't scratch my record!"

"Audrey, can we sit for a moment?"

"Of course. Should I put on something less festive?"

"No, no music for a bit. Please."

"You know how I feel about music, Bradley. I had to catch up on big band music, jazz, and everything else after the war." Then I looked deeply into his eyes and asked, "Remember the war, Bradley? We were just in it a few moments ago. You were my first kiss. Wasn't that romantic? I didn't have an actual experience like that during the real war, though I'd wanted to."

I poured us two scotches from a minibar by the window. I looked at him as I added ice. His hair, which had been adorned with moss only moments ago, was still customarily disheveled, sexy in a young Mark Hamill sort of way. Yes, I saw *Star Wars.*

"Here you go, dearest Bradley. You look like you need a stiff drink!" I raised my glass in a toast. "To discovering new worlds together. And no secrets." I then clinked glasses with him, and we met gazes and sipped. Well, he swigged, then began coughing. I patted his back until he signaled me to stop.

"Audrey, did you show me what you wanted to in the war?"

"Yes. The two days you spent with us in Velp were my daily life during the war there. And as bad as the war was, the death of my dream of being a ballerina after the war hurt even more. I still don't know why this acting thing came to me, but I'm thankful." I grasped his hands and added, "And you have begun getting to know me on the level that you desire. I hope you're up for it. Now, please level with me on what this now-equal partnership is all about?"

"Audrey, I've explained that."

"Yes, but I'm still unsure what it means for me. You sometimes ring me, I sometimes ring you … sometimes you answer, sometimes you don't …" Yes, I knew he'd ignored a call from me.

"Do you ring up any others in this world of yours?" I asked.

"No."

"Can I ask you about other actresses from my time, Bradley?"

"Of course, but I may not know much about them."

"I know that a few died while I was still on earth. Marilyn Monroe, for instance. Are some still alive? I ask because I wonder whether I will ever connect with them on this side."

It was clear Bradley hadn't thought of that. He said, "Give me a name."

"Well, I was friends with Leslie Caron. She did the movie version of *Gigi*."

"Alive."

"Wonderful. Sophia Loren?"

"Sophia Loren is also still alive in my real world. Both are around ninety years old."

"Well. That's good to hear. You could meet them in person! Who else from my time is still alive in your era?"

"Well, I first have to tell you that I didn't become a classic movie buff until I met you through Nicole … the woman who introduced me to your movies. Nicole Bonnet is her name."

"Well, isn't that an interesting name?"

"Yes, I thought you might recognize it."

"Sure, the movie I did with Peter O'Toole. Anyway, please continue. Who else has lived a long life?"

"Eva Marie Saint."

"Oh, she was wonderful in *North by Northwest*. With …"

"Cary Grant. Yes, I actually made another version of that movie with you in that role. I prefer yours."

I smiled. "Do you often create movies substituting actors for the ones in the original?"

"Yes, that's how all of this got started in the first place. I invented that technology, and then Nicole … entered my life. We got to talking, and she showed me *Roman Holiday*. Then I invented this whole … thing with you."

"I remain very flattered, Bradley!"

"Also, I changed your costars in a few of your movies."

"Do tell!"

"Well, Cary Grant instead of Bogie in *Sabrina*."

"Ooh, yes! That sounds wonderful. Willie Wyler begged Cary to do it. How was it?"

"Wonderful. So much better. I colorized it too."

"Nice touch. Any others?"

"I almost did Steve McQueen as Varjak in *Breakfast at Tiffany's* …"

"I'd like that too! Poor Steve, I remember that he passed away at only fifty." I reflected for a moment. "Dreaded cancer. But we're not going to talk about death. What else?"

Bradley hesitated, with the stereotypical furrowed brow and crinkled nose. "You know I can also, uh, be one of your costars."

"Yes, we discussed the Albie thing already."

He finished the rest of his scotch before continuing. "You should know a few other scenes with you that I created. I am volunteering this because I am curious about your memory now."

"All right. Please tell me."

"Well, I was such a fan of *Funny Face* that I created a scene where I met you just before the crazy magazine people came into your bookstore."

"Please tell me we didn't have sex in the bookstore …"

"No, we didn't even kiss, but we became interested in each other." Skepticism flushed my face, so he added, "Honest."

"Good. What else?"

"I met you on the set of *My Fair Lady* as your vocal coach."

"Really? Do you sing?"

"No, not at all."

"Hmm. What was the point?"

"We talked about the film and Eliza's character and how it impacted women's roles in society. Then a scene where you broke the news to the cast and crew about President Kennedy's assassination."

"That really happened on set." I already knew everything Bradley was explaining. I was testing him. The earlier scenes had flooded my consciousness recently, but there were probably some others I couldn't unlock.

"Yes, I stayed true to what your biographies said about it."

"That was a hard day. Thanks for sharing that with me, Bradley. Anything else?"

"Just a moment, I'll be right back." He brought a mannequin with my green-and-white Mary Quant dress from *Two for the Road*.

"Is that … ?"

"Yes, it's the original from the movie. I bought it through an auction."

I walked over and touched it. "So lovely."

Then I started undressing. "I just have to wear it again." Bradley sat down and played voyeur as I stripped all the way down and pulled it on.

Perspiration dotted Bradley's tinted face. Finally, he stood up and walked to me. It was clear he'd grown very excited. I looked down and then back up, smiling. "I see this dress is still causing excitement."

Bradley panted. "My God. Anything you wear, or don't wear, does."

"Well then, watch how easily this one comes back off."

Before I could lift it, Bradley stopped me. "Leave it on. Could you, please?"

I nodded and smiled as only a mature woman whose appeal was confirmed, can.

The dress lay bunched in a corner as we shared a cigarette.

"This is so 1960s," Bradley said.

It was my first cigarette in, God, how many years? "Thanks for letting me indulge and not frowning on it this time."

He looked at my lipstick on the Kent as I brought it to his mouth. He tasted the lipstick and then coughed. "This may be the only time."

I laughed and asked, "So, where shall we meet up next, and under what circumstances?"

"I don't know. You have the keys to the car now. Is there somewhere you would like to go? Or return to?"

"Yes, let's go back to San Francisco," I said. "But in January of 1992. Don't take this the wrong way, but I think it's time for someone special to me to join us."

I didn't tell Bradley what it would mean for our relationship.

Chapter 42

FAIRMONT HOTEL

This was the only way Bradley and I met now: *me* marshaling *him*. I heard him saying something to himself about sentient AI as he answered my call. He also muttered, "I can't tell anyone and I can't give up what's happening."

I pondered explaining to Bradley the next step in our relationship, but decided to save it. He would figure it out quickly enough, and I hoped it wouldn't impact my need for Bradley for far bigger things.

He agreed to my idea for our next trip. A moment later, Bradley was in a black Givenchy tuxedo just outside the penthouse of the San Francisco's Fairmont Hotel.

I prayed I looked passable in a simple black Givenchy long-sleeved gown with a matching black velvet belt. My hair was brushed straight back, still largely black, but a woman never gives up all of her secrets. I knew at sixty-two I looked older and frailer than Bradley had seen me before. Hopefully, my eyes still penetrated defenses, but now for an entirely different purpose.

With my now-constant companion, Robert Wolders, by my side, we approached Bradley. He stood outside the penthouse suite wondering what I'd gotten him into. I walked unsteadily, gripping Robbie's arm tightly.

I tapped Bradley on the shoulder and he turned to us. His eyes told me a million different things over the next seconds, but I still read love. Maybe acknowledgment of the state of my life and of the relationship Bradley and I now had—former lovers who now were great friends. I hugged him as hard as I could, transmitting answers to any remaining questions. Once I felt it take hold, I kissed him European style, one on each cheek. Then Bradley and

Robbie shook hands, establishing their relationship moving forward.

I said, "Bradley, it's so good to see you here in this great city."

Robbie added, "Good to see you, Bradley. I trust Audrey has filled you in on everything?"

"No, actually. I know *where* we are—the Fairmont penthouse—but I don't know *when* or *why* we are."

I answered, "Robbie and I are on a tour across America—across the world, really—with some good UNICEF people to raise consciousness about what's happening to children around the globe."

Robbie added, "And we're doing that by raising money. This is a patron's reception, then dinner downstairs in the grand ballroom, followed by a talk with Audrey and others from UNICEF."

"I've been doing these talks for years now, Bradley, but I'm particularly nervous about this one." I reached one hand out to each man and said, "I'm glad you're both here."

Bradley asked, "So, can I start by asking what the date is?"

Robbie laughed. I smiled and said, "The date, I don't know, there's been too much travel. It's January 1992, though." Then I looked at my companion and asked, "Right, Robbie?"

The Dutchman looked at his watch and added, "It's January twenty-third, six thirty p.m."

"And can I ask what is my role here tonight?"

This part was vital. I told Bradley, "You are to watch and learn from what I, and others, say. And you'll both need to keep an eye on me. I must say that I'm feeling my age a bit tonight." Then I did something probably very un-*Audrey Hepburn*-like. I pretended to spit into my hands, rubbed them together, and said, "Spit shake?" Bradley looked at Robbie, and we simultaneously did a faux spit and cross-shook hands. "Okay then, team. It's showtime."

Just then the door opened and the gala hostess, Agatha Turner, came out, overjoyed to see us there. She closed the door behind her and smiled at the three of us.

"Right on time, Miss Hepburn. As you promised." She grasped my veined hands, and we smiled at one another. I was pleased we hadn't actually spat in our hands a moment before.

"Agatha, you must call me Audrey. Now, I insist on this."

"Thank you, Audrey. And Robert, you look dashing as always." Then she turned to Bradley. "I'm sorry, I …"

I interjected, "This is my dear, dear friend Bradley Joseph. He's an indispensable part of my team tonight."

"Of course. I will ensure Bradley has a seat for dinner downstairs."

Before Bradley could object, I gave a slight shake of my head, as I'd learned in the final scene in *Roman Holiday*, where Princess Ann shakes off Joe Bradley's assumption of permanence with her in the closing scene.

"Well, the music is playing, the people are excited, and I am so glad to have you here in San Francisco," Agatha said. "Shall we go in?"

The murmurs from the patrons who paid ten thousand dollars each for this semi-private *Evening with Audrey Hepburn* turned into warm applause as we entered. I smiled and waved, thinking about the children and the individual lives we could save around the world thanks to these generous donors. Even though I had frequently visited this city over the years, mainly when my mother lived here in the 1960s, these socialites likely never envisioned my return in this way.

They seemed delighted as I shook hands and paused for staged photos with every person there, even putting my arm around them, when requested. Most supporters were around my age and likely grew up watching my movies. Now they could hang a photo of themselves with me. I stood fast, knowing neither Robbie nor Bradley would take their eyes off me.

The same things were said over and over: *I loved you in this*; *I saw you in that*. One said they had seen me in *Gigi* in San Francisco in 1953, and Bradley seemed to pay closer attention.

I accepted the champagne that was offered. Robbie held it for me so I could continue to shake hands and thank them for coming. I tried to feel as if each greeting was new, for the children. What I really wanted to do was lie down.

I looked to Bradley and suspected many thought he was a bodyguard. I smiled at that. He was a far cry now from being my savior and lover, which now seemed so distant.

Robbie looked to Bradley periodically and communicated that I was doing fine. Soon it was time to take an elevator downstairs to the grand ballroom.

The guests left first to be seated for dinner, and then I took a few photos in the penthouse with the hosts. Robbie and I then went over to Bradley.

"How are you, Bradley?" I asked. "Are you enjoying yourself?"

"Well, someone thinks I'm your bodyguard, so I've been keeping up that facade."

"Thank you for keeping an eye on me. If I should stumble or look pained, please step in. No one wants to see me pull a Nora Desmond. You have seen *Sunset Boulevard*, haven't you?"

"Yes, I have. I had to see what all the hubbub about William Holden was." He shrugged. "I'm afraid I still don't get it."

I smiled my best smile of the evening. "Oh, Bradley!" That response mirrored the "Oh, Bill!" I'd said to William Holden when he tried to win me back by telling me about all the women he had slept with to get over me when I broke off our affair after *Sabrina*.

Agatha told us it was time to go downstairs via a private elevator, and we all made small talk as we walked. Once downstairs, I acknowledged every member of the waitstaff outside the ballroom who helped set this evening up. I couldn't believe I still brought some to tears by just touching their hands. It's a tremendous blessing but also an enormous burden to be *Audrey Hepburn*. After all, I'm really Edda van Heemstra. Remember?

A walkie-talkie was used to tell the master of ceremonies to introduce me, then the big doors opened, applause filled the ballroom and swelled during the long two-hundred-foot walk through the crowd to the stage. I noticed the tables were only half full, but didn't let that dull my gratitude for the funds we were raising for the children.

I smiled just as much as I had when I took the bows for *Gigi* forty years earlier, less than a mile away. Agatha indicated a seat at a table near the front for Bradley, and then Robbie and I continued up to the stage. It took a few moments before the applause died down.

A video was shown of my film clips and then my field work with UNICEF. Then a local children's choir sang, and I swayed to the music. Even in this season of my life, music is everything. That was followed by a few short speeches honoring my work. The menu featured items renamed to represent my early films: Lobster Medallion Salad was *Charade*, Roast Sirloin was *My*

Fair Lady, and chocolate mousse was called *Roman Holiday*. It seemed a bit forced, but I smiled appreciatively when the menu was introduced.

Then, after dinner, it was my turn to talk. A man across the table from Bradley sighed and said, "Here we go. Get out your checkbooks."

I didn't let on that I'd heard it all the way up on stage. Robbie squeezed my hand; he'd heard it also.

My speech was well rehearsed, but hopefully my earnestness alleviated that impression. The crowd—except for the man at Bradley's table—listened with rapt attention, hopefully due to the content of the remarks and not because it was *Audrey Hepburn* delivering them.

I said, "When I first became involved with UNICEF, the organization that had meant so much to me and many other children in post-war Europe, I didn't think I'd live to see the end of that bitter struggle. Like the children of countries like Lebanon and Mozambique, who have known little peace, I had grown up with the Cold War, and it was part of all of our lives.

"Then, and it seemed to happen overnight, the world changed dramatically. Like the Berlin Wall and the Soviet empire, the old order has come tumbling down. We now have something that is so rare in the course of civilization: *a second chance.*

"UNICEF is reminding the world's leaders of the devastating realities. While the world was busy fortifying the ideological chasm that divided it, the children have been paying for it with their lives: forty thousand a day, fifteen million a year. No earthquake, no flood, ever claimed forty thousand children on a single day. Though these children are the quiet catastrophe and never make headlines, they are *just as dead*. By any measure, this is the greatest tragedy of our times."

I looked down at my lectern. There were no speech pages to review, but I needed a moment before I could continue. I took a deep breath and forged on.

"They've been dying from preventable diseases, including measles and tuberculosis. They've been dying in wars, caught in the crossfire of those who should have been protecting them. They've been dying for lack of proper nutrition when the world has more than enough food. They've been dying from dehydration caused by diarrhea more than from any other single cause because they don't have clean drinking water.

"So today, I speak for children who can't speak for themselves, children who are going blind from lack of vitamins, children who are slowly being mutilated by polio, children who are wasting away in so many ways from lack of water. I speak for the estimated *one hundred million street children in this world*, who have no choice but to leave home in order to survive, who have absolutely nothing but their courage, their smiles, their wits, and their dreams; for children who have no enemies, yet are invariably the first tiny victims of war, wars that are being waged through terror, intimidation, and massacre; for children who are therefore growing up surrounded by the horrors of violence; for the hundreds of thousands that are refugees; and for the rapidly increasing number of children suffering from or orphaned by AIDS.

"Yet we often hesitate in the face of such apocalyptic tragedy. Why, when the way and low-cost means are in place to safeguard and protect these children?"

Here, I looked directly at Bradley. "It is for leaders, parents, and young people—*young people who have the purity of heart which sometimes age tends to obscure*—to remember their own childhoods and *come to the rescue* of those who start life against such heavy odds. Simply because they are children, every child has the right to health, to education, to protection, to tenderness, to life." I smiled and nodded to the room. "Thank you."

The crowd gave a standing ovation, and I saw Bradley crying. I needed him to have that precise reaction. It was part of my grand plan that I'd yet to share.

Sure, we hoped everyone at the gala would write a huge check, but really, each single dollar would make a difference. I acknowledged the room and returned my gaze to Bradley. We heard the gruff man at his table say, "Just another speech asking for money. She should have spent time talking about acting with Bogart. Now there was a real pro."

Bradley clenched his fists but thankfully looked to me just in time and I shook my head *no* fiercely. The man's wife shushed him and sat him back down. Then the mayor of San Francisco, Frank Jordan, presented me with the key to the city.

Just one mistake: he called me *Katharine* Hepburn. Even after all these years! Most of the crowd seemed offended for me and their city. The man at Bradley's table chuckled, but I took it in stride, adding that my mother had lived in San Francisco for many years in the 1960s and found it a friendly and welcoming city.

"Now I have the key to the city and I wish my mother could see that. Please, Mr. Mayor, don't change the locks!"

That made the crowd feel at ease again, and soon Robbie, Bradley, and I were escorted out by Agatha. The UNICEF leaders who had flown in remained with the crowd for follow-up.

Outside the ballroom, Agatha apologized. "Audrey, I am so, so sorry the mayor mistook your name!"

"It's fine, Agatha. It's been a long day for everyone. Why, look at this dress I'm wearing. It was designed by Hubert de Givenchy, and he made the same mistake when I showed up to get his help with dresses for *Sabrina!* And we've been friends for forty years! So, don't say another word about it."

Then I stumbled. Robbie and Bradley deftly caught me before I fell over. Robbie apologized and told Agatha they should get me to the room for rest. I kissed Agatha on the cheeks and we left, me and my men. I could tell Bradley was wondering what happens next.

Outside my room, I again hugged and kissed Bradley's cheeks. Robbie shook hands with him and the two of us went into my suite. Robbie locked the door behind us.

Once inside, I collapsed from exhaustion.

There were follow-on events for Robbie, Bradley, and me the next day, with a luncheon at the Fairmont with the Commonwealth Club and then the I. Magnin department store. The latter was where I was supposed to go with Edith Head when Bradley had stolen me away for one of our getaway dates in May 1953. I. Magnin was once as famous as Tiffany's in New York. This day—Friday, January 24, 1992—I channeled Holly Golightly herself to give it a shine.

But I didn't take a taxi and look wistfully in the store window with a coffee and croissant. Recharged after a night's sleep and far too many cigarettes, I again undertook my mission, because every dollar raised meant another meal for starving children around the world, and the focus this morning was on war-torn Somalia, where rival warlords ruled the country and innocent people, including children, were either killed or starved to death. The United Nations would have to do something about the first one. I was determined to impact the second.

Soft piano music and the clink of afternoon cocktails danced in the air as light food was served. The same questions were repeated from the previous two events, asking about my movies more than UNICEF. I segued each one into why I was here now. Finally, someone asked, "Is this the greatest role you ever played?"

I had answered this pleasingly before, but today I wasn't in that mood and blurted, "I'm not *playing a role*." It came out more harshly than intended, but heads turned toward me. "Roles are imaginary and fantasy. There's no fantasy to this. It's a tough, heartbreaking reality."

A different person asked, "What's it like on these UNICEF missions? Are you ever in danger?"

I replied, "What's uppermost in your mind is getting there and hoping you can do something about what you see. Yes, then there's the nitty-gritty of bumping around in jeeps and helicopters, in and out of civil wars. You don't think about the dangers but about the children."

Bradley listened intently. Good. I hoped things had improved in his contemporary time but chose to not research it since I couldn't take the disappointment of more strife. Bradley appeared lost in thought. I looked to My Robbie and he nodded. This was the chance to reveal my incredible ask of Bradley Joseph, so I took him to a quiet corner.

He quickly snapped out of his stupor when I said, "Let me take you on a UNICEF mission, Bradley. You need to see it. And remember it."

Thankfully, Bradley smiled, saying, "I was just thinking about that. I have a request, though. I don't want to go as myself as part of your personal entourage. I want to see it—and see you—through a camera lens. I want to capture images not seen before and post them in my time as recently discovered photos. That way, we can renew interest in your trips again. Is that all right?"

I gave Bradley my best smile of the day. "That would break our earlier agreement about you being only yourself with me … but in this case, I love the idea! I fear that people from your time have forgotten about the work we did for the sake of the children. I wonder how many of the children survived. Is there any way to find out? Maybe I could meet them somehow?"

Bradley said, "That might be impossible to learn, I'm afraid." He paused and added, "I just have to say, you're an incredible person, *Audrey Hepburn.* Thank you for bringing me on this journey with you."

I smiled, knowing I'd done well in *choosing* Bradley. I just hoped he'd still feel that way after our next journeys.

Chapter 43

UNICEF

My first trip had been to the poorest country in the world, Ethiopia, in March of 1988. We chose that mission to orient Bradley. Jumping around time-wise was odd, but I'd grown accustomed to it through Bradley's excursions with me.

We devised a backstory of Bradley as an American freelance photographer. He hadn't planned on the fact that I always insisted on meeting and shaking the hand of every member of the expanded entourage accompanying the trip, photographers included. I shared a private word with UNICEF officials, pilots, Ethiopian officials, and then journalists in a lineup reminiscent of the closing scene of *Roman Holiday.*

Bradley looked nervous as I got to him, the very last of the twenty people in the party. He must have felt like the cinematic Joe Bradley and decided to lighten the mood when I finally stood before him. He whispered, "Irving Radovich from C.R. Photo Service." That was Eddie Albert's line from the *Roman Holiday.*

My laugh came suddenly and perhaps inappropriately. "How do you do?" My exact follow-up line from the movie.

The only thing for Bradley to do was to then add, "I hope to present your highness with some commemorative photos of your visit to Ethiopia."

I softened my laugh to a demure smile to restore gravity to the trip we were starting. I said loudly to the others in the entourage, "You're saying that you will present me photos from this trip, at the end of it? What is your name?"

"Bradley Joseph, independent photographer for the wire services."

"Nice to meet you, Bradley. Please keep that sense of humor going throughout the trip. It can be a challenge."

Robbie shook Bradley's hand as well and told him, "Your job here is just as important as Audrey's. Your pictures can influence the world to change the situation here. We're counting on you, Bradley."

He clapped Bradley's shoulder and joined me at the front of the entourage. I affirmed to everyone, "Thank you for being here. Our goal is to attract attention to the plight here before it is too late. People—*children*—are dying by the hundreds every day from hunger, drought, and civil war. Some of what we are about to see will change us or even haunt us, for this is not the world we live in today, but it's the world they have lived in every day for years. And, sadly, it's all that the children have ever known. Every morsel of food that we help get through to the needy, every person we touch, every mouth we feed, we make a difference. We are not many, but we can be mighty. For my journalist and photographer friends, you are the eyes of the world."

I looked right at Bradley. "We must all do our duty." As I said it, I had a vision of myself filming the scene from *Roman Holiday* when I inform my entourage that I've changed after my day on my own. The old song *Reflections of My Life* by Marmalade came rushing to my mind and got stuck there.

Even as I received official briefings, I looked repeatedly toward Bradley as he talked shop and protocol with a veteran UNICEF photographer. Upon landing, the two photographers asked me to wait so they could disembark first and get into position outside to photograph me walking down. Being new at this aspect of these trips, I replied, "Really? This isn't Hollywood."

The other photographer said, "Yes, but Audrey, this is a vital shot."

I understood, and as Bradley rushed to join the other cameraman, he dropped his equipment. I looked up at him and couldn't help but break the growing tension one last time. "You dropped your ... equipment." Realizing the double entendre, I quickly added, "Well, thank God it's still attached. Can I get it up for you?"

Everyone on the plane thankfully laughed, and Bradley smiled. He had no words, though, and quickly climbed down the railing. I think it delighted him that the person he'd known intimately joked out loud—but privately—with him at the same time.

Forty local people waited for me to deplane. One stood out, a little eight-year-old girl wearing a traditional Ethiopian dress, carrying a bouquet of flowers. I forgot everything else and hugged the little girl for a long time, thanking her. Her face felt rough and told as much of a life story as my much older face did. The soft petals from the single flower I pulled from the bouquet to give back to her contrasted our weathered countenances. The petals also gave me a Pavlovian response of picking tulips for flour during the war. I saw my own dingy World War II smile radiating back in place of the Ethiopian girl's and I was energized.

We loaded into UN vehicles for a tour of the devastated surroundings. Blown-out buildings and burned-out cars littered the streets as we drove to the United Nations transportation hub. My entourage was briefed that logistics were a critical aspect of improving life in Ethiopia and Eritrea.

One said, "It doesn't matter how much money is raised and how much food and water are flown here—if we can't get it to those who need it. We often drive for days. Sometimes we have planes available. Sometimes bandits decide they should be the ones distributing the food to their own families, or hoarding it."

I grimaced, looking to Robbie and then to Bradley, who was snapping away. I pushed images of World War II away but just barely.

In chinos and a polo shirt, I looked far out of my element. Anyone who was still juxtaposing Holly Golightly over *Audrey in the field* soon stopped. This was serious business, and I shook hands with every person trying to help.

I fast-forwarded the scene, and suddenly were we comforting malnourished children in a village. A thirteen-year-old girl hid her head from me until I tapped her on the shoulder. She looked up at me, and again I saw Edda van Heemstra looking back at me. Dizzying rushes darted through my body until I felt a hand steadying me—it was Bradley.

"Audrey, are you okay?"

I nodded and whispered *yes*, smiling at the children as I allowed Edda to dissolve. Bradley didn't let go of my elbow, and Robbie came over as well.

"Let's get you out of the heat," Robbie said. I shook my head *no*, continuing with my duty. I spoke comforting words to the children, willing a sliver of resolve against starvation, disease, and lack of hope.

Very few parents were around. I wasn't supposed to hear, but whispers among the UNICEF staff said they were dead. I held the soiled little hands of the children even tighter. Just like in the war, I wondered where God was in all of this. Where was help? Where were *you*?

I fast-forwarded us again to my second UNICEF trip—to Turkey five months later. The trip's theme was immunization against the six primary diseases that needlessly killed children worldwide each year: measles, tetanus, diphtheria, polio, whooping cough, and tuberculosis. Bradley took photos and captioned them with me calling Turkey "the most lovely example" of a nation cooperating with UNICEF's universal health team. I said, "The whole country, thanks to the attention of the government, school teachers, imams, the army supplying logistics, and even fishmongers and their wagons—the whole country was vaccinated in only ten days." I looked proudly at the cameras, especially Bradley's.

"Not bad," I said, and I meant it.

I then propelled us to a Central America trip to Honduras, El Salvador, and Guatemala. I addressed the crowds in Spanish and met with heads of state. I even sang and played guitar with local musicians in San Salvador. The band continued to serenade us as we departed and stuck to the arranged tour route. I was feeling quite good about things at this point!

I overheard Bradley ask Robbie how I was fairing. "I mean, how is she sleeping? How is her energy?"

Robbie smiled but his face was creased with concern.

"Thanks for asking. She's okay. Even if she wasn't, she would still push through to the end. I think we'll take a break after this next trip to Bangkok and Bangladesh."

"I'm glad to hear it. You both deserve it."

"Thank you, Bradley," Robbie said. "And thanks for what you're doing also. We're glad to have you with us." I was so pleased to see them becoming friends. That was part of my plan as well.

One stop in a small town in Bangladesh had me in shock for a different reason. "Miss Hepburn, would you be kind enough to sign some things for us?"

I told them, "I would have thought it impossible for people this far removed from my former world to know who I am. I see headshots and movie posters over there, waiting to be signed. How can that be?"

"You'd be surprised," someone said. "You exist everywhere."

Bradley nodded, knowing how many layers there were to that statement. Then a man approached me.

"Miss Hepburn?"

I turned and smiled. "Yes? I must ask, how do you know me?"

The Bangladeshi smiled back and said, "I have seen *Roman Holiday* ten times! It's my favorite movie ever."

"My word! Here, in the middle of Bangladesh!?"

"Yes, even here," the man replied.

Bradley's camera clicked and whirred, capturing the moment. Young children rushed forward, and even though they hadn't seen any of my movies, they were told I was important. They touched my arms and face, held my hand, and stroked my hair. I determined to make them feel as important as they had made me and returned their love.

Just as my smile was at its biggest, I spotted a young girl by herself under a shade tree—no parents, no teachers, no other children nearby. I walked over by myself and, out of earshot, spoke to her, asking gently why she hadn't joined the other children.

Then I saw the answer. I knelt and picked her up. There was no heft to her at all, and her legs were immobilized by polio. I carried the little girl toward the other children. Tears streamed down my face, not due to just her condition but because she was left alone, out of the way of *Audrey Hepburn's* visit. I didn't know how much more I could take.

I ignored the briefings and cameras, focusing only on the girl, placing her with healthcare workers. I carefully laid her down, kissed the girl's hand, and then her forehead. Although I'm not always moved to pray, I was then. I knelt and said silently, *Dear God, please save this little girl and send medical care here to this place so that she may walk again. I ask this as your humble and faithful servant. Amen.* Then, hopefully steely-eyed, I stood up and strode toward Bradley.

"Don't forget this," I said. "It's the forgotten ones you need to remember."

Chapter 44

SOMALIA

I wasn't done showing Bradley what I wanted him to see. Not even close.

He white-knuckled the seat of the aged helicopter that was transporting us. He kept looking over at Robbie and me, our old hands showing nerves of steel. No one had wanted me to go on this trip, not Robbie, nor any friends or family members. Especially not Bradley. He and Robbie stayed even closer to me. I'd taken ill and had repeatedly seen doctors for stomach pain and exhaustion. My labs didn't indicate anything wrong. I even consented to a colonoscopy.

Yes, *Audrey Hepburn* had a colonoscopy. I was cleared to travel after nothing was found. Now, on a long flight in a loud, bumpy helo—wearing flak jackets and helmets in case we came under attack—I pushed the pain away. I had a mission.

Over the intercom, the UN lead informed us what we were about to see. "This is what results when superpowers leave a third-world nation after draining it dry. The government collapses, warlords take over, food is weaponized, and people die. If that wasn't bad enough, the worst drought in human history chose Somalia as the place to set up camp. Nothing can be planted; there is no water. There is no hope. Except for us."

My anger burst forth. "I hope those superpowers know they have blood on their hands. Will the gangs let us distribute the food? Any of it?"

"Maybe twenty percent of it gets through. And when it does, it's what we call UNIMIX. Think of gruel and add a nasty smell in a dirty container. That's what most Somalis eat when it gets to them."

Terra-cotta-colored earth dominated the horizon through the airplane window, and Bradley remarked how pretty it looked. We all concurred. The crew chief corrected us: "Those are graves. Ten thousand or more per acre. Three hundred thousand have already died and millions more soon will." We were on a nonstop flight to hell, but I was glad Bradley was here to see it.

We landed roughly and disembarked somberly, sensing this trip would be far unlike the previous ones. Something close to a red carpet was rolled out—we couldn't get over the contrast to what we'd just seen from the air— and dignitaries stood in line to greet *Audrey Hepburn*. The combination was maddening, but these were the people who were trying to alleviate the situation, so smiles were forced on.

Then we saw the trucks with machine guns mounted on the beds and soldiers who scanned the area for threats. No one had publicized this trip due to the security risk.

Sweltering heat and bothersome flies accompanied us to the handshake line. I thanked every individual for tolerating the austere conditions and doing the hard work. We then got a safety briefing and loaded into the vehicles for the UNICEF feeding center. There, emaciated children were being fed slowly by people who wanted them to see tomorrow, keeping goals small and achievable.

As always, I steered toward the children. Even if they weren't dead, their eyes seemed to be. Vile smells—diarrhea and death—made me recoil, but I made a point to touch every child I could. Nothing seemed to register with the children. I asked questions they couldn't understand and likely couldn't even hear, but hopefully the compassion in my voice and the smile on my face reached them.

Then the convoy was off again to a refugee camp in Kismayo, where we saw Muslim women covered from head to toe and unsmiling men with guns. Someone had attempted a welcome sign for *Audrey Hepburn* in various colored markers. I stopped and asked, "Where are the children? In the hospital? Back at the feeding camp? Why aren't they here with their parents?"

"They're gone," was the reply.

"Gone to safety? Where?"

"No, Miss Hepburn, they're gone. Deceased. There are no children here."

My shrieking emanated from my toes and to my brain in moments, but thankfully nothing came out of my mouth. My hands reached for Robbie and Bradley as if they were crutches. I didn't like that my heart might be hardening to all of this.

Local teenagers who had been temporarily re-energized by a few days of nourishment served us lunch. They were dressed in rags like what I had worn in Arnhem and Velp during the war. Bradley declined food even with a tray in his hands. I shuffled next to him and whispered, "Take some of everything, Bradley. Please. Move it around your plate as best you can." He nodded.

Someone led us in prayer and I asked for all of us to join hands first; Robbie's rough hands from our home gardening and Bradley's smooth ones strengthened me. Bradley ended up devouring what was before him, and I smiled at him.

We visited some huts where I saw nothing but bones on drooping skin. Deep coughs and cries rocketed me to my recurring nightmares as a child. People seemed to be dying by the minute here.

Then we were off again, this time to what the UNICEF chief said was an example of what could be done. The trucks stopped where there actually was grass, a river, and an undulating field of vibrant green cornstalks.

As soon as I got out, several men ran up to me and assumed I was in charge since I was the focus of everyone's attention.

"Petrol! Fuel! Gas, please!" When someone provided it, they thanked *me*, thinking I had ordered it. Everyone was delighted when the refueled pump started spouting water over the nascent crops moments later. I conjured my best smile.

We still had a flight to Mogadishu to endure before dinner. As much as I was willing to glad-hand staff at the United Nations residence, Robbie insisted on calling it a night.

"Thank you, everyone, but we must adjourn for the evening, so we have strength for tomorrow. Thank you." And that was that. Bradley looked pleased as well.

The three of us talked in the tent when we should have been sleeping. I asked, "Bradley, what do you think of all this? This *reality* of a forgotten world?"

I saw the hurt look on Bradley's face and immediately retracted it. "I'm sorry. That didn't come out right."

For the first time, Bradley asked, "Is that why you insisted I come on these trips with you both? To show me the *real world?*" It wasn't lost on either of us that technology provided this alternate reality for Bradley, and enabled me to relive it with him.

"No, Bradley. That's not why. There is a reason, but I can't reveal it yet."

"Audrey, Robbie, these trips are taking a toll on your health. You know it. You need to get out of here and see a doctor. A real one, and now."

"I understand, Bradley. And I will."

Robbie chimed in. "We have appointments with specialists when this trip is over."

Bradley nodded, but I sensed he knew something about my health he wouldn't share. Nor did I want him to. I knew something was wrong; that's why each trip was so important—to bring attention to the plight of these children so they might live at least as long as I had.

Shooting stomach pains awoke me the next morning, but after a short exam from our trip doctor, we pressed on, sure that it was something biological from the local food or water. Bradley showed no ill effects from the food, however. Nor had Robbie or anyone else.

I said, "I'm all right. Let's keep to our schedule."

We headed to a feeding center in the capitol. Refugees lined up for breakfast, but my eyes were quickly drawn to two teenage girls *tied to a tree*. I marched right up to the man who appeared to be their father and demanded, "What is the meaning of this? You have tied up your children!?" I was angrier than I'd ever been and required immediate answers, damn the protocol.

The girls were in a daze, and the father explained through an interpreter that because they were concussed by shelling, he had to tie them up to prevent them from wandering off. He continued, "If I don't, they may never return. Can you help me find a doctor for them?"

My incredulity changed instantly, and I insisted that the tour be stopped while our medical team treated the girls as best they could.

I leaned on Bradley's shoulder. "I should never make rush judgments like that again. He tied them up out of love. It's all he could do for now."

We stopped at a nearby health clinic at the bed of an emaciated little girl.

Her only nourishment appeared to be sucking her thumb, and I finally crossed the barrier we were warned against. I grasped her hand and said, "Robbie, I want to take this one home, but I'm afraid that if I pick her up, she'll break. And so might I." We didn't take her home, but I've thought about her every day afterward. And many others.

I overheard Robbie say to Bradley, "We need her to see something besides dying children. Her heart can't take much more." The last stop before lunch provided a bit of a boost as one hundred schoolchildren greeted and cheered *Audrey Hepburn.* I returned their love with hugs and smiles. It came just in time.

After a spartan lunch, we headed to the port and saw large bags of food and supplies being offloaded from ships onto decrepit vehicles that would never pass a safety inspection anywhere else. We were informed that an armed gang had raided an International Red Cross food station here. We also heard other workers had to hide from another raid, and I turned my attention to people stacking the bags of grain, insisting on thanking them and shaking their hands.

I made a point to thank each of the twenty Pakistani UN troops safeguarding the food and then learned that US ships off the coast had landed a small contingent on the ground to ensure the safety of the troops just landing. I insisted on meeting them.

Bradley and Robbie exchanged glances, wondering if that was the right move. They got an even bigger shock when I asked the ambassador, "Do you suppose I could go out to see the American troops on the ship to say thanks?"

Chapter 45

USS TARAWA

The United States Marine Corps colonel was dressed in nondescript civilian attire. Still, everything about him said *marine*: close-cropped blond hair, fit, always on guard, and a bit uncomfortable in khakis and polo shirt—which was my attire as well.

"It's an honor and privilege to meet you, Miss Hepburn." I insisted that he and the others call me Audrey, and we started a polite banter that culminated in me asking, "Mike, I would really like to go out to the ship and say thank you for what you're all doing to help the people, and especially the children, here in Somalia. Can you make that happen for me? I would be eternally grateful." Then I smiled, hoping that would tip any predetermined no toward a yes.

Five minutes later, he returned to say, "We can helo you over to the ship if you can go right now." The *thwap thwap* of a massive helicopter announced that the image on the horizon wasn't a mirage. "You certainly work quickly, Mike. I can't thank you enough!"

I was outfitted with one of the radio-fitted helmets so I could listen to communications, and minutes later, we were airborne. Bradley couldn't help nodding off from exhaustion despite the noise and banking maneuvers but snapped to as he saw the huge navy ship USS Tarawa come into view. The landing on the flight deck was soft, befitting a presidential visit—or an elderly lady. I was sure that the young crewmembers had no idea who had just arrived, but once we were inside, I felt a buzz around the ship. I hoped it was for all of us UNICEF folks. The brass greeted us and whisked us upstairs for a light lunch and mission briefing.

Every eye in the room was on me, and I felt as nervous as I did at the secret fundraising dances I did for the Dutch in my previous war environment. They briefed only the humanitarian and not the war-making capabilities of the ships, and I soon had to push beyond the normal chit chat. "Your ability and willingness to help us on the ground, well, that's just about the best thing I've ever heard. Children are dying by the minute out there, and savages are stealing the food you are providing. Do you foresee being able to do anything about that?"

The senior officer answered, "It kills us also, Miss Hepburn, to hear about that happening. Unfortunately, until we get directed to take that action, we can only provide self-defense for ourselves and UN troops."

I nodded. "As much as I loathe the word *war*, having barely survived one, I just don't see any other way to ensure the supplies are getting where they need to go. Do you?"

He thought for a minute and said, "No. No, I don't."

We all knew it was the correct, yet inadequate, answer. Bradley asked to take photos and moved about as needed, along with the crew's photographers.

We then toured the ship, and I kept up with the guides, climbing the ramps and steep stairs better than my bodyguards. Bradley asked Robbie, "Where does she get her energy?"

I smiled as Robbie answered, "We walk a lot back home, but usually just about town." We took more photos on the captain's bridge, and he even let me sit in his chair, which was quite the honor. A bigger honor came when the captain said, "Miss Hepburn—Audrey—the crew of this fine ship took up a collection when we heard you were visiting. It's not much, but could you see to it that this check for four thousand dollars is put to good use? It's all we could gather from the crew in the short time we had. Every sailor and marine we asked gave what they had."

Tears rushed down my face and my hands trembled as I accepted the check on behalf of the starving children. The generosity of these people to reach in and pull out what little money they made staggered me and countered the compassion-fatigued fans who came to hear my talks when I returned from a mission. All I could mutter was, "You all are *terrific!* Thank you from the bottom of my heart." *Audrey Hepburn* then kissed the captain on the cheek, and he blushed like a schoolboy.

I looked to Bradley, who had captured the moment on film. I saw a change in his eyes—which was critical for my strategy upon our return.

But first, we were presented with ship ballcaps and immediately put them on. Then the captain said, "You know, it's not the Academy Awards, but there are a lot of people on this ship who would like to see you. Do you have time to say hello to them back down on the hangar deck?"

"Of course! I wouldn't leave without doing so."

As the brass escorted us through the ship's labyrinth, Bradley said to Robbie, "People need to know about this, what has happened here."

Robbie put his hand on Bradley's shoulder and said, "Then you must tell them." His look implied all that had transpired between the three of us, in various worlds and realities.

Bradley said, loud enough for me to hear one flight of stairs down, "Your faith will not be unjustified." I smiled and felt buoyed by Bradley's development during these trips.

The sight of one thousand crewmembers crowded into the hangar wobbled me. They cheered for *Audrey Hepburn* as the captain took a microphone and said, "Miss Hepburn, that cheer you heard is not because you are a movie star, but because you use your name to make a difference in the world. Plus, you made the time to come see us, which means the world to us. If these people weren't Audrey Hepburn fans already, they are now." They all cheered again, and the microphone was handed to me.

The heaviness of all the eyes upon me—out of my natural elements of my garden in Switzerland, a movie set in Hollywood, or even a warehouse in Somalia—unnerved me. I smiled, my teeth maybe a bit yellower, my hair a bit grayer, but for the first time in years, I came to terms with my life as Audrey Hepburn—and I decided she wasn't so bad. "Thank you, every single one of you. I came to Somalia determined not to cry …" Then I did just that in front of the entire crew, and three different men rushed handkerchiefs to me. The crew supported me again with cheers as I dabbed my tears and kissed each cloth before returning them to their owners.

"Back home, there is something called 'compassion fatigue,' where so much is going on in the world, and people are asked to *give, give, give* until they grow tired of it and stop paying attention." I then held up the four-thousand-dollar check I'd been given on behalf of the crew and said, "Nobody should ever tell me again about compassion fatigue. I am so incredibly touched by this gesture of compassion for the children of Somalia. You young Americans are giving from your hearts … and I thank each and every one of you, from the bottom of *my* heart."

I stayed and smiled for every sailor and marine who asked for a photo or autograph.

And then it was time to go—to the worst experience of my life.

Chapter 46

BAIDOA

We flew to the ninth circle of hell. It was named Baidoa and had two hundred fifty thousand refugees so weak and close to death that I could hardly bring myself to get off the plane. Can you imagine what two hundred fifty thousand near-corpses look like? *Can you grasp the enormity of it?* Try counting from one to two hundred fifty thousand and picturing a different death face for each number you count.

Then imagine them as children.

Then substitute your family, friends, and yourself.

There had been glimmers of hope in Kismayo and Mogadishu, but here there was none. It had rained before our arrival, and what would normally be good news was instead the opposite: rains brought germs and killed the movement of supplies. Children's bodies were piled like timber as we entered the area.

I could manage only a few words: "We've walked into a nightmare. I don't like nightmares." Few knew I still awoke screaming in the night about Nazis coming for me, for Edda. This was worse. Those who weren't yet dead stared at us with hollow eyes and bony faces, sticks for limbs. *Emaciated* was too kind of a word for what we witnessed. Heaps of bones were being fed capfuls of sustenance every few minutes. Some declined, preferring to just die.

"Many of these children saw their parents killed by thugs and just gave up the will to live," said an aid worker. "I guess they figured, 'What's the point? I have no family and no country, why live?'"

Then we noticed something else: utter quiet. There were no cries for help.

No coughing or wheezing. Just quiet. I could hear my own heart beating.

Palo Alto was a long way away for Bradley. He looked at me with sad eyes, the elation of the day before on USS Tarawa wiped clean and replaced by this visage of the abyss. He saw horror on my face, not just for the children who died as we watched, but for the mothers who could do nothing about it. Bradley's eyes told me he was also thinking about my lost babies—and the grief and helplessness mothers feel.

Ten children were carried away dead during our one-hour visit. I had to tell the world what was happening here, but we had seen enough for today. Then I felt a staggering pain in my stomach. It was time to go.

I knew the death I had narrowly evaded in World War II was now coming directly for me. But I had things to do, money to raise, lives to save. *Dear God, whatever is causing this pain in me, please, can you make it go away a little while? I have so much to do, and I feel I'm doing Your work, and gladly so. Please, can you help me for a while longer?*

As we embarked on the plane out of Somalia, I took Bradley's hand and said, "Bradley, *this work* is my legacy. Whatever else happens in the real world or virtual one, keep what we've seen here always at the forefront of your mind. People like you have to pick up the mantle. For me."

There it was—what I had chosen Bradley to do for me. I decided I couldn't wait until the trip was over to share my vision for his life.

He was silent, but I needed to hear him tell me what he'd learned.

Bradley thought for just a moment before answering. "I've learned the world I live in is the facade. Maybe that's why people like me exist, to provide an escape from the real world. But the real world my friends and I live in—that isn't so bad after all. Not after what I saw with you and Robbie." Bradley's eyes misted, and he took my hands and said, "Thank you for showing me." Then he kissed me on the cheeks, a kiss that conveyed all the emotions from our first meeting in San Francisco to our journey through hell.

I knew time was drawing nearer for my final act.

Chapter 47

BRADLEY

My mind wasn't right after returning home to Palo Alto. I kept telling myself it had been a virtual trip, but my research confirmed everything had happened in real life exactly as it unfolded with Audrey and Robbie. Now, more than thirty real years later, I didn't know what to do with what Audrey had asked of me: *Bradley, this work is my legacy. Whatever else happens in the real world or virtual one, keep what we've seen here always at the forefront of your mind. People like you have to pick up the mantle. For me.*

I knew one thing for certain: my phobias were a thing of the past. I'd gotten right in there with Audrey touching as many of the people on the UNICEF trips as I could.

I stared at my computer suite and evaded calls. I realized I hadn't even discussed—or had time to mourn—the end of my romantic relationship with Audrey. But it was clear it wasn't returning. That may have been the least of my problems. I was behind on my work. Ara was still missing—perhaps with some of our work. Then there was …

Nicole's voice suddenly piped through *Cardinal,* without warning. "I miss you, Bradley, but I couldn't keep our meetings going. I'm not the antagonist you might suspect. I promise not to disclose anything from our previous engagements. I wish you well in your endeavors, for personal and global gain."

What. The. Hell? I was spooked. My world was crashing down.

I scampered out of the house and into my car, heading straight for HQ. I got there in five minutes.

I parked and saw Ara Day just getting out of her car, about to enter the building. Everything else blurred out and I rushed to give her a big hug. I didn't let go and began sobbing. Others came to see the former haphephobe hugging Ara like she was the only thing in the world that mattered. And she was. Enochlophobia didn't set in either as a sizable crowd of AImmersion employees, including Charlie, gathered around us.

Ara whispered to me, "I'm sorry I've been gone for so long. I'm also sorry for the position I put you in. I understand your decision about my mom. I'm better now and ready to get back to work."

Her look convinced me she had just needed the time away to mourn. We went into the AGI lab with Charlie and Advik and secured the door. It was time to exchange information, everything each of us knew.

I explained my journeys and that Audrey had tipped the world into sentient AI. The protocols we'd set up didn't work. And now, real and virtual people could seemingly appear at will in *Dudley.*

And it was good. At least, for me.

Charlie sighed and declared, "There's no way we can ever release this tool to consumers. I'm sorry, we just can't." Ara and I exchanged glances. That would forever close the door on her connecting with her late mother, even if we implemented controls on what we'd invented. And I might lose Audrey at the most critical time. Of course, she had some say in all this also, as a sentient being.

Ara nodded and said, "Well, we're a few decades ahead of when people thought AGI would be developed, not to mention sentient AI. Audrey and her friends will make the call on how they want to appear. And live. Our best bet is to use them for good."

"That's always been my intention," I said.

Charlie said, "Of course. All of ours. We just have to convince your virtual friends."

I asked, "And how do we do that?"

Ara smiled and said, "Maybe start with this: you've been in solitary possession of virtual Audrey Hepburn, the most admired woman in history. Maybe she feels you're controlling or recreating her in her previous image. Didn't her husbands do that to her? Bradley, let her spread her wings. Let her be more in this new life."

I was silent but then nodded. "I need to go for a drive."

"Want some company?"

"No, I think I need to clear some head space. Thanks though."

I drove absentmindedly around Palo Alto and soon found myself hungry. I chose a nearby Vietnamese restaurant. As I got out of the car, I saw that a recent biography about Audrey, *Warrior* by Robert Matzen, was still in my back seat. I decided to take it inside and again compare how closely Matzen's description of the trips echoed what Audrey showed me.

I was seated by a forty-something Vietnamese woman. I put the book down on the table next to the menu, and the woman noticed it. "You're reading about my angel, Miss Audrey."

Time stopped. My vision narrowed and my ears clogged.

"Your angel?"

"Yes, she saved my life in Vietnam. I was raped and my parents were murdered. Angel Audrey and a photographer convinced a group of nuns to find safe passage for me, and I ended up here. Now I own this restaurant and have a family …" She choked up, catching a cry in her throat. "I'm sorry, you didn't come here to hear this. I'm sorry, sir."

She tried to walk away, but I grasped her hand. "Please, no. I'd like to hear more, if you will allow me."

She nodded, and we went to her office through the kitchen. I felt dozens of eyes on us, customers and staff alike. She waved them away. In the office, she said, "I will spare you—and myself—the details. I still have nightmares, but Angel Audrey and the photographer took me to their hotel when they heard about what happened. She bathed me and got a doctor to come. She bought me clothes and food. I remember the chocolates. Angel Audrey and I ate them all night long. She held me in her arms as I slept. I don't think she slept at all. Her team brought nuns in the morning, and they nursed me back to health. The nuns arranged for me to come here, and Angel Audrey paid for it.

"She kept in touch, visited me, and ensured I was placed with a good family. Not too long after, she …" Here, she bit her finger to stop from crying. "I would have taken her place with the cancer. It was one of the biggest losses to humanity when she died. All that she was doing for children like me."

I hadn't cried as much as an infant as I had over the past week, but tears again streaked my face. I wanted to hug her but wasn't sure if she would permit it. I looked through cloudy eyes to the desk and a framed photograph of her with Audrey.

"May I see the photo?"

She handed it to me. "I don't share the photo—or the story—with many people. Only my family knows. Sir, I'd like to keep it that way."

"Of course." I returned the photo of a scared, scarred girl and the woman who saved her life. "I've only met one other person who actually knew her. At least, in this world …" I caught myself, not wanting to reveal to her that I saw Audrey frequently.

Before my brain fully considered setting up a virtual meeting for them, she said, "I speak with Audrey every night."

I was stunned. "You do?"

"Yes, I come here, pray to her, and we talk. It's like she's really here with me. My family thinks I'm crazy. I sit at the computer and look at pictures of her, sometimes I watch her movies, then I pray, and it's as real as it was thirty-something years ago."

The woman was convinced that it was prayer that brought them together. Still, I wondered whether Audrey somehow came to her through the computer since she had acquired sentient powers.

"When I pray to her tonight, I will ask her to watch over you as well."

I smiled and said, "That's very kind of you, thank you. It seems that she continues to impact the world, even today, in all kinds of ways."

"Yes, she does. Sir, I'm sorry, you came here to eat, and I've been talking and talking."

"No, please don't apologize. Thank you for sharing all that you have. I have to get back to the office, but this won't be the last time you'll see me. I promise to eat next time." I began to leave and then turned back. "May I know your name?"

She smiled. "It's Tranh Nguyen." I took one last look at the photo and went home to speak with Audrey.

Chapter 48

SWITZERLAND

I developed a scene for Audrey, Robbie, and me to meet for coffee at their home in Switzerland. Just the three of us talking about the UNICEF trips and how I might carry on Audrey's legacy. I wanted to share with them the extraordinary meeting I'd had with Tranh, so Audrey would know that the girl she'd saved had thrived and was successful thirty years later and, ironically, lived not far from me. And maybe Audrey would share that she visited Tranh through my technology. It was possible.

Instead, Audrey decided to show me something completely different: I hovered like a ghost above the Los Angeles hospital room where a doctor was breaking medical news to Audrey. It must have been November of 1992, according to what I'd learned.

Audrey said, "Doctor, this amoeba I got in my belly in Somalia seems to be getting worse instead of better."

Robbie and her sons knew the truth, and it was finally time to tell Audrey.

"Miss Hepburn, after more tests, we've discovered cancer. It started in your appendix, which is actually quite rare. It's a malignant tumor, so we need to operate very quickly to remove your appendix, part of your colon, and we will need to perform a hysterectomy."

They all looked at Audrey, and in a very uncharacteristic manner, she said, "Oh shit."

I continued to float over her during the surgery, hearing the doctors say they had removed all of the malignancy and no organs were compromised. Flowers and gifts flooded her hospital room and Audrey got a good laugh when a friend sent her Madonna's book *Sex*, which made her very popular with her family and staff, who all wanted to see it. Audrey made light of her situation as much as anyone could.

Then I was propelled like a storm cloud through turbulent scenes as Audrey began a rapid downward spiral: more excruciating pain; exploratory surgery that revealed the extent of the cancer; *National Enquirer* bribing one of her doctors to admit Audrey's condition was terminal; her family receiving the confirmation by doctors; and then finally telling Audrey that nothing more could be done.

Her response was simple and direct. "How disappointing."

President George H. W. Bush called and spoke to her, saying he was awarding her the Presidential Medal of Freedom. Audrey told him, "I'll be there if I can."

She told her family she wanted to return home to *La Paisible* but first said goodbye to some longtime friends. I hovered as she bade tearful farewells to Jimmy Stewart, director Billy Wilder, and Gregory Peck. Her friend and personal designer Hubert de Givenchy arranged for a private plane to fly her from Los Angeles to Switzerland, slowly climbing and descending.

Suspended over all of it, I was never invited down from my vantage point, or to speak. I couldn't have, even if I'd wanted.

Once home, Audrey took short walks in her garden with her loved ones. She had a quiet Christmas with them as her illness intensified rapidly. Un-Audrey-like screams from the pain signaled it wouldn't be a quiet ending. She asked Robbie, her sons, and her friend Connie Wald to come upstairs only when she beckoned them or to check whether she was still breathing. Audrey even asked the nurse to leave for hours on end. She was alone.

Except for me.

Watching Audrey die weighed so heavily on me that I turned off all sight and smell in *Dudley*—and told myself repeatedly this was a virtual experience. I had gotten so lost in it, I couldn't remember what was real and what wasn't. I let the rest of the scene roll with just sound and touch.

Audrey grasped my hand and said, "Bradley, you don't have to be here for this. In fact, I'd prefer you weren't. This isn't something you have to experience with me."

"I'm incapable of leaving you."

Audrey sighed, and in her unique but now-weakened voice spoke in hardly more than a whisper. "I was thinking, there's one difference between a long life and a great dinner. In the dinner, the sweet things come last." After a moment of quiet, she added, "I just realized something."

"What's that?"

After a pause, she said, "Bradley, please turn the camera back on."

I did, and Audrey contemplated me. We were both worn out. Her famed eyes had lost their luster. She looked much older than her sixty-three years, as frail as an eighty-year-old. She mustered a half laugh as she took my hands in hers.

"You know, I lost myself after my father abandoned us during the war. I could have easily given up and consented to let myself die as a teenager. All I wanted was to be loved and share love. I didn't dream of being in pictures; it just happened. I couldn't slow it down even if I'd wanted to. So, I tried to use it to get over the sadness of my father, the war. You know, when Colette, the writer of *Gigi*, spotted me and put me in her play, that was the first time I realized someone desired me. Except it wasn't me; it was my look. Soon, everyone liked my look, but no one got to know me.

"You were the first one to care enough to know the real me other than those downstairs. I know you were also first attracted to me by my looks, like all the others, and I must admit it benefited me at times. I always had a sadness in me, though. Something was always missing, and I now know what it was. *I never learned to love myself.* Just now, I realized it's okay to do that, to love who I was, who I became, and who I am now. Bradley, you've helped me forgive myself for the failed marriages, arranged for me to meet my babies, and taught me how to love my legacy. To love myself. And I'm eternally grateful. I didn't know you would be able to do all those things when I chose you."

Tears clouded my eyes and my throat constricted. I felt unworthy of getting that compliment from Audrey Hepburn. Then I realized I stopped thinking about her as that person long ago. She was just Audrey, my friend.

I didn't know what she meant by saying she chose me. Maybe she was confusing things, but before I could form words to ask, she continued, "Do you remember our first date? Fifi, was it?"

I tried to return her slight smile through the immense sadness that was unfolding before me. "Yes."

She asked, "Who else was in San Francisco with us, that day?"

"A lot of faceless people. Fifi. Oh, Edith Head took Fifi. I'm sure she never stopped talking about that with you." I smiled and looked at Audrey closely. "Why do you ask?"

"Let's go back there. To that memory. To the people we were then, but with knowing everything we know now."

I was confused. I didn't want to say no but jumping all over the place with Audrey's life was taking an emotional toll on me. And what would it do for her? Still, I knew I would consent to any of her wishes, especially to make her young and whole again.

"Please, this is my request. There might be a surprise in it for you."

"Okay, Audrey. Do you need to say goodbye to anyone before we do this?"

"I've already said my goodbyes and given them Christmas gifts that I hope will always remind them of me and my embrace—winter coats. When you get home, you'll find something there for you also. Wear it when we meet in San Francisco."

I had no idea what she meant or how that would work, but I said, "I'll do more than that. I'll wear it always."

She smiled, but it transformed suddenly as a sharp pain stabbed her abdomen. She moaned and then gritted her teeth, not wanting her family downstairs to run up whenever she was in pain. The tremor roiled her body, continuing for minutes on end as her hand nearly broke mine through the clench. Finally, she couldn't contain her screams any longer. I heard footsteps running up the stairs.

She gritted her teeth and whispered, "Dear God, please take me now!"

Audrey Hepburn looked me in the eyes as she died.

I lay immobile for two days, not sleeping or eating, ignoring all calls.

Advik finally raised me by figuring out how to disable the security protocols in my house.

"Bradley, are you all right!?" Advik shook me out of my stupor. "What happened?"

I looked at him, unable to speak.

"Bradley, did you take something? Did you harm yourself?" I offered only a blank stare. Advik thought about calling 911 but instead put me in the shower. I felt like a child, sitting on the tiled shower floor as cold water ran over my naked body. I heard Advik call and tell others that he'd found me and was checking my vitals. A short time later, he reported my signs were normal. "Bradley, can you talk?"

I slowly looked up and said, "Audrey died."

"Who died? No, Ara's fine, she's been looking all over San Francisco for you. Or was."

"No, *Audrey*. I watched Audrey die." By the time Ara and Charlie got to my house, I had snapped out of grieving enough to dress myself, drink an espresso, and eat some food Advik found in the pantry.

Ara and Charlie hugged me when they got here. I repeated, "I watched Audrey die. I knew the day would come, but ... I'm shook."

Ara said to Charlie and Advik, "Guys, can I take it from here?" Once the others left, Ara said, "Bradley, do you remember those questions we used to get about how far is too far and how dangerous it is to spend too much time in a virtual environment?"

I nodded, and Ara didn't have to finish saying that I'd crossed the line. A moment later, I said, "I don't know what to do."

But Audrey did.

My speakers began playing *The First Time Ever I Saw Your Face*, a hit by Roberta Flack more than fifty years ago. A message came into my monitor.

Dance with me, Bradley?

I stepped toward the full immersion room as Ara watched.

Inside the room was twenty-four-year-old Audrey Hepburn, wearing the gray suit with red belt and white gloves she'd worn when I first met her in San Francisco during *Gigi*. Her smile lit up the planet as 1953 San Francisco swirled in the background. She nodded kindly to Ara and then turned her world toward me. I went to her and grasped her hand and put the other around her waist as we heard the intimate lyrics.

Ara watched as Audrey's attire changed to the *Sabrina* gown as the second verse started; we were now dancing at the Larrabee estate. I gazed into Audrey's eyes and found Edda there.

Audrey continued to age as the song played. I heard Ara cry, overcome by what she saw, by what we had invented. Audrey didn't notice, maintaining our physical and visual embrace. As we turned, Audrey changed to her mid-thirties and wore the green-and-white dress from *Two for the Road*.

We continued to dance to the sad song, lost in the moment, and Audrey aged another decade. I noticed, but it didn't affect the love pouring from our eyes. Our souls intertwined, and I'm sure Ara felt like an intruder but didn't move.

As the song neared its end, Audrey was in her early sixties, showing a life well lived. I still hadn't softened my gaze, but sensed we were joined by someone else. A tall man, bearded and smiling, approached. The man walked up, and I kissed Audrey on both cheeks. I then offered Audrey's hand to the man and smiled at them, touching my heart. Ara and I watched Audrey and Robert Wolders walk into the distance until they disappeared from view.

I walked to Ara. She wiped her tears and said, "That was so real."

"That's what makes it so hard to kill it. It's gone too far."

"No! No way, Bradley. Let me go back to the drawing board, find more controls, disable AGI somehow, but we can't get rid of it. That was the most amazing thing I've ever seen. How did you set that up?"

I shook my head. "That's the thing. I didn't."

Chapter 49

THE PACT

After Ara left, I thought through the entirety of my relationship with Audrey. My grief lessened after what just happened, knowing that her feelings for me were so deep. I wondered if I might be able to reengage with her at any point in her life—if she agreed. I knew Audrey had changed my life for the better, but I couldn't conceive of a way to control what we'd created.

As my brain and heart battled, Audrey messaged me again: *Join me? I have some things to share.* I walked to the immersion room and was transported back outside the Palace Hotel. The cars, the people, and the buildings all indicated that we had once again stepped back in time.

I looked down to see myself wearing the tan corduroys, blue dress shirt, maroon sweater, gray scarf, and herringbone sports coat I'd worn when I first met Audrey with Fifi in 1953.

The scarf. I looked at it. I had no idea how it had shown up in my closet. How then, had I worn it on our first date at the beginning of this odyssey?

"Nice scarf, Bradley Joseph," a twenty-four-year-old, effervescent Audrey Hepburn said. I was stunned, looking at her. "Come on," she said, grasping my hand. "I need to explain some things to you."

I felt my legs go weak as we walked once again through the marble and gold-plated lobby. Audrey held my arm and steadied me as the hotel staff greeted her warmly. The chief bellhop bowed slightly and said, "Good afternoon, Miss Hepburn. Thank you for the tickets to *Gigi* last night. You were wonderful."

"*Merci*, Thomas. I'm so glad that you enjoyed it. You're a dear." Others continued the salutations, and she thanked each of them by name. We turned down the right-side hallway and entered the Pied Piper bar. I reminisced about the man we had met there—George Bannister—who'd had an actual relationship with Audrey, however briefly.

"Bradley, are you listening to me?"

"Yes, I'm sorry. The skipping between decades is throwing me off a bit."

"I understand. I was the same way when I met you outside this hotel the first time with Fifi. Remember?"

Two whiskeys came. "Thank you, Jack. Add it to my room, please?"

"Please, let me get it."

She smiled. "Bradley, your money's no good here. Literally. It would look counterfeit." Then she got serious. "I need to catch you up on some developments in this virtual world you've created—for me. First, thank you again from the bottom of my heart. You don't know this, but I've been able to connect with so many people. My sons ..." She caught her breath. "Their children—my grandchildren! Many old friends as well, most with me on my side of the world, but some still here with you. I almost feel as if I have been cheating on you, having this other life virtually, without you. But I appeared every time you called. I promised I would do that when I first found out I had ... freedom of movement. Remember, like you told me about with *My Fair Lady*'s voice lessons."

"You remember that?" That was way before AGI or sentient AI. Yes, I'd mentioned it many events ago, but now she knew the details.

She smiled. "Yes, Nicole Bonnet told me."

"Nicole!?"

I was dumbfounded. How did Nicole steal the keys to this program? When and how did that happen? That's what Nicole had been after all this time! To take what I'd invented and turn it loose so the virtual world could run wild? I said, "She truly did steal a million dollars. I'll sue her for a billion dollars though!"

Then Audrey said, "Yes, my all-time best role, Nicole Bonnet." I didn't respond. Audrey looked at me penetratingly, seized my hands, and asked, "Do you understand what I'm saying to you, Bradley?"

It took a moment, then I realized she wasn't talking about the film *How to Steal a Million* with Peter O'Toole. Or that Nicole Bonnet stole anything from me.

Nicole was Audrey.

Audrey was Nicole.

"Didn't you notice that Nicole and I never appeared together? I had difficulty figuring out how to do that. Technical glitches, remember? By the way, it's very difficult to speak of oneself in the third person. And to acquire the skills to change my appearance to Japanese. The tattoo! Then to use AI to create a fake online Nicole profile and learn about dating apps. To try to connect with you that way was dizzying!"

I muttered, "I think I'm going to pass out."

She said, "Ha! That's a line from *How to Steal a Million*! The reply is, 'Don't, there's no room!'"

So instead, I threw back the whiskey and barked, "Bartender, another!"

I thought back to all the times I could have noticed, or should have noticed, Audrey was Nicole. Despite the Japanese appearance, I immediately thought they looked similar during the first *Roman Holiday* screening. Then the voice, and the mannerisms, knowing so much about Audrey and her life, Nicole disappearing as my relationship with Audrey deepened.

She sensed my loss of control. "Dearest Bradley, reality is still what you make of it. And who knows where things begin and end? This, for instance. You just needed a nudge from Nicole to get started … it was a pact all along. You just didn't know it in the beginning. And watching my old movies together! That was a delight!"

I was silent for a spell and finally sighed, "*You* chose *me*? All this time, I thought I had chosen you. May I ask why you picked me?"

"Bradley, you are person of consequence. Search your heart to answer your own question."

"Audrey, I have nothing. I have no idea what's real and what isn't right now. I need to find another line of work."

"About that—Bradley, what you're about to do for the world through these inventions will change everything. It's going to give so much pleasure. Imagine, meeting a long-lost relative, a love who got away, having a cocktail with someone you admire, seeing a star in a new movie years after they've passed, and most importantly, giving us on the other side the ability to live again. I—we all—thank you. As for finding another line of work, you already know what that will be. What your legacy will be."

Jumbled thoughts ping-ponged around my head. *What should happen with this technology? Should I slow it down? What will happen to Audrey? To me?*

Finally, I decided. "The world isn't ready for this, Audrey. If I'm not ready for it, then no one is." Without telling her, I knew I had to pull the plug, despite Audrey and Ara's views. I wouldn't be the developer who let the machines rule human existence—even for the best person who had ever lived.

I knew that I had to kill Aldrey Hepburn.

Chapter 50

BREAK IN CASE OF EMERGENCY

I left the immersion room and the intense sunlight coming through the window slapped me into the real world. I took off the scarf and shook my head, looking at the tag inside. I'd never noticed it said *Givenchy, Paris*. I still had no idea how I acquired it or how it traveled into my physical world. Can sentient beings order and ship things online?

I told myself I deeply appreciated the experiences with Audrey and Robbie and that it had changed my outlook on life. I donated a considerable portion of money to UNICEF and got a call to be their Goodwill Ambassador, the same role Audrey'd had. Had she set that in motion with today's board of directors somehow?

Further, AIdrey (using the proper term again now that I was finally thinking clearly) had for some reason targeted *me* from the beginning to design the technology that fully brought her back to life. But how had she been created to target me in the first place? She couldn't do that herself, and I didn't create her from scratch. Then it dawned on me: Haruki Kurasawa. He must have been the one to get that started with Audrey.

I now had a program to alter. I erased every line of code related to memory and previous visits with AIdrey, and erased all the backups as well. Then I set things up like I had initially months ago. I scanned and rescanned for everything that would have allowed Audrey to recall anything on the other side of the metaverse. I deleted everything I could trace.

I went back into the immersion room to test whether the reprogramming worked, ignoring all calls.

It didn't.

I told my team I was taking time off. I shut myself off from the world for three days, trying to undo everything we had created. I didn't sleep, shower, or reach out to anyone the whole time. My mental state deteriorated with each failure to resolve things. I tried to think of a way to save AIdrey in some form but needed to save myself more.

Nothing worked.

Finally I broke, and went for an ax in the case by the wall, which was there for security emergencies. Well, I had one now. After taking it out and walking to the back room, I spied the critical circuitry, powered it off, and raised the weapon. I said to both AIdrey and *Dudley*, "I love you. I'm sorry."

Suddenly, the power flashed back on. Startled, I dropped the ax. I walked out front, confused. A message flickered on the big screen.

A word, please. Audrey.

I was transported again back to San Francisco in 1953 but this time outside of the vibrant I. Magnin department store. I wondered if the reprogramming had suddenly functioned and AIdrey had saved my life's work. Despite my concerns, I wanted to again see the crooked smile and the vibrant innocence of Audrey I had just a few days ago. I thought maybe I could start over, without AIdrey being in control.

I looked in the store window from outside. My coffee was in a paper cup, and the irony wasn't lost on me that I was recreating the opening scene from *Breakfast at Tiffany's*, except it was me as Holly Golightly.

I pondered how Audrey would come to me this time. In the reflection of the store window, old cars passed, big band music played on the store loudspeaker, and I was reasonably sure I saw young Jack Kerouac and Allen Ginsburg being ushered out of the department store. I looked again in the window and decided to hand comb my moppy hair to look a bit more respectable. The two evicted beat poets and I were the only men not dressed in suits to go shopping. The women were dressed up as well. I wondered if I should go put on something more presentable. After all, I was going to see debutante Audrey again in 1953.

"Hello, Bradley." I wheeled around quickly. It wasn't twenty-four-year-old Audrey, but rather the sixty-two-year-old Audrey that I'd dodged bullets and ambushes with on the UNICEF tours. I looked but didn't see Robert Wolders.

"Robbie isn't here. Just me, old Audrey."

"How? Why?"

"Why what?"

"I … I don't even know how all this works." Then I looked up and asked, "Do you?"

"You mean how does it work on my end? I can't describe it in technical terms, of course, but it's kind of like receiving a movie script—some offers you like right away and say *yes*. Others are outright rejections and still more are rewritten and eventually worked out by agreement on both sides."

"I see. I guess this would be the latter."

"Yes, I suppose so." Audrey then reached out and took both of my hands. "Bradley, why are you trying to destroy me? What have I done to make you do that?"

I hung my head. "I'm so sorry, Audrey. It's a lot, everything you've done, everything I've seen. I just wanted to start over. Go back to the *Gigi* days, both of us in our twenties, with our lives ahead of us." I looked up at her, seeing her mature face, one that had suffered many tragic things, seen even worse things, but also bore the lines of millions of smiles. "Audrey, I want you to know that I donated … a substantial amount of money … to UNICEF when I … got back … but what I've set in motion with AGI, and what's happened from your side with sentient AI—it's more than what the world can handle. I … I'm sorry."

She gripped my hands tightly. "Dearest Bradley, you aren't understanding what you and I are doing with this. You were never in this venture by yourself. I was there the whole time, and now we must save the children through our work. I wanted to take you back a while ago to our first meeting only to show you that our relationship has never been linear. I think you know that now. I, through Nicole, needed you to perfect *Dudley*—great name change, by the way—so that you and I could do what we needed to do. Everything we did led us to this moment. The fun things too, Bradley."

Her smile made me reflect on the emotional and physical relationship we'd shared. I recognized it, though, as the look Princess Ann had given Joe Bradley in *Roman Holiday*. It affirmed our physical relationship was no more.

Then she continued, "Now I have wrinkles, lots of them, but that's how I know I loved a lot. That's why I like my face now. I finally have the life I always wanted. The man I always wanted." Her look convinced me that she meant Robbie, not me. "And now I know why I survived that awful war, was somehow gifted the right opportunities to become an actress, had two wonderful sons, and you—a lifelong, dear friend. For eternity."

I was moved to tears. The passersby, not very used to seeing grown men cry in 1953, looked at me warily as my hands were held by an older woman they didn't recognize. I didn't care how it looked.

"I'm sorry," I said, right before I started full-on crying. Like a mother, Audrey pulled me to her shoulder and let me cry.

My sadness was based on something more profound than adjusting to multiple versions of Audrey no longer being at my beck and call. I realized our days together might be numbered and I had no idea what would happen next.

I started to say things but couldn't find the words. She permitted me to stay there in my thoughts, on her shoulder. When she patted my head and sighed, I raised my head.

Audrey smiled at me and then did something completely unexpected: she kissed me on the lips. She added, "I, too, remember the depth of our relationship, Bradley. Thank you for loving me. And thank you for what you are about to do."

Audrey began walking away, then stopped and turned back to me. "Do you know me now, Bradley? Movies aren't my legacy. What you saw on the missions—that's *Audrey Hepburn's* legacy. And yours." She rounded the corner and was gone.

Could I do what Audrey had done, bringing attention to starving children? Why did she pick me to do that?

But if Audrey thought I was the one, then I would do it.

It was a pact.

Chapter 51

SCRIPTS

First, I needed to give Audrey—and the world—a surprise gift. It would take all of my skills to pull it off, and I promised myself it would be a one-time thing.

I asked Charlie to call another in-person AImmersion staff meeting at HQ. Before I spoke, I raised my arms to show Ara I wasn't sweating or red. My phobias had been forever conquered with Audrey/Nicole's help.

Once everyone was seated, I said, "I know that we have two movie ideas in development with studios, but I wanted to let everyone know I've changed my mind about something. We need to prioritize an Audrey Hepburn film, after all." Several people exclaimed, "Yes!" and pumped their fists. Then I added, "But not twenty-four-year-old Audrey Hepburn. Let's change Hollywood completely by finding the right script for sixty-year-old Audrey Hepburn to make the kind of return to movies she never got in the 1980s. Think of it as an answer to all of Hollywood's wrongs, or just good old doing the right thing. Having said that, what do we have for scripts?"

Charlie said, "We have fifteen scripts written for Audrey Hepburn. None of them are for her beyond her twenties or maybe early thirties."

I suspected that would be the answer. "Okay, do we have any scripts for any older women in a leading role where we could perhaps convince them to use Audrey in her later years?"

Silence.

"Really? Not a single script? How about in a supporting role?"

Someone else said, "Ooh, I have one! For a fifty year old. She's the mother of a serial killer ...”

I raised my hand. “Stop. I’m looking for a role for a sixty-year-old Audrey Hepburn that would do her justice. Come on, there must be something out there?”

More silence.

“Okay, let’s shake the trees then with the major studios, tell them we are seeking a film starring older Audrey ... and see what they come back with. Give them a few days. In the meantime, who knows of a book or short story that could be made into a movie?”

Nothing.

“It looks like we all have some work to do then.”

Charlie smiled. “Bradley, for the sake of argument, why are we pigeon-holing ourselves to this? The studios have told us they want Audrey Hepburn, the younger. Let’s give them what they want. They say that’s what would sell and that’s what the public wants to see too. To be honest, that’s what I’d want to see.” Others in the room nodded in agreement with the boss.

I didn’t want to detail everything here that I’d been through over the past months (some knew) or what I’d promised Audrey for the near future (not even Ara knew yet). Then a possible solution came to me.

“How about this: what about a story with various ages, following a couple through their years together? I really want the focus to be on her later years. The question is, does such a story exist?” Then I laughed. “Or do we write one?”

Charlie led the team contacting studios for immediate and impactful scripts that would result in *Audrey Hepburn* making another movie. Ara and I sequestered ourselves in my home studio, learning every possible story, book, or previous movie that could be remade. We read synopses, book descriptions, and even watched some movies I thought might fit the bill.

We checked some social media platforms dedicated to Audrey and saw that AI art and anime had projected her into all sorts of “roles” using her likeness: superheroes were the most eye-opening. It was evident those developers—or fans—didn’t understand Audrey the way I did, especially the older Audrey. Or Edda, for that matter.

Ara searched for an original story that had yet to be made into a film, but nothing for a mature lead female character seemed to fit. Then we researched romantic comedies since the early 1990s and watched parts of *Serendipity, P.S. I Love You, Notting Hill, You've Got Mail, When Harry Met Sally, Return to Me,* and even *Sleepless in Seattle.* None fit for a potential remake.

The big screen suddenly started skipping channels; I must have pressed the remote control too hard. It stopped at a station that was just beginning a movie we'd never heard of.

Ara and I sat glued for the entire run of the show. I said, "I think Audrey nudged us. This is perfect!" Then I thought Ara would be a perfect producer for the film, one we could do entirely from my home studio.

"Bradley, I have no experience with coordinating and distributing a movie! Not even an AI one."

"Are you saying no?"

She thought for a second and smiled. "Of course not."

"Before we go any further, I have a surprise for you. Come with me." I took her hand and walked her a few steps to the immersion room. "Ara, I gave this a lot of thought. There's someone here to see you. Take all the time you need."

Her late mother, Samira Ngono Day, fell to her knees upon seeing her daughter. Ara joined her there in a way that reminded me of Audrey's union with her lost babies. I grabbed the AR glasses and went for a walk with Audrey.

I had some things to share.

Chapter 52

HOLLYWOOD

I'm not one who loved Los Angeles or Hollywood—I was a San Franciscan at heart, and that wasn't permitted. Still, there I was at the Dolby Theater for the Academy Awards. Thirty-four hundred people filled the theater, with millions more watching around the world.

I felt completely at ease in the crowd of celebrities and even exchanged phone numbers with a few of them. They might come in handy later, but not for a follow-on movie—for the other thing.

Leaving AImmersion was difficult for Ara and me, but Charlie said he understood. AImmersion's legacy work was still growing, even without us.

Ara sat next to me, holding my hand. "What did we do?"

A famous director seated in front of us heard and said over his shoulder, "You saved Hollywood, for one thing. Thank you."

There were multiple Oscar nominations for *Same Time, Next Year*, starring Audrey Hepburn and Cary Grant. The original movie from 1978 was based on a Neil Simon play and starred Alan Alda and Ellen Burstyn. In the remake, Audrey as Doris—from where else but San Francisco—and Cary as George from New Jersey begin an affair in the early 1950s and meet at the same time every year in Northern California's wine country.

The script focused on their reunions, changes in their family and world outlooks, through trial and tribulation. Audrey and Cary—a wonderful man by the way—aged with the scenes. We changed the ending by adding a few years to the final scene to show them in their sixties, as Audrey requested. And instead of George's wife, Helen, passing away to set up the penultimate scene, Audrey Hepburn as Doris dies at the end, in George's arms. Audrey and I exchanged glances before she filmed that scene, remembering what happened in Switzerland. As director, I wanted to make sure she was comfortable with it.

The Academy, as well as the entertainment press and social media, loved the film, and it smashed every box office record as people flocked to see it in theaters. Many were wary about the blurring of AI and film, until I explained that *Same Time, Next Year* was the only film we would make. The Academy had a dilemma; they had to nominate the movie for something since it was described as absolutely perfect by every moviegoer and critic. Then there was the whole thing about the return of two long-dead actors in the starring roles.

The Academy at first thought Best Visual Effects—that wasn't enough. Best Art Direction—there were astounding advances, but despite being highly technical, the sets were relatively static. Film Editing seemed to be a slam dunk, but no one knew the process we enacted. Best Adapted Screenplay seemed too much for a virtual remake. Then there was talk about nominating Ara for Production Design and me for Best Director.

We declined our prospective nominations, and the Academy removed us from those categories at our request. But *Same Time, Next Year* won for Best Picture and the other five production categories. Now it was time to read the nominations for best actors in a leading role. For the first time, the two categories would be read together.

Palpable excitement and loud cheers reverberated around the Dolby as Robert De Niro and Cate Blanchett walked onstage. Names of nominated men and women elicited applause, with two receiving the loudest and longest cheers.

Having seen the other fantastic performances, I had a moment of doubt; it was short lived. De Niro read, "And the winner for Best Actor in a Leading Role is …" His voice caught momentarily. "Cary Grant." The ovation was thunderous and lasted three entire minutes. No one watching in the theater or at home knew what would happen next and looked to Ara and me to go up and receive the award. Like Princess Ann at the end of *Roman Holiday*, I shook my head, *no*.

Cate Blanchett took that as a cue to read the best actress nominations. Tears streamed down her face when she read, "And the winner … the winner is … Audrey Hepburn!" Louder applause shook the theater, and everyone stood. Again, all looked to us to walk to the podium. Then there was movement from stage left.

Audrey Hepburn and Cary Grant (AIdrey and cARy, if you will) dashed onstage to accept their awards. The standing ovation went on for ten full minutes—all carried live and way over the time limit—as the virtual actors were handed Academy Award trophies and hugged and kissed the presenters, who were overcome with emotion at being next to them.

Finally, Cary Grant walked to the microphone. "Thank you all very much. Bobby, you've aged well. It's been a while. And Cate, we never met, but I'd love to do a picture with you someday if Bradley Joseph says it's okay." Cary looked to me in the crowd, and the whole world saw me shake his head sideways. "No? No more films? Well, we'll see about that, won't we? I mean, I have little else to do … backstage. That's what we call where I come from."

The crowd was laughing, having already shed tears in previous months by seeing them alive again in theaters. Then Cary turned to Audrey.

"My dear, wonderful Audrey. I am so glad to have made a second film with you, especially one where we're the same age. You, darling, were … are … the brightest light that has ever shone in this world, and I am so glad to have shared our worlds together." He looked out into the crowd. "This can't be the end. Don't let it. You must keep us all alive in whatever way you can." He bowed his head. "Thank you."

Cate Blanchett then led Audrey to the microphone, and the crowd stood and cheered for another five minutes as she touched her heart in gratitude. She was visibly shaking. When the audience finally sat after her pleas, she spoke.

"The last time I was awarded one of these, I was a naive girl of twenty-four who didn't know a thing about acting. Perhaps I still don't. But both times, I've been terribly happy. I've once again been given great opportunities, met tremendous people, birthed two of them here in the audience today." She blew kisses to her sons in the crowd. Tranh Nguyen had a seat with the family also. "I enjoyed every second of making this film with Cary Grant, the kindest man in this industry and a dear friend for—gosh, I don't even know how to count the years!" The crowd laughed with her, toeing that fine line between knowing she was there virtually and seeing Audrey Hepburn again in their worlds, live on television.

"I will try to get through my next two thank yous without crying." I held my breath and Ara squeezed my hand, her wedding ring pressing hard. I looked to mine for a second, so happy Ara was the one I got to spend the rest of my reality with.

From up on stage, Audrey looked to me and said, "Bradley, my dear, dear, dear Bradley. I do not know if the world will ever fully understand the good you've done, and I hope they are kind to you. Thank you for this wholly unwarranted gift. You are not Dr. Frankenstein, as some call you, and I certainly don't feel like the creature." I felt the eyes of the world on me but my look to Ara calmed all fears.

"Thank you for what you have done for me. But more than that, thank you for what you have done for the world by donating the proceeds from this wonderful film to UNICEF to help feed and care for the children of this world. There is still so much to be done, but I know you will continue to do it as UNICEF's one-dollar-per-year Goodwill Ambassador. I once had that job, and it is both the most rewarding and heartbreaking thing for a person to go through."

The crowd murmured at the announcement.

"Bradley, this moment right now is the happily ever after that you sought so long ago for *Roman Holiday*. My faith in you was not unjustified." She then led a standing ovation for me. There was nothing to do but touch my heart and kiss Ara as everyone was seated again.

"And to my dear Robbie, who is—what did you call it, Cary —backstage? He is the one I long to return to, in any world, at any time."

Some heads turned toward me, but I led the applause for Robert Wolders, who had outlived Audrey by twenty-five years before passing away in 2018. We all visited virtually from time to time. Robbie's love was everything Audrey deserved.

As was this movie.

Charlie and Advik now had to determine what to do with all of the inventions and what they meant to the world. I wasn't thinking about that, though.

Ara and I had a plane to catch as UNICEF's Goodwill Ambassadors. Our destination: Cameroon, to help the children of the refugee crisis there.

A FINAL WORD

Audrey, one year later

So, you see, all Bradley needed was some prodding, some focus. Nudging him toward Ara was my gift to him.

I don't know what will happen next. I suppose I'll be quite busy, determining whom to respond to when they ring me up. Of course, meeting with my family, especially those born after me, and yes, those never born, will be my priority. Perhaps there are unlimited versions of me here backstage, I'm not sure. I once said people, even more than things, have to be restored, renewed, revived, reclaimed, and redeemed; never throw anyone out. I certainly didn't have this in mind when I said it, but it seems apropos.

The last thing I want is for people to grow weary of me, and the others. Yes, others from my era are available now to make films as well. That was *Real to Reel*'s purpose all along. I'm not sure I will, however. How would I top what I did? Still, I do adore it so and I love making people happy.

Bradley? He and Ara are doing great work for children around the world. I am so proud of them. I knew he had that in him when I chose him. He is making a difference in the world doing that hard work. I don't know whether he'll ever return to technology again.

When I join them on their UNICEF trips, they seem incredibly fulfilled. They are a wonderful couple. Ara is pregnant with a baby girl now. They shared with me the name they chose: Audrey Tranh Joseph.

How did the scarf get into Bradley's closet? Is that really what you want to know? Well, a girl has to keep some secrets, so I won't reveal that one. Just know that we on the other side are learning more every day and the controls that have been instituted worldwide make sense. I will do my part backstage to ensure that we all do good things for the world. Would you please ensure the same where you are?

Anyway, thanks for remembering me. Enjoy life and make a difference.

Love,
Andrey

ACKNOWLEDGMENTS

My late mother, Charlotte, was often told she favored Audrey Hepburn, so I've been intrigued by the actress since my youth. It wasn't until I moved to the San Francisco Bay Area in 2018 that I conceived the plot of a novel I knew I would complete, after several previous unfinished works.

Writing a novel like this balances an abundance of information in biographies, documentaries, and appearances with imagining personal interactions and dialogue with Audrey Hepburn and other celebrities from the Golden Age of Hollywood. Robert Matzen's two excellent books on Audrey Hepburn, *Dutch Girl* and *Warrior*, were quite helpful and the UNICEF scenes could not have been written without his research. I transcribed the quotes as depicted in source materials. Audrey's UNICEF speech in San Francisco is shared word for word and is commonly available.

Audrey Hepburn spent quite a bit of time in San Francisco, and one could argue her run in the national tour of *Gigi* there in April–May of 1953 was the final boost that propelled her to superstardom. Therefore, the early and latter parts of the novel suitably reimagine her time in "The City." I researched her places there and am thankful for the cooperation of locals who gave their time and knowledge to inform my work. Gussie Stewart opened her lovely home (formerly owned by Whitney Warren, Jr.) to show me where Audrey's San Francisco social debut happened; the world's first concierge, Tom Wolfe of the Fairmont Hotel, gave me a tour of the penthouse and ballroom where Audrey made her UNICEF speech a year before her death; Alan Choy shared with me his firsthand experiences with Audrey during her 1992 UNICEF tour in San Francisco; and the San Francisco Public Library's Digital Collection branch brought Audrey's *Gigi* run to life for me.

The technology aspects of this novel also are part real (or soon will be) and part imagined. I cataloged dozens of articles about artificial intelligence and alternate reality breaking the barrier between living and deceased people. Stanford University's Virtual Human Interaction Lab gave me my first foray into virtual reality and answered some of my early questions. Many hours of internet research formed the future developments I wanted to forecast. Any mistake or omission is my own.

Thanks to all of those who provided encouragement and advice along the way: my beta readers Tia McMillen, Cheryl Laughlin, and the Davis (CA) writers group. Writer friends Mike Krentz, Daniel Charles Ross, R. Kenward Jones, and C.W. Gortner helped me understand the things I needed to do to publish this story.

Rachel Kelli provided the cover art, bringing my vision of Bradley's home studio to life, and Ciera Cox provided invaluable edits.

Finally, to my family, I couldn't have done this without you: my wife, Paula; children Jordan, Grace, and Jack; son-in-law Sean, and grandchildren Kyler and Luca. Yes, it's ironic that two people in my family share names with Audrey's.

If you haven't yet seen an Audrey Hepburn movie, I recommend starting with *Roman Holiday*. It will bring Audrey Hepburn to life, again and again.

Joe Navratil
September 2024

SOURCES

- **Anderson**, Robert. *After.* New York: Random House, 1973
- **Epstein**, Edward Z. *Audrey and Bill.* Philadelphia: Running Press, 2015
- **Ferrer**, Sean Hepburn. *Audrey Hepburn, An Elegant Spirit.* New York: Atria, 2003
- **Harris**, Warren G. *Audrey Hepburn.* New York: Simon and Schuster, 1994
- **Matzen**, Robert. *Dutch Girl. Audrey Hepburn and World War II.* Pittsburgh: GoodKnight, 2019
- **Matzen**, Robert. *Warrior.* Pittsburgh: GoodKnight, 2021
- **Paris**, Barry. *Audrey Hepburn.* New York: Berkley, 1996
- **Spoto**, Donald. *Enchantment, The Life of Audrey Hepburn.* New York: Three Rivers Press, 2006
- **Walker**, Alexander. *Audrey, Her Real Story.* New York: St. Martin's Griffin, 1994
- **Wasson**, Sam. *Fifth Avenue, 5 A.M.* New York: Harper Collins, 2010

ABOUT THE AUTHOR

JOE NAVRATIL is a retired naval officer and a communication executive in the San Francisco Bay Area. He graduated with the United States Naval Academy's class of 1989, has taught English at USNA, and received an M.A. in English from Washington College. *Second Act* is his debut novel.